desperate measures

# Also in the Port Aster Secrets series

*Deadly Devotion*
*Blind Trust*

# desperate measures

*a novel*

## SANDRA ORCHARD

Revell

a division of Baker Publishing Group
Grand Rapids, Michigan

© 2015 by Sandra J. van den Bogerd

Published by Revell
a division of Baker Publishing Group
P.O. Box 6287, Grand Rapids, MI 49516-6287
www.revellbooks.com

Printed in the United States of America

Library of Congress Cataloging-in-Publication Data
Orchard, Sandra.
    Desperate measures : a novel / Sandra Orchard.
        pages ; cm. — (Port aster secrets ; Book 3)
    ISBN 978-0-8007-2224-1 (pbk.)
    I. Title.
PR9199.4.O73D47 2015
813'.6—dc23                                                                 2015001798

Scripture quotations are from the King James Version of the Bible.

15  16  17  18  19  20  21      7  6  5  4  3  2  1

To my children,
whose part-time greenhouse work
originally sowed the inspiration for this series,
and whose love and support helped grow it to fruition.

# 1
---

Squinting against the bright grow lights, Kate Adams slipped into her fruit cellar in the back corner of her basement and shut the door. She couldn't risk anyone discovering her little greenhouse. Enough people had already died.

The musty humidity in the tomblike room squeezed her chest. The walls were concrete, but mildew had already infiltrated the wooden ceiling, like GPC Pharmaceuticals' insidious blight in her life. Mildew was a price she'd gladly pay—if it meant getting her dad back.

She blinked away the image of him lying in a coma in a nameless hospital and forced herself to focus on the plants. She pressed her fingers into the soil of the nearest pot to gauge its dampness and smiled at the new buds peeking past the succulent, dandelion-shaped leaves. The virtually extinct plants were thriving in the tropical microclimate she'd recreated.

Her heart hiccupped. If only Vic Lawton hadn't run her father off that ravine to try to recover the plants, she might be enjoying a sweet reunion with Dad even now. Part of her didn't want anything to do with the plant that had cost her so much. But after Detective Tom Parker's "executive decision" to send her father back into hiding, figuring out what gave amendoso the extraordinary curative properties it seemed GPC would stop at nothing to exploit might be her only hope of ever convincing the people safeguarding Dad to let her see him again.

*Why, Lord? Why bring my father back into my life, only to take him away again?*

No answer came. Not that she'd expected one. Lately she felt as if even God had abandoned her.

She squirmed at the irreverent thought. Her dad hadn't really abandoned her by faking his death twenty years ago. No matter how much it felt like it. He'd been trying to protect her and her mother. And if she were honest with herself, lately she'd probably been shutting God out, more than the other way around. How many times had Daisy reminded her to take God at his Word, not trust emotions that surged and ebbed like the tide?

Kate rubbed her knuckles over the ache in the vicinity of her heart. She'd have an easier time leaning on God if Daisy hadn't been murdered and every other person she'd ever trusted hadn't lied to her face or hid things from her—big, monumental things, like the fact her father was alive.

Shoving aside the thought and ignoring for a few more minutes the paint job awaiting her upstairs, she snatched up her spray bottle and misted the plants. "What's your secret?" she whispered as she deadheaded a spent aster-like flower.

What could be so special about this plant that a multinational pharmaceutical company would burn down a remote Colombian village to control it? So special that her father would sacrifice a lifetime with his family to keep it out of their hands? So special that all these years later, his former employer, GPC Pharmaceuticals, would track it down to Port Aster and kill a man to safeguard its existence?

Kill *her* if they found out she had it.

Her chest squeezed tighter. If she ever needed police protection, it was now. But with GPC vying to partner with the research facility where she worked, she didn't dare tell anyone about the plants.

Detective Tom Parker least of all.

If he'd separate her from her comatose father to ensure her safety, he'd never allow her to experiment with the plant responsible for Dad's fate.

She jerked the mist bottle's trigger. *For her own protection*, he'd said. And she appreciated his concern. She sincerely did. But she couldn't trust him not to do the same thing again.

The doorbell sounded.

She froze. Who'd come around on a Saturday morning? Especially this early?

Glancing down at the painting clothes she'd tugged on first thing, she palmed the perspiration from her brow. *Pull yourself together. No one's gonna suspect you're up to anything.*

The doorbell chimed a second time.

She closed the fruit cellar door and hurried upstairs, still puzzling over who could be here. Tom would call first. *Unless* . . .

Her pulse quickened. Had he finally brought good news? That her father was out of his coma, that she could see him again?

She peeked out the front door's peephole, her hopes deflating like a pricked balloon. She turned off her security alarm and unlocked the dead bolt. "Patti, what brings you by on a Saturday?" Kate did a double take at her lab assistant's faded jeans and the ratty T-shirt straining at her ample hips. Since Patti had started dating the mayor's son, Kate hadn't seen her in anything that wasn't designer fashion. "What's wrong?"

Laughing, Patti pulled her long, dark hair into a ponytail and snapped on a hair elastic. "Nothing. You said you were painting your bedroom this weekend. I came to help."

She had even worn an older pair of glasses instead of the funky new ones she'd been wearing lately, Kate couldn't help but notice. "Really?"

"Don't sound so shocked. I do know how to paint."

"No, I—" Kate motioned her inside. "I just assumed you'd be hanging with Jarrett. You two have been insepa- rable lately."

Patti shrugged. "A girl's got to spend some time with her girlfriends. Right?"

Speechless, Kate relocked the door. Patti was her assistant, a graduate student, her co-worker. She'd never really thought of her as a girlfriend. But she'd missed having a friend to turn to with her former roommate, Julie, newly married and Daisy, who'd been so much more than a colleague, gone and Tom . . . not an option. "I'd love some help. Thank you." Kate led the way to her empty bedroom, her heart lightening at having company. "I laid old bedsheets over the carpet so I wouldn't have to worry about paint splatters."

"Smart idea." Patti grabbed the stepladder and set it up along the far wall. "I can do the top and bottom edges with a paintbrush if you want to handle the roller."

"That would be awesome." Kate poured half of the

lemongrass-green paint into the tray, then set the can on the ladder's pail shelf for Patti's easy access.

Patti started in immediately, saying little except that she liked the color.

Kate loaded her roller and concentrated on making long, smooth strokes. "You seeing Jarrett later?"

Patti shrugged.

"Did you two have a fight?"

"No, nothing like that." Patti's brushstrokes grew jerky, as if it was *exactly* like that.

A real girlfriend would commiserate with her. But Kate couldn't. Truth be told, she'd be happy to see the pair break up. She didn't trust Jarrett. It was too coincidental that he'd started dating Patti at the same time Kate took her on as a research assistant, especially when his father—the mayor— was so set on helping GPC partner with the research station.

Kate slanted an uneasy glance in Patti's direction. Was there more to her assistant's visit than a little altruistic bonding?

Patti jabbed her brush into the paint can. "Whoa. You might want to wear a ball cap. You're speckling your hair green."

"Red and green. Terrific. I'll be all set for Christmas." Kate set down her paint roller and ran her palm over her long waves. Yup, she could feel the wet, sticky spots.

Patti muffled a giggle.

"What?" Kate pulled away her green-smeared hand and groaned.

"At least it's not speckled anymore." Patti returned to her painting, still chuckling.

Kate went to the bathroom and washed out the paint as

best she could, then squashed a ball cap over her hair. By the time she got back to the bedroom, Patti had already cut in the tops of three walls. "Wow, you paint like a pro!"

Grinning, Patti slid the ladder in front of the final wall needing to be edged, climbed two rungs, then swayed precariously.

Kate dropped her roller and lunged for the ladder, scarcely stopping it from toppling, along with the can of paint.

Patti stumbled off the bottom rung and struggled to recover her balance. "I'm sorry." She pressed her palm to the side of her head. "I don't know what's wrong with me. I keep getting these bizarre dizzy spells. Last night I tripped up my porch steps."

"You should see a doctor."

Patti dropped her hand and laughed off the suggestion. "I don't think it's that serious. Probably just low blood sugar or something."

"Then let me get you a glass of apple juice."

Patti retrieved the roller Kate had set on the drop sheet. "That's okay. I can get it. How about you finish edging the top of the wall and I'll take over the roller?"

"Okay, but"—Kate pried the roller from her hand and set it in the tray—"first get yourself that juice. There's a bottle in the fridge."

Patti saluted and headed down the hall.

Kate climbed the ladder and continued painting where Patti had left off. But when Patti hadn't returned by the time she reloaded her brush for the fourth time, she called out, "You okay?"

No response.

"Patti?" Kate dashed down the hall. An empty juice glass

sat on the table, but Patti was nowhere in sight. Kate skidded to a stop at the top of the basement stairs beside the kitchen. "Patti?"

Halfway down the steps, Patti whirled at her name. "Ahhh!" Her arms windmilled, and in that sickening millisecond when she knew she'd fall and couldn't stop herself, sheer panic blazed in her eyes. She tumbled backward, catching her heel on the tread. Her head slammed into the cement floor, half her body sprawled on the steps.

She shifted awkwardly and her screams escalated.

"Don't move!" Kate raced down two steps at a time. "You might have broken some—" *Oh, no.* Bile stung her throat at the sight of Patti's badly broken leg. She was lying at such a horrible angle; Kate prayed the leg was all that was broken.

Patti collapsed back against the floor. "I can't believe this. I saw you'd left a light on, and"—she gasped for air in short, painful sounding gulps—"I was just coming down to turn it off for you."

Kate's gaze shot to the fruit cellar. The door was closed like she'd left it. But no light that she could see seeped around the edges.

Was Patti lying? Had she snuck into the fruit cellar? Had she seen the plants?

The derelict Potter farmhouse crouched like a duck blind in a haggard marsh of overgrown hay fields, a quarter mile in from the road. Trespassing calls weren't normally his territory, but Tom had a hunch this particular trespasser might be the missing teen he'd been trying to track down. The place was a runaway's dream home.

Unwilling to risk a busted axle, Tom parked at the end of the driveway, if it could still be called that, and buttoned his sport coat to conceal his shoulder holster before climbing out.

He scanned the horizon for signs his arrival had been noticed. The young Conner family, who'd made the call, lived to the south of the twenty-acre property. Their youngster stood on a tire swing, pointing Tom's way. Shading her eyes, Mrs. Conner followed the direction of her son's finger. Tom waved, then radioed dispatch to alert them in case Mrs. Conner mistook him for another trespasser thanks to his unmarked car.

Beyond the fields to the north lay the Goodman place, a virtual castle, fortified by a six-foot stone wall. If the person Mrs. Conner saw wasn't his missing teen, he could be someone scouting out the estate Kate's research assistant recently inherited.

Too bad it was Saturday morning. Questioning Patti Goodman about any suspicious activity she might've noticed on the adjoining property would have been a great excuse to stop by Kate's lab.

Remembering Kate's parting words, *There is no we*, after he'd arranged, against her wishes, for her dad to go back into hiding, he kicked the dirt. Yeah, wake up and smell the weeds. Stopping by wouldn't change anything. If he weren't the only connection to her father—as tenuous as that connection was—she probably wouldn't talk to him at all. Never mind the danger he feared she was still in.

Despite his certainty that GPC must have recovered the plants Vic Lawton stole from her father after running him off the road, the pharmaceutical company was still maneuvering for a stake in Port Aster's research station. And Lawton's subsequent murder proved they didn't leave loose ends.

Tom returned his attention to the task at hand. Multiple bicycle-tire-sized ruts through the grass confirmed someone had been around. He scoped the area for any evidence he might walk into more than he bargained for, like some gang's hideout.

A murder of crows perched on a dead tree limb, cawing noisily as if to warn of his arrival. But no shifting shadows at the windows betrayed a response to the birds' alarm.

He tried the front door. It held fast, and from the look of the crusted edges, it hadn't been opened in years. A glance through the dirty window revealed only an old sofa, its stuffing puffed out the corner, in an otherwise bare main room. A staircase with ratty carpet curling on the treads stretched to the second level. In the dim light, it was impossible to tell if anyone had recently traipsed across the floor.

Tom strode around the perimeter, but the hard-packed mud revealed no footprints . . . like every dead-end lead in this case. A pillared wooden porch spanned the length of the house's driveway side, its paint gray and peeling, its shingles curled, its floorboards pitted with rot, but he'd seen teens hole up in worse. Much worse. He yanked open the storm door and reached for the doorknob. It turned easily. The reek of animal waste bit his nostrils as he stepped inside. A chrome-legged kitchen table and faded red vinyl chairs sat in the center of a floor layered in years of dust and . . . man-sized scuffs.

"This is Detective Tom Parker. Anyone here? I just want to talk to you."

Skittering from inside one of the kitchen cupboards answered his call, nothing more. The footprints were concentrated outside a closed door in the back corner of the kitchen. He jerked it open and shone his flashlight down rickety stairs leading to a mud-floor cellar. "Anyone down there?" Hearing no scuttling, he descended slowly into the cool, dank cellar, batting cobwebs from his face. He flicked his light into every corner, but there was no sign of anyone, just old farm baskets and gardening implements and shelves upon shelves of ancient canning jars, many still filled with food. He returned to the kitchen, then moved from one room to the next, checking closets. Although someone had clearly wandered through the place, nothing suggested anyone lived there, besides mice and a feral cat or two. Tom grabbed the stair rail, glanced up the open staircase, and tested the bottom step.

His cell phone rang. He cocked his head toward the top of the stairs, thinking he'd heard movement. The phone rang again. Seeing his dad's name on the screen, he punched it on. "Just a second, Dad." Tom stole up the stairs and quickly scanned the top floor. The three bedrooms with slanted ceilings were empty, save for threadbare sheers dangling from the narrow dormer windows. He edged aside the sheers at a window with a view of the hip-roofed barn he still needed to check and unmuted his phone. "Sorry about that, Dad. What is it?"

"I just heard on the police scanner that an ambulance was dispatched to Kate's house."

Tom's heart pitched. "Did you catch any details?"

"No, but I'm on my way over now."

"Thanks, Dad," Tom said, already hoofing it back downstairs. The scanner had been a fixture in their house since Dad's days on the local police force. But he'd been paying much closer attention to it since Vic Lawton's death intensified their fears Kate might be next. "I'll be right there." Tom bolted outside just as a motorcycle roared up the rutted driveway.

Tom took cover behind a porch pillar, his hand settling on his gun.

The bike swerved to a stop at the foot of the porch, kicking up a cloud of dust.

"Hold it right there," Tom shouted.

The driver yanked off his helmet, revealing dark hair and blue eyes Tom would know anywhere—Jarrett King, the mayor's son. "What's going on, Detective?"

Leaving his weapon holstered, Tom refastened his sport coat. "What are you doing here?"

"My girlfriend lives next door."

Right. Patti Goodman. How could he forget, after catching the pair nosing through Kate's house little more than a month ago? Was it only a month? Tom glanced at the yellowing fields of late September. Seemed like a lot longer with Kate avoiding him most of the time.

Jarrett tucked his helmet under his arm. "I saw the car at the end of the driveway and got curious."

"The neighbors saw someone skulking around the place and called it in. Has Patti mentioned seeing anyone?"

"No." Concern rippled Jarrett's brow. "Are we talking kids, or someone she needs to be worried about?"

"I don't know yet, but if you notice anyone around the place, I'd appreciate you giving me a call."

"Will do." Jarrett yanked on his helmet and wailed out of the driveway before Tom's long strides ate a quarter of the distance.

But instead of turning north toward Patti's, Jarrett turned south. So why had he really happened by?

On the sidewalk outside her brick bungalow, Kate spun from the departing ambulance to a car screeching to a stop behind her.

*Oh, no!*

Tom jumped out of his car, looking way too good with his dark hair newly trimmed.

She should've known he'd follow his dad here.

*His dad! Where'd he go?*

She darted a glance back to the house. Was that a basement light that just flicked out? By the plants! "What are you doing here?" she snapped at Tom.

"A 911 call from your house, Kate? Where do you think I'm going to be?"

Yes, of course he was here. He was always here for her when she needed him. She darted another glance at the basement window. Whether she wanted him or not.

His gaze travelled up her paint-splattered clothes. "What's going on?"

"Oh." She waved her arm mindlessly toward the house. "Nothing you need to worry about. Patti was helping me paint and fell and broke her leg."

"I'm sorry."

Spotting his father through the living room window, Kate crowded Tom back toward his car. "I appreciate you checking on me, but I need to go to the hospital."

"You might want to clean up first." He reached out a hand to her cheek.

She jerked back, then felt foolish when he presented a lemongrass-green-smeared fingertip. She swiped at her face

18

with her shirtsleeve, trying to ignore the tingle on her skin where he'd touched her.

He was sweetly gallant, but his protectiveness had already cost her too much. Before her father was run off the road, he understandably might've still thought of her as a little girl that needed protecting, but Tom should've known better. She didn't need other people making her decisions for her, and she couldn't sit around waiting for someone else to make a family reunion possible. Even if it meant keeping her own secrets.

Tom jutted his chin toward Patti's car blocking hers in the driveway. "If you give me the keys, I can move her car out of the way for you while you change."

Kate glanced helplessly down the now-empty street and groaned. "Patti took her purse with her."

"No problem. I can give you a lift to the hospital."

"Uh . . ." If her insides were already doing gymnastics over keeping secrets when he was being so nice, they'd be nothing but knots after a twenty-minute car ride together. She'd probably end up confessing to digging up the plants and everything.

And he'd take them away, just like he did her dad, and she'd never figure out what was so special about them and gain enough leverage to get him back.

Squinting at her blocked car, she shifted from one foot to another, not wanting to depend on Tom. "Aren't you supposed to be working?"

He shrugged as if it was no big deal. "I'll take an early lunch."

Oh, she was in trouble.

Tom's father emerged from the house. "Since you said

you'd be going to the hospital with your friend, I emptied your paint tray into the can and sealed it up and washed your brushes in the basement."

"The basement?" She swallowed a gasp, then tried to cover with an innocent smile. "That was nice of you. Thanks."

Tom's eyes narrowed, and Keith gave him a look she couldn't read but that made her stomach churn.

Did he know? Would he tell Tom? "Um . . . I'll just go get changed real quick." She hurried inside, dead-bolted the door behind her, and raced downstairs. Her pounding heart roared in her ears as she opened the fruit cellar door. At the sight of the grow lights still burning, she exhaled, then charged back upstairs and snuck a peek out the front window. Tom and his father were in deep conversation. *Okay, that might not be good.* She quickly washed and changed and raced back outside. "Ready," she said, breathlessly.

The smile that crinkled the corners of Tom's eyes as he held open his passenger door for her sent a too-nice zing right to the center of her chest. Oh boy.

He hadn't even turned the corner before diving into the questions she'd dreaded. "Dad said Patti was at the bottom of the basement stairs, but that all the paint and brushes were upstairs. So why did she go downstairs?"

"Uh . . ." Kate clutched her thighs to still her fidgeting hands. Tom was far too adept at reading her body language. Maybe Patti had just been going to turn off the light, like she'd said, but Kate wasn't sure she believed her. "She said she saw a light on and she was going downstairs to turn it off."

Tom glanced from her lap to her face. "Hey, it's not like you pushed her. It's not your fault."

Softening at his caring tone, she tried to relax, except one look at his deep blue eyes and her anxiety only morphed into guilt over how nice he was being. Of course it was her fault. She was harboring a fugitive plant in her basement.

He reached across the seat and squeezed her hand. "I'm glad *you're* okay. I was afraid GPC had gotten to you."

She stiffened at his touch. GPC *would* be after her if they knew. And Tom would have a hairy canary fit if he knew.

Tom put his hand back on the steering wheel and sighed. "Kate, you have to know that I'm doing everything I can to figure out a *safe* way to reunite you with your father."

"I know," she mumbled, sorry that he'd misread her reaction, taken it personally. But she couldn't explain. So she turned to the window and watched the landscape sliding by. She'd been deprived of her dad for twenty years for her own safety. Now that she knew he was alive, she intended to do whatever it took to be reunited, safe or not.

Tom parked near the ER, and as he guided her inside with a gentle touch to her back, she tried not to think about the last time they'd visited the ER—the night Vic attacked her in the woods, the night he rammed her father's car over a ravine, the night Tom finally told her the truth.

Her heart ached at the memory of the precious few minutes she'd had with her long-lost father.

As if reading her thoughts, Tom rubbed soothing circles on her lower back.

She arched away from his touch, willing her anger at the unfairness of it all to dispel the impulse to turn into his arms. She didn't have time for a pity party. Patti needed her.

The ER doors slid open and Jarrett, looking way too pale, pushed through the door separating the waiting room from the patients.

Kate ran to him. "Is she okay? Have you talked to the doctor? How did you know she was here?"

"I called him when you were changing," Tom whispered.

Jarrett raked his fingers through his hair. "It's bad. A displaced fracture, the doctor said. They won't be able to cast it until the swelling goes down. They just sent her for a CT scan. She hit her head hard."

"This is all my fault." Kate sank onto a molded plastic chair standing by itself next to the door, as disconnected from the others as she felt. "As soon as she told me how dizzy she'd been feeling, I should have told her to rest."

"You knew she was dizzy?" The urgency in Jarrett's voice made Kate's heart race. "Did she suspect what caused it?"

"She said maybe low blood sugar."

A nurse carrying a clipboard interrupted them. "Are you Kate? Miss Goodman said you'd be able to tell me the policy number for your work's medical insurance."

"Oh, yes." Kate dug into her purse and produced the card. "The group policy number is on the top." She frowned uncertainly at the number beneath it. "But I don't know her personal ID number."

The nurse tapped her pencil in a quickening staccato as she studied the card. "You work at the research station?"

"Yes."

"Could Miss Goodman have drunk an experimental concoction that might have caused the dizziness?"

"No, we don't ingest things we're studying."

The nurse handed Kate back her card. "Of course. Well, if you think of anything she might've consumed that could explain the dizziness, please let us know."

As the nurse walked away, Tom pulled up a seat beside

Kate. "This scenario sounds too uncomfortably like your friend Daisy's."

Kate stared at him, her heart pummeling her ribs. "You think someone poisoned Patti?"

"No, I—"

"Daisy had complained of dizziness a few times before she di—" *Oh no. Oh no. Oh. No.*

Tom pulled his seat even closer. "Kate, it's okay. Take deep breaths."

"It's not okay. *It's not!* What if they poisoned Patti to get to me?"

# 2

Tom risked putting a calming hand on Kate's shoulder. Relieved when she didn't pull away, he steered her into a small alcove outside the ER's waiting area, away from curious stares, and lowered his voice. "We don't know that *anyone* has poisoned Patti." He slanted an uncomfortable glance at Jarrett joining them. As much as Jarrett seemed to care for Kate's research assistant, Tom wasn't convinced that her welfare was his primary concern. His father was too eager to ensure that GPC partnered with the research station, which made Jarrett's relationship with Kate's assistant smack of ulterior motives.

But what would he gain from Patti being poisoned?

*If* she was.

"Who are *they*? And why would they poison Patti to get to you?" Jarrett asked, his voice low and insistent.

"Allegedly poison." Tom threw Kate a cautioning look.

"I don't know what I'm saying." Kate hunched forward and stroked her temples with her fingertips. Her hair tumbled off her shoulders, the long soft curls shielding her face from view.

Tom's heart ached at her defeated posture. There had to be dozens of possible explanations for Patti's dizziness, but he wasn't about to ignore the possibility that she'd been deliberately targeted to somehow get to Kate, no matter how remote the chance. He rested a palm on her shoulder. "We'll know more once the doctor runs his blood tests."

Jarrett narrowed his eyes, clearly not pleased by the brushoff. "The doctor asked a lot of questions about the plants they work with. They wouldn't show up in a normal tox screen."

Kate's gaze snapped up, her hair blazing in the light slanting through the window, looking as fiery as her voice suddenly sounded. "What does the doctor *think*? That we test the tinctures we formulate on ourselves?"

"Do you?"

"No, of course not! You just heard me tell the nurse."

Jarrett leaned closer, his voice deepening menacingly. "But you think someone poisoned her. Why?"

Tom squeezed Kate's shoulder. "Kate's colleague died of poisoning less than five months ago. It's only natural she would react so strongly to the suggestion that Patti's been poisoned." He cupped Kate's elbow to coax her to her feet. "Why don't I take you home now? I'm sure Jarrett will see to Patti."

Kate pulled her arm tight to her side. "I can't leave her."

Tom fought the urge to tighten his hold. Any attack on Patti was potentially research-related, which meant *anyone* connected to the research was at risk.

But he was still on duty. And he had a missing kid he needed to find.

He blew out a deep breath. Chances were he was over-reacting to the Patti incident anyway. If Vic Lawton, who'd seen Kate going after the plant in the woods, or the GPC salesman Peter Ratcher, who'd seen her at her father's bedside afterward, had reported as much to GPC, surely they would have taken Kate out before now. Tom fisted his hands. But that didn't mean they weren't still monitoring her and her research assistant. His mind flicked to the boot scuffs at the old Potter place, the upstairs window with a perfect view of Patti Goodman's house. *Maybe watching Patti from the vacant property next door.*

He glanced at Jarrett, still not certain he could be trusted, especially given his sudden appearance at the property this morning, but this was as safe a place as any for Kate to be for the time being. By the list of procedures still ahead for Patti, it sounded as if she'd be stuck here for a few hours more. "Okay, I need to get back to work. Call me when you're ready to go home and I'll swing by to give you a lift."

"That's not necessary."

Tom tamped down a twinge of hurt at the cool note to her voice and mustered a smile. "I want to."

He was rewarded with a flicker of emotion in her eyes, fol-lowed by a soft "Thank you." *Baby steps.* Just because Kate could see logically that hiding her father had been the safest option didn't mean it was easy for her, and unfortunately, he was the nearest target for the injustice of it all.

He hoped one day she'd be able to get past his betrayal to the place they'd been. Because he couldn't imagine his future without her.

He headed outside, debating whether to ask his dad to stop by the hospital and play bodyguard. From inside his car, he scanned the hospital entrances, the grounds, and the parking lot. He had no compelling reason to think GPC had anything to do with Patti's condition or that Kate was in more imminent danger than she'd been—or hadn't been, as the case may be—for the past few weeks.

Except for the twisting in his gut.

He started his car. No point in enlisting Dad's help just yet.

Driving back into Port Aster, Tom passed the long-term care facility and made a quick U-turn. His priority was locating their missing teen, but if he wound up unearthing evidence pointing to GPC spies at the old Potter place, he didn't want it thrown out of court on a technicality. And gaining the property owner's permission to search would be easier than securing a warrant.

His earlier visit to the Potter house had been by the book, thanks to the concerned neighbor's 911 call. He couldn't say the same about his next one.

Climbing out of his car, Tom nodded at the seniors sitting outside the entrance, enjoying the sunny autumn afternoon. The setting reminded him of his previous visit here with Kate. He smiled at the memory of her feisty determination to visit her neighbor despite his protests. Truth be told, he'd enjoyed playing bodyguard. And as crazy as her stubborn pursuit of the truth drove him sometimes—most of the time—he wouldn't have her any other way.

"May I help you?" a woman behind a plate-glass window asked the moment he stepped inside the main doors.

"I hope so." He showed his detective's badge to the sour-looking receptionist. "I'm looking for Mrs. Francis Potter." When he'd gotten this morning's call to the old Potter place, Carol, on dispatch, had said the home's owner had gone to the nursing home years ago, following a stroke. He prayed she'd long since recovered enough to give him informed consent.

Someone tapped him on the shoulder—a young woman in a pale pink uniform. "Follow me. I just wheeled Fran to the TV room."

"Thank you." Tom nodded to the tight-lipped receptionist and followed the young nurse's aide. "How is Fran's state of mind? Will she be able to answer my questions?"

The nurse chuckled. "Oh, that won't be a problem. Fran is as quick as a whip. She'll talk circles around you. Before you know it, an hour'll go by."

Tom glanced at his watch. "I don't have that much time."

"Compliment her new hairdo then."

Tom lifted an eyebrow.

"Trust me. Compliments always disarm her." The aide's eyes traveled down his physique. "And coming from you, they'll probably disarm her more than most."

*Okay.* The sudden churning in his stomach wasn't from a missed lunch. What had he gotten himself into?

The aide led him into a bright, sunny room with a giant-screen TV at one end and a half dozen wheelchair-bound residents angled toward the talk show playing a dozen decibels higher than was comfortable.

The nurse leaned close to a handsome woman with perfectly coiffed blue-white hair and then wheeled the woman's chair toward him. "This is Fran."

"Pleased to meet you." Tom extended his hand, which she took in a firm grip that surprised him. The twinkle in her clear brown eyes suggested that his surprise pleased her. He smiled, liking her already. "I'm Detective Tom Parker. May we talk privately for a few moments?"

Fran turned those twinkling eyes toward the nurse's aide. "Ooh, did you hear that, dear? This handsome young man wants to see me *privately*."

Tom fought back the grin tugging at his lips. "Actually it might be helpful if Miss . . ." He looked to the aide.

"McKay."

He nodded his thanks and returned his attention to Mrs. Potter. "If Miss McKay could join us."

"Pooft," Mrs. Potter spluttered. "Let's get on with it then."

Tom exchanged an amused glance with Miss McKay, who wheeled Mrs. Potter to a table in the empty dining area. Miss McKay jerked her pointed gaze from him to the older woman's hair.

"Oh," Tom mumbled, taking a seat opposite Mrs. Potter. "May I say that your hair looks stunning," he said.

Mrs. Potter patted the bottom of her hairsprayed, not-going-anywhere-for-a-week curls, looking utterly discombobulated.

Mirth danced in the aide's eyes as she mouthed, "Told you."

"Why thank you, young man," Mrs. Potter finally said. "Now, how can I help you?"

"Well, I'd like to help you. There have been reports of someone trespassing on your property, and I'd like your permission to conduct a thorough search of the grounds and buildings."

"Oh my, of course. I do hope children aren't playing around in there. It isn't safe. I suppose that's why my real estate agent hasn't had any luck selling it in all these years."

"Who's your agent?" There wasn't a FOR SALE sign on the property that he'd seen. The agent probably wasn't doing anything to advertise the place.

"The only Realtor in town." Mrs. Potter's nose scrunched as her gaze drifted upward. "I can't remember his name."

"Westby?" There were others in town these days, but he'd been in business the longest.

"Yes, that's it."

*Just great.* The guy hadn't been the least bit cooperative when Tom had asked him for the name of the business-man interested in buying Verna Nagy's wooded property after Kate found the amendoso plants growing there. And he wouldn't be happy to find Tom nosing about on another of his listings.

Hiding his frustration over that minor glitch, Tom laid the form he'd brought on the table. "That's no problem, Mrs. Potter. If you could sign this, I won't keep you any longer." Technically, the request was overkill, but where GPC might be connected, he didn't want to take any chances. By dinnertime, Mrs. Potter might have forgotten granting him permission. The woman signed her name with a flamboyant script that matched her lively personality, and he fought a smile.

Somehow he imagined this woman once had fiery red hair like Kate's. He pictured Kate at her age, just as feisty. A pang nipped his chest. He hoped he'd be in her life long enough to find out.

Returning to his car, he put a call in to dispatch to have a K-9 unit meet him at the Potter place to see if the dog could pick up their missing teen's scent.

"All available units are at Short Hills, tracking a missing girl. What's your situation?"

"That's okay. It can wait." Tom punched the gas. Caleb's parents wouldn't agree. But he'd do a thorough search with or without K-9.

A minute later dispatch called him back.

Hopeful they'd freed up a dog, Tom clicked on the call. "Yeah?"

"The chief wants to see you."

"He say why? I'm in the middle of something."

"It's about your runaway."

*Terrific.* At the best of times, his former high school buddy seemed to take too much pleasure in micromanaging Tom's investigations, but with Caleb's parents continually phoning for updates, his missing teen case was fast approaching a flash point.

At the police station ten minutes later, the chief cut him off the instant Tom stepped inside. "Where have you been?"

"Securing permission to search the Potter property." Tom pulled the signed form from his pocket, thankful he'd decided to stop on his way back from the hospital. Hank didn't need to know what else he'd been doing. He'd made his opinion of Tom's "all-consuming" interest in Kate's welfare abundantly clear on more than enough occasions already.

"Why? What did you see?"

"Size ten or eleven shoe prints."

"That'd be about the kid's size."

"Which is why I need to get back. What's going on?"

"Hold on a sec." Hank moseyed to his office, looking like he'd spent too long in a saddle.

Tom grimaced. *More likely from wrangling over the reins on my cases.* Tom plunked behind his desk and fired up his computer, needing to satisfy the itch to take another look at Molly Gilmore's file while he was here. Or more precisely to compare witnesses' descriptions of Daisy Leacock's symptoms before her death to Patti's symptoms. Molly's image appeared and her smug look irked him. To frame her ex-boyfriend, the woman had shamelessly poisoned Kate's colleague and then tried to kill Kate when she threatened to expose her. Then to add insult to injury, the judge dismissed the murder charge for insufficient evidence *and* let Molly out on bail, pending her trial for her attempted murder of Kate. Was it any wonder Kate got so distraught over the suggestion Patti had been poisoned?

Not that they had any reason to suspect Molly this time. But he wouldn't put it past GPC to mimic the incident to exploit Kate's fears.

Hank returned with a laptop under his arm. His expression soured. "What are you doing searching Gilmore's records? We have open cases to deal with. Not your wannabe girlfriend's."

"Give me a break."

"I've given you enough breaks. I already told you when you were pushing to prove Vic Lawton's swan dive wasn't suicide that not everything's a conspiracy."

Tom bit back a retort. Hank didn't know that Tom suspected GPC of being behind Vic's death. Telling him would've invited too much scrutiny of the man Vic had supposedly felt inconsolable remorse over killing. The man that nobody, except Tom and Kate and the team that took him into hiding, knew was Kate's father.

Hank flicked off Tom's computer screen and slapped the laptop he'd grabbed onto Tom's desk. "You need to forget trying to win Kate back and find our runaway."

Tom ignored the jibe and scrutinized the laptop. The initials CM were scratched onto the bottom. His adrenaline surged. "This is Caleb's. Where did you find it?"

"A friend of his just turned it over. Claimed Caleb loaned it to him before he disappeared. Said he didn't know we were looking for it."

Right. Tom snorted. "I'll want to talk to him."

Hank passed him a memo. "His name, number, and address."

Tom didn't recognize the name from the two dozen friends and classmates of Caleb he'd already talked to.

An hour later, Tom shut the laptop. There was nothing on it to suggest the sixteen-year-old had planned to run away. Barely anything to suggest the kid might be discontent. Unfortunately, teenagers were experts at hiding destructive behavior. And whether he was nabbed or ran of his own volition, every passing week made the likelihood of finding him too small to want to think about.

Tom crushed the empty coffee cups littering his desk and tossed them in the trash. His time would've been better spent scouring the rest of the Potter house and property. He'd do that now, then stop by the real estate office to see what he could get out of Westby. The fact the property was next door to Kate's research assistant's home was too coincidental to not suspect GPC might somehow be connected.

At the main intersection outside of town, he flicked on his right turn signal to head toward the Potter property and glanced at his dashboard clock. Patti had already been in the hospital more than four hours. And he had a bad feeling that Kate would leave without calling him if Patti were released.

He pulled to the side of the road and clicked Kate's number on his cell phone. After four rings, it went to voice mail. He tried her home number. Same thing.

Okay, he didn't like this. Inhaling, he squinted in the

direction he should be heading—the Potter property. *Face it, man, your mind won't be on your game if you're worrying about Kate the whole time you're searching the place.*

He flicked his turn signal the opposite way and turned toward the hospital. The twenty-minute drive gave him lots of time to mull over what little facts he had on his missing person case.

Caleb was the youngest of three, the only boy, and had always been a good kid. Got good grades. Was never in trouble at school. Hung out with clean-cut kids, kids who seemed as baffled as his parents at Caleb's sudden disappearance.

The parents had been out of town for the weekend, visiting his older sister at college. But they could account for his whereabouts until Sunday morning. The teen had been at a friend's Friday evening, then biked home. He delivered his Saturday papers, checked in with his parents regularly, and according to the neighbor had been home Saturday night with no visitors. The phone company logged his last cell phone call just before nine Saturday night. But they'd had no success tracking its position since. Even more disturbing, they'd only gotten a handful of tips after plastering his picture all over the news stations.

An ambulance swerved up to the ER doors as Tom parked in the hospital lot. Paramedics burst out the rear door with a young man on a gurney, blood everywhere. A couple trailed behind them, their shell-shocked expressions looking too much like those of the parents of his missing teen. Tom offered a silent prayer for the young man and prayed he'd find Caleb in better shape, and soon.

Tom checked in at the ER desk and was redirected to the fracture clinic, one floor up. He took the stairs and arrived in time to hear the nurse's report to Kate and Jarrett in the otherwise empty waiting room.

"Your friend is fortunate. Only a broken fibula. The doctor splinted the leg for now. Patti will need to come into the fracture clinic Monday after the swelling has gone down to have a cast put on."

"So she can go home?" Kate asked. "Her CT was clear?"

"She has a concussion and will need to be on pain meds." The nurse handed Kate a piece of paper. "These are symptoms you need to watch for."

Kate looked from the paper to the nurse. "What do you mean?"

"The doctor doesn't want her to be alone until he pinpoints the cause of her dizziness."

Jarrett snapped up the paper. "No problem. I'll stay with her."

Kate shot him a horrified look. "You can't stay with her."

"Why not? We've been dating for months."

"Because you're not married!"

Jarrett laughed, his gaze shifting as Tom stepped into the room, nodding his agreement. Jarrett immediately sobered. "Don't tell me you agree with her?"

"Yeah, I do," Tom admitted, as much as he didn't want to encourage Kate to stay with Patti instead.

"I'll stay with her," Kate said.

Yup, just what he didn't want.

The nurse motioned them to follow her. "Why don't you let our patient decide?"

Tom caught Kate's arm as Jarrett left the waiting room ahead of them. "I don't think staying with Patti is a good idea."

"It's better than Jarrett staying with her. I don't trust him. How do we know he didn't slip her something to make her dizzy just to give himself an excuse to move in with her?"

"Why would he do that?" Tom didn't bother trying to keep the exasperation from his voice. Why couldn't she be as worried about what GPC might do to *her*? Then he might have a fighting chance of keeping her out of trouble.

Kate crossed her arms defiantly. "To take advantage of her. Patti's too naïve and rich for her own good."

"She's twenty-one years old. Obviously her parents thought she was mature enough to manage her inheritance or they would've assigned a trustee."

"She's blinded by love—at least what she thinks is love. Add pain pills to that and who knows what foolish promises she might make."

"This morning you seemed to be more worried that GPC got to her. Weren't you?"

Kate's glare slipped to the vicinity of his chest. "Maybe. I don't know. You've got me so paranoid."

Tom stroked his thumb along her jaw and gentled his voice. "And you should be, Kate." His cell phone rang—the Lone Ranger ringtone reserved for the chief. "Excuse me a sec. I need to take this." He stepped ahead to block her exit.

"Where are you?" Brewster barked before Tom could spit out his name.

"Why?"

"The Conner woman called again, ten minutes ago. Dispatch couldn't reach you and wanted to know if she should send someone else."

"No, I'll check it out."

As he pocketed his phone, Kate brushed past him. "You've got to go. I can call a cab for Patti and me."

"Wait, you're not thinking this through. If GPC is connected somehow, you could put Patti in worse danger by moving in with her. After all, if anybody, it's you GPC is after."

Biting her lower lip, Kate wavered. "I need to do this. She fell down *my* basement stairs. I feel responsible. And I do not want her staying alone with Jarrett."

Tom matched Kate's step and whispered close to her ear. "What if I told you that someone may be spying on her house?"

Kate halted abruptly and whirled toward him. "Who? Why?"

"I don't know. And until I do, I'd prefer you weren't in the vicinity."

Ahead of them, Jarrett's steps slowed.

Kate lowered her voice. "I can't have her stay at my house. My spare room is jammed with furniture from the room I'm painting." She motioned to Jarrett now disappearing into a room at the end of the hall. "I have to catch up before he talks her into agreeing to let him stay."

Tom strode alongside the stubborn woman, reminding himself that her sense of duty and loyalty to her friends was what he'd first admired about her. "I wish you cared as much about your own welfare as your friend's."

She stopped outside Patti's room. "I thought you had a call to get to."

"Yeah, to the old Potter place next door to Patti's." He prayed this delay wouldn't cost him. "I can drop you and Patti off. Then"—he paused until she gave him her full attention—"after I check it out, we can *finish* this discussion."

"Sounds good," Jarrett said from inside the room. "I rode my motorcycle. Won't work with Patti's leg splinted."

Patti beamed. "Jarrett offered to stay with me at the house while I recuperate."

Kate rushed into the room. "I'd rather you let me stay with you." She leaned over Patti's wheelchair and added a few words that brought a pink blush to her friend's cheeks.

As far as Tom knew, Patti didn't share Kate's religious convictions, but whatever she'd said must've hit its mark.

Patti's hands twined in her lap, her fingers tracing a line around her bare ring finger. "Yes, you're right, of course. I appreciate your offer, Jarrett, but it would probably be better if Kate stayed to help me instead."

Jarrett pressed a kiss to the top of her head. "We'll talk about it when we get you home."

Kate's frown betrayed her distaste for Jarrett's slippery non-acceptance of Patti's decision. Tom didn't like to leave the young woman at Jarrett's mercy any more than Kate, but he liked even less the idea of Kate being miles outside of town with who knew who hiding in the house next door.

# 3

Tom in full cop mode was almost harder to bear than Tom in his caring, compassionate mode. Suffocating from the silence between them, Kate opened the car window to suck in a breath of fresh air.

Doped up on pain pills, Patti had dozed off in the back-seat within minutes of leaving the hospital, but Kate didn't want to argue with Tom about her decision to stay with Patti when she might overhear. Not that Kate could explain her compulsion. She didn't understand it herself, considering she'd planned to spend every spare minute doing more experiments on the plants in her basement. Except . . . it had been nice having Patti's company this morning.

Kate inhaled another deep breath, not wanting to think about how lonely she'd been lately. Besides, a tiny corner of her mind worried that Patti's motives for going to the basement this morning weren't entirely innocent. The extra time together should help her decide if Patti could be trusted not to feed Jarrett sensitive information.

A twinge of self-reproach coiled through Kate's middle. Maybe she was being too harsh on Jarrett, reading too much of his father's slick political motivations into his interest in Patti. If he were anyone else, she would've thought his offer to stay with Patti while she recuperated was sweet. But she'd rather err on the side of caution.

"Whoa, who lives there?" Kate exclaimed as a massive stone wall came into view.

Tom shot her a curious look. "You've never seen your research assistant's place?"

"Are you serious? Patti lives there? Alone?" The wall looked like it ran for miles. What she could see of the house set on a hill far back from the road looked like a castle, complete with parapets.

"Yeah, her father's landscape design business must've been lucrative, huh?"

"I'll say." They wouldn't need to worry about any GPC goons getting to them here. Except that she'd have to climb to the second story just to see who might be parked at the road. Although from the look of the security cameras mounted every few hundred feet along the top, Patti probably had a bank of closed-circuit monitors covering every inch of the property and surrounding fields.

"What's he doing here?"

Tom's question jerked Kate from her thoughts. "Who?"

"Westby." Tom slowed his car and motioned to a pair of vehicles parked at the end of an overgrown driveway just before Patti's property.

Kate's heart missed a beat. They hadn't been able to verify that the real estate agent had been trying to secure Verna Nagy's property for GPC. But the fact amendoso—the plant the company had destroyed her father's life over—had been growing there made the theory pretty much a certainty. The same real estate agent looking at an abandoned farm next door to her research assistant couldn't be a coincidence.

And the rigid line of Tom's jaw confirmed he shared her concern.

Yet he cruised right on past the property.

"Wait. Aren't you going to talk to him? Find out who's looking at the place? It could be"—Kate stole a peek over her shoulder as Patti stirred—"someone you want to talk to," Kate finished vaguely.

"I'll drop you two off and go back."

"But they might be gone by then." Kate twisted in her seat to get a glimpse of the agent and his client, only to have Patti's fortress walls cut off her view.

Tom pulled up to the wrought-iron gate guarding the driveway. "How do you open this?" The urgency in his voice betrayed how anxious he was to get back to the Potter property.

Patti rummaged through her purse and pulled out a remote.

"What do you do if the electricity goes out?" Kate asked.

"A backup generator automatically kicks in. My dad thought of everything."

Kate's heart panged at the affection in Patti's voice. She scarcely remembered the house she'd lived in before her dad died—she heaved a sigh—before he *left them*.

The instant the gates began to creak open, Tom edged the car past them.

As nice as the property was, Kate would have felt like a prisoner growing up here. The only thing missing was a moat. Giant oaks shadowed the pristine grass, blocking their view of the house as Tom started down the long, winding driveway. The gate closed behind them with a bone-shivering clank.

They emerged from the canopy of leaves at the foot of a small hill topped with a massive two-story Victorian. Flowers of every description flowed down and around the hill and steps to the driveway, hugging the gentle curves.

"Wow," Kate said breathlessly. She'd known her assistant's parents had been rich, but . . . It was a wonder Patti bothered to work!

"It's getting a little shabby looking with the cooler September weather. Now that I've wrecked my leg, I'll probably regret letting my gardener leave early for his winter in Florida."

"You have a gardener?" What was she saying? Of course she had a gardener. With a full-time job, she'd be working every night and weekend to keep these grounds looking this good otherwise.

Patti pointed to a quaint cottage at the back of the property. "He and his wife live there. She cleans for me, used to cook for our family too, when I was little." She pressed a hand to her generous tummy. "Cooked a little too well." Her twittery laugh made it sound like her meds were doing more than kill her pain. "They've been with us as long as I can remember," Patti chirped on. "Even stayed through the winter last year to keep me company after Mom and Dad died so suddenly, but they really don't like the cold." Her tone dropped, her words stalling.

Kate's heart reached out to her. They shared much in common.

Tom swerved around the circle and pulled the car to the

hewn stone steps carved into the hill. "Is there an easier way for you to get inside?"

"Yes, see the Y off the circle ahead? It leads to a garage built into the hill."

"Wow," Kate repeated as a door in the hill yawned open at the push of a button on Patti's remote.

"Dad didn't want to spoil the Victorian look of the house by attaching a garage, so this was his solution. The elevator opens into the kitchen to make it easy for bringing in groceries."

Tom didn't comment, probably thinking about getting next door to find out what the real estate agent was up to.

Kate hurried out of the car and helped Patti hop out on her good leg. "I can take care of Patti from here. You go check out your call."

Tom glanced around the state-of-the-art garage and, seemingly satisfied they were safe, said, "I'll be back as soon as I can."

Kate opened her mouth to say there was no need. She didn't feel like arguing with him again over whether or not she should stay with Patti. She closed it again when she remembered that she wanted to know who the real estate agent was showing the neighboring property to.

Patti pushed a button on her remote. "The gate will open automatically as you leave. When you come back, just press the speaker button and we'll let you in."

Tom nodded and hurried off.

Kate handed Patti the crutches the hospital had supplied and trailed her to the elevator.

"You'll have to give yourself the grand tour." Patti clip-clomped into the elevator like a pro and hit the Up button.

"I'd love it if you could make us a couple of sandwiches first, though. I'm starved."

"No problem. Is your bedroom on the main floor?"

"I'll stay in my parents' old room. Be easier than trying to manage the stairs. If you could bring down my clothes and stuff later that would be great."

"Sure, not a problem."

Patti chattered on even more rapidly than usual, and Kate hated to think how she'd feel when her pain meds started to wear off.

"There's a couple of guest rooms upstairs. Pick whichever one you'd like. I really appreciate you staying with me."

"I'm happy to."

Patti's eyes glistened with unshed tears. She blinked rapidly. "It'll be nice having company. The house is way too big for one person."

Kate knew that feeling well, and her house was a tenth the size.

The elevator opened to a massive kitchen with Italian slate floors, gleaming granite countertops, and shiny copper pots hanging over a center island practically the size of her entire kitchen. "Oh. My. I see what you mean."

Patti's crutch caught on the corner of the cupboard and she let out a yelp as she inadvertently put weight on her fractured leg. Leaning heavily against the counter, she said breathlessly, "Mom liked to bake, so Dad wanted her to have the best."

Letting her gaze travel the open shelves of decorative canisters and jars, Kate pushed chairs clear of Patti's path. It would take a bit of time to go through the expansive collection of dried herbs and tea mixtures to see what might have caused Patti's dizzy spells.

Patti levered herself through the kitchen, then plopped on a plush leather sofa in front of a cozy-looking gas fireplace in an equally expansive great room.

*Wow.* Kate tore her gaze from the baby grand sitting in a brightly lit round alcove in the far corner of the room and pinched her nose at the sudden bite of orange-blossom fragrance.

"Oh, sorry." Patti finished rubbing the smelly lotion into her hands and snatched up the bottle from the end table. Rising, she hooked the bottle's spout between two fingers as she clutched her crutch handle. "I forgot the fragrance bothers you. I'll put it away and go wash it off."

"Thanks." Kate lowered her hand, feeling bad about causing Patti the trouble, but orange blossom was one fragrance that tended to trigger her migraines. That was probably the bottle of hand lotion management had supplied their lab and Kate had told her to bring home. "I'll run up and use your other bathroom before I make those sandwiches," she said, needing to get away from the scent almost as much as she wanted to see if she could spot Tom and the real estate agent.

Leaning heavily on the crutch supporting her good leg, Patti pointed her other crutch in the general direction of the sweeping staircase that curved up to the second story. "First door on the right."

At the top of the stairs, Kate beelined to a south-facing window. From this height, she could easily see the entire Potter property beyond the fortress walls. She squinted toward the driveway and traced the faint path leading from the cars parked at the road. No sign of Tom. Could he have already made it up to the house?

Or was he still sitting in his car, waiting for backup?

desperate measures

She squinted back at the cars, wishing she had binoculars. She'd have to grab hers when she went home to pack an overnight bag. Movement at the Potter house caught her eye. Tom emerged from behind a thicket as two men stepped out of the house—one of them bald like Nagy's real estate agent.

Kate tensed. Her fingernails bit into her palms and she chided herself. It wasn't as if Tom was catching them doing anything that should provoke a shoot-out or something.

Then again, if the agent's client was from GPC . . . he was capable of anything.

"Kate, is that you?" Patti's voice drifted up the stairs.

"Be right down," Kate called, torn between watching to ensure Tom would be okay and getting Patti her sandwich. She noted the exact moment the men spotted Tom. They stopped on the porch, no doubt preferring the advantage of their higher position. "Lord, please keep him safe," she whispered, and waited, certain Patti would forgive her a few more seconds.

An ear-piercing scream split the air.

Having parked at the end of the property's almost impassable driveway, Tom reached the Potter house as the real estate agent and his client stepped out the side door onto the dilapidated porch. The agent's narrowed eyes left little doubt he recognized Tom from their last interaction.

The man buttoned his suit jacket and stepped to the edge of the porch. "May I help you?"

Tom anchored a foot on the steps, effectively blocking their exit. "We had a call about a trespasser on the place."

46

"As you can see, we're not trespassers. I'm showing a potential buyer the property."

Tom turned to the darkly tanned, twentysomething buyer, whose sandy-blond hair and week's worth of whisker growth made him look more like a beach bum than an aspiring farmer. "And you are?"

Recognition flickered in the man's eyes.

Tom tilted his head, noting the broad nose, the bushy black brows incongruent with his sand-colored hair, the familiar smirk. "Crump?" He hadn't seen Molly Gilmore's former fiancé since her bail hearing. He'd quit his job as the research station's publicist, a position acquired with a fake name and credentials manufactured by Molly's wealthy father, and left town. "What are you doing back here?"

Kate had liked to think that Jim Crump giving her the house he'd inherited from her murdered research partner was a sign he'd changed. The plain black pickup at the end of the driveway was certainly a step down from the flashy Porsche Boxter Crump used to drive. But the fact the broken-down place he was looking to buy stood next to the wealthiest estate in the area suggested he was still playing whatever lucrative angle he could find.

Crump caught Tom's hand in a firm grip. "Came back to make sure Molly gets her due."

"Oh?"

"Yeah, her father tried to pay me to disappear again so I wouldn't be around to testify against her."

Tom raised an eyebrow. "You willing to testify to that?"

"He didn't exactly say it in so many words. Nothing prosecutable. But the intention was crystal clear."

"And you turned him down?" Tom failed to keep the skepticism from his voice.

"I was seriously tempted, let me tell you. But those blasted Bible verses Daisy was always spouting kept hammering my brain and I couldn't do it. Daisy's about the only person who's ever believed in me. I can't let her down now."

"I see." Tom squinted at him, far from ready to take his explanation at face value. "And what's your interest in the old Potter place?"

Crump gave one of the porch columns a firm slap. "I know it's probably hard for you to believe, but I'm pretty handy with a hammer. I figured I could repair the place and then make a tidy profit selling it."

Okay, now that sounded more like the Crump Tom knew.

"Not that it's any of your business," the real estate agent interjected, reminding Tom of Westby's foiled attempt to help GPC acquire the Nagy property to get its hands on the amendoso plant.

Tom let his gaze travel over the fields surrounding the Potter place—full of weeds now, but formerly used for corn or hay or wheat. Not a tree in sight, beyond the ones in the yard. Not a habitat that would support the plant responsible for all Kate's troubles. Tom refocused on Crump. "Were you looking over the place last night too?"

"No, just got in this morning." Crump hesitated a fraction too long for Tom to believe him. Only, if he'd been here to look the place over, why not admit to it?

"And"—the real estate agent shuffled toward the steps—"we were just heading back to my office to take care of the paperwork." He shouldered past Tom. "If you'll excuse us."

Crump didn't immediately follow. His gaze shifted to the

horizon, or more specifically to the Goodman estate. "Do you have a lot of trouble with drifters in these parts?" His tone sounded concerned, like maybe he was rethinking his offer.

"No," Westby barked.

"Not as a rule," Tom confirmed. "Have you looked at other places?"

"If you don't mind, Detective," Westby cut in before Crump could open his mouth. "My wife's expecting me home for supper, and I'm sure my client would like to be on his way before dark." He motioned to Crump to follow him down the driveway.

Tom handed Crump a business card as he passed. "If you return and notice evidence of a trespasser, give me a call. We think he may be a runaway we're looking for."

Nodding, Crump pocketed the card.

The "Just the Way You Are" ringtone reserved for Kate blasted over Tom's cell phone. Snatching it from his hip, he leaned against the stair rail. "Hey, Kate, what's up? Everything okay?"

"Someone's in the house."

His pulse spiked at the frantic edge to her voice. "Who?" He sprinted past Crump and Westby, glancing across the field at what little was visible of the Goodman mansion over the stone wall. "Where are you?"

"I'm upstairs," she whispered. "I heard Patti scream, but when I reached the stairs, I heard a man's voice. Now I don't know what to do."

"Are you sure it's not Jarrett? He came through the gate as I was leaving."

"He did?" Hope crept into her voice. "But then why would Patti scream?"

"I don't know." Tom jumped into his car and had it spitting gravel from the tires before he had the door closed. "I'll be there in two minutes. Can you get to a control panel to open the gate for me?"

"I don't know where it is. But a house this size must have a back stairwell. I'll try to sneak down and—"

"No. Stay where you are." Chances were Jarrett had merely startled Patti. But what if the guy he'd seen on the motorcycle wasn't Jarrett?

"But—"

"Hold on." Tom stomped on his brake in front of the speaker box at the entrance. The house was scarcely visible through the trees, but if he announced himself and there was a prowler, he'd have lost any chance of surprising him. He scrutinized the spikes at the top of the wrought iron gate. From the hood of his car, he could probably scale the gate without skewering himself. *Probably.* "Kate, can you still hear voices? Does Patti sound distressed?"

"No, I don't hear or see anyone!" Kate's voice had that high-pitched tone of someone on the edge.

"Okay, stay calm. And stay where you are. I'm coming." Tom leapt onto the hood of his car, knowing he'd look like an idiot if this turned out to be a false alarm. He gripped the bars and swung his legs over. Better to look like an idiot than risk Kate's safety.

A black pickup screeched to a stop next to his car.

Tom ducked behind a giant oak tree as Jim Crump jumped out.

He glanced in Tom's car, shook the gate, then squinted through the bars.

Tom jerked back out of sight.

"Detective?" Crump called out, and Tom swallowed a ticked response. Even with the abundance of trees and shrubs on the park-like grounds between the gate and the house, he wouldn't be able to sneak up to it with Crump shouting after him.

Another thought triggered an uneasy ripple through his chest. What if Molly's ex was working with whoever was inside? In seconds his cohort could open the gate.

With no time to lose, Tom stole down the edge of the winding driveway, using the trees as cover. "Kate, you still there?" he hissed into his phone as he ran. "Kate?" He glanced at his phone, only then realizing he must have pressed the Off button when he vaulted the fence. He didn't dare risk ringing her back.

The squeak of hinges sounded behind him. *The gate.* Who opened it? Slipping deeper into the trees, he squinted up the drive. There was no way he could make it to the attached garage built into the hill at the far side of the house without being spotted. He glanced at the security cameras on either end of the roof. Yeah, might already be too late. He sprinted toward the solarium attached to the nearest side and crouched behind a bush twenty feet from the front door, then called dispatch for backup.

Crump's black pickup rumbled up the long driveway as the front door burst open and Kate bounded outside.

The tightness in Tom's chest eased at the sight of her. "Kate, over here," Tom called in a hushed whisper, closing the distance between them in long strides.

"You were right. It was Jarrett. He let himself in and caught Patti by surprise. I'm sorry I worried you for noth—"

Tom pulled her into his arms. "You never have to apologize for being cautious."

She returned his embrace as if it were the most natural thing in the world, as if she didn't blame him for concealing her father's existence and then ripping him from her life once more.

But there was no time to relish the sweet moment. He quickly maneuvered both of them behind the bush next to the solarium. "Who opened the gate?"

Kate bucked against being shoved behind a bush, clearly confused. "Jarrett. I told him it was you—" She choked on the last word as Crump's truck pulled to the front of the house. "Who's that?"

"The man Jarrett let in," Tom growled, pushing Kate behind him until he could figure out what had possessed Crump to follow him. "Stay here."

Crump came around his truck and jolted at the sight of Tom striding toward him. "There you are."

"What are you doing here?"

Crump eyed the holstered weapon visible under Tom's open blazer and lifted his hands. "I heard you say Kate's name on the phone, then saw your car at the gate, and from the way you ripped out of my driveway, I thought she might be in trouble."

"I appreciate your concern, but the situation is under control." Tom glanced back at the bushes concealing Kate, half expecting her to pop out to greet him.

"That's great." Crump lowered his hands. "Then I might as well say hi while I'm here."

Tom clenched his fist in frustration. Of course he'd want to say hi. Considering the man had handed her Daisy's house on a silver platter, Kate would be eager to see him too. But apparently, she hadn't recognized him yet. "Kate,"

Tom muttered toward the bushes. "Come meet Patti's new neighbor."

The bushes jostled, but Kate didn't show herself.

"Kate?"

Another long moment passed before she emerged from behind the bush, and even then her gaze warily slanted back over her shoulder before connecting with Crump's. She blinked. "Edward?" she said, calling him by the alias he'd used during his last stint in Port Aster.

"Hey." Crump extended his hand and flashed Kate the kind of smile guys used at a party to pick up women. "I go by Jim now."

Tom curled his arm firmly around Kate's waist and straightened to his full height. At over six feet, Crump had a good two inches on him and a build that probably took hours a day in the gym to maintain, but Tom wasn't about to let him think Kate was available. He wasn't even sure the guy could be trusted.

Surprisingly, Kate didn't quiz him on what he was doing back in town. She slipped her hand from Crump's and motioned toward the front door. "Come in and meet Patti."

And if Kate's lack of curiosity wasn't bewildering enough, Tom didn't know what to make of Crump's nervous glance at the door. Given his previous modus operandi, Tom sure wasn't ready to dismiss his sudden interest in property neighboring Kate's wealthy research assistant as coincidence.

The distant wail of a police siren reminded him to cancel his call for backup. He caught up with Crump at the steps. "Hey, what happened to Westby? I thought you were heading to his office to sign papers."

"I was, but when I saw you veer into Patti's driveway like

there might be trouble, I told him I'd meet him at the office tomorrow morning."

The hair on the back of Tom's neck pricked to attention. "How did you know her name was Patti?"

A telltale flush crept into Crump's cheeks.

"I just said her name," Kate chirped, but the instant relief that relaxed Crump's shoulders told Tom that *that* wasn't how he knew.

Apparently Kate's newfound reluctance to take anyone at his word only applied to him, not to the would-be philandering neighbor.

Kate hurried up the porch steps. "Patti broke her leg this morning, so I'll be staying with her for a while until she's back on her feet."

The concern Tom had seen in Crump's face earlier steamrolled into his voice. "Is she okay? How'd it happen?"

Hovering at the threshold to the house, Kate flinched. "She fell down my basement stairs. It looked horrible, but the doctor assured her it should heal all right."

As they led Crump to the great room, Patti hunched forward on the sofa, cupping her hands to her head, her broken leg propped on a pillow.

Kate dashed to her side. "What's wrong? Do you feel sick?"

"She said she felt dizzy again." Jarrett set an empty juice glass on the end table next to the sofa.

"She was fine a minute ago. What did you give her to drink?" The accusation in Kate's tone was unmistakable, and Crump's gaze snapped to Jarrett, his eyes narrowing.

"Whoa, I didn't cause it." Jarrett backed up a step. "I gave her orange juice from her fridge *after* she said she felt dizzy."

Crump's attention shifted to Patti and his expression

softened. No, transformed. Transformed to a compassion that verged on something several shades stronger than affection.

Tom bristled, instinctively certain Crump was laying on the charm in anticipation of a new score.

Jarrett must've noticed too, because he shot Crump a glare that would've combusted a lesser man on the spot. "Who are you?"

Crump didn't seem to register the question. He kneeled in front of Patti and gently lifted her chin. "Do you feel like the room is spinning or tilting?"

Patti took a moment to focus on him, but surprisingly, even then didn't pull away or ask who he was. Eventually his question must've sunk in and she shook her head. "Not spinning. I just feel dizzy."

"Do you feel worse when you walk?"

"No." She squeezed her eyes closed. "I don't know. I feel like my head's floating."

Crump nodded as if her description made perfect sense. "Are you on medication?"

"The hospital gave her anti-inflammatories and pain pills," Kate interjected.

Again Crump nodded, but his gaze never left Patti's face. "When's the last time you ate?"

"Who are you?" Jarrett yanked hard on Crump's shoulder, knocking him off balance.

"What are you doing?" Kate shoved Jarrett away as Crump pushed to his feet. "Can't you see he's trying to help her?"

Tom wasn't so sure, but he kept his opinion to himself.

"It's okay." Crump extended his hand toward Jarrett. "I'm sorry. I should've introduced myself. I'm trained in first aid and thought maybe I could help. I'm Jim Crump. I'm buying the place next door."

Jarrett snorted, obviously having seen the same besotted look as Tom had in Crump's face.

Patti sat back and squinted up at Crump. "You look familiar. Have we met before?"

Tom didn't know what to make of the pleased smile that accompanied Crump's negative response. He didn't know how to read the guy at all. And that was more worrisome than his suspicion that Crump was angling to fleece Kate's friend, because for all Tom knew, the guy could still be loyal to Molly Gilmore.

And if he was, Tom didn't want him anywhere near Kate.

Crump studied Patti's face a moment. "I don't think so."

"Actually, she does know you," Kate corrected, then turned twinkling eyes to Patti. "He used to go by the name Edward Smythe."

"Edward?" A rosy blush bloomed on Patti's cheeks. "Of course! I can't believe I didn't recognize you. You changed your hair color. I was an intern at one of the greenhouses when you worked at the research station." And if Tom had to guess, she'd had a big-time crush on the guy.

Crump reached for Patti's hand and gave it a gentle squeeze. "So nice to meet you."

"You too," she murmured, apparently as mesmerized by his face as he'd been by hers.

"Why the name change?" Jarrett growled, steam all but billowing from his ears.

"Um, maybe you should visit again when Patti's feeling better," Kate suggested.

Tom caught Crump's arm. "I'll walk you out. You can give

me a lift to my car, if you don't mind." It was as good an excuse as any to ensure that Crump didn't make any detours or pit stops on his way off the property. The sun was fading fast, leaving him little time to make a thorough search of the Potter property. And the sooner he saw Crump out, the sooner he could do just that.

Tom dug his hand into his pocket for his keys, tamping down his irritation that he was no closer to identifying their phantom trespasser. Was it the missing teen?

Tom's gaze strayed back to Kate and Patti. *Or someone more dangerous?*

# 4

As soon as Tom and Jim Crump disappeared down the drive-way, Kate slipped outside and hurried to the solarium. When Edward—Jim, she was going to have a hard time getting used to using his real name—first arrived, she'd been so distracted by the plant she'd spotted while hiding in the bushes next to the solarium, she hadn't even registered who Tom was talking to. She'd been concerned only with getting them away from the solarium before they spotted the plant too. She had a thousand and one questions for Jim. But the compulsion to scope out the plant had had her way too distracted to form a single intelligent question.

Next time she saw him, she'd have to do better.

When he left town three months ago, he'd been so broken—ashamed of his trust in Molly and of his own lies and that Daisy, even knowing he wasn't really her long lost nephew, had still left him her house. He'd signed the house over to Kate, but she'd hoped that with time, he'd find his way back to the *real* home Daisy had been trying to show him.

Reaching the door at the far end of the solarium, Kate jiggled the knob. *Locked.* Cupping her hands around her eyes, she squinted through the glass wall near where she'd been hiding. Had she seen what she thought she'd seen?

Colorful blossoms dangled from hanging baskets. Half a dozen tropical trees—lemon, lime, fig, avocado, star fruit, bay leaf—stood in massive planters scattered throughout the glass-enclosed sanctuary dominated by an ornamental waterfall in its center. Dozens of unusual plants completed the serene setting. But Kate zeroed in on the lone pot set on a bench in the corner.

Her breath caught. *It* is *an amendoso plant.* Her eyes hadn't been playing tricks on her. She pressed her hand against her hammering heart. How did Patti get it?

And what did she intend to do with it?

Tires crunching on the driveway startled Kate out of her thoughts. *Tom.* She couldn't let him see her peering into the solarium. He'd want to know why, and she wasn't ready to tell him about her discovery. It would make him suspicious of Patti and all the more concerned about the danger of her staying here.

She emerged from the bushes, her pulse escalating. She could just imagine what Julie would say of her reasoning. *Too stupid to live.* How many times had her best friend compared her to a horror-flick chick who treks to the basement to investigate an eerie noise instead of racing out of the house and calling the police?

Missing her recently married confidante, Kate let out a bittersweet chuckle. But running away wasn't an option.

Neither was informing the police.

She had no idea who could be trusted. If GPC had an inkling

that Patti had an amendoso plant in her possession, she hated to think what tactics they'd resort to, to get their hands on it.

Kate shivered. Okay, maybe she was too stupid to live. Because if Patti had had the plant in her solarium all along, she would've said something about it! Did she acquire it herself, or . . .? Kate fisted her hands in frustration. She'd wind up second-guessing herself to death, when the fact was that figuring out why GPC so desperately wanted to control the amendoso plants was her only leverage to convince the FBI or CIA or NSA—or whoever Tom had enlisted to hide her father—that they needed to let her see him.

And she didn't dare reveal their existence until she figured out the secret. She had to believe that her dad wouldn't have kept the plant from GPC, let alone gone into hiding and let his family believe he was dead, if his employer had intended to use the plant for the good of humanity. He had to have been afraid they planned to exploit something else about it, something dangerous.

Tom parked at the foot of the steps that climbed the hill to Patti's front door. Halfway up the steps, he stopped, his attention jerking in her direction. "Kate?"

She hurried toward him.

"What are you doing out here?" His gaze shifted over her shoulder to the thicket of shrubs and the solarium beyond.

"Oh"—she fluttered her hand toward the end of the house as her mind scrambled for a believable excuse—"I wanted a feel for the lay of the land."

Not even a lie . . . metaphorically speaking.

"C'mon, I'll take you home."

"What? No way. I already told you I'm staying with Patti." Especially now.

"I know. I meant to grab your car and a suitcase."

"Oh, right." Kate forced thoughts of the plant in the solarium from her mind and started up the steps ahead of him. "I don't want to be gone long. I'm not so sure I believe Jarrett didn't have anything to do with that last dizzy spell." She bit her lip, realizing Tom might ask her what she was doing outside when the man was in the house alone with Patti.

"Do you think Patti's been experimenting with a weight-loss formula?"

"Huh? What are you talking about?"

"Her dizziness. And she seems self-conscious about her weight. Maybe she was too embarrassed to mention it in front of Jarrett?"

Kate paused at the door and faced him. "She'd have said something about it to me back at my house, I'm sure."

"I don't know." Tom looked skeptical. "Sometimes people are funny about things like that."

Kate nodded, but not because she thought Patti was taking diet pills on the sly. Maybe she'd been secretive because what she was really experimenting with were amendoso infusions. Maybe she'd managed to translate more of the Spanish documents she'd downloaded about the plant than she'd let on. Drinking amendoso infusions might explain her dizziness. And if she *was* experimenting with it on herself, she wouldn't want to admit to something so foolhardy.

Just because an online article claimed it was innocuous didn't make it true.

How did Patti even find the plant? Kate never told her where it was growing. A light came on inside the house, and Kate glanced through the window. *Jarrett.* He'd tailed her through the countryside that one day, last month . . . the same day Patti had given her the info she'd found online. A coincidence?

Or had she all but led him straight to it?

"What's wrong?" Tom cupped her elbow. "You've gone white."

"I have?" Kate pressed her palms to her cheeks. "I'm just tired. It's been a long day."

He reached around her and, twisting the doorknob, pushed open the door. "Then we'd better let Patti know that we're going to make a quick trip to your house."

"But I still have to make her a sandwich."

"Taken care of." Jarrett emerged from the kitchen, carrying a plate of sandwiches, as she and Tom stepped into the great room.

*Good*. The sooner she got back from her house, the sooner Jarrett could leave and she could find out what Patti was up to with the plant. This could turn out to be a great place for her to run her experiments . . . if she could be sure that Patti hadn't dug up the amendoso with more insidious motives. Kate could handle aspirations of making a research coup; she just needed to ensure that Jarrett didn't have other ideas.

As soon as he left, she'd figure out a way to get to the truth.

Jarrett helped prop Patti a little higher on the sofa and handed her a sandwich.

"Jarrett's offered to stay in the gardener's cottage until I'm feeling better. Isn't that great?"

Kate's jaw dropped. She quickly clapped it shut. "That's not necessary. I'm happy to stay."

"Oh, I still want you to. And you might as well drive my car back here. Jarrett, could you grab her my spare car key from the dish on the mantel behind you?" Patti bit into her sandwich, then danced her fingers over her mouth as she chewed. "Jarrett just figured we might appreciate extra security. He said there'd been reports of someone lurking around the Potter place. Is that right, Detective?"

For the first time since they'd entered, Kate glanced at Tom. His expression looked grimmer than her mood.

"Your neighbor reported seeing someone on the property and a light in the house. Yes."

Kate stifled an involuntary shiver. Someone hiding out at the Potter place couldn't have anything to do with her. No one could've foreseen her ending up here tonight. Not when she'd never been to her research assistant's house before.

"C'mon." Tom steered her back to the front door. "We better get going. It'll be dark soon and I still want to take another look around the property next door."

As the door clicked shut behind them, Kate whispered, "Do you think it might've been Jim Crump that the neighbor saw? You know, checking out the place?"

"That's one possibility. Although he claims not."

"You don't believe him?" She had a pang of alarm at the memory of Jarrett and Jim Crump vying for Patti's attention. She was too emotionally vulnerable right now to see things clearly.

Tom prodded Kate down the hill to his car. "Crump doesn't exactly have a reputation for being honest."

The grave tone of his voice intensified her concern and told her Tom's objections to her staying here hadn't subsided either. She squirmed at the uncomfortable realization that he likely saw her as similarly alone and vulnerable. Was that why he wanted to protect her—not so much because he had feelings for her as he just didn't want her hurt, the same as he'd feel about any person in trouble?

She shook away the thought. It didn't matter. Climbing into the car, she refocused on Patti's situation. The compassion on Crump's face when he'd looked at her didn't jibe with someone working toward nefarious ends. Kate was pretty sure they didn't have to worry about any trouble from him. Unless . . . Jarrett's jealousy got out of hand.

Kate rested her head against the passenger window and stared at the purple-gray clouds streaking the late afternoon sky. How was she supposed to win Patti's confidence, let alone experiment on the plant, with Jarrett constantly around the place? "I don't trust Jarrett alone with Patti."

Tom turned the car and sped down the driveway. "You'll be back in less than an hour. There's nothing he can do today that he couldn't have done any other day."

"But she's more vulnerable right now. I can't believe she agreed to let him stay in the gardener's cottage."

"I think it's a good idea."

"You trust him?" Kate lifted her head, her voice rising with it. She couldn't help it. Tom was supposed to be on her side. "That's like asking the fox to guard the henhouse!"

"He seems genuinely concerned about her." Tom glanced across the seat with a smoldering gaze that left her weak in the knees. "I know how that feels."

He did?

"If I'd known Patti was open to putting someone up in her gardener's cottage, I'd have volunteered to stay in it myself."

Kate's heart skittered at Tom's rumbly words. She rubbed her arms, trying to ignore how appealing the idea sounded. She needed to stay focused on studying the amendoso plant—

the plant Tom couldn't know about. "At least I wouldn't have to worry about *you* drugging Patti's orange juice," she quipped, only half joking.

"True." His look turned serious. "And I wouldn't have to worry about you running headlong into more trouble."

She let out a mock snort.

The gate opened ahead of them.

Tom pulled his car through and waited at the end of the driveway as the gate closed. "I'm serious. You go full tilt watching out for anyone you think's in trouble, without giving a second's thought to the danger." He turned onto the road toward her house. "Not to mention what your risks do to my blood pressure."

"Is your blood pressure elevated?" she asked, ever so innocently. "Because I have hawthorn tea that'll bring that right down."

It was his turn to snort. "You're changing the subject."

"Am not. You mentioned your blood pressure. I was—"

"Forget my blood pressure. We're talking about the risks you're taking."

*And he only knew half of them.* Pressing her lips together, she glanced back at Patti's fortressed grounds disappearing behind them and suddenly felt much too hot for the rapidly cooling air. "Now that I've had time to think about Patti's dizziness and my conclusion-jumping back at the hospital, I highly doubt Patti's been poisoned, let alone that GPC is responsible."

No, the more she thought about it, the more certain she was that Patti had been experimenting with the amendoso plant. "After all, what possible motive would GPC have to poison Patti?"

"Like you said, this dizziness, and now the broken leg, has made her vulnerable and more receptive to Jarrett drawing closer."

Kate gaped at him. "You just said you believe Jarrett's concern for Patti is genuine."

"Sure, but that doesn't mean he doesn't have ulterior motives."

Kate threw enough clothes into her suitcase to last for a few days and then gathered her laptop and the papers about amendoso that Betty from the B and B had translated. She should've guessed Patti's discovery of the online Spanish journal praising the plant's almost magical healing abilities would pique her interest, especially after she'd searched every corner of the internet in her effort to help Kate identify the plant. Kate reached for the page she'd removed from the stack this morning, the one with the instructions on how to make it into a salve. Rereading Betty's neat printing, frustration that her experiments would now be delayed even longer warred with the need to get back to Patti's and get her alone long enough to find out what the plant was doing in her solarium. Except . . .

Kate raced down to the basement to initiate the experiment she'd hoped to start this weekend after a little more background research. She'd have to forgo the research part, but a short delay getting back to Patti's wouldn't do any harm. Like Tom said, Jarrett wasn't going to get anything out of her this afternoon that he couldn't have gotten yesterday. And as long as he was hanging around, Kate wouldn't get anything either.

She prepared a salve from the amendoso leaves, exactly as

Betty had transcribed, and prayed that both the original and Betty's translation were accurate. The Spanish missionary who wrote the blog claimed the plant healed everything from dysentery to gangrene, and once she confirmed whether a fraction of the claims were actually true, she'd have a better idea of where to begin to determine how it worked. Step one was to prove it could kill harmful bacteria.

As she added the salve to petri dishes with different strains of bacteria, the scientist in her—the one Daisy had conscientiously trained to follow protocols and never rush the process—wrestled with the daughter in her who wanted to see her father *now*. Because without answers, she didn't have a hope of that ever happening.

Her mind flicked to Tom. She'd half expected him to stick around while she packed a bag so he could follow her back to Patti's house. Thankfully, another police call on the drive into town had nixed that possibility. He'd scarcely stopped long enough in her driveway to see her safely inside. Not like him at all, especially when he'd made his opposition to her staying at Patti's abundantly clear.

She pushed the thought aside and set the petri dishes in the incubator Daisy had bought from the research station when they upgraded theirs, then recorded the needed data. If by the time she returned the bacteria levels had significantly declined, she'd have something to go on.

Satisfied, she hurried back upstairs and grabbed the fixings for the supper she'd planned to cook. With extra rice and vegetables, she could easily stretch it to feed three instead of one. She loaded everything into Patti's car, then checked all the windows and doors and armed the alarm. *Oh! My binoculars.* She snatched them from the top of the closet by the door and slipped outside, seconds before the alarm's exit delay finished beeping.

Clouds huddled on the horizon, blocking the setting sun. The days were getting way too short. At this rate, unless that call Tom got was quick, he wouldn't make it back to finish checking over the Potter place before dark. Of course, whoever had been there likely wouldn't have stuck around after the real estate agent showed up with Crump.

Kate focused on getting herself back to Patti's. Whatever was going on at the Potter property wasn't going to affect her. Not with a six-foot block wall topped with an electrified wire and enough cameras to rival London's city streets standing between the two places.

As she pulled through Patti's gate, she spotted Jarrett on a stepladder at the south wall, reorienting a security camera. *That might keep him busy for a few minutes yet.* She stepped on the gas and sped up to the house. Of course, it took her a good three minutes to figure out which button on Patti's remote control opened the garage door, but the instant it yawned open, she nosed the car inside and made short work of unloading her stuff into the elevator.

The house was quiet. When she reached the kitchen, she set the supper fixings on the counter and carried her other luggage to the great room. Patti was nowhere in sight. "Patti?" Kate set her bags at the foot of the stairs and checked the washroom. Empty. "Patti?" she said more quietly this time as she padded toward the main floor bedroom. The door was closed. Repeating Patti's name one more time, she lightly tapped the door. When no response came, she edged it open. The room was massive, dominated by a king-size, dark mahogany sleigh bed. Patti lay sound asleep in the middle of it.

Kate soundlessly closed the door and hurried back to the great room. This was her chance. Standing on her tiptoes, she peered out the front window until she spotted Jarrett, still preoccupied with a camera on the wall. *Perfect.* She rushed down the hall leading to the solarium. The doorknob turned easily in her hands, but the door didn't budge.

She pushed. She pulled. She muscled her shoulder into it. Nothing. Great. Why on earth would Patti lock her solarium? Kate glanced around the dark hall. And where would she keep a key?

Kate felt her pockets for Patti's car keys. Empty. She must've dropped them on the counter, along with the food. She sprinted across the great room to the kitchen and snatched them up. Eyeballing each one, she hurried back across the great room.

"What's on fire?"

She startled at the sound of Jarrett's voice by the front door. The keys went flying. "Oh, I didn't hear you come in."

Chuckling, he scooped up the keys and tossed them back to her. "Sorry, didn't mean to scare you. Patti still asleep?"

"Yeah, I, uh"—Kate motioned from the kitchen to the bedroom to her bags still sitting at the bottom of the stairs—"brought stuff to make supper, but I was just going to take my suitcase upstairs first."

"I can do that."

"No, no." Kate reached for her bags before Jarrett closed the distance between them. "I need to freshen up anyways." And there was no way she wanted Jarrett snooping through her papers. Bringing her amendoso research here hadn't been the smartest move. She'd have to keep it hidden in her room until Jarrett went out to the gardener's cottage for the night.

"Okay, I'll be in the security room if you need me." Jarrett headed in the direction of the hall that led to the solarium.

"The security room?"

He stopped at the first door on the right in the hall. "Yeah, right here. Stop in after you're done and I'll show you how everything works."

Kate took the stairs two at a time and slung her bags onto the bed. Not bothering to unpack, she paused only long enough to peek out the window with her binoculars. Seeing no sign of Tom or anyone else next door, she set them on the night table and headed downstairs.

She found Jarrett sitting in front of a bank of monitors, his gaze fixed on one he was fast-forwarding. It showed the solarium. Her pulse quickened. Had he seen her peering inside? She squinted at the image, which showed not only the outside of the solarium, but sections inside the glass-enclosed construction, not concealed by the shrubs. Which meant even if she snuck in when he wasn't around, he still might see her if he played back the feed. "How long is the data saved?" she asked a little too breathlessly.

He gave her a funny look as if he'd noticed. "It's on a twelve-hour loop."

She shifted her attention to the other monitors and paused at one that offered a near-perfect view of the Potters' drive-way. "Hey, does Tom know about the recordings? Have you scanned this one?" She pointed to the monitor, anticipation welling in her chest. "It may have caught an image of the trespasser."

"Yeah, I did. But all the cameras were angled to moni-tor Patti's property and a tight perimeter around it, not the neighbors'. I just adjusted the angle on that one so I can keep a better eye on the Potter place from here on out. And I've tapped into the feed so that I'll be able to monitor the images from the cottage on my laptop at night."

Wow, he was taking Patti's security seriously. Which was actually kind of scary. "How do you know how to do all this?"

"It's not hard."

"Maybe not for a computer genius."

He shrugged. "I'm a security consultant."

"Oh." She remembered her hairdresser—the last woman he dated—saying he was a consultant when asked why he traveled so much. But she hadn't said anything about him being in security. No wonder he'd offered to stick close after hearing about the trespasser, on top of Patti's unexplained dizziness. "Do you think whoever has been hanging around next door is planning a break-in?"

Jarrett tapped a couple of buttons, changing the perspective of the view on the screen he was studying. "You secure yourself behind a towering wall, people are going to assume you have something they'll want."

"I suppose." Kate hugged her middle, suddenly feeling vulnerable despite the state-of-the-art security. "The whole walled perimeter does seem like overkill. You'd think Patti's dad had the Hope Diamond squirreled away in here or something."

"I suspect his primary motive was to protect his wife and daughter." Jarrett's tone was deep and serious, conveying the authority of one intimately acquainted with security clients' motives and fears.

"Kind of ironic, don't you think? He probably put them in more danger by making the place look like a place worth breaking into."

71

"He was afraid we'd be kidnapped."

At the sound of Patti's voice, Kate spun on her heel and gaped at her lab assistant standing in the doorway, her face as white as her fingers clenching the handles of her crutches. "Why?"

Patti's gaze flicked to Jarrett, then the security monitors. "It was a silly paranoia. Now that he's gone, I should probably get rid of all of this."

"Kind of a big paranoia to go to this extreme."

Patti turned away. "He had his reasons," she muttered as she awkwardly maneuvered her crutches out the door. She seemed a lot wobblier on her feet than she had earlier.

"What reasons?" Kate whispered to Jarrett.

He frowned, his gaze dipping to the keyboard he'd been manipulating before she came in. "Patti," Jarrett called after her. "If she's going to stay here, she should know the risks."

"Risks?" Kate's breath caught as Patti whirled back around.

"My grandparents never forgave my dad for taking Mom away."

"O-kay . . . ," Kate said, as her brain scrambled to make sense out of the statement.

"Away from the family business," Jarrett clarified, although Kate still couldn't wrap her mind around how that translated into the kind of security in this room.

Patti, resting against the door frame, stared at her, clearly expecting her to say something.

Kate shook her head. "I'm sorry. I still don't understand. He thought your grandparents would take her back by force?"

Patti rolled her eyes. "The family business is the mob."

# 5

The first rays of dawn speared Tom awake. Stretching out his still-sleeping arm, he squinted at the dashboard clock. 7:00 a.m. Only four hours of sleep. Not nearly enough. But when he'd finally left the scene of last night's investigation, it had been too late and too dark to finish searching the Potter property. At the time, sleeping in the Potter driveway and waiting for dawn had seemed like a smart idea.

He winced at the prickle in his waking arm. If he'd been smart, he would've gotten more info from dispatch on Kate's 911 call before racing over there yesterday morning. His dad could've handled it without him.

Tom choked down the last half of his stone-cold coffee that even when hot hadn't come close to the taste of his favorite blend from A Cup or Two, then climbed out of his car. The chilly morning air slapped him awake as well as any cold shower. Eyeing the quarter-mile hike up the deeply rutted so-called driveway to the house, he zipped his jacket and buried his hands in his pockets. Brrr. By the time he reached the door, he might be firing on all cylinders.

He squinted across the field toward the Goodman estate. A light flicked on in an upper story bedroom. *Kate's*. His pulse quickened as he zeroed in on it. The curtain shifted, and reflexively he puffed out his chest. But the window was too far away to tell if she'd actually looked out. His face heated at the thought of her taming her wild mane after a restless night.

He revisited her harried call last night. Considering Patti's mobster grandparents had been dead for six years, leaving only uncles and cousins far less likely to carry a grudge, he suspected Jarrett had been angling to scare Kate out of bunking up with Patti rather than anything more devious. But the information about the camera feeds she'd given him when she called was good to know. He wished he'd been able to scan the images from yesterday morning before they got recorded over. At least Jarrett would have no good reason to cover up seeing Caleb, the missing teen, on the feed. If whoever had been around the Potter place was spying for GPC, that might be another story.

Pausing at the foot of the stairs, Tom stared at the porch screen door. It hung cockeyed on one good hinge, and he strained to recall if that's how it had sat after Westby and Crump came out yesterday afternoon. He studied the ground for signs of another set of footprints. But the path to the porch was so overgrown that the footprints were indistinguishable.

Flicking on his flashlight, he wedged the broken screen door and pushed open the interior one. The kitchen looked the same as it had the day before. He wasted little time re-checking the rest of the house, upstairs and down. Aside from two new sets of man-sized shoe prints—Westby's distinctive

74

heeled dress shoes and Crump's athletic treads, different than the court shoe style treads he'd noticed yesterday—nothing had changed. He wished he'd taken fingerprints from the stair rail and doorknobs yesterday, before Westby and Crump had traipsed through. He might've at least confirmed that the kid had been here.

Stepping back outside, Tom pulled the door closed behind him. It was the barn he was most interested in combing this morning.

"Hey!" Kate waved from the field of chest-high grass and quickened her stride, her arms moving like a champion swimmer's, sweeping aside the grasses. "Find anything?"

Her early-morning smile kicked his heart up a notch, but he checked the urge to meet her halfway in the grass and . . . Wrestling that romantic notion out of his brain, he growled, "What are you doing over here?"

Her head jerked back at his less-than-friendly greeting. "Good morning to you too."

"Sorry, I didn't get much sleep."

She finished her diagonal swim from the corner of the property and stopped in front of him, sporting a playful smile. "And you're kind of grumpy before your morning coffee?"

"That too," he mumbled, since five-hour-old, cold, truck-stop coffee didn't count. "I trust you knew I was here before you came wading across the field."

"Sure. I saw you from the window. So did you find any clues?"

"Not yet." He pressed his palm to the small of her back and a whole different tingling awakened in his arm. "I was about to check out the barn. Care to join me?"

She tapped her finger to her chin, her eyes twinkling. "I don't know. My gran always warned me never to go in a barn alone with a boy."

Tom laughed, glad she hadn't been able to read his thoughts about being in a meadow with one. "Wise woman. I promise to be on my best behavior."

"You better be." She smirked. "You never know when Jarrett might be watching. Did you know he's a security consultant?"

"Yeah." Tom slid open the barn's bay door to let in more light and motioned Kate forward. "I did a background check on him at the same time I did Patti's, after I found them nosing around your house last month."

Kate worried her bottom lip between her teeth as if she might have more to say, then abruptly turned her attention to the rusty farm implements littering the floor. "What are we looking for?"

Tearing his gaze from her tortured lip and still wondering what she'd been thinking, he looked around dumbly for a full two seconds. "Uh . . . any sign someone's recently been in here."

"But Jim and the real estate agent probably were. Wouldn't you think?"

"Unfortunately."

The haunting blast of a train whistle carried across the fields, followed by the distant rumble of the wheels on the tracks.

Kate shivered. "If Caleb's been around all these weeks, why hasn't anyone spotted him? His picture is plastered everywhere. How's he getting food? Warm clothes? The nights are getting colder."

"I don't know. Maybe he's long gone, and the neighbor just spotted some vagrant or neighborhood kids. Because if it was Caleb, the bigger question is, why hasn't he just gone home?"

"You got any ideas?"

He shook his head. "The kid's parents seem terra firma. The kid does well in school. Seemed well liked by teachers and classmates. There isn't a single red flag in the file."

"And he wasn't carrying a cell phone the police could track?"

"He was, but the best we could confirm was that he was still in the area Saturday night." Tom shone his flashlight into the loft of the large barn, striped by the morning sun slanting between weathered boards. "Looks like up there's the only decent hiding place in here."

"Yeah, aside from that pile of musty straw bales over in the far corner, down here looks like a machinery graveyard."

"Touch as little as possible and keep your eyes peeled for a scrap of snagged clothing or candy wrappers or footprints, anything like that." He tested the rickety wooden ladder leaning against the loft. "I'll be right back." A rung cracked under his weight.

"Be careful!"

He tightened his grip on the sides and climbed faster. Reaching the top, he gingerly tested the floorboards.

"Don't you dare fall through," she called after him. "You'll be impaled by a harrow."

Hmm. Nice picture. He spotted a rope dangling from the rafters and a muddle of small shoeprints near the edge, too small to be Caleb's. "Looks like the local kids use the rope to swing into that straw pile. A place like this would've been heaven when Hank and I were kids."

"Would explain the bike trails in the field too."

"It would, but Caleb's bike went missing with him, so we can't assume anything." Tom combed through the thin layer of hay covering the loft and let out a sigh as he reached the window. "Unfortunately, from the size of these shoeprints, there's no sign that anyone over four and a half feet has been up here recently. But there's a great view of Patti's place."

Inside the barn, Kate stepped from behind an old red Massey Ferguson tractor, her hair shimmering in the narrow shafts of sunlight stealing between the wallboards.

"Mmm, this view's even better."

She smoothed her fleece jacket and tugged a stray piece of straw from her hair. "Cute."

He grinned. "That too." Out of the corner of his eye, he caught motion outside the barn door. He grabbed the rope and threw himself out of the loft. As the rope swung toward the bales of straw in front of Kate, he scarcely restrained a Tarzan call. But at least he managed to let go of the rope *over* the straw pile and land on his feet, with maybe only fifty rope slivers burning into his fingers.

"What are you doing?" Kate cried in surprise.

"Shh." Muffling her question with his lips rather than his sliver-covered hand, he caught her by the waist and tugged her behind the cover of the tractor tire. Wow, her lips were soft. His breaths came shorter, faster. Not from his precarious leap, or the stranger skulking outside, but because she was kissing him back. He groaned at her timing and moved his lips closer to her ear. "Someone's outside. Stay here."

Her shoulder trembled beneath his hand.

"It'll be okay. Just stay put." He unzipped his windbreaker

for easy access to his shoulder holster before stepping away from the tractor. Unless the guy was deaf, he had to know there were two of them in here—a man and a woman—but that didn't mean he had to see her.

"Hello-o-o," the man called, friendly like. "Someone in there?"

Tom picked his way around the machinery and joined him at the barn door. The guy wore loud plaid pants, the kind you only saw on a golf course, no doubt to throw off the opponent's swing, with a bright green windbreaker and a ball cap from the local golf club. "What can I do for you?"

"You my competition?"

"Pardon me?" Tom glanced around the corner, thinking this was some crazy *Candid Camera* set up.

"You the one putting an offer on the place?"

"Not me."

"Oh, 'cause Westby said he had an offer coming in today, so I thought I'd better rush over before my tee time to look at the place. I should've figured he was conning me. You know how these guys operate. Trying to get you to act faster or bid higher."

"Who did you say you were?"

The man extended his hand. "Selby." His grip was firm and self-assured.

"Afraid this time Westby's telling the truth. Someone has made an offer on the place."

Selby scratched his beard and peered around Tom, into the barn. "You doing a building inspection or something?"

"Yes." Or something. Tom maneuvered him further from the door, then took out his cell phone and while pretending to check messages, snapped his photo.

The man squinted at the house and shook his head. "I'd tear it down and go new. Wouldn't you?'"

"I wouldn't buy it." Tom glanced around to ensure the guy wasn't a diversion while his partner did something else.

The guy chuckled. "Would it be all right if I look around inside?"

"Not much point if you're going to tear it down, is there?"

"I mean the barn." Selby sidestepped him and paused at the open bay door. "She's a beaut. You don't see many old hip-roofed barns in such good shape these days."

"I'm afraid you're probably too late for this one. You'd best give Westby a call."

Selby took a step inside and peered into the loft. "He here? I thought I heard someone else a minute ago."

Uneasy at the guy's persistence, Tom feigned an embarrassed look. "That would've been my girlfriend."

"Ah, sorry. Say no more." He lifted his hands and backed up a step. "I didn't mean to interrupt."

Kate's head popped up from behind the tire, with straw in her hair and her cheeks an adorable shade of pink.

Selby tipped his ball cap, ogling her with an intensity that made Tom's skin crawl. "Sorry, little lady. I'll be going now." He elbowed Tom suggestively as he strutted out.

Tom cringed, feeling like dirt for dragging Kate through the guy's gutter of a mind. She was the last person Tom wanted a guy like him spending another second thinking about.

As Selby hurried toward the dark green Taurus parked at the end of the driveway, Tom snapped a photo of it with his cell phone. But when he tried to zoom in on the image, he couldn't make out the license plate.

Kate clasped his arm. "Why'd you let him think we were fooling around in here?"

Reining in the grin that threatened to burst loose, Tom turned and tucked a strand of hair behind her ear. He'd like nothing more than to continue that kiss where they'd left off, but—his gaze dropped to the frown curving her lips—she clearly didn't have the same idea. In fact, she looked down-right disturbed. "It seemed like the fastest way to get rid of him." He brushed his thumb along her lower lip, trying to coax a smile. "You forgive me?"

"He has the same beady eyes as the businessman Westby showed Verna Nagy's property to. I think he might be the same guy."

Tom's gut plunged. "The guy who tried to buy it for GPC?" At least that had been their theory. The real estate agent hadn't been cooperative about confirming it.

"Yeah, when I saw him back then, he didn't have a beard, and he dressed a lot nicer, and he didn't act so slimy. But those eyes. I'm sure it's the same guy."

"What about his voice?" Tom tried again to zero in on the guy's license plate, but he couldn't make it out on the cell phone image.

"I never really heard him talk. Only hiss under his breath to Westby."

"Let's go." As they hurried after the guy, Tom dialed Westby's number. After five rings it went to voice mail. Tom punched it off. "He's not answering."

"It is kind of early. What are you thinking?"

Watching the Taurus speed off in the direction of the golf course, Tom scrubbed his hand over his day's growth of whis-kers. "I'm not sure. C'mon, I'll drive you back to Patti's. Then

I think I'll happen by the golf course. See if this guy was telling the truth." He held open the passenger side door for her, and as she slipped inside, Hank pulled up in his Jeep. Tom closed the door and walked over to Hank's open window. He was the last guy he wanted to mislead about Kate's purity, and he hoped Hank didn't draw the same conclusion Tom let the other guy draw. "What's up, Hank? I mean, Chief."

His former-buddy-turned-boss tended to act less threatened when Tom used his title. And with the way everything he did seemed to tick Hank off lately, Tom figured he could stoop to a little bootlicking to stay on his good side.

"I bumped into Mrs. Conner last night at the Pizza Shack. She said more than an hour passed before you showed up at the Potter place after she called the second time."

"I had business to finish at the hospital first."

"That *business*"—Hank's tone flipped from conversational to hostile—"have anything to do with Kate Adams?"

"Why would you ask that?"

Hank's eyes narrowed on Tom's car, or more precisely, on Kate sitting in the front seat. "Your obsession with the woman is affecting your work."

Tom laughed, but it sounded forced, even to his own ears. "I've been working night and day, between last night's investigation and trying to track down Caleb Marshall."

"You're telling me you were parked here half the night watching for a runaway?"

"That's exactly what I was doing." Only, how on earth did Hank know where he'd been all night? "And this afternoon, I'm going up with Abe to check over the back of the property, see if I can spot any trails." And get a bird's eye view of Patti Goodman's expansive property while he was at it, to evaluate it for potential breach points. "On my own time, I might add."

"What do you mean *up*?"

"In his plane."

Hank seemed to choke on whatever he'd been about to say.

"What's really bothering you?"

Hank tipped back his hat, betraying a hint of uncertainty. "The mayor called."

*Ahh.* Tom wasn't the only one working to stay on the good side of those in power.

"He said you got his son's girlfriend in a dither with some far-fetched story about criminals spying on her property."

Tom raised an eyebrow. "Far-fetched? She has a top-level security system precisely because the possibility isn't *far-fetched*, wouldn't you say?"

Hank's jaw muscle ticked, his gaze still fixed on the back of Kate's head.

"I'd have thought the mayor would be pleased with our thoroughness." Unless, of course, he was worried Tom might uncover someone spying on the place. Someone connected to the mayor or his pet project?

Kate set the chocolate-and-cream-cheese cupcakes she'd baked on the counter and peeked into the great room. Removing her oven mitts, she muffled a frustrated sigh. Jarrett hadn't left Patti's side since she'd emerged from her bedroom at 10:00 a.m. At this rate, Kate was never going to get a chance to ask her about the amendoso plant in her solarium. She almost wished she'd tagged along with Tom.

No, that wouldn't have been smart. Her hand strayed to her lips, her thoughts returning to his kiss. What had she been thinking, kissing him back when he'd just intended to shush her?

Only . . . that kiss had felt like he meant it.

She yanked her hand from her mouth and stuffed the oven mitts back in the drawer. At times like this she wished Julie were still her roommate. Maybe she should call her.

Uh, then again, she knew exactly what Julie would say. *It's about time you kissed him!*

Yeah, she'd be no help at all. Besides, considering how prickly Tom turned after his heated powwow with the chief, he probably already regretted kissing her. And Julie had no idea what it was like to be alone. She'd gone straight from living at home with two parents and brothers, to rooming with Kate, to being married. Besides that, Kate couldn't explain about her dad, so Julie wouldn't understand at all.

Letting out another sigh, Kate glanced into the great room once more. At least if she'd gone with Tom, she might be learning something, because the more she pictured the beady eyes of the guy who showed up at the barn this morning, the more certain she was that he was the guy who'd wanted to buy Verna's land. And she could only think of one reason he'd now be interested in the old Potter place, the barn in particular: the great view of Patti's estate from the loft.

She shivered. Maybe she didn't want Jarrett to totally buzz off. Knowing he was monitoring the surveillance cameras was kind of reassuring—except for the one filming the solarium.

Okay, so if she couldn't check out the solarium, maybe she could figure out what caused Patti's dizziness. She perused the canisters of tea and herbs. A few in Patti's collection—

valerian and coenzyme Q10, in particular—were known to cause lightheadedness, but someone as knowledgeable of their properties as Patti would've made the correlation if she'd been taking them. Kate scrounged through the fridge and cupboards, searching for diet pills as Tom had suggested. Nothing.

This time she didn't bother to muffle her sigh. Patti must've been experimenting with the amendoso plant. And it was time they had a heart-to-heart.

She plopped a couple of cupcakes onto a plate, grabbed napkins, and carried the offering into the expansive great room, where Patti languished on the sofa reading a novel and Jarrett sat in a nearby armchair working on his laptop.

"Oooh," Patti squealed the second Kate set the plate on the little table between the sofa and the chair. "I thought I smelled baking." She dropped her book and snatched up a cupcake. "Kate's baking is to die for," she said to Jarrett. "She brought these to the research station's summer picnic and they were gone in ten seconds flat."

Jarrett leaned in close and kissed away a crumb on Patti's mouth. "Mmm, delicious."

Kate's heart kicked at the cozy scene. Would she and Tom ever enjoy such a homey—?

She caught her hand straying to her lips and shook her head at how she kept torturing herself. She turned her attention to the window with a view of the solarium. She itched to get a closer look at the amendoso plant but didn't dare risk drawing Jarrett's attention to it, on the off chance he still didn't know. She trailed her fingers along the shelves of books.

Waiting was driving her crazy. If she'd been home, she would've been back from church an hour ago and already in the basement, running more experiments. She circled behind Jarrett's chair, glancing at his laptop screen, and gasped. He was perusing a jewelry site, diamond rings to be exact.

With a silencing glare, he instantly clicked onto another browser window.

He needn't have worried about her spilling his secret. She had way too many reservations about him to breathe a word to Patti about him shopping for a diamond. The last thing she wanted was her research assistant getting any cozier with the mayor's family. Not when she was still far from convinced that his interest wasn't purely mercenary.

She glanced back at his laptop and nearly choked at the view the browser had reverted to. "You're doing a background check on Jim Crump?" Her voice rose higher than she would've liked, but she couldn't help it. *She* had good reason to be wary of Crump's motive for buying the place next door, but what was Jarrett's?

Patti's jaw dropped. "Are you serious?"

Jarrett shrugged as if it had just been a way to pass the time.

Kate sent Patti a wink. "Maybe he's worried he has a little competition."

"Yeah, right," Jarrett said in a tone that clearly meant *no*. "Any guy who changes his name warrants a thorough background check if he's moving beside my girl."

Patti's eyes lit at his protective endearment.

A twinge of guilt needled Kate's conscience. Maybe she'd misjudged him.

Patti closed her book and sat a little straighter. "What's that noise?"

Kate cocked her ear and heard a faint drone. "It's coming

from outside." The drone grew louder, seeming to circle the house.

"That's a plane." Jarrett snapped shut his laptop and strode to the bay windows facing the driveway. As he craned his neck to scan the sky, he muttered something under his breath and marched to the door. "Stay here. I'll check it out."

"Wait," Patti cried. "What do you mean you'll check it out?"

But Jarrett had already gone.

Kate tugged on her shoes to hurry after him. More than likely it was just a tourist plane, but the thought streaked through her mind that it could be GPC scouting the lay of the land. Maybe Beady Eyes.

By the time Kate stepped onto the porch, Jarrett had planted himself under the arching branches of a maple tree and was peering up at the circling plane through . . . *a pair of binoculars?*

Where did he get the binoculars?

And why hide under a tree when he could get a better view of the thing from the front porch?

The only possible reason congealed in Kate's throat. He'd been expecting trouble.

Stepping back into the shadow of the house, Kate squinted at the plane as it made another pass. She recognized the plane instantly—Abe's. He was always taking folks up for scenic flights over Niagara Falls. Usually people he knew. But not always. Sometimes sightseers stopped by the small local airport, hoping to talk a pilot into a tour. Her pulse quickened. *Or maybe people just pretending to be sightseers.*

What kind of sightseer would ask him to keep circling over Patti's property?

Still half watching the plane, she scrolled through her phone's contact list and hit Tom's number. When he picked up, the drone of the plane's engine sounded ten times louder. "Where are you?"

"Look up."

Above her, the plane did a rollover.

"*You're* in the plane?"

"Yeah, with Dad and Lorna."

*Lorna?* His dad's new girlfriend. What were they doing playing in a plane? He was supposed to be trailing Beady Eyes.

"It's amazing what you can see from up here."

*Oh, good plan.* "Uh, about that." She lowered her voice. "Jarrett seems really concerned about who's up there or what they're gonna see."

"How do you mean?"

"He's spying on you with a pair of binoculars from under a tree." Only now he'd pocketed his binoculars and was on his cell phone.

"Interesting. Don't tell him it's me." Tom instructed his pilot to head in. "I'll see you soon."

"Wait—" she called out, but he'd already disconnected. As she turned to go back into the house, the muffled *twerp* of a car door being remotely unlocked startled her. The sound came from the garage.

Jarrett headed her way, a familiar-looking set of keys in his hand. "Tell Patti I need to borrow her car. I'll be back in a couple of hours." He swerved toward the garage door and disappeared inside before she could snap shut her gaping mouth. Ten seconds later he sped down the driveway.

What was up with him?

The front door opened and Patti peered out, leaning hard

88

on her crutches. "What's going on? I heard the garage door open."

"Jarrett borrowed your car."

She slumped against the door frame with a dejected *humph*. "Did he say why?"

"No." Kate urged her back inside. "He said he'd be back in a couple of hours." Which meant this was the chance she'd been waiting for—a chance to talk to Patti about the plant without risk of Jarrett overhearing. But first . . .

Instead of following Patti into the great room, Kate veered into the security office and studied the control panel. She'd asked Jarrett a bunch of questions when she found him sitting in here this morning. She'd wanted him to rewind and zoom in on the feed monitoring Mrs. Potter's driveway to get a better look at Beady Eyes. That hadn't worked, but in the process, she was pretty sure she'd figured out how to pause a camera's recording. From the computer screen's pull-down menu, she clicked on Review mode; a virtual image of the buttons for a digital recorder appeared. She clicked on Camera 6, the camera dedicated to the solarium, and clicked the Pause button. The image on Camera 6's monitor continued to display in real time, but red letters flashed on the screen warning the image wasn't being recorded. *Perfect*.

Figuring she'd gauge Patti's reaction to the possibility she might discover the plant, Kate hurried back to the great room. "I'd love to check out your solarium if you don't mind."

Patti froze in the middle of fluffing the pillows she'd been propping her leg on. "Uh."

Yup, based on Patti's unenthusiastic response, she was worried. *Not good*. So much for hoping she'd have an ally in Patti, someone she could trust to help her expedite the research that would buy her leverage to see her dad.

Instead, she had a bad feeling that her worst fears were true—Patti worked for the other side.

Kate eased Patti's leg onto the pillow. "It's okay. You can stay here."

Patti's face paled. "No, I'll come." She grabbed her crutches and pushed to her feet.

Kate managed to school her expression, not wanting to give away that she already knew about the amendoso, which she was positive was what had Patti so bent out of shape.

"I'm not sure if I ever told you that my dad grew many of the plants he used in his landscape designs," Patti babbled in an overly bright voice.

"Oh?"

"Yeah, he liked to offer his clients, uh . . . unique plants, ones that would winter well."

"I remember that was one of his trademarks." One of the reasons he could charge twice as much as any other designer.

Patti teetered, one second looking like she'd lead the way to the solarium, the next looking like she'd plop back onto the sofa.

"You sit," Kate said. "I'm fine going on my own." And she had no idea how much time she had before Tom would show up.

Patti sucked in a deep breath. "There's something I need to tell you first."

Kate waited expectantly. A cool breeze wafted through an open window in the alcove, teasing the creamy white sheers, as sunlight and shadows chased each other across the top of the gleaming grand piano.

"Do you remember that amendoso plant I found all that information on for you?"

Kate's heart pounded in her ears. "Yes."

"Part of the reason I worked so hard to track down the information for you was because I recognized the plant as one my dad had."

Kate reached out and clasped the back of a chair to steady *her* suddenly teetering legs. "Your dad grew it?"

Patti's eyes glistened. "Yeah"—her voice cracked—"he found it while out hiking, but he'd never been able to identify it."

Kate's heart squeezed. She'd been so caught up in her own issues, she hadn't considered the extent of Patti's pain.

"He even posted pictures and descriptions of it to a bunch of online gardening forums," Patti rushed on, visibly squirming. "Experts, both genuine and the armchair variety, asked tons of questions, some even hazarded a few guesses, but no one really knew."

He posted pictures of it online? Which meant anyone who knew what it was would know where to find it. Ambitious pharmaceutical researchers looking for new research possibilities likely scoured those kinds of sites regularly. "Did your father give his real name or make up a username?"

"Huh?" Patti looked confused. "Oh, you mean in the forum. I'm not sure. We could look it up. I still have his computer." Patti hobbled to a desk in the corner and powered on the computer sitting atop it.

As Patti slid into the desk chair and opened the internet browser, anticipation bubbled in Kate's chest. If she could see who responded to Mr. Goodman's inquiry, they might get a lead on who tracked the plant to Port Aster. If the person contacted Patti's dad, he might've unwittingly given away the plant's exact location. It would explain how GPC knew where to find it.

Patti tapped a bookmarked link in the computer's toolbar. "That's weird."

"What?"

"The forum's gone."

"The whole site?"

Patti tapped a few more buttons. "No, not the main site, but my dad's thread on the plant has been deleted. He used to check this site every night after supper." She typed "help ID plant" into the search box and two images appeared on the screen, neither of them the amendoso. "It's gone. Why would they delete the thread?"

"Was it a private discussion? One you had to be logged in to participate in?"

"I don't think so."

"Go to a new tab and try accessing it from his computer's cache." Her father had been dead for more than ten months, but if Patti was like most people, she'd probably never cleared the browser's history.

Patti clicked on last November's history. "There it is." She clicked on the description and a memo came up saying, "This content is no longer available. Would you like to view a cached version?" Patti clicked Yes.

Kate pointed to the "Plantman" avatar next to the original question. "Was that your dad?"

Patti blinked rapidly. "Yeah."

"Click on his avatar."

The account info appeared on the screen, but other than listing a few blogs he followed, it didn't publicly display any identifying information. Not even an email address. "Go back to the last screen." She did, and Kate scanned the responses to Plantman's question. The conversation had been dominated by very specific questions from "#1 Gardener," but at no point did #1 Gardener ask for contact information. "That's weird."

*And kind of creepy scary.*

This had to be how GPC found out about the plant. But they must've hired a hacker to break into Mr. Goodman's account or browsing history or something to find out where he lived. And then strong-armed the web host to delete the discussion from the boards so no one else would see it . . . maybe. Kate shuddered.

Patti powered off the computer and levered herself back up on her crutches. "Anyway, Dad tried using the plant in a couple of designs, but it was too temperamental." She clomp-hopped toward the solarium. "He said it'd been growing in a rare, almost tropical microclimate that he just couldn't seem to replicate, so he gave up."

"But he kept growing the plant here?" Kate swallowed, trying to process what else this could mean. Patti's parents had died in a fatal car accident just before Christmas. Only . . .

What if it *wasn't* an accident?

# 6

The prospect that Patti's parents' deaths were tied to everything else made Kate's head swim. Was she letting her imagination run amok, as she'd done last night after hearing Patti's
grandparents had been mobsters?

She blindly followed Patti down the hall to the solarium,
weighing the implications. GPC must've found out about
the plant from the online forum and . . .

Kate shook her head. No, that was crazy. If GPC had already known about it way back in December, they would've
sent someone to break in and steal it long ago. Unless . . .
Patti's dad had disclosed the location where he'd found it.
If he'd given away its location, they might've decided to buy
the property and kill him before he became a liability.

Kate's heart stuttered. Had they now decided Patti was
a liability?

Patti stopped at the door at the end of the hall and reached
above the door frame. "Dad kept one plant in the solarium,
as a conversation piece more than anything." Collecting a
key, she unlocked the door.

"So he showed the plant to a lot of visitors—business associates?"

"He always invited clients to walk through the solarium so he could get a sense of what types of plants appealed to them. When you described the plant you'd found, it sounded so much like Dad's that I really wanted to find out what it was. If it's half as beneficial as the information I downloaded from the internet for you says, it—"

"Wait, I thought you said you couldn't translate it."

She grinned. "Turns out Jarrett's pretty fluent. I didn't tell you, because you'd already flipped out when I told you I'd talked to him about it." She dismissed the revelation with a wave of her hand. "Anyway, it would be a great plant for me to write my master's thesis on. I was hoping you'd help me convince the university. Maybe help supervise the research."

*Whoa.* Kate hadn't seen that one coming. The research station acted as a satellite campus for some of the university's courses, and staff supervised a number of interns every year, as Daisy had done for her and she was now doing for Patti.

A tingle prickled Kate's arms at how much she and Patti had in common. She could sure identify with Patti wanting to finish what her father had started. And the project could be a godsend. Patti wouldn't have to know why Kate wanted to study the plant. Except they couldn't get formal approval. They couldn't tell anyone. Not a soul. Not until she'd used whatever they discovered to enable her to see her father. Only . . .

The solarium's hot, humid air coiled in Kate's lungs, tightening her chest. "Does Jarrett know you have the plant?"

"Sure. He asked for a tour of the solarium the very first time I invited him in after a date."

No doubt the reason he'd started dating her in the first place. His father was the kind of rich professional who'd hire a landscape designer like Patti's dad. He could very well have been GPC's first spy, then convinced his son to continue the job for them.

Or worse.

Patti's last dizzy spell happened when she'd been alone with Jarrett. Kate closed her eyes and strained to reel in her crazy suspicions. Half an hour ago, the man was browsing engagement rings!

Patti slid the crutches from under her arms and eased onto a bench. "When I told Jarrett about you finding the plant growing here in Port Aster, he'd been as eager as me to find out more about it."

*Oh, yeah.* Kate didn't doubt that. Except Verna's grandson had said that the interested buyer had made an offer on the property already, way back in April, long before Kate told Patti about the plant. So Patti's dad must've given one of GPC's goons the location before he died. It made sense that they'd wait until spring, until after they'd actually seen it sprout, before making the offer.

Kate stared at the amendoso plant, her heart racing. *So maybe Jarrett's not a bad guy?*

She needed to tell Tom about all this. He needed to know that Patti's parents may have been murdered. But not by the mob, as she'd foolishly imagined last night.

*Then again*—Kate gripped the table's edge, forced down a deep breath—*maybe Tom already knew.*

And was keeping *her* in the dark.

Again.

Her gaze shifted to the bush outside the solarium's glass

wall. Tom had whisked her father into hiding almost as fast as he'd pushed her behind that bush last night, which meant he must've had the help of someone both powerful and eager to thwart GPC's plans.

But he must not know about Patti's plant or he would've confiscated it already—the same way he took away her father—and then said it was for their protection. So what should she do? She was past playing it safe. That route had already cost her twenty years with her dad. But she couldn't knowingly endanger Patti.

Although considering Patti's dizzy spells, it might already be too late. She examined the plant for signs it could've been the culprit. No leaves appeared to have been snapped off, but the plant was devoid of flowers, so Patti might've used those to brew an infusion. Thoughts of the tests she wanted to run on the plant tumbled through Kate's mind. If she agreed to help Patti, they could do the research twice as fast. She could suggest they do some experiments before approaching the university so they'd have something worthwhile to show them.

Shuffling sounded from behind her, where Patti had settled onto a bench near the waterfall. "Did Jarrett say where he was going when he took off?"

"No." The question smothered Kate's thoughts like a wet blanket. Until she got Jarrett fired from guard duty, they wouldn't be able to do any research. Because even if he was a good guy, there was no way she could risk word of what they were doing getting back to his father, who she knew was slimy enough to do anything to win GPC's favor.

Kate pinched the bridge of her nose to ease the throb in her head. It didn't work.

Tom was bound to be here any minute. Maybe she should

just let him take the plant. It would ensure Patti gave up her thesis idea. A thesis that would never see the light of day if GPC caught wind of it.

Kate joined Patti on the bench. Before she made her decision, she needed all the facts. Drawing a deep breath, she paused to let the sound of the water cascading over the rocks quiet her frenetic thoughts. She shifted in her seat to face Patti directly. "Have you mentioned your interest in this thesis to Jarrett?"

"Yes." As if the question signaled agreement, Patti straightened, eagerness written all over her face. "Although he actually didn't think it was a good idea."

"Did he give a reason?" Kate didn't imagine it would've been the real one—that GPC Pharmaceuticals didn't like competition. Then again, maybe he wasn't cozy with GPC. If he was, why hadn't he just secreted the plant away months ago?

Patti plucked a leaf from the plant beside her and rubbed it between her fingers. "He said that if the plant is so rare and hard to keep alive, it wouldn't have any commercial value." She hesitated, no doubt trying to gauge Kate's reaction. "He didn't think I'd be able to get a research grant or any other kind of funding because of that."

"He's probably right." And it was better not to apply. The more people who discovered the nature of her research, the more danger she'd be in.

Patti let the leaf fall through her fingers, into the water. "Except that I don't need a grant, just access to a lab. My parents left me more than enough money to live on. If it came down to it, I could build my own lab."

Ooh, that would be perfect. Kate wouldn't have to use the research station's lab equipment on the sly. Of course, if Patti had said as much to Jarrett, he may have been trying to protect her, in his own way. And if she was that eager to study the plant, she might . . . "Have you ingested an infusion from the plant?"

"No." Patti snorted. "I'm too chicken, but I've been collecting and drying the flowers so we'd have plenty to work with."

Kate nodded. Okay, so her dizziness theory was out. Maybe she needed to push on the Jarrett button a little harder. Never mind his engagement ring shopping. That could have been a ploy to win her trust.

Patti glanced at her watch. "Are you sure Jarrett didn't say where he was going?"

"I promise that I would have told you if he had. When you came over yesterday, you seemed upset with Jarrett about something. Was it his reaction to your thesis idea?" That would explain why she'd come to Kate's house rather than go to a closer friend's place.

"No." Patti poked her finger around the edge of her leg splint. "This thing is so itchy."

Kate stilled her arm with a touch. "What's really bothering you? Does it have to do with Jarrett? Because, to be honest, I was kind of surprised you invited him to stay here."

Patti gave her leg one more scratch, then tucked her hands in her lap, her cheeks reddening. "I saw Serena leaving his house yesterday morning."

*Whoa.* "As in Serena Duncan? His ex-girlfriend?"

Patti winced. "Yeah."

*Ouch.* Considering how early Patti had shown up to paint, that must've been one early visit—or a late one. No wonder she'd been upset. Except if she knew he was two-timing her . . . "Why'd you let him come here?"

99

Patti let out a chest-deflating sigh, snatched up her crutches, and levered herself to a standing position.

"Because it meant he wanted to be with me instead of Serena." Patti headed for the door, her crutches lifting in wide arcs that bisected every poor, helpless plant in their paths.

Kate scrambled after her. "Did you ask him about what you saw?"

Patti stopped so abruptly, Kate almost plowed into her. "Do you think I should?"

"Of course! I would've demanded an explanation before I ever let him step foot on my property again."

"But I don't want to be like those clingy women who never trust their boyfriends." Her voice sounded hollow and uncertain, not anything like the Patti she knew.

"Hello? You saw a woman leaving his house in the early hours of the morning." It was awful how insecurity over a man's affection could make a woman so desperate.

Patti slumped onto a wrought-iron chair near the door, her gaze drifting to the glass walls. "I didn't exactly see Serena *leaving*. She was standing on the porch and he was standing in the doorway talking to her."

"So she could have just dropped by to talk to him?" Not that Kate particularly wanted to stick up for Jarrett, but she could see Serena stalking him, begging for a second chance. She was Kate's hairdresser, so Kate knew firsthand how poorly Serena had taken being dumped. She'd handled the news of his new flame—Patti—even worse.

Hope lit Patti's eyes. "Do you really think so?"

"I honestly don't know." She'd never understood what Jarrett had seen in the flighty hairdresser in the first place. Sure, she was gorgeous, in a three-hours-in-front-of-the-mirror kind of way, but she was four years older than him and not even close to his intellectual counterpart on any subject outside of aesthetics.

The light blinked out of Patti's eyes. "He's been very quiet since my accident. Not himself. I thought maybe he was feeling guilty about two-timing me or something."

Yeah, it was the "or something" she worried about.

Patti shook her head. "Never mind him. What do you think of my thesis idea? Will you be my advisor? I know one plant isn't enough to work with. But you found more, right? When you snapped that picture you emailed me, asking if I knew what it was. So we can dig a few up. Well"—she glanced at her busted leg—"you'd have to do the digging."

Kate gave a relieved sigh that Patti apparently hadn't seen the plants in her basement.

"You'd have to dig them up soon," Patti went on, "before it gets any colder. Then through the winter, we could take some cuttings. And—"

"Hold on." Kate held up her hand stop-sign style. "I haven't said yes yet."

A beep sounded above the door.

Patti sprang from the chair. "Jarrett's back! I've got to buzz him in." Patti clomp-hopped down the hall toward the great room.

Clueing in that the beep had been for the front gate, Kate hurried after her, but first she took an extra thirty seconds to relock the solarium door. Jarrett had the remote, so it must've been Tom that beeped, and she didn't want him to find her here. She needed more time to think everything through first. Legally, he probably couldn't confiscate the plant, as much as he'd want to, and he sure wouldn't want to explain to Patti why he wanted to take it, especially at the risk of Jarrett hearing about it.

Kate's breath caught in her throat. She needed to warn Patti not to mention her thesis idea to him again. Kate sped after her.

"C'mon up." Patti spoke into the speaker at the end of the hall as she buzzed open the gate.

"Is it Jarrett?" Kate asked. "Or Tom? Because I think it's probably better if you don't say anything about the plant or thesis idea to either of them, or to anyone."

That hopeful gleam returned to Patti's eye. "Does that mean you'll help me?"

"I'd like some time to think about it." Her head still spinning with disjointed theories, Kate meandered to the bay window in the great room that looked out over the long driveway, but instead of Patti's white Honda or Tom's sedan, a black truck pulled up to the front of the house. Her heart jerked. "Who did you let in the gate?"

"Hope you find the kid," Abe, Tom's pilot and his dad's longtime friend, said as the Cessna's wheels touched the runway.

Dad leaned forward from the backseat, where he'd ridden with Lorna, whose jolly disposition always made Tom think of Mrs. Claus. "You get a chance to talk to the kid who turned in Caleb's computer?"

"Yeah, he said it was Caleb's old computer and he'd lent it to him months ago after his died." Then he'd gone back to the Potter place. And yeah, okay, he wanted to watch

102

Kate's back. He had a funny feeling about this. Maybe the chief was right. Maybe his interest in Kate was messing with his perspective. "Could you do me a favor and keep digging on Crump?" During Dad's thirty years on the force, he'd made connections with just about every useful contact in the region, but unfortunately he had come up short on Tom's latest request. "I need to know where he's been these last few months and what's really brought him back here."

"He went to Venezuela," Lorna said blithely, as if Dad hadn't spent hours on the internet and on the phone trying to track his whereabouts.

"Venezuela?" they said in unison. Tom's mind reeled. *Venezuela.* Why on earth would he go there? "How do you know?"

Lorna laughed. "Because I'm his travel agent."

Dad hugged her to his side. "To think I had an ace in the hole and didn't even think to ask her."

Tom unlatched his safety belt and turned in his seat. "Any idea what he was up to?"

"I assume relaxing on the beach."

He certainly had the tan to vouch for that.

"There are a number of nice resorts on the ocean," Lorna went on, "but he said his accommodations were taken care of so I can't say for sure. Or he could've been taking a rainforest tour. Those have become quite popular."

"Interesting. Seems to me I read that Gilmore recently acquired an emerald mine in Venezuela—diversifying. Maybe Crump went looking for compensation."

"Ooh," Lorna said, looking way too eager to weigh in with a theory. "Or maybe he went to exact revenge."

"I'm not so sure he cared enough about Daisy Leacock

103

to risk his own neck to avenge her death." Tom reached for the plane's door handle as Abe gave them the all clear. He stepped onto the wing and pulled the seat forward, making it easier for Dad and Lorna to climb out of the back.

"His fiancée framed him for the woman's murder!" Dad said, joining him on the wing. "I know Crump's let himself be bought off more than once, but the man's got to have some pride, don't you think?"

"Okay, say you're right. Then why'd he come back here?"

"Maybe to do exactly what he said—testify against Molly. What better revenge than to ensure she pays for her crime and make sure that there's nothing her daddy's money can do to protect her?"

Tom jumped to the ground. "I wish I could believe that, but after the way he cozied up to Patti Goodman, I have a bad feeling he's up to his old tricks. And I don't like that the newest conquest in his sights appears to be Kate's research assistant." Tom waited for his dad to give Lorna a hand down before continuing. "Or what if Crump was in Venezuela because he's on Gilmore's payroll? For all Kate's insistence that she can't trust anyone, she seems all too ready to take Crump at his word."

A telltale smirk tugged at the corner of Dad's lips as he threaded his fingers through Lorna's. "Do I detect a hint of jealousy?"

Lorna swatted him. "Stop giving your son a hard time. He was up half the night, watching out for his girl. I think that's sweet."

Tom's gaze jerked back to his dad. If he was going around telling people he was playing bodyguard, was it any wonder that Hank was complaining? "What did you tell her?"

Dad looked as shocked as Tom felt. "Not that."

Lorna rolled her eyes. "I wasn't born yesterday."

Tom groaned. "I'd better get going."

"Son, coincidences do happen. Just because Crump wants to buy the property next to Kate's assistant doesn't mean he poses a threat."

"I hope you're right." He lifted his hand to Abe. "Thanks for the tour. Appreciate it."

"Anytime."

Tom winked at Lorna. He'd been a little taken aback when Dad said he was coming along for the ride, with his exact words being "wouldn't want to let those back seats go to waste" and his eyes twinkling with a light that Tom hadn't seen since Mom was alive.

His heart panged. Not that he begrudged Dad a second chance at happiness. It was good to see him embracing life again, and Tom couldn't think of a nicer lady for him to share it with, now that Mom was gone.

No, the pang had been envy, pure and simple.

As he walked out through the hangar, a couple of young pilots flagged him down. "Hey, were you guys looking for pot from up there or something?"

Tom pushed up his sunglasses for a better look in the dim light at who was asking. "Just sightseeing. Why?"

"The mayor's son barreled in here a few minutes ago and asked if we knew who was up with Abe. We figured he was worried you'd spotted his stash."

Tom raised an eyebrow. "Jarrett King grows marijuana?"

The guy laughed as his friend's face tinged red. "Who knows? We were just joking. But you gotta wonder why he was so fired up."

*Yeah.* Tom glanced around the parking lot.

"He took off as fast as he came in," the guy added.

"Thanks for letting me know." Tom hurried to his car and drove straight to the Goodman place, not sure what to make of Jarrett's fishing expedition. Tom had spent the last ten minutes of the flight mulling over what might've spooked him.

Had he feared would-be thieves were scouting his girl-friend's property?

Or was he afraid of what might be spotted from the air?

Whatever the reason, it was a complication Tom didn't need right now.

Every year a farmer or two would find a small plot in the middle of their cornfield usurped by a teen secretly trying to grow a few marijuana plants. But ever since the police department started using heat sensitive cameras to scout the fields from the air, most attempts to grow an illicit stash were quickly squashed.

While up there today, he hadn't spotted any signs that a plot had slipped through the surveillance net. But he'd spotted several trails crisscrossing the overgrown backfields of the Potter property and disappearing into the woods beyond—woods that also backed onto the Goodman estate.

Tom pulled up to Patti Goodman's gate and pressed the call button.

Patti's voice came through the speaker, sounding breathless. "Come on up!"

"Patti?" What was she doing running for the bell in her condition? "Where's Kate?"

The gate clanked open without a response.

"Patti?"

Silence greeted him. Had she walked away without hearing the question? Tom blasted past the gate, his mind whirling. Kate attracted trouble as readily as an unguarded Brink's truck. What could have happened now?

As the house came into view at the end of the winding driveway, so did his answer.

Jim Crump.

Tom parked behind the man's black truck.

Kate and Crump stood on the porch talking feverishly. As Tom strode toward them, Patti maneuvered out the front door on her crutches.

Tom planted a foot on the porch's bottom step. "What's going on?"

Crump slid a too-smooth smile in Patti's direction. "Just paying a visit to my new neighbor." Crump helped Patti sit on the porch swing.

Turning to Kate, Tom lifted an eyebrow to silently question her take on Crump's "visit."

She was trembling and clearly flustered, and he scarcely resisted the urge to reach for her hand. She folded her arms over her midriff. "Edward, I mean, Jim, says he came back to Port Aster to make sure Molly gets her due."

Nodding, Tom propped his foot on the top step and rested his forearm on his leg. "Yeah, he told me."

She moistened her lips. "Did he tell you that he thinks Molly poisoned Daisy because of our research?"

"What?" Tom swung his attention back to Crump. "Why would Molly care about Kate's research?"

Crump set the swing swaying gently. "Remember what she said after you arrested her?"

An uneasy feeling burned Tom's gut. "Refresh my memory."

"She said, 'This isn't what it looks like. You don't know my father.'"

"Why would a diamond baron care about herbal research?" Patti asked.

Tom's gaze reconnected with Kate's, and his heart crunched at the uncertainty flickering in her bottomless green eyes. Between GPC's push to partner with the research station and the trouble that kept finding her, they'd theorized more than once that she'd been targeted because of her research. After arresting Molly for Daisy's murder, he'd even dug into Gilmore's potential family ties to GPC, speculating that the G had once stood for Gilmore before the company went public. It hadn't. And Jeremiah Gilmore was *not* a major shareholder. Tom had even dug into the numbered companies that were major investors to rule out the possibility that Gilmore was concealing the fact.

"It makes no sense," Kate murmured.

"I know. Right?" Crump nodded. "But Gilmore's connected. I'm sure of it."

"How can you be so sure?" Tom cut in.

"For one thing, Dick and Gilmore are close. Real close. Former college roommates. The best man at each other's wedding."

Panic glazed Kate's eyes. "Dick as in Richard Wolfe, GPC's CEO?"

"One and the same," Crump confirmed, sounding way too pleased with himself.

Tom clenched his fingers into a fist against his thigh. They attended the same college. How had he missed that? He should've caught the connection. Kate's father must've known. That had to be why, after he'd seen the newspaper coverage of Molly Gilmore's attempt on Kate's life, he'd been so afraid GPC had figured out she was his daughter. But it didn't explain why Gilmore would risk his own daughter's neck to help GPC gain access to Kate and Daisy's research.

Crump leaned forward, closing the gap between him and Kate. "I went to see Molly's dad after her arrest and overheard him talking to Wolfe about a plant. Is that the plant you and Daisy were experimenting with?"

Patti and Kate exchanged anxious glances.

"How's she supposed to know what plant they were talking about?" Tom interjected, before Kate said something they might regret . . . if she hadn't said too much already. They'd been talking way too intensely when he showed up.

Crump lifted his hands in surrender. "Hey, I'm on your side. The way I see it, if we can figure out what Gilmore wants with Kate's research, her lawyers will have a better chance of convincing a jury that Molly's attempt on Kate's life was premeditated."

"The woman came to my hospital room with a syringe full of ladder-to-heaven!" Kate blurted, her face red. "Of course it was premeditated."

Tom tilted his head, scrutinizing Crump, wondering if he was really on their side.

He sat back, as coolly as the mayor when facing down disgruntled constituents. "Only, the syringe went missing before the contents could be tested, so there's no proof of what was in it. She'll argue that she made it up to scare Kate out of pursuing the case because she was afraid I'd be accused of killing Daisy." Crump's voice cracked.

Patti touched his arm. "I'm sorry for your loss. Your aunt was a very special lady."

Crump didn't correct her on the aunt part, just appreciatively brushed his thumb over Patti's knuckles in a too-slick move that set Tom's teeth on edge. And despite her months-long relationship with Jarrett, Patti visibly melted at his touch. The woman would be putty in his hands if he chose to ply her for information about "the plant."

And with the internet research she'd done to help Kate ID it, she likely knew just enough to be dangerous.

Especially if Crump wasn't on their side as he claimed.

Tom blew out a breath. Between Jarrett's response to sighting the plane, Crump's sudden appearance in town, Gilmore's connection to GPC, and the still-unaccounted-for trespasser next door, Tom felt like a juggler with one too many balls in the air. He needed to start eliminating imagined threats so he could focus on the real ones. He turned to Patti. "Have you heard from Jarrett?"

He'd expected her to shrink from Crump's touch at the mention of her boyfriend's name, blush even. Instead, she squared her shoulders and lifted her chin. "Not a word."

Crump edged forward on his seat. "I guess I'd better get going."

"You don't have to," Patti protested.

Crump glanced at Tom as if assessing his opinion on the matter.

Tom took a step back, signaling that Crump should leave. He would've liked nothing more than to grill Crump here and now on what he knew about Gilmore's connection with GPC and what he'd been doing in Venezuela, but not in front of Patti. "Did you make an offer on the place next door?" Tom asked instead, as Crump pushed to his feet.

Crump grinned. "Yup, and the old lady accepted. The

lawyers should be able to take care of all the paperwork this week, and then she'll be mine. The lady said I could get started working on it right away though."

"You don't mind if I take another look around the grounds, do you?"

Without a second's hesitation, Crump swept his arm in the general direction of his new property. "Go right ahead."

"Appreciate it." Tom hadn't expected Crump to be so accommodating. Not that he had a choice, since technically the property still belonged to Mrs. Potter. Or that it meant he could be trusted. Tom wasn't ready to believe Crump's story when he might very well be back on Gilmore's payroll and merely pretending to be on Kate's side to find out what she knew.

A finely tuned engine hummed up the driveway.

Kate tilted her head at the sound. "Did you leave the gate open?"

"It must be Jarrett." Patti squinted through the trees that shielded most of the driveway from the porch's view. "He would've used my car's remote."

"It doesn't sound like your car," Tom said, and a moment later, Jarrett's sporty Cadillac coupe pulled up to the house.

"What happened to my car?" Patti sprang to her feet but immediately yelped, jerking up her bad leg. Crump rushed to her aid as Jarrett stalked up the hill toward the porch, glowering at him.

Jarrett looked pointedly at Crump's hand on Patti's elbow before meeting her gaze. "Your engine was knocking, so I left it with my mechanic."

"But then how will I drive her to the hospital tomorrow, and then to work?" Kate asked.

"You can use my car."

Her jaw dropped. "You're going to let me drive your sports car?"

"Sure. It'll be more comfortable for Patti than your Bug anyway."

Tom grunted, acutely aware that his boring midsize didn't stand a chance of eliciting the same look in Kate's eyes. "What do you mean by *knocking*?" His heart kicked at the instant anxiety that hollowed out Kate's starry eyes.

"Knocking. Like it could use a tune-up," Jarrett explained. "Don't worry, my mechanic will take care of it."

"He's open on a Sunday?" Kate questioned, apparently not as starry-eyed as he'd thought.

"He's a friend." Jarrett lasered in on Crump, prodding him off the porch as proficiently as a sci-fi tractor beam.

Kate's gaze slammed into Tom—clearly skeptical.

Yeah, he wasn't ready to drink Jarrett's Kool-Aid either.

# 7

Kate caught Tom's arm as Crump drove off. "You're just going to let everyone walk away?"

His gaze shifted from Jarrett helping Patti back inside to Kate's hand on his arm to her face; his eyes, the color of the clear blue sky, softened to lavender. "I'm not walking away." His breath whispered across her cheek in a gentle caress as he steered her toward the door.

Her heart somersaulted at his tender promise, which only compounded her guilt over asking for his help at the same time she was keeping secrets. Of course, at the moment, whether to tell him about Patti's plant seemed the least of her worries. If Edward—Jim—continued his obvious advances on Patti, Kate couldn't trust her not to talk about the amendoso, let alone their potential research. And what was she supposed to think about his revelation that Jeremiah Gilmore *and* GPC were after it?

Tom pushed open the door and urged her inside.

Pausing to slip off her shoes in the foyer, Kate glanced

toward the hallway leading to the solarium and the amendoso plant—a possible motive for an attack on Patti. A motive Tom knew nothing about.

She sucked in a breath. Oh no. She'd forgotten to reactivate the camera monitoring the solarium.

Tom toed his shoes off next to hers on the slate floor. "Do you think Crump suspects you and Patti of harboring an amendoso specimen?"

"What?" Kate jerked her gaze from the security room's door, and swallowed the squeak in her throat. "I mean, why would you think that?"

Oh no, she was actually trembling. She had to have "guilty conscience" written all over her.

Tom squeezed her shoulder consolingly. "Crump was clearly fishing. And Patti glowed under his attention. The man knows how to pour on the charm when he wants to."

Kate shivered at the thought of how easily Crump could win Patti over, especially with how mistrustful she was of Jarrett at the moment. Kate was glad she hadn't admitted anything to Patti about her own stash of amendoso. Before Kate could quiz Tom on his opinion of Crump's story, he prodded her toward the sound of Jarrett's and Patti's voices.

The pair sat in one of the love seats grouped around the great room's unlit fireplace. But the cozy scene failed to coax away the chill that had iced her veins ever since Crump mentioned Molly's father's connection to GPC.

Patti must've felt it too, because she powered up the gas flames. "Jarrett tells me he went to the airfield to see who was flying over my place and learned it was you. Should I be concerned?"

Tom joined Kate on the sofa opposite Patti, his weight on

the cushion drawing her close to his side. "Until we figure out who's been hanging around at the place next door, you'd be wise to stay on your guard."

Jarrett cradled Patti's hand between his own, his attention directed toward Tom. "Did you see anything from the plane?"

"A few trails leading into the woods behind the property."

"Woods that back onto this place too." Jarrett leaned forward, looking very concerned. "Who do you think made them?"

"Could be deer trails, or kids, or my runaway."

Jarrett's eyes darkened. "Or someone spying on Patti's place?"

"Or that, yes."

The heavy note in Tom's voice thrummed through Kate's chest. Then, as if he sensed her tension, his hand found hers too, its solid grip making promises she probably didn't deserve.

Jarrett pulled binoculars from a side pocket in the leg of his pants. "I've kept these handy so I could keep an eye on the place like you asked. But I haven't seen anybody."

So that explained the binoculars. He really was worried about Patti.

As if he'd read her thoughts, Tom squeezed her hand. "I'll have a better idea what we're looking at once I get over there and check out the trails at ground level. I wanted to talk to Patti about Crump first."

Patti shrank back against the sofa. "Me? I hardly know him."

"I know." Tom's voice gentled. "And from our experience, you can't always take what he says at face value. Since he'll be a witness in the court case against Molly Gilmore, I'd

115

appreciate it if you don't talk to him about anything to do with the research center or your work with Kate. You never know how people will twist information for their own purposes."

Pink tinged her cheeks. "Oh." She tucked her hair behind her ear. "No. Of course I won't."

From the way Jarrett was grinding his jaw back and forth, Kate imagined he'd appreciate it if Patti didn't talk to her new neighbor at all.

Patti seemed to avoid his gaze, focusing instead on positioning her injured leg on the ottoman, her expression pinched—whether from pain or Jarrett's brooding, Kate couldn't be sure.

Tom rose. "Okay, then. I need to head next door and search the woods behind the Potter place."

Kate sprang to her feet and hurried after him. "But what are we going to do about Crump?"

"How about you join me and we consider our options while I search?"

"But"—she flicked a glance back to the great room, her mind veering the opposite direction to the security camera she had yet to unpause—"I probably shouldn't leave Jarrett alone with Patti."

Tom pulled on a shoe. "Oh, c'mon. Didn't you see his face? He genuinely cares about her."

Yeah, she'd noticed, as much as she hated to admit it, because it left her no good reason to urge Patti to send him packing. "And he's crazy jealous of Crump. This afternoon, I caught him looking at diamond rings on his laptop."

"Is that how a woman can tell a man's sincere?" A smile danced in Tom's eyes as he teetered on one foot to pull on his other shoe. "I'll have to keep that in mind."

A little thrill burbled through her chest at the intimation. He really was a good man. Sweet, conscientious, protective—in a my-way-or-the-highway kind of way. She let out a despondent sigh. "Just a sec." She slipped around the hall corner and into the security room. Only, the control panel screen was black. Holding her breath, she wiggled the computer mouse to wake up the screen. The main menu came up, not the play and pause controls. Oh, no. Had Jarrett already been in here?

"What's going on?"

"Ah!" Kate nearly jumped out of her skin at the sound of Tom's voice. "I"—she glanced from him to the control panel, to screen number six, which now had a little red dot on it, showing it was recording—"Nothing." Not unless Jarrett asked Patti who paused the solarium camera and why. Kate's gaze flailed about the room for an excuse. She snatched up a remote for the front gate. "I figured we could use this." Oh, it was scary how easily the little white lies had started to come.

Tom headed to the front door.

Kate grabbed her coat and hopped out after him, one shoe on, one shoe in hand. She really should tell him about the plant in the solarium. It could be what Crump was trying to weasel his way into Patti's good graces to find out.

Tom was already halfway down the porch steps.

"What's going on, Tom? Do you think Crump's come here to spy on Patti? On our research? Is that why he bought the house next door?"

Tom caught her arm and steadied her as she pulled on her other shoe. "I don't know. But like I said to Patti, I don't want you talking to him about anything to do with your research or Molly Gilmore." He lowered his voice. "Or your father's plant."

"Trust me. I wouldn't," she said a little too forcefully. She ducked her head. Yeah, listen to her—after lecturing him on how he should've trusted her with the truth about her father, here she was keeping an equally ginormous secret from him.

His thumb tenderly brushed over the pulse point on her wrist. "Hey, don't worry. I'll keep my eye on Crump. It's going to be okay."

Only, as he tucked her arm under his and led her down the steps, everything felt a long way from okay.

This was not a good idea. But considering how many weeks it'd been since Kate had shown any eagerness to spend time with him, not to mention not shy away from his nearness, let alone his touch, Tom hadn't been able to resist inviting her to join him.

Besides, between all the comings and goings at the Potter place in the last twenty-four hours and the plane circling overhead, he had no doubt that Caleb, or whoever had been there, would be long gone. Tom just hoped he'd find something that'd point to Caleb's whereabouts. He hugged Kate's arm snug against his side and steered her around the back of Patti's house.

Kate's steps slowed. "Where are we going? We can't get to the Potter place this way. The stone wall goes all the way around the estate. And there's an electric wire on top. We can't go over it."

"No, but from the air, I spotted a possible breach point in the back corner. I want to check it out."

Kate buried her free hand into her jacket pocket and scrunched her shoulders as if fighting a chill.

Welcoming the excuse to draw her closer, Tom curled his arm around her shoulders. She didn't pull away, didn't even stiffen. Just the opposite. She seemed to melt against him. A smile tugged at his lips. Maybe his patience was finally paying off.

Or Crump's visit had seriously spooked her.

A cloud blotted out the sunlight, casting a shadow across their path. Reflexively, Tom's fingers curled more securely about her shoulder. "What else did Crump say to you before I got here?"

"That he wants to make sure Molly gets her due." Kate half-turned, bringing her face within inches of his. Her breath caught, uncertainty shimmering in those beautiful green eyes. "That's good, right?"

Tom blinked to unscramble his brain from the effect of those eyes, of her warm breath on his cheek, of her flowery fragrance invading his senses.

Oh boy, his all-nighter camped outside the Potter place had clearly caught up with him. He forced himself to wedge a little more space between them and realign his focus on her protection, on figuring out what game Crump was playing. "Unless he thinks her due is to be exonerated."

"Yeah, that thought had crossed my mind too. So what should I do?"

"Nothing." He muffled a chuckle at her scowl. Even with as much trouble as her plucky determination got her into, he couldn't help but admire it. "I'd just as soon you avoid

Crump as much as possible until I can figure out what he's really doing here. What did you tell him about the plant before I got here?"

"I didn't say anything. I was trying to figure out if he meant the plant Daisy and I were researching, or Dad's plant, or if he thought they were the same thing."

"And *how* exactly were you trying to figure that out?"

She jerked free of his hold. "Don't take that condescending tone with me. I'm not an idiot. I didn't tell him anything."

He patted the air as if he was trying to calm down his overactive nephews. "I'm sorry. I'm more furious at myself for not making the connection sooner. Your dad told me it was the newspaper coverage of Molly's attempt on your life that made him worry GPC had connected you to him. But he never told me her father was the CEO's best friend."

His NSA buddy's remark that he should've known Tom would be a thorn in his side if he got involved in Molly Gilmore's case suddenly made perfect sense. His mind drifted back to their phone conversation, outside her father's hospital room.

"What's Gilmore got to do with anything?" Tom had asked.

And his buddy had scoffed. "You're kidding, right?"

At the time, Tom thought Zeb had been referring to his protectiveness of Kate. His fingers itched to phone Zeb on the spot. Get some straight answers for once.

"Dad knew?" Hurt flared in Kate's eyes, her arms crossing protectively over her chest.

Tom wanted to kick himself. Why'd he have to go and mention her father, when she'd finally seemed to be moving past . . . ?

"So Crump really is onto something."

"Or playing us. But if he is, he's going to regret showing his hand." The breeze whipped a strand of hair across her cheek, and Tom tucked it behind her ear. "Don't worry. We'll get through this, Kate. We'll figure it out."

She flinched at his touch, and with a sickening thud in the pit of his stomach, he realized he'd made the same promise after he broke the news about sending her father into hiding.

The echo of her adamant "there is no we" rang in his ears as loudly as the day he'd confessed the arrangements he'd made behind her back. Except he hadn't imagined the way her breath had caught at his nearness only moments ago, or the way she'd melted at his touch. They were a "we," whether she was ready to admit it to herself or not. She looked as if her thoughts were miles away, and something told him he didn't want to know where they'd gone.

"C'mon." He clasped her hand and started walking again. They had more pressing issues to deal with than her flip-flopping feelings for him. "Did Crump mention anything to you about his trip to Venezuela?"

"Venezuela?" She quickened her steps to keep up with him, sounding relieved at his change in subject. "No. Why'd he go there?"

Tom veered toward a patch of pine at the southeast corner of the property. "I'm not sure yet." But as soon as they finished searching the Potter property, he was going to have a long powwow with his NSA buddy about Crump, the Gilmores, and GPC. "Except that apparently Gilmore owns an emerald mine there. One more reason I'm not ready to take Crump at his word."

"No one is ever what he seems," she said, parroting his

investigation motto. But deep down, he knew she was thinking it about him as much as referring to Crump, because while Crump and Molly Gilmore may have taken the shine off her Pollyanna faith in people, his not telling her about her father had destroyed it. At least this new turn of events seemed to be getting her mind off her father for the time being.

He shoved thoughts of her father and how he'd let her down from his mind and focused on the task at hand. He had a runaway to track down. And too many leads to investigate. Leads he needed to track quickly and quietly, because the chief would hit the roof if he heard Tom was following up on anything remotely connected to Molly Gilmore and Kate.

Weaving through the pine trees, he inhaled deeply. The air was crisp and cool, nothing like the humid, tropical feel of the Nagys' woods, where Kate had found the amendoso plant. The strip of woods on the other side of the estate wall was likely similar—not a place where Crump or anyone else would be planning to propagate the missing plants.

They emerged from the trees smack against the stone wall. Kate followed it to the back corner. "I don't see any way to get out. Do you?"

He tugged at the decaying branches piled haphazardly along the base of the wall. "This way." He pointed to a ditch hollowed out near the back corner, probably for drainage in the spring. "Wait here a second. I'll check it out." He dropped to his hands and knees and poked his head through the opening, also strategically concealed by a bush on the other side. He swept it aside for a better view, then backed his way to Kate. "Lots of rabbit prints under there, but no footprints or any other sign the opening's been used by humans. We might as well drive around and scout the trail from the other side."

"Why not crawl through? It would save us a lot of time hiking in from the road."

His gaze traveled over her light-colored jacket and new-looking jeans, trying not to notice how they hugged her legs in all the right places. "You'd have to go on your belly."

"No problem." She skirted past him, slipped to her knees, and shimmied through the opening, her feet disappearing before he could stop her and say he should go first.

"Stay down," he hissed as he dragged himself through the opening after her.

"Watch the—"

"Ouch!" Tom jerked his hand from the ground and lurched to his feet. "What was that?" Tom scrutinized the tiny red welts exploding on his palm.

"Stinging nettle. Hold on a second." Kate intently studied the ground in ever-widening circles.

"What are you looking for?"

"Dockweed."

"Dockweed?" he repeated stupidly.

"Yes, it's the antidote. Antidotes to toxic plants often grow close by. My grandmother used to say it was like a gift from God."

Good to know. Too bad there wasn't an antidote to make her forget that he'd kept her father's secret from her. That'd be a true gift.

"Here it is." She broke off a broad leaf and crushed it between her fingers, then reached for his arm. "Let me see."

Her touch sent a pleasant tingle dancing up his arm. And the way she moistened her lips and focused so intently on rubbing the leaf over his palm and the underside of his wrist made him wonder if she'd felt it too. "Some people say that formic acid in the nettle hairs causes the sting, but the concentration isn't really high enough to be an irritant," she babbled. She tended to do that when she was nervous, and he decided it was a sound he could happily listen to for hours. "My botany teacher said it's the histamine and serotonin that does it. The sap of the dock leaf contains a natural antihistamine."

He offered an appreciative smile. "It's starting to feel better already."

Her lips curved in response, but she didn't look up. Not that he was complaining. Not as long as she was holding his hand so tenderly. She turned his wrist to examine the other side, and her hair tumbled over her shoulders, the rich red waves shimmering in the sunlight, so invitingly touchable.

She looked up then, still cradling his wrist in her palm. "How's that?"

"Much better. Thanks." For a blessed moment, she held his gaze and his hope resurged.

"Hey, you two see that runaway?" a man's voice called across the field. Crump.

Kate dropped Tom's hand like *she'd* been stung and stepped back.

Crump jogged over to them. He looked from the leaf Kate's hand was strangling to Tom's wrist. "What's going on?"

"The stinging nettle got me." Tom pointed it out. "You'll want to get rid of that."

"Oh no," Kate cried. "Nettles are a favorite place for several species of butterflies to lay their eggs. You don't want to eradicate all of them."

Crump shrugged. "If it doesn't bother me, I won't bother it." He winked at her, oozing charm.

"What were you saying about the runaway?" Tom griped.

"Asked if you saw him. I was exploring the place and came across . . ." He motioned toward the house. "C'mon, I'll show you." He started walking, with Kate and Tom trailing behind. "Where'd you two come from anyway? I didn't hear you drive in."

"The back way," Tom said quickly, before Kate could launch into a more detailed account. The Potter property backed onto a narrow strip of woods that backed onto another farmer's field that bordered the next road over. Hopefully, Crump would assume that's from where he'd meant.

Crump squinted in its general direction. "And you didn't see any sign of the kid you were looking for?"

"No. What did you find?"

"Evidence he's been here, I think." Crump veered toward the hip-roofed barn he and Kate had searched that morning.

Tom let Kate fill the gap between him and Crump, taking a few extra moments to survey the field's trodden-down grasses more closely, just in case Crump's sudden appearance was a ploy to distract them from other evidence.

Crump glanced over his shoulder. "So, you two finally a couple?"

Kate's jaw dropped at Crump's casually tossed question, but in two long strides, Tom caught her hand. "Yeah, we are." He winked at Kate, hoping that she wouldn't disagree in front of Crump, despite her previous edict on the subject. If the guy was a spy for Gilmore, and by extension GPC, better he think Kate had a detective taking a special interest in her. Unless Gilmore's lawyers decided to use that to cast doubt on his testimony against Molly for her attempt on

Kate's life. He groaned under his breath. It was a no-win situation all around.

"I figured when I heard the ringtone he has on his cell phone for you," Crump said to Kate.

"Oh?" Her voice rose curiously.

"Just the Way You Are." Crump chuckled. "A guy's got to be serious when he uses that one, because if any other woman hears it, they know they don't have a chance."

Kate's widened eyes shifted to Tom's.

He gave her a "What can I say?" shrug and took heart at the beautiful shade of pink that immediately splashed her cheeks.

"What about Patti? Is she dating Jarrett?" Crump went on.

"Why do you want to know?" Kate countered before Tom had a shot at the question.

"Just curious." Crump continued his trek toward the barn in silence.

"She and Jarrett have been dating for a few months," Kate offered.

"Are they serious?"

The question sounded nonchalant, but Tom had read on Crump's rap sheet about too many of the cons he'd pulled on rich old ladies to believe it. "You should probably ask them."

Instead of walking to the barn's giant sliding door, Crump led them to the back of the building and pivoted a loose board on the single nail that held it in place, revealing a gap large enough for someone to slip through. A couple of mangy-looking cats scattered. "I noticed a dog nosing around out here and thought it might be onto something." Holding the board, Crump motioned them in. "Take a look."

Tom hunched over and scanned inside. "Someone's hollowed out a hidden room in the straw bales."

"Really?" Kate leaned down for a look. "I checked over the stack of straw bales inside the barn this morning and didn't see any sign of a hole like this beneath them."

Tom flicked on his flashlight and shone it up. "Whoever's been holed up in here rigged boards across the top to keep the overhead bales from crashing in on the room." The light beam danced off something shiny. Tom aimed it into the corner of the musty straw cave. "Looks like there's a bunch of canning jars in here."

"He must've found them in the old root cellar," Crump said.

"Yeah." Tom mentally upbraided himself for not checking the root cellar more thoroughly. He should've called in a K-9 from another station when their men weren't available Saturday. If he had, Caleb might already be home with his parents . . . if this hideout was his. "He's got peaches, beans, beets. Oh man, I hate to think how old this stuff is." The metal rings holding on the lids were pure rust.

"I guess that answers the question of what he's been eating," Kate said, shifting her head next to Tom's for a better look. "There's a bunch of empty ones over there, and a bowl and spoon. Those are probably what the dog smelled."

Tom wiggled through the loose-plank opening and spotted a fluffy bed of straw in the other corner, along with a few crumpled granola bar wrappers. "He's certainly been making himself at home." Tom flicked his flashlight toward Crump's face, now peering through the opening. "Have you touched anything in here?"

"Nope. But it looked like the dog had been lapping up a

spilled jar of peaches, which made me think the kid might've taken off in a hurry. I was trying to see if I could pick up his trail when I saw you two."

"You never saw him?"

"No."

Tom scrutinized the jars. "I should be able to lift prints off of these to see if we're looking at our missing youth." He swept his flashlight beam over every square inch of the ingenious hideout. "No evidence of a scuffle." Tom crawled back out of the room and surveyed the ground outside the entrance. "Not out here either. My arrival yesterday might've spooked him, but there's no evidence to suggest he'd been in danger."

"Except that he has to be hiding for a reason," Kate said.

"Yeah." The question was why? Tom pulled out his cell phone to call in K-9 and every available officer.

Kate crawled through the opening.

"What are you doing? You'll disturb the scent trail."

"I thought I saw something." She plunged her hand between two bales and pulled out a small coiled-ring sketchbook. Kate hurried back through the opening, beaming. "Is your runaway an artist?"

"He is, yes. His bedroom is papered in sketches."

Kate flipped through the pages, displaying sketches of animal caricatures. "He's talented."

Tom pointed to one of a lion. "That one's face looks like his dad."

"They all have people faces." Kate flipped a page. "Oh, look at this poodle."

Tom laughed. "I think that one might be his sister." He punched the police station's number on his cell phone. "This is Detective Parker. I need a K-9 search unit and as many others as you can send at 1159 Ridge Road. We have a lead on the whereabouts of Caleb Marshall."

"Tom." The nervousness in Kate's voice sent his senses into high alert.

Crump shoved his hands in his pockets and backed up a couple of steps, his gaze flicking from the sketchbook to Kate's face. "I guess I should get out of your way." He tripped over a rock, righted himself, and backed another couple of steps.

"Hold up a minute. I'll need to ask you a few questions first." Tom scanned the image Kate was staring at—a sketch of a . . . "What is that?"

"A lemur." Kate gulped, her fingers tightening on the edges of the sketchpad.

Tom's chest tightened. "Do you recognize the face?"

Kate's gaze skittered over Crump, her throat working double time.

Tom jerked his attention to Crump. "Do you?"

Crump's gaze slid to the paper, then bounced back to Kate's. "No one I know."

Tom tried to read in Kate's eyes what she wasn't saying. The sketch clearly had her panicked. Tom nudged up her chin and waited for her to meet his eyes. "Who do you think is in the sketch?" he whispered.

Her gaze flicked to Crump.

Okay, clearly she didn't want to say anything in front of him. Tom opened his notepad and got straight to his questions, so Crump could be on his way and Tom could focus on what had Kate so spooked about the lemur's face.

"I already told you I didn't see the kid," Crump said in

answer to Tom's questions. "I was just walking around the property when I spotted the dog and came over for a closer look."

Sirens wailed in the distance.

And the muscle in Crump's cheek twitched in response. He handed Tom a business card. "That's my cell number if you think of anything else you need to ask me. I'm staying in town at Betty's B and B until the sale goes through."

"Thanks." Tom pocketed the card, and once Crump rounded the corner of the barn, he turned to Kate. "Okay, now tell me whose face you think is on the lemur?"

Kate's gaze skittered over Crump's departing back. "Do you think your runaway drew that picture?"

"That's why I called in K-9. Yes."

"But why would he draw *him*?" Her jaw trembled. She covered her mouth with her hand, her gaze drifting toward Patti's estate. "And why here?"

The wobble in her voice cut him to the core.

Tom tugged Kate's hand from her mouth. "Who's the man in the sketch?"

Twin lines creased her brow, her gaze dropping once more to the image. "He has the same beady eyes, pointy nose, stubby ears, and recessed chin."

"Who?"

"The guy I saw with the real estate agent on Verna Nagy's land."

"GPC's guy?"

"Yes."

Not good. Not good. *Not good.* He could not risk her sleuthing into this. Especially if there turned out to be a connection between what happened to her father and what

was going on with Caleb. He already didn't like the way
that guy this morning had eyed her. "Kate, this sketch is
proof my runaway was here. Nothing more." He softened
his voice. "I know I told you that you needed to be on
your guard. But this sketchbook means our prowler was a
kid, not some wannabe burglar." He nudged her shoulder
cajolingly. "You should be happy. I'm actually investigating a case you haven't landed in the middle of for once."
He hoped.

She shook her head. "I'm telling you, the face looks like
Westby's client. Caleb must've seen him spying on Patti's
place." Kate's voice cracked. "You said yourself that the loft
offered a perfect view."

"Sure, but it didn't look to me like anyone over four and
a half feet had been up there in a long time. And if someone
had been, Caleb wouldn't have seen him, if he was holed
up in his cave." Tom texted Hutchinson to tell him to find
Westby for questioning

"Maybe he wasn't in the cave when the guy showed up."
She sucked in a breath. "Maybe the guy saw Caleb and came
after him."

"But waited for him to finish his sketch first?" Tom barely
managed to keep the amusement out of his voice. The more
he considered the idea, the more he was certain that her fears
were unfounded. He rubbed Kate's arm. "There's bound
to be a more rational explanation. I'll show the sketch to
Caleb's parents. It's probably a caricature of one of his
friends or relatives, who just happens to resemble the guy
you saw."

Kate shoved the sketch closer to his face. "Take a good
look and tell me that doesn't look like Beady Eyes."

The nickname hiccupped in Tom's chest. "You're talking about the guy who showed up here this morning?"

"Yes, I'm sure they are one and the same. And after seeing this picture, I'm positive he's the guy who was trying to buy Verna's property too."

Tom narrowed his eyes, liking the sound of this less and less, especially after how intently the guy had ogled her. He pulled up the picture of the golfer he'd snapped with his phone and zoomed in on the guy's face. "I don't see the resemblance."

"The beard and clothes threw me too. I think that's what he'd been hoping, but"—she tapped her finger on the screen—"look! His eyes are the same."

Okay, yeah, the eyes looked similar, but . . . "Kate, lots of men have beady eyes." He resisted the urge to tell her she was overwrought. That would only annoy her more. He touched her cheek. "Listen, if that guy who came here this morning had been spying on Patti's place, do you really think he would've meandered up to the barn and introduced himself?"

"Did you find him at the golf course after you dropped me off?"

"Not at the local one, no." And unfortunately he hadn't been able to trace his license plate to get an ID on him, or to get Westby to answer his calls. But that didn't make her theory any less out there.

The wail of police sirens grew louder, reminding him how edgy Crump got after seeing the sketch. He'd just finished telling them GPC was connected to Jeremiah Gilmore. And Tom wasn't so sure Crump wasn't too. Which meant if Kate's theory was right—Tom's gut clenched—Crump had to suspect she'd recognized the face. Would he tell Gilmore? Was that why he'd been in such a hurry to get out of here?

Tom pressed his hand to Kate's back, urging her toward the front of the barn. The K-9 officer's SUV turned off the road and plowed down the rutted driveway toward them.

But Crump was already long gone.

# 8

*I need to tell him.* Kate grew antsier by the second as Tom directed the newly arrived officers to the search grid, spread out on the hood of the K-9 officer's SUV. The sun was sinking fast, coloring the sky with smudges of purple and crimson. Smudges too much like the nasty bruises that had covered Dad's face after Vic Lawton's attack, the night they'd both gone after the plants.

Kate swallowed hard. She didn't know for sure who'd hired Vic to dig up the amendoso from Verna's property, but it stood to reason it was the guy who'd wanted to buy the place—Beady Eyes.

And if Tom knew Patti had an amendoso plant—a reason for Beady Eyes to sneak around and spy on her place—then maybe he'd listen.

Kate shoved away the niggling thought of her own hidden specimens. Not a soul knew about those, and as long as she kept it that way, there was no reason to fear this guy would break down her door. In fact, if they turned over Patti's plant to the police, the guy might think it was the only one they had.

Okay, probably not. More likely, he'd invade Patti's place and hold them at gunpoint until they handed over every stalk, stem, cutting, or dried blossom she had of the thing, and then kill them anyway.

Like he killed Vic.

*Oh.* Her breath froze in her lungs.

"Kate, what's wrong?" Someone shook her. Tom.

She blinked and his chin came into focus in front of her.

He was holding her arms, his eyes shadowed in concern, and her heart shifted at the sudden errant memory of what Crump had said his ringtone for her meant. "Are you okay? You looked ready to faint."

"No." Her gaze shifted to the officers watching them and she ducked her head. "I'm fine."

"I'll take you back to Patti's."

"Wait!" Her heart climbed to her throat, pounding wildly. She tugged him out of earshot of the officers and lowered her voice. "When did Caleb go missing?"

"The Sunday before last."

"Sunday? You're sure?" She massaged her throat with her fingertips, vainly trying to slow the erratic thrum of her pulse. Vic Lawton's car went off the ravine Friday night, and if Caleb saw—

"Yes." Tom stroked her hair, his hand coming to rest at the base of her neck, his gaze deeply concerned. "His parents called it in Sunday evening, when he didn't come home for supper and didn't answer his cell phone."

*Oh.* Her chest deflated, even though she should've been relieved that Tom had probably been right about there being no connection between the sketch and Westby's client.

Tom's head tilted, his gaze probing hers as if he might read her thoughts. "Why did you want to know?"

"It doesn't matter. It's not when I thought."

"What day were you thinking?"

She shook her head. "You'll tell me I'm being paranoid."

His thumb skimmed her jaw, his lips slanting into a lop-sided grin. "Hey, I'm the king of paranoid. Or have you forgotten my infamous 'C-4 in the dahlia pot' theory?"

A smile trembled to her lips despite the terrible situation.

"So . . ." His eyebrows lifted. "When did you think he went missing?"

"Two days earlier. The night Vic supposedly committed suicide."

She saw by the shifting light in his eyes the moment Tom made the connection. "You think Caleb had something to do with Vic's death?"

"I think maybe he saw what really happened. Like maybe he saw Beady Eyes do something to Vic."

Tom pulled out his phone and tapped a contact's name on the screen. "Hutchinson, got a name from Westby yet on his beady-eyed client that looked at this place this morning?" Tom held out his phone so Kate could hear the answer too.

"Just left his place. He claims he doesn't know what we're talking about. Says Crump is the only one who's asked about the place in over six months." Kate exchanged a triumphant look with Tom.

"Did you show him the picture I forwarded you?" he growled at the phone.

"Yeah, he didn't recognize the guy."

"Do you believe him?" Kate blurted. She wasn't surprised Beady Eyes didn't contact Westby about the Potter place, but he still should've recognized him as the client interested in Verna Nagy's land.

"Tom?" Hutchinson said haltingly.

"Answer her question."

"He didn't look to me like he was lying."

"Okay, thanks." Tom clicked off the phone.

"Now do you believe me?"

An inscrutable look creased his face. "The golfer's not Westby's client."

"Exactly!"

He gave his head an abrupt shake as if he hadn't heard right.

"Don't you see? The guy lied about what brought him here this morning. He must've heard scuttlebutt at A Cup or Two or police radio chatter about a potential lead on Caleb's whereabouts. You saw how eager he was to see if anyone was hiding in the barn."

Tom's jaw worked back and forth as if he was having a hard time swallowing that she might be right.

"And for the record, I still think he was the same guy who Westby showed Verna's land to last month. I didn't recognize him in that golfer's disguise at first either. You need to show Westby the lemur sketch."

"Okay, say Caleb did see something that Friday night. Why wouldn't he go to the police? Why hide out here?"

"I don't know." Her voice pitched higher. "Maybe he was terrified the guy would come after him too!"

Tom looked contrite. "I wasn't criticizing, just trying to rationalize what he might've been thinking."

"I'm sorry. You're right. If he'd been terrified, he wouldn't have waited until Sunday to run away."

Tom frowned, his gaze unfocused, as if his thoughts were miles away.

"What?" Kate prompted.

His eyes drifted to the officers searching the property. "Caleb's parents were out of town for the weekend, visiting their daughter at college."

"So Caleb *could've* been missing since Friday?"

Tom shook his head. "He delivered his newspaper flyers Saturday morning as usual. Answered his parents' call that night."

"But—"

Tom's radio beeped. He snatched it up, lifting a finger to signal he'd be a minute. "Yeah, what do you have?"

"Rex lost the scent at the railroad tracks, but we found an abandoned bike that fits the description of the kid's. He must've hopped a freight train."

"Okay, bring the bike in. We'll get a list of the trains that have been through here in the last forty-eight hours. And go from there." He clicked off and motioned to another officer. "I need a lift to the Goodman estate so I can pick up my car." He prodded Kate toward an SUV. "I need to get you back to Patti's. This search just got a lot wider."

She gripped his arm, felt the flex of his muscles beneath her fingers. "What if I'm right about that guy hunting down Caleb? He could be listening to the police radios. Already looking up which trains went past here."

His grip on the radio tightened, his knuckles turning white. "In my experience, bad guys don't go to that much trouble. They just get out of town."

"But—"

He jerked open the vehicle's back door. "Kate, it's just a

sketch of a lemur. Please, I need you to let this go. Trust me to do my job."

She prickled at what he was really saying—he didn't want her sticking her nose where it didn't belong. But if Caleb's disappearance was somehow connected to Vic and her father, her nose most certainly *did* belong in the middle of this investigation. And she'd been about to tell him why. To tell him about the amendoso plant in Patti's solarium.

He impatiently cocked his head toward the backseat.

She climbed silently inside. He was worried she might be onto something. She could tell. And he was shutting her out!

Acting like her idea was too farfetched so . . .

What? So she wouldn't get herself into more trouble?

She'd get into a lot less trouble if he'd tell her what he was really thinking, what he planned to do. As he climbed into the front seat next to the officer driving them, she turned to watch the men sweeping the field for clues. *Lord, I know Tom's stressed about finding Caleb. And that it has to be his first priority. But what if I'm right?*

*Finding the man in Caleb's sketch may be the key to linking GPC to the attack on my father, to finding out what they want with the amendoso plant. To getting Dad back.*

*I can't just let it go.*

Monday morning, long before she needed to wake Patti and help her get ready for her appointment at the fracture clinic, Kate slipped out of the house, armed with the printout of the sketch she'd spent half the night doctoring. If Beady Eyes had been trolling the area for the past few days, maybe someone in the area had noticed him. After all, there were only a few houses on the quiet country road and not much traffic. It was exactly the kind of area where people paid attention to strange comings and goings. Why else would Mrs. Conner have called the cops in the first place?

Kate's stomach quivered as she climbed into Jarrett's car. "He gave you permission to drive it," she said aloud, hoping that hearing it might squelch the sudden feeling she was doing something she shouldn't. Never mind that he'd meant for her to take Patti to the hospital. He'd been intrigued by how, using software on her laptop, she'd transformed the photo she'd snapped of Caleb's sketch from a lemur caricature to a pretty good likeness of a man. And better than that, it had got him off her case about tampering with the surveillance controls in the security room. She'd printed off two versions. One with a beard, like yesterday's golfer. And a second of how she remembered the buyer in Verna Nagy's woods, clean-shaven and businesslike. After all, the neighbors would think she was a lunatic if she went around asking if they'd seen a lemur in the area.

She turned on the engine and took a few minutes to acquaint herself with all the gadgets, suddenly feeling a lot more nervous. Nervous that she might hit the wrong button and eject out of her seat or something crazy.

Okay, maybe she was just stalling. She glanced across the seat at the sketch and inhaled. What was the worst that could happen? The neighbor would complain about her coming to the door too early. Not the end of the world. Certainly nothing Tom needed to fret over her doing.

She tugged her cell phone from her pocket and glanced at the screen for the dozenth time since she awoke. No missed messages.

Scenarios of why Caleb had left Beady Eye's sketch in the barn had plagued her dreams all night.

None of them good.

She'd thought that Tom would at least call to update her on the progress of the search. Then again, he probably didn't want to encourage her . . . no matter what ringtone he used for her number. She shoved her cell phone back in her pocket. Clearly, caring for her didn't translate into keeping her in the loop.

But if they could catch Beady Eyes and connect him to GPC and Vic's murder, they could put a stop to GPC's reign of terror once and for all—make it safe for her dad, and Caleb, to come home where they belonged.

She stepped on the gas, thankful that at least the morning was clear and bright. As she waited for the security gate to open at the end of the driveway, she flicked on the radio.

The broadcaster ran through the weather report, the traffic report, and the baseball scores. Not a word about the search for a missing teen. She heaved a sigh. So they couldn't have found him yet. That would've been all over the news.

Seeing the kids who lived on the other side of the Potter place standing at the road, waiting for their school bus, Kate decided to start by asking them. She pulled up beside them and lowered her window. "Hi guys, I'm Patti's friend, staying at the big house over there." She motioned to the wall hiding the property. "And I was wondering if you could help me."

"We're not supposed to talk to strangers," the eldest girl said.

"She's not a stranger if she lives on the street," a younger boy countered.

"Yes, she is," another girl insisted, as if he were dense.

"I'd just like to know if you've seen this man around," Kate said quickly, before they used up the time arguing. She held out the printout of the sketch just as the school bus rounded the corner.

The kids all looked at it and shook their head. "Nope," they said in unison. She held out the second one, in which she'd added the beard.

The youngest girl piped up. "Uncle Ralph has a beard like that."

"It's not Uncle Ralph, goofball," the boy argued. "He lives in California."

The bus pulled to a stop behind her car and the children scurried toward it. That's when she noticed their mother stalking down the driveway. Kate waited for the bus to pull away, then turned into the driveway and parked.

"What were you doing talking to my kids?" the woman demanded.

"I'm sorry. I know I should've asked your permission first, but the bus was coming and I didn't want to miss the opportunity." She pushed the sketch out the window. "I'm wondering if you've seen this man around here lately."

The woman squinted at her suspiciously. "You helping the police look for that runaway boy?"

"Ah," Kate stuttered, not so sure the police would see it as helping. Tom sure wouldn't. But if she got answers, they would help. "Yes, that's right. We believe this gentleman might know his whereabouts or why he's hiding."

"Last night they showed me a picture of a guy with a beard."

Kate's heart leapt as she grabbed the second sketch she'd printed off. So Tom had taken her theories seriously, just like she'd thought. She pushed the second picture out the window. "You mean this one? It's the same man, just without the disguise."

The woman studied the pictures. "Sorry, I can't say that I have. But you might try old Mr. Harris, across the road. He's always sitting on his porch, watching people's comings and goings."

"Thank you, I appreciate your help."

Kate drove across the road and parked at Mr. Harris's. The man was raking leaves out of his front flower bed but stopped and leaned on his rake when she climbed from her car.

His eyes twinkled. "To what do I owe getting such a pretty visitor this fine Monday morning?"

Kate introduced herself and showed him the pictures.

"Like I told the police last night, the bearded guy tromped around the Potter place for a few minutes yesterday morning. But that was the first and last time I seen him. A dark-haired young man has been there a few times, though. Always wears a blazer. Drives a black sedan."

"Yes, that's Detective Parker, the officer in charge of the investigation."

"Then why isn't he here asking the questions?" The man returned to his raking. "What'd he think? I'd be more likely to tell him what he wanted to hear if a pretty gal was asking?"

She chuckled. "No, I can assure you that was the furthest thing from his mind."

The man gave the leaves a brusque swipe with his rake. "Call me old-fashioned, but if this guy in the picture is dangerous, I sure wouldn't send a pretty woman around asking about him. The next thing you know, he'll get you in his sights."

A creepy feeling like the pitter-patter of a hundred spider feet chilled the back of Kate's neck. She glanced at the road, neighboring yards in the distance, the Potter place across the road. "Now, how would he know that I'm asking about him?"

The man snorted. "People talk, girl. It's the favorite pastime of us old fellas sitting around the checkerboards in front of the hardware store and of those old biddies sipping tea in that flowery-smelling Cup or Two shop."

For some reason, her mind flashed to Jim Crump. He'd said he didn't recognize the guy in the sketch, but she'd been too edgy herself to judge whether he'd been telling the truth. She pasted on what she hoped looked like a smile. "Well, I trust I can count on you to not give me away?"

He winked. "Not me."

Returning to her car, Kate bristled at the thought of what Tom would say if he heard she was flashing a sketch of a beady-eyed guy around the neighborhood. She glanced at the dashboard clock: 8:40 a.m. Less than an hour before Patti's fracture clinic appointment. She'd better hurry back and help her get ready. Save the visits to the rest of the neighbors for later. Or maybe forgo them altogether, since Tom had apparently done the job. Had he quizzed Jim again too?

She sped back to the house and parked in the garage, then took a moment to call Jim before going in. His voice mail picked up.

"Jim, I'm taking Patti to the hospital in about an hour and hoped we could meet for coffee in the lobby. I have a couple of pictures I'd like you to look at." With any luck, the prospect of seeing Patti would be all the enticement he needed to agree.

The smell of coffee greeted Kate as she rode the elevator

to the kitchen. Expecting to find Jarrett, she jolted at the sight of Patti. "You're up!"

Patti spun at Kate's voice and teetered on the crutch under her arm.

Kate rushed forward and grabbed her tilting plate. "Sit down. I'll carry your breakfast to the table."

"Thanks. It really is awkward trying to do stuff on one leg."

"I'm impressed you made breakfast and dressed without help."

"That was the easy part." She lifted a flap of her skirt. "Wrap around."

Laughing, Kate set the plate of toast and eggs in front of her. "I don't mind helping, so don't push yourself."

Deep down, she'd hoped that once Patti got her cast, she'd be able to cope on her own. Otherwise, Kate would never get any closer to figuring out amendoso's secret, unless she took Patti up on the thesis idea, which wasn't an option as long as Jarrett or Jim Crump were hanging around. "Hey, where is Jarrett?"

"He had to leave early for a meeting in Toronto this morning. Took his motorcycle."

Kate poured herself a bowl of cereal. "He doesn't need to stay here anymore, now that we know it was just the runaway hiding out next door."

"You don't like him much, do you? You know he wasn't bawling you out for mistakenly pausing the security camera, right?"

Kate snorted. "Yes, he was." Although she'd almost forgotten about that. He'd laid into her about playing around with the controls the second she got in the house yesterday. But at least he'd just assumed she'd been playing.

"I really appreciate you taking off work to drive me this morning."

"I'm being purely selfish, I assure you." Kate winked. "I'd have to be crazy to pass on a chance to drive Jarrett's car."

Patti shuffled her eggs around her plate. "You given any more thought to my thesis idea?"

Kate shoveled a spoonful of cereal into her mouth and nodded.

"And?"

Kate swallowed. "These things don't happen overnight. I'm still thinking about how we might make it work."

Patti's face lit up. "Oh, Kate, thank you!" Patti chattered giddily as Kate, feeling slimier than a worm, finished her breakfast in silence. "You ready to go?" Patti chirped, as if she were off for a carefree day of shopping instead of having her leg encased in plaster.

Twenty minutes later Kate vroomed up to the hospital's main doors. Or at least as close as she could get. Cars were lined up, waiting to drop off patients. "Just park," Patti said. "I can manage."

"If you're sure." Kate's gaze skittered over the hospital's flower beds as she drove past. They needed a good watering. She cringed to think about the state of the plants in her fruit cellar. Maybe after Patti got her cast, they could swing by the house. If she told Patti that she just had to grab a few things, Patti wouldn't want to bother getting out of the car.

Kate circled the lot twice and finally snagged a parking spot not far from the door.

Instead of getting out, Patti slunk down in her seat.

"What's wrong?"

Patti slanted her head toward the window, eyes bulging. "It's her."

"Who?" Kate peered out Patti's side window. "Serena?" Patti's blonde bombshell nemesis appeared to be enthusiastically scurrying toward them as fast as her ridiculously high heels would allow.

"Shh, she'll hear you."

"Through the window?" Kate couldn't help snorting. "Why don't you want her to see you?"

"Because she's obviously still after Jarrett. Can you imagine what stunt she'd pull to get him back if she found out I was laid up with a broken leg?"

"I highly doubt that Jarrett would fall for any of her stunts, and if he did, he doesn't deserve you." Kate gave her a nudge. "C'mon, hold your head high."

Kate pushed open her door and stepped out.

Serena skidded to a stop ten feet from the car, her mouth gaping. "Kate? What are you doing driving Jarrett's car?" She slanted her head and peered at the tinted passenger window. "Is he hurt?" She reached for the door handle, apparently under the misconception that Jarrett was sitting inside.

Patti slapped on the lock as Serena gave the door an ineffective tug.

"Jarrett's fine." Kate rounded the car's hood and used the remote to unlock the passenger door. "He asked me to give Patti a lift since he had a meeting."

Serena snatched her hand back from the handle as if she'd been scorched. "Oh." She smoothed her hair and lifted her chin. "I see. Well, nice seeing you. I guess I'll see you next week for your usual trim?"

"I'll be there."

Serena flounced off, leaving a thick cloud of musk in her wake, without so much as asking what was wrong with Patti.

Patti speared her crutches into the pavement. "Thanks for not telling her what's wrong with me."

Kate shrugged. From the way the hairs on the back of her neck prickled, she suspected Serena was watching their every move, no matter how uninterested she'd wanted them to believe she was in Patti.

As if Patti felt it too, she hesitated, glancing around, then levered herself out of the car.

Her assistant's self-esteem was shakier than she'd realized. The stark opposite of Jarrett's.

Of course, maybe Jarrett liked her that way—easier to control.

Oh boy, she was getting way too cynical.

As they headed for the front door, the feeling they were being watched intensified, and the warning of Patti's elderly neighbor reverberated in Kate's head. *The next thing you know, he'll get you in his sights.*

Her cell phone shrilled, making her jump. Snatching it from her pocket, she buried her free hand in the other pocket to hide how it trembled.

"Hey, Kate, I just got your message," Jim Crump said. "Can we meet at the car pool lot, just off the highway instead? I'm heading into the city but can't afford the time to detour up to the hospital."

"Sure, I can be there in about eight minutes."

"Great, see you then."

"You're leaving me?" Patti's voice quavered.

Kate held the door open for her and then pointed to the signs that would lead her to the fracture clinic. "I won't be

148

long. I'm sure I'll be back before you're done, but if I'm not, you can wait for me in the lobby. They have nice couches and a TV here now. Okay?"

Patti suddenly looked twelve instead of twenty-one, and Kate felt like a heel. "You'll be fine. You know how long hospitals always make you wait. And I won't be long. I promise."

Patti nodded reluctantly, and Kate walked her to the clinic door before deserting her. Then hurrying back out to the parking lot, she prayed the traffic lights would be in her favor.

"I should have prayed the parking meter would be," she muttered, trying for the third time to get it to accept her payment and lift the bar. Finally it lifted and she zoomed out of the lot, forgetting for an instant that Jarrett's car went from zero to fifty in a lot less time and with a much lighter touch than her old Bug.

The commuter lot, or kiss-n-go as she liked to call it, was just outside of town, only a few blocks from the hospital. As she maneuvered through traffic, she reached into her bag for the sketch she wanted to show Jim. Minutes later, she turned onto the road she wanted, steering clear of the narrow shoulder that dipped away into a scary-deep ditch.

She gave the car more gas and a horrific racket erupted in the front end. Then the car yanked right. Straight for the ditch!

She slammed on the brakes. They squealed in protest for a breathless second. Then the car jerked to an abrupt, scarily tilting stop.

Her breaths piled up in her lungs as she clenched the steering wheel, not daring to move for fear the car would tip into the ditch. She peered out the windshield, then at the mirrors. Not a car or home in sight. But she was only a mile or so from the commuter lot. She'd call Jim. She warily eased her grip from the steering wheel, and when the car didn't topple nose first into the ditch, she shifted into park, flipped on the hazards, and turned off the engine. As she reached for her phone, the air seeped from her lungs on a prayer.

Jim answered on the first ring. "Kate, I've been here five minutes already. Where are you?"

"I . . . I'm just up the road. I think I blew a tire. And I'm afraid to move because the car is sitting kind of precariously. Can you come help?"

"I'll be right there," he said, like a true knight hurrying to aid the damsel in distress, despite his impatient tone only seconds earlier. And although she considered herself pretty self-reliant most of the time, she'd take every ounce of chivalry he had to offer at the moment.

Two minutes later, he drove past her, turned, and parked behind her lopsided car, flipping on his own hazards. He strode to her door, whisked it open, and smiled cheekily. "Happy to see me?"

"Yes!" She edged toward him, terrified the car would tip if she moved too quickly. "Is it safe for me to get out? It won't tip in without my weight to counter bal—?"

He actually had the gall to chuckle when her pulse was still racing the Indy 500. "Your tire is not dangling suicidally over the edge of the ditch, if that's what you're thinking. It's just flat."

"Oh."

His gaze shifted to the car's interior and his grin slid away. "Come on out."

Okay, that didn't sound all that chivalrous.

"But first pop the trunk so I can grab the spare." He walked around the hood and scrutinized the front passenger-side tire. "Wait. I need you to straighten her out so I have a place to stand."

Her hands shook ridiculously as she reached to turn the key in the ignition, but she couldn't stop them. "Direct me," she shouted through the window. "I don't want to go for a swim in that ditch."

He motioned her to back up, but she didn't have a lot of room with his truck sitting behind her. When she'd reversed as far as she dared, she turned the steering wheel toward the road and pulled forward until the car was more than half on the pavement. "Is that far enough?"

He frowned. "I'll make do." Within minutes he had the jack in place. He handed her the hubcap. "Hold this so I can put the lugs in it, will ya?" Once she had a grip on it, he tugged it toward him, catching her off guard. "Stand on the other side of me. It'll be easier."

Recovering her balance, Kate eyeballed the scant few inches of muddy shoulder between where he was crouched and the ditch, and turned to head the long way around.

"Where are you going?"

"I can't get past you that way."

With a look that said "stop being a sissy," he leaned into the lug wrench he was muscling.

*Fine.* A shining knight he was definitely not. "What's got you in such a foul mood?" she asked as she edged behind him.

He jerked up, lug wrench swinging. "You don't ge—"

The wrench slammed into her gut. She gaped at him, the air whooshing from her chest as her body catapulted backward into the ditch.

Her head whiplashed painfully off the dirt an instant before she sank into the cold water. She clawed at the air, desperate to keep her face above water. "Help me!" she screamed, sputtered a mouthful of dirty water.

Her head fell back a second time, water rushing over her face as Jim stood at the top of the ditch just staring.

# 9

Tom stood with the foreman in the center of the manu-
facturer's yard, watching the K-9 officer check out railcars.
"These are all the freight cars that came in yesterday?"

"Yeah. The engine unhitched on the side track, hitched on
the railcars we were sending on, and kept going."

From the looks of it, Caleb hadn't been on them. Tom
rubbed his gritty eyes, wishing he'd grabbed a second coffee
on his way in. He'd been up half the night trying to track
down Caleb. Updating the boy's parents had been the hardest
visit he'd made in a long while. The mother hadn't been able
to stop crying, and the father looked as if he'd aged twenty
years in the past two weeks.

The K-9 officer strode his way, shaking his head. "Sorry,
Rex isn't picking up anything here."

"Okay, thanks for trying. I'll give you a call if we get any
more leads." Tom shook the foreman's hand. "Thanks for
your time." *Terrific*. This meant Kate's theory about the
sketch was the only lead he had left, considering that any

hope the caricature had been of a friend or relative or teacher had evaporated after speaking with Caleb's parents. And chances were good she was right about the kid witnessing Vic's murder. Vic died on a road between Caleb's home and the friend's he'd been visiting Friday evening.

Tom followed the K-9 officer to the parking lot.

Tom's dad pulled in and emerged from his car holding out a coffee. "I figured you could use this."

"Thanks." Tom inhaled, taking a moment to appreciate the aroma of his favorite brew. "What did Crump have to say?" His dad, a retired police officer, had been the perfect choice to do the legwork Tom wasn't ready to officially document. The idea that GPC or the Gilmores were somehow connected to Caleb's disappearance would *not* go over well with the chief.

"Crump wasn't at the B and B. Betty said he left in a rush about an hour ago."

Tom sipped his coffee. "What's the rumor mill at A Cup or Two churning out this morning?"

"Everyone's buzzing about the picture of the bearded man you showed the neighbors last night."

Tom groaned. "I should've seen that coming." His phone rang, and at the sight of Zeb's ID on the screen, his hopes surged. "I'm going to take this in the car." He slid in and closed the door so he wouldn't be overheard before answering. "Zeb, where've you been? I've been trying to call you all night. I need answers."

"What kind of answers?"

Tom pointed to the pen and pad on the dash as his dad slipped into the passenger seat. "Hand me that, will you?" he whispered, and then to Zeb said, "Why's the NSA really interested in protecting Kate's father?"

Zeb laughed. "You can't be serious. Tom, we hid him as a favor to you. That's all you need to know."

"Right. Do I sound like I just fell off the turnip truck? You don't want to mess with me—I'm operating on too little sleep. If you don't tell me what I need to know, I'm liable to leak something you don't want the world to hear to national news reporters."

An odd sound skipped over the line, like Zeb might've been trying to choke down that little morsel. "I have no idea what you're talking about."

"Okay, then let me shed some light on the situation. I've got a kid who went missing on the same night Vic Lawton died." *More or less.* Tom ignored his dad's raised eyebrow. As wild as Kate's ideas sometimes seemed, she had good instincts. And although Caleb's parents hadn't been able to identify the face in Caleb's caricature, they'd sure recognized it. Said they'd seen the same guy watching the house more than once from a car on the street, and thought he was with the police. "You remember Vic Lawton? The guy who almost killed Kate's father." Tom paused, giving Zeb a few moments to let the facts sink in. "I'm thinking the kid saw who killed Vic. In fact, I'm pretty sure I have a picture of the guy."

"From where?"

Tom smiled to himself. Zeb was hooked; now he just had to reel him in. He recounted where they found the kid's hideout and the sketch. "But here's the thing. The kid was hiding in a barn right next door to Kate's research assistant's place. Odd coincidence, don't you think?" He wasn't so sure it wasn't just a coincidence. But he'd spent too many hours wrestling with how Crump, Gilmore, and GPC might all fit into the equation not to throw out the full bucket of bait and

155

see what he caught. "And if that weren't suspicious enough, Jim Crump just bought the property."

"Who's Crump?"

"We got him," Tom mouthed to his dad, then to Zeb said, "You must remember Crump. Molly Gilmore's ex-fiancé. Funny thing about that too. He paid his former father-in-law-to-be a visit and ran into none other than GPC's CEO. Kind of makes you wonder why she really killed Daisy Leacock, doesn't it?"

"Okay, fax me the sketch and I'll try to get you a name. But leave the rest alone."

Tom drilled his pencil into the notepad. "Not a chance. Crump says he's here to make sure Molly gets her due. But I'm not so sure that means what he wants us to think it means. You wouldn't happen to know anything about his recent trip to Venezuela, would you?"

Silence followed the question, although Tom was pretty sure he heard the muffled sound of Zeb talking to someone else, as if he'd covered the phone. "No, can't say that I do," Zeb came back a moment later.

"Put your colleague on then. Maybe he can help me." Tom ground the words through his teeth. "Because Zeb, if I lose this kid, I—"

"Fax me that sketch," Zeb cut in, "and I'll see what I can do."

The phone clicked off before Tom could respond. He slammed it onto the seat.

His dad clamped his shoulder. "You're not going to lose anybody."

"If that kid hopped a freight train, he could be anywhere by now."

"Anywhere is not dead. And if you catch the guy you think he's running from, the kid will come back."

Tom scrubbed his hand over his face. "I don't know. We called every depot between here and Montreal. No one's seen the kid. What if they already got to him?"

"What if they haven't? Or what if there's nothing to Kate's theory? All you can do is follow the leads you're given. So get that sketch faxed and move on with what you do know."

"You're right." Tom shoved back his cuff to check the time on his watch. The graze of the fabric against his wrist brought to mind Kate's touch when she'd soothed dockweed over his stings. He inhaled, and unbidden, the scent of her hair when she'd leaned in for a closer look filled his senses. Irritation grated his chest. If he was going to protect her, he needed to stay focused. Not be thinking about how he'd happily walk through a meadow of nettle if it meant she'd look at him that way again.

As if his dad knew exactly where his thoughts had veered, he asked, "Have you called Kate with an update this morning?"

"No." Tom picked up his phone and swept his thumb over the screen. He should call her. She'd been ticked with him for shutting her out last night but might forgive him if he kept her in the loop.

"You know she'll start sleuthing again if you don't."

Tom frowned. *Yeah.* He scrolled down his contact list, but noticing a missed message alert, clicked it first.

"Tom, this is Patti. I didn't know who else to call." Patti's frantic voice sent Tom's heart ricocheting off his ribs for fear something had happened to Kate. He held the phone so his dad could hear too. "Kate dropped me at the fracture clinic, then went to meet Jim Crump at the car pool lot by the highway. She said she'd be back before I was done. But she's not here. And she's not answering her phone. And now I'm in the ER, because I had another dizzy spell, and the doctor wants to see her. I don't know what to do. Please call me. He thinks we might have been poisoned."

Poisoned? Tom checked the screen for the time the message was sent—seven minutes ago. Too much could happen in seven minutes. Before he could click Patti's name to return the call, the phone rang—Julie, the name of Kate's friend, appeared on the screen.

Another foreboding feeling rippled through his chest as he clicked Talk. "Julie, have you seen Kate?" Tom snatched up the photocopy of the sketch, jotted Zeb's fax number on the front, and shoved it into his father's hands. "Can you get this faxed for me?" he whispered, missing what Julie said. "What was that?"

"I said, 'no, she'd be at work,' but Tom, you're not going to believe who I saw at A Cup or Two this morning. Kate will probably kill me for telling you before her, but I thought you should know."

"You mean Crump? She knows."

"Crump's back in town? She never told me that. Huh, then I don't feel bad about calling you first. Did he change his mind about giving up Daisy's house or something?"

"No, nothing like that. Look, Julie, I'm in a hurry." Tom turned the ignition key. "Who did you want me to know was in town?"

Dad stopped in the middle of closing the door, his gaze flicking back to Tom.

Tom braced himself for the only other possible person Julie would feel she needed to warn him about—Peter Ratcher,

GPC employee, former friend of Kate's father, and the one man who could seriously expose her . . . if by some miracle GPC didn't already know who she was.

"Are you sitting down?" Julie asked a little too breathlessly.

"Just tell me!" Tom gulped his now-tepid coffee in a vain attempt to tamp down his rising impatience.

"Sorry. It's Molly."

The coffee sprayed from his mouth. "Who did you say?"

"Molly Gilmore."

Tom held his father's gaze. "Molly Gilmore's in Port Aster? You're sure?" *Molly Gilmore, the woman who poisoned Daisy Leacock.*

"Yes, I saw her with my own eyes. She was wearing a floppy hat to hide her face and has dyed her hair blonde, but I'd know that woman's strut anywhere. Never mind that no one in Port Aster would visit the local coffee shop in a thousand-dollar Dolce pantsuit. Not even the mayor's wife."

"You're sure it was her?" Tom repeated, swiping at the coffee with a napkin as he wracked his brain for a logical reason why she'd risk showing her face in their town, one that didn't involve Crump, Kate, or revenge. Was there a hearing scheduled that he hadn't heard about?

"I'm as sure as I am that you're head over heels in love with Kate."

Tom forced a chuckle that sounded more like a grunt from a blow to the gut. "Okay, thanks for letting me know." Dad slid back into the passenger seat as Tom ended the call and immediately clicked Patti's number.

It went straight to voice mail.

"I can't catch a break. How am I supposed to protect Kate when she's got enemies crawling out of the woodwork?"

"Considering your feelings for her, are you sure you're not seeing threats where there aren't any?"

"Didn't you hear what Patti said? The doctor thinks she's been poisoned. And now Kate's missing!"

"Or just late and not answering her phone. None of the rest necessarily has anything to do with Kate."

Tom tried Patti's number again. "Are you willing to take that risk?"

"No, of course not. But you're not going to help her by reacting with your heart instead of your head. You've—"

Patti's "hello" cut off the last of Dad's lecture.

"Patti, have you heard from Kate?"

"No, but I called Jarrett, because I remembered he subscribes to one of those GPS things that can locate the car if it's stolen." Her voice rose frantically. "It says she never made it to the car pool lot. The car is stationary on a desolate road and no one is answering the car phone!"

Kate lurched up, gasping for breath.

Jim scrambled down the ditch's steep side and landed knee deep in the muddy soup. She reached for his hand, but he stumbled forward. "What are you—?"

He fell against her, knocking her under again.

She gasped and got a mouthful of dirty water. Spewing it out with the last of her breath, she shoved frantically at his chest.

But he didn't budge.

Water stung her nose. Her lungs burned. She flailed blindly under his weight, sinking deeper into the mud. Desperate to inhale, she rammed the heel of her hand toward his face.

He grabbed her by the wrist and jerked her up.

She gasped again. Air this time.

"Are you okay? I'm sorry. I lost my footing."

She pushed away from him, hungrily gulping air.

"Is she okay?" asked a man in faded jeans and cowboy boots, standing at the top of the ditch.

"I think so," Jim called back. "You are, aren't you?"

Kate stared at him, too stunned to speak. *He'd been trying to kill her!* She spun away from him and clawed her way out of the ditch.

"Should I call an ambulance?" the man asked.

Kate scrambled toward her rescuer, before Jim could wave him on his way. "Thank you for stopping." She swiped dirt-smeared hair from her face. "I don't need an ambulance."

The guy headed for his truck parked on the other side of the road.

"You're not leaving!"

"I have a blanket it looks like you could use. You're shivering."

Wrapping her arms around her waist, she stood with the car between her and Crump, who was still mucking around in the ditch. The muddy water had seeped through her clothes and smelled faintly of sewage. "What are you doing?"

"Trying to find the lug nuts that went flying out of the hubcap when you fell."

*Fell? Don't you mean when I was pushed?*

The man returned to her side and dropped a saddle blanket over her shoulders that smelled faintly of leather cleaner. "Why don't you sit in my truck, out of the wind, and I'll give your friend a hand changing that tire?"

"Thank you." She hurried into the safety of his truck,

not anxious to go anywhere near Jim and the flat tire. Once inside, she murmured her thanks to God for sending along this Good Samaritan, even as a voice in the back of her mind said she shouldn't have been here in the first place. Yeah, who was she kidding? He wouldn't approve of her keeping secrets or taking risks any more than Tom. Was it any wonder she was struggling to pray these days?

Chocolate-colored water dripping from his shirtsleeves, Jim emerged from the ditch with the hubcap and hopefully the missing lug nuts.

The pair quickly changed the tire, and as Jim carried the flat to her trunk, her rescuer opened his truck door. "You're good to go," he said, offering her a hand down. "Take it easy."

"Thank you so much." She handed him back his blanket.

"You're welcome. Take care." And before she could say anything more, he climbed into his truck and took off.

Jim rounded the back of her car, wiping his hands on a dirty rag, seemingly oblivious to her mistrust. "What was it you were so desperate to talk to me about?"

"Oh. I—" She opened her car door, then quickly shifted to hide the sketch from his view as she scrambled to come up with another reason for wanting to talk to him. "I was wondering . . . I mean . . . I didn't get the chance yesterday to ask . . ." The perfect question sprang to mind like a flash of light. "I was wondering if you'd read Daisy's Bible I gave you before you left. Had any questions."

He crushed the rag in his fist. "That's what you were so desperate to talk to me about?"

She shrugged sheepishly. "I didn't think you'd come if—"

"Kate, I thought you needed to talk about something important. I have things I need to do *today*. We can talk about that any time."

She climbed into her car. "Of course, I won't—"

A car engine sounded behind them, as another car slowed in front.

Jim slapped the car's roof. "I've got to go. We're blocking traffic." He strode back to his truck, and she realized she recognized the car slowing to a stop on the opposite side of the road. It was Keith's.

As Jim's truck eased around her and sped off, she spotted the other car in her rearview mirror. Tom's. Both men descended upon her with fierce expressions.

"What's going on? Are you okay?" Tom asked.

"How'd you know I was here?"

"Patti called. She's frantic. You're not answering your phone."

"I didn't hear—" She reached into her pocket and pulled out the water-soaked phone. "I guess it stopped working."

His expression morphed as his gaze skittered over her mud-streaked hair and soaked clothes. "What happened?"

Her heart took off at a gallop as uncertainty gripped her. Had she only imagined that Jim tried to kill her? It could have been an accident. She spewed out the whole story, and somewhere along the way, Tom opened her car door and pulled her into his arms. "I don't know why I thought he was trying to kill me," she blubbered. "It's not like he could have known I'd get a flat tire out here. I mean, he knew I'd be at the hospital and I did feel like someone was watching us, but . . ." She buried her face against his chest. "I don't know what I'm saying. I probably imagined it all." And the last thing she should be doing is seeking solace from Tom. It would only make him more protective. Except with the taste of mud in her mouth and stench of sewage in her nostrils, and her breath still bottled up in her lungs, she was okay with that.

Keith reached around the door and popped the trunk. A moment later, he said, "Tom, take a look at this."

Tom walked to the back of the car, still hugging her to his side. "What did you find?"

Keith held up what looked like a scissors' tip. "Wedged in the rubber."

Kate gulped.

But Tom didn't give away what he was thinking, except for the telltale flick of his cheek muscle that said he didn't like it. "Check the lugs. Make sure they're tight."

Keith grabbed the wrench and headed to the newly mounted tire, a few seconds before Tom's concern sank in.

"You think he'd deliberately leave them loose?"

Tom's forehead furrowed as if he couldn't believe she'd ask. "You thought he tried to kill you. Why would you think he'd suddenly stop trying?"

"Yes, but—" She tried to swallow, but couldn't choke down the fear balled in her throat. Tom was supposed to be her voice of reason. Tell her she was jumping to conclusions. Not . . . "*You* think he tried to kill me?"

Tom didn't answer.

"The bolts are all tight," Keith reported and Kate's breath swooshed from her lungs.

"Could be thanks to your Good Samaritan," Tom reminded her. "What were you thinking meeting Crump out here?"

Keith tossed the wrench into the truck and closed the lid. "Do you want me to pick up Patti and meet you back at the house?"

"That would be wonderful," Kate said, feeling as wrung out as a dirty mop.

"Actually"—Tom cupped her elbow and steered her back to the driver's seat—"Patti's doctor wants to see you. You okay to drive? Because I could call a tow truck and drive you myself."

"Yes, no." She shook her head, trying to remember the question. "I'm fine to drive."

"Okay, I'll follow you." As he opened her door, his attention shifted to the papers she'd shoved off the seat. "Where did you get that sketch?"

Her stomach plunged at the sight of beady eyes glowering up at her from the floorboards. "I made it from a photo I took of Caleb's sketch."

He snatched it up. "Who else has seen this? Crump?"

"No, I was going to show him, but after—" Had he seen it? Was that why his mood had suddenly soured? Why he tried to kil—? She swallowed, unable to think it. "He may have seen it."

The muscle in Tom's cheek twitched big-time. "Who else knows about it?"

She shrank at his irate tone. "Patti's neighbors. I—I showed it to Patti's neighbors," she stuttered, then added more softly, "and Jarrett."

# 10

Parking next to Kate's car in the hospital lot, Tom wished he could be in three places at once. Here, ensuring Kate was really okay, as well as getting the lowdown on the poison the doctor found in Patti's blood; in Crump's face, finding out what had really happened back on the road and if Kate's mock-up of Caleb's sketch had anything to do with it; and out there finding Caleb.

Kate stepped out of her car and he dropped his coat over her shoulders.

Dad, who'd followed them to the hospital, hurried ahead to find out where Patti was now.

"You don't have to stay, Tom, honest. Your dad will keep an eye out for us. You must be anxious to get back to looking for Caleb."

Tom held the hospital door open for her, a myriad of unsuitable responses running through his head. The search *couldn't* wait. And she *shouldn't* be more important than a missing boy. But the truth was, without more information,

166

he didn't know where else to look. In fact, this attack, on the heels of her showing that sketch around, was the freshest lead he had, but she didn't need to know that. "I have time," he said instead.

"This better not be a ploy to get me to see a doctor." Kate's strained whisper ended on a cough as passersby gawked at her muddy clothes and bedraggled hair.

Tom steered her down the hall behind his dad. At least she'd stopped dripping, and she'd managed to get her face cleaned with the tissues he'd given her. "Patti's doctor said he wanted to talk to you." And it was the perfect excuse to ensure she got checked over too.

"I don't understand why he'd want to talk to me."

"I guess we'll find out." Tom hedged, not wanting to worry her with Patti's claim they'd been poisoned before he had all the facts. After all, Kate hadn't shown any concerning symptoms. At least none that she'd admitted to. Which wasn't all that reassuring, considering what else she'd done behind his back. Maybe she had been poisoned—might explain her obliviousness to the danger she could bring on herself by showing that sketch around.

Dad poked his head into a room ahead, and a moment later Patti appeared, sporting a leg cast. "Kate! You're all wet. What happened?"

"I fell in the ditch when I was helping Jim change the tire."

"That's terrible." Patti backed back into the room and motioned Kate inside.

Tom paused in the hall and cut off a nurse hurrying past. "Will the doctor be long?" He lowered his voice. "He wanted to speak to this woman ASAP about a poisoning, so we didn't take time to check in, but she's aspirated water and needs to be examined too."

The nurse glanced at the room number. "I'll let him know," she said, already hurrying away.

"I'm so glad it wasn't anything worse," Patti was saying to Kate as he stepped into the room. "I was so worried when I couldn't reach you on your cell phone."

He grimaced at the thought of how much worse it *had* been. *Maybe.* He needed to figure out which threats against Kate were real and which were imagined. Before it was too late. "Kate mentioned feeling as if someone was watching her when the two of you arrived at the hospital. Did you notice anyone?"

Patti's eyes widened. "The flat wasn't an accident?"

"No, we found a broken scissors tip embedded in the rubber."

"Serena," Patti said on a gasp.

Tom glanced at Kate, whose mouth had dropped open. "You didn't mention Serena."

"Because she wasn't sneaking around, watching us. The second she saw Jarrett's car, she rushed right over. I'm sure she thought she'd scored a chance to corner him."

"Yeah." Patti snorted. "And considering how *not* thrilled she was about seeing me and you in the car, I could see her sneaking back after we were inside to sabotage a tire."

Tom exchanged a look with his dad. The probability that the blown tire was the vindictive act of a scorned girlfriend would've been more reassuring if the ex-boyfriend weren't Jarrett King. If he wanted a mishap to come to the two researchers causing GPC the most grief, how better to make it happen than to manipulate a jealous ex into doing his dirty work. Tom ground his teeth. "I'll have a chat with her as soon as we see you safely home."

Kate shivered, probably as much from thoughts of the attack as her wet clothes, and Tom scrounged through the cabinets looking for a blanket. "What's taking the doctor so long?"

"You don't need to hang around," Kate said. "I'm fine to drive without an escort."

Locating a blanket, he tucked it around her and rubbed his thumb across a smudge she'd missed on her cheek. "I'm *not*."

Kate's warm smile curled in his chest, squeezing out the last of the fear that had lodged there from the instant he'd gotten Patti's phone message. Maybe now, finally, after all this, she'd listen to him.

"I'm Dr.—" The young man rushing into the room jolted at the sight of all of them. "Who are you?"

Tom extended his hand. "Detective Tom Parker."

"A detective, good. You'll want to hear this."

Kate shrank into a chair. "What's going on?"

"Are you Miss Goodman's supervisor?" His eyebrow arched as his gaze slid over her wet clothes.

"Yes, Kate Adams."

"She was pushed into a deep ditch, Doctor," Tom spoke up. "I'm concerned she's aspirated water. Could you check her over? We didn't want to delay meeting you by stopping at triage first."

"That's not necessary," Kate protested, shooting Tom a caustic scowl.

"No, the detective is right," the doctor said. "People can die hours later from secondary drowning after inhaling only a small amount of water." He fitted his stethoscope in his ears and listened to her lungs. "Have you noticed any abrupt change in her energy levels or personality?" He slid a monitor over her fingertip.

Tom smirked. "No, she's always been this uncooperative."

Kate stuck her tongue out at him. But the corners of her lips edged into a smile.

The doctor scrutinized the monitor's readout. "The oxygen levels in your blood look good at the moment, but if you notice any sudden drop in energy, you should come in immediately. Okay?"

"I will. Thank you, Doctor."

"Okay, now that that's taken care of." The doctor propped his hip against the counter and picked up a file. "I wanted to speak with you, because Miss Goodman tells me the two of you work in the same lab."

"That's right."

"And she told you we found significant levels of an industrial toxin in her previous blood work that could explain the dizziness?"

"No!"

Patti's gaze shot to Tom's. "You didn't tell her?"

Kate's gaze narrowed. "You knew?"

He shrugged, cringing on the inside. He should've known he'd be in the doghouse again for keeping information from her. "I brought you here to hear what the doctor has to say," he deflected, then turned to the doctor. "What kind of industries are we talking?"

"It's found in a widely used chemical found in everything from common disinfectants to manufacturing to mining."

Tom's gut kicked at the mention of mines. Molly Gilmore's

father owned diamond mines. And according to Julie, Molly was back in town.

"So, wait a minute," Patti interjected. "You think this toxin is something we've been exposed to accidentally?"

"Possibly. That question would be better explored by the detective." The doctor slanted Tom a look that implied he should. "The good news," the doctor went on, "is that the body is remarkably efficient at ridding itself of the toxin if exposure ceases. But if levels build, the effects can become debilitating. We took additional blood samples from Miss Goodman following her dizzy spell in the fracture clinic to compare to her previous results, and if we may, I'd like samples from you, Miss Adams."

"You think the exposure is coming from their lab?" Tom clarified.

"It would be my first guess, and the easiest to eliminate if Miss Adams's blood doesn't show any exposure."

"Yes, of course, you can take a sample," Kate said.

The doctor pulled out a lab order form and ticked a half dozen boxes. "Have you been noticing any dizzy symptoms yourself?"

"No."

"Miss Goodman tells me you stayed at her house the past couple of days. Have you experienced any unusual symptoms during your stay?"

"No. But other than the one episode Saturday afternoon, Patti hasn't either." Kate exchanged a concerned glance with Patti. "Have you?"

"Not until an hour ago."

"Her symptoms this morning were not nearly as acute as when I saw her Saturday morning." The doctor closed his file. "Exposure is typically through the skin, so you'll both need to be extra vigilant until we pinpoint the source."

Tom mentally cataloged what that could be. The disinfectant soap dispenser on their lab wall, any number of chemicals they used in their experiments, something in the soil mixtures they used.

The doctor handed her the requisition and opened the door. "Stop by the lab before you leave to have your blood taken."

"Could you put a rush on those lab tests?" Tom asked. "The sooner we can narrow in on the source, the better. Especially if this turns out to be deliberate."

"I'll do my best."

Tom muffled a sigh. It would still be like looking for a needle in a haystack, even if the source turned out to be from Patti's home. Between makeup and facial cleansers and household cleansers, it'd be nearly impossible to pinpoint the source without testing every product. As they all headed to the lab, Patti called back Jarrett to let him know Kate was safe, no thanks to his ex-girlfriend.

Anxious to speak to Serena and at least confirm their suspicions about the sabotaged tire, Tom entrusted his dad to see Kate and Patti home safely and headed straight to Serena's hair salon. The door chimed a falsetto tune he suspected she'd be echoing when he presented her with the snapped scissors his dad had pried from Jarrett's tire.

"Hey, Tom," Linda called from the washtubs at the back of the shop, where she was squeezing some foul-smelling treatment on Mrs. C's curler-filled head. "You in for another trim already?"

"No, I need to talk to Serena. She around?"

"You'll have to get in line. Jarrett beat you to her."

Terrific. The man was looking less trustworthy by the second. He'd told Patti he was in Toronto for meetings. "Where'd they go?"

Linda fiddled with the cotton batting wrapped around the base of Mrs. C's curlers, her gaze zigzagging between him and it. "Uh, Jarrett said he wanted to talk to her in private."

"Where'd they go?" Tom repeated more insistently.

"The back room," she said at the same moment Serena's voice shrilled, "The way we kissed was not nothing!"

"It was a mistake," Jarrett growled as the back room's door jerked open. "I thought I made that clear eight months ago. You need to move on. And stay away from Patti." Jarrett blindly plowed out of the room, bumping Tom's shoulder in his rush.

Tom grabbed him by the elbow, not quite ready to believe the performance wasn't for his benefit. "She admit to puncturing your car's tire?"

Icy fury darkened Jarrett's stark blue eyes. "More or less. I don't want to press charges. This should be the end of it."

Tom stretched the kink out of his neck, ignoring Linda's and Mrs. C's open-mouthed gawking. "Kate might. It was her life Serena endangered."

Jarrett's expression morphed into a you-can't-be-serious face. "She fell in the ditch changing the tire," he seethed, hopefully low enough that the pair behind them didn't hear.

Tom resisted the urge to point out she almost drowned, certain Kate wouldn't want that rumor making the rounds in town. "I thought you were supposed to be in Toronto?" A two-hour drive away.

"I blew off my meeting the second Patti called about Kate being missing. So I'm sure you can appreciate how steamed I was when she called again with her suspicions that it had all been Serena's doing." Jarrett yanked open the shop door and stormed out.

Serena emerged from the back, lines of black mascara streaking her cheeks.

Tom almost felt sorry for her, knowing too well how it felt to not have feelings reciprocated.

"Did Jarrett send you?" she asked, hatred burning through her voice.

Not taking it personally, he motioned her into the back room once more. "Why don't we talk in here?"

"He doesn't know what he's talking about. Yeah, I saw Patti at the hospital. But I didn't shove any scissors into her tire, like he said."

Tom held out a plastic baggie with the two matching pieces of a broken pair of hairstyling scissors—one pried out of Jarrett's tire, the other found in the garbage canister on the curb near where the car had been parked. "Then I don't suppose you'll mind letting me take your fingerprints to eliminate any matches with the prints on this."

"I—" She looked at her hands, and Tom couldn't help but notice that two of her otherwise perfectly manicured, hot pink fingernails were broken, recently by the looks of it. "Okay, I did it. I was mad. I didn't mean to hurt anyone, especially not Kate. I like her." She swiped at the fresh onslaught of black tears pooling on her cheek. "I just . . . I was mad! Jarrett strung me along for months, then suddenly drops me like a hot curler, acting surprised that I should be stunned."

174

Yeah, Tom had a bad feeling he wasn't going to like whatever game Jarrett was playing with Patti either.

An hour later, Kate's spirits lifted at the sight of her house. Jarrett had assured Patti that they were welcome to continue to use his car, but when Patti admitted she didn't feel up to going into work that afternoon, Kate had jumped at the opportunity to retrieve her own car so she'd have the freedom to come and go as she pleased. And thankfully, after following her and Patti home to make sure the spare tire didn't give them any problems, Tom's dad hadn't minded waiting while she had a quick shower and changed into clean clothes. "Thanks for the ride," she said to Keith as he parked in the driveway. "It will be nice to drive my own car again."

"Happy to help. Got to say that it's good to see you and Tom together again." He winked.

Not knowing how to respond, she hesitated, half afraid her shaky smile said more than she wanted it to. Over the past few months, Keith had come to treat her like a daughter, which, as wonderful as that was, only made her miss her father more.

"I know it was hard for you to accept Tom's reasons for not telling you your father was alive, but you never know what you'd do until you're in the situation."

"Yes, I can see that now." *Too well*. She tamped down thoughts of the secrets she was keeping. She'd never been so happy to see Tom as when he showed up this morning. He'd certainly proven she could count on him. If only he could understand why she'd risk anything to be reunited with her father, maybe she wouldn't have to keep him at arm's length.

Stale air assaulted her as she pushed open the front door with a farewell wave to Keith. If she weren't expected at work in less than an hour, she'd open all the windows. She dropped her laptop onto the sofa, quickly disarmed the alarm, and settled for opening the window over the kitchen sink. While she was at it, she put out the garbage she'd forgotten about, then hurried down to the fruit cellar.

One of the grow-light bulbs had burned out, but the plants hadn't seemed to suffer for it. She grabbed a replacement from the box under the bench, and by the time she'd fitted it in, perspiration beaded her forehead. The room was like a sauna.

She propped the door open to circulate the air, then, eager to see if the tincture she'd added to the bacteria had killed them, she collected the petri dishes from the incubator and carried them to her microscope in the other section of the basement. The phone rang as she prepared the first slide with a Gram's stain. She ignored it. It was probably a tele-marketer. None of her friends would expect her to be home in the middle of a workday.

She slipped the slide under the lens and her heart fell. The bacteria had multiplied, not died. If the amendoso tincture acted like an antibiotic, like the information they'd found online implied, there should be less bacteria, not more. Here she'd anticipated needing to take the specimens to view under the electron microscope at the research station, but clearly the amendoso had no effect on streptococcus. She reached for the next petri dish.

"Kate, where are you?" Tom's voice drifted down the stairs.

The petri dish flew out of her hand and shattered on the cement floor. "Hang on," she called, straining to keep the panic from her voice. "I'll be there in a minute." She snapped off the microscope light and sprinted toward the fruit cellar to close its door.

"Kate, you've got five seconds to pick up or I'm going to come—"

"Beep." The answering machine cut off his threat.

She jolted to a stop. *He's not here.* But . . . if she didn't call him right back, he soon would be. Leaving the cellar door open, she raced upstairs and dialed his number.

Voice mail picked up.

"Tom, I'm okay. I just couldn't get to the phone in time. Okay? There's no need for you to come over. I need to leave for work in a few minutes." She slammed down the phone. Why was she wasting time leaving a message she wouldn't know if he got? She dialed his number again, but again it went to voice mail.

"Argh!" She grabbed her bleach bottle from the laundry room and raced back downstairs. If she hurried, she could quickly prepare a slide from the third dish.

She poured bleach over the shattered petri dish on the cement floor to kill the bacteria, then hurriedly prepared a slide from the third dish. Two minutes later, she let out a heavy sigh. These bacteria were alive and kicking too. Maybe she hadn't prepared the tincture correctly, or maybe Betty mistranslated the instructions. She'd have to check later, because she'd left the translation at Patti's.

Kate hurriedly swept up the broken petri dish and returned the other two to the incubator in the fruit cellar.

At the phone's shrill ring, she spun on her heel toward

the door and sent a bucket of potting soil sailing off the table. The dirt puffed into the air, getting into her nose and mouth as she rushed out and up the stairs. She grabbed the phone a second before it would have clicked over to voice mail. "Tom! I'm here."

A cheery computerized voice said, "Hello, I'm your—"

Kate slammed down the phone. Tom must not have gotten her message. She tried his number again, without success. Spying her laptop on the sofa, she wondered if she had time to look up the blog on the amendoso plant before he got here. She pulled it out of the bag and hit the power button. It wasn't as if she had to hide looking at a website anyway, and if she could get the instruction page for the tincture printed off, she could drop it by Betty's on her way into work and ask her to see if she'd missed something in the translation.

Her boss would understand if she was a few minutes late. After the morning she'd had, she had a good excuse. The instant the computer finished starting, she went online and clicked the bookmark for the blog.

A box appeared in the middle of the screen, proclaiming no such site existed. She checked her browser history and clicked on the last page she'd visited at the site—the one with the photos.

The same message appeared.

*What's going on?* The memory of Patti's unsuccessful attempt to view her father's forum discussion skittered through Kate's mind. Was GPC systematically trolling the entire internet, hunting down and deleting any and every reference to the plant?

She checked her history list again and tried a different page. Same message. Another box popped up at the bottom of the screen—her virus software saying it had blocked an attempt to infiltrate her computer.

Heart pounding, she clicked off the computer's Wi-Fi.

The doorbell rang, followed immediately by insistent knocking. "Kate, are you in there?" Tom shouted.

Kate hurried to let him in. "I tried calling you back. I—"

"What happened?" He stepped inside. "Why are you covered in dirt?"

Huh? She glanced down at her white shirt, dusted in a fine layer of potting soil. She moistened her lips and tasted the dirt there too. Great, the bucket she'd spilled had spewed dirt all over her. And . . . *oh no*, she'd been in such a hurry to answer the phone that she hadn't closed the fruit cellar door! She couldn't let Tom go down there. She flung herself into his arms. "Oh, Tom, I'm so glad you're here!"

# 11

"I was on the computer and someone tried to hack in or something," Kate blabbered frantically. "All I could think of were the flames that burned through the webcam image of me on my work computer last month."

Tom's arms slid around her, solid and reassuring. "You're okay," he murmured, sounding as if he was saying it as much for his own peace of mind as hers.

She leaned into his comfort, momentarily forgetting the pretense that had thrust her into his arms. He was so protective and sweet. And anyone with two eyes could see he really cared about her. If only she could trust him not to take the plants away, she'd tell him everything. She'd feel a lot better confiding in him. But she couldn't. Because her well-being was more important to him than reuniting her with her father.

She pressed her palm to his chest to put some distance between them as her mind raced for a way to get herself out of this mess. Tom's heart pulsed rapidly against her fingers, betraying the depth of his concern.

Feeling utterly unworthy of it, she ducked her head.

He clasped her hand and tugged her toward the laptop. "Show me what happened."

She bit her lip, swiped at the dirt she tasted there, and quickly brushed it off her clothes and Tom's shirt. Okay, admitting to still searching the internet for more information on amendoso was a lot safer than telling him about the plants in her basement. Maybe his computer forensics guy could even track down who'd deleted the sites. *Site*. She couldn't tell him about Patti's father. Not yet. She sucked her lip between her teeth once more, wavering over maybe at least telling him that much.

"Kate?"

Tom sat in front of the laptop, staring at the innocuous no-such-website-exists message. The Trojan alert had long since slipped from the bottom corner of the screen.

She explained what happened, and to her surprise, Tom didn't give her a hard time about trying to revisit the blog. He searched her virus reports, his brow furrowing deeper with every click of the mouse.

"What's wrong?" If someone from GPC had hacked into her computer and scanned her hard drive, they'd know she knew about the plant. She'd always assumed it, but that didn't stop the panic from suddenly welling into her throat. "Patti's poisoning and my near drowning weren't accidents, were they? Crump must be working for—"

"Take it easy." Tom spun the office chair to face her and caught her hand. "One of the reasons I called was to let you know that Serena admitted to jabbing the car tire."

"She did?"

"Yes, and from the blowup I overheard between the two of them, I doubt Jarrett conspired to get her to do it."

"Jarrett's in town?" Her voice edged even higher. "He's supposed to be in Toronto."

"He said he blew off his meeting after Patti's call," Tom said, but his clenched jaw said he didn't know what to think.

"Jarrett saw the sketch I doctored," Kate reminded him.

"I know. Do you need your laptop at work today? Because I'd like to have our computer forensics officer check it over."

"Go ahead. I want to know that no one's spying on my every key click before I work on it again."

"Me too." He powered it down and closed it up. "So what were you doing that got you all covered in dirt? I thought you were in a hurry to get to work."

"I am." She glanced at her wrist before she remembered it was empty. Her watch had died along with her cell phone in the ditch water. "I'm probably already late."

"Did you try throwing your watch and cell phone into a bowl of rice?"

"Yes, but the man at the store I called said it could take a few days for the phone to dry out."

"I figured." Tom pulled a cell phone from his pocket. "I didn't want you to be without, so I picked up a prepaid phone for you to use for the time being. It's a different phone number, which means if GPC is onto you, at least they won't be able to track you." He pressed it into her hand, and both the warmth of his touch and his thoughtfulness left her speechless. "I've programmed in my cell and house number. Okay?"

"Yes, thank you. I—"

He brushed stray dirt off her sleeve, renewing her fear that he'd start asking about it again.

"I'd better get to work," she said a little too breathlessly.

"I'll follow you in. I need to check over your lab and alert your supervisor to Patti's poisoning. I've already asked Patti to make a list of possible sources in her house." Tom scooped up the laptop and positioned himself by the alarm pad, clearly not planning to leave until she did.

But she hadn't watered and fed the amendoso plants yet, or closed the door of the fruit cellar. Through the window, she spotted Verna stepping onto her back porch and grasped at the diversion. "Do you have that printout of the sketch I doctored? Because I was thinking you should show it to Verna. Ask her if she remembers the man's name. Her grandson told me someone made her an offer back in April. It's probably the same guy, and maybe he left a business card." Kate gasped in a breath, only then realizing that her mile-a-minute chattering would make Tom suspicious, especially given that at any other time she'd be insisting on accompanying him. "It'll give me time to change my shirt," she improvised.

"No need. I spoke with Verna yesterday. You go ahead and change. I'll wait."

"You did? What did she say?"

"Same as Westby. That the guy called himself Smith, not Selby. He gave her the same business card he'd given Westby. And the phone number on it is no longer in service."

Kate shuddered.

"Don't worry. One way or the other, I intend to get to the bottom of this. Now get yourself changed."

Kate teetered a second, wondering if he'd question her going downstairs instead of to the bedroom. If her laundry room was down there, she could've talked her way around him. But it wasn't. It was no use. She'd just have to go to work with her handsome bodyguard and pray he didn't get it into his head to follow her back to Patti's after work. Then she'd be able to detour here and see to the plants first.

She ignored the nervous flutter in her stomach at the thought of returning alone, at night, with GPC possibly watching the place. Maybe she should've stuck to driving Jarrett's car, donut tire or not.

"Kate? Is there a problem?"

"Oh, no." She stuffed the cell phone he'd brought into her purse and then hurried to the bedroom and pulled on a new shirt. Thankfully, Tom was still standing by the alarm pad when she returned.

"Ready?"

Not by a long shot, but what choice did she have? She allowed him to escort her to the research station, grateful that at least he hadn't suggested she ride along with him. She'd never be able to return to experiment on the plants if she didn't have her own wheels. And given the disappointing results from the first experiment, she clearly had a lot of work left to do.

Two hours later, long after Tom had finished combing through the lab for potential sources of poison, she struggled to focus on the spectrograph readout for the presentation she needed to prepare on their depression medicine for next month's symposium. It was positive proof that the parasite they'd introduced to the plant had significantly modified its chemistry. Kind of like what the information she was still keeping from Tom was doing to her gut.

Her mind flashed to how warmly he'd wrapped her in his arms when she pretended to freak out over the Trojan warning. She'd felt like a heel. Not that she hadn't really been freaking out on the inside. She squirmed at how easily she'd let him slip back into her life. Maybe she should tell him what she was hiding and put an end to . . . *No, I made the right decision. I can't do anything that will jeopardize being able to see Dad again.* She set down the readout and then squirted soap from the dispenser onto her palm to wash her hands before the next test.

Tom's and the doctor's warnings about limiting her exposure to chemicals resounded through her brain. What was she doing? She hurriedly rinsed off the soap without lathering.

This was crazy. How was she supposed to do her job without touching any chemicals? She snatched a pair of latex gloves from the box on the shelf but froze at the sight of the powder inside. What if these had been tampered with? Did Tom even think to check these? She rummaged through the cupboard for an unopened box and fished a pair out of it.

Picking up a scalpel, she took a scraping from the next plant.

The lab phone shrilled, startling her. The scalpel slipped. "Ouch!"

Blood pooled inside the nicked finger of her glove. Tearing it off, she lurched for the sink and slapped on the tap water. Her heart rampaged as she thrust her hand under the running water, desperate to rid it of the glove's powder before it could get into her bloodstream. Staring at the red tinted water swirling off her finger, she let the phone ring. "You're being paranoid. The box was sealed, remember?" She knocked the tap closed with her elbow. If GPC wanted to get to her, there were far more expedient ways to do the job than pouring toxic powder into her latex gloves.

The phone's ring seemed to get shriller with every ring. It

could be Patti needing something since she didn't have her new cell number.

Kate pressed a paper towel to the cut and hurried to the phone. At the sight of a 1-800 number on the screen, she turned away. *Figures, I slash my finger for a salesman who conned reception into putting the call through. Except . . .* She jerked her attention back to the caller ID. No name, but the final digits were the same as her alarm company's phone number. She snatched up the phone. "Yes, Kate Adams here."

"Miss Adams, we're receiving a fire alarm from your home and have dispatched the fire department."

*Fire?* Her pulse skyrocketed, her mind flailing in a dozen different directions. GPC must've found out about the plants. "Thank you. I'll be there as soon as I can." She grabbed her purse and bolted out the door.

*Oh, please, Lord, don't let the plants burn.*

Kate's heart sank at the sight of all her neighbors gathered on the sidewalk around the fire truck. When she'd called the alarm company back from her cell phone on the way here, they'd said the firefighters couldn't see any sign of the fire from outside. Thinking only of saving her father's plants, she'd given them permission to pry open the door, all the while hoping against hope that the reason the fire wasn't visible wasn't because her grow lights had sparked the fire in her windowless fruit cellar.

She pulled to the curb behind the fire truck and hurried toward the firefighters standing on her lawn. "I'm the owner. Where'd it start? Is it contained?"

A young firefighter pulled off his helmet and gave her a

reassuring smile. "Looks like a false alarm. But I'm afraid you'll need to fix your lock now."

Relief washed over her. "Oh, thank you! A lock is the least of my worries."

"The chief's still inside trying to figure out what triggered the alarm. He said to send you in when you arrived."

Her relief fled as quickly as it had rushed in. Had the chief found her plants? What if he thought she was growing some exotic drug and notified the police? What if the firefighters who saw the plants mentioned them to the wrong people? She strode stiffly toward the door, forcing a little more starch into her backbone with every step. She was an herbal research scientist, for crying out loud! Half the town knew it. If she didn't appear concerned by what they saw, they'd have no reason to be suspicious about it. She lifted her chin. No reason at all.

She bypassed the front door, which didn't appear to be damaged, and skirted around the house to the back door, thankfully out of view of the gawkers, save for Mrs. C, leaning over the fence.

"Kate, dear, so glad you're here. I called Tom for you. He should be along any minute too."

Kate's confidence flagged, but she pasted on a smile. After all, Mrs. C had meant well. "Thanks, I appreciate that." She hoped the Lord would forgive her the little white lie, and the bigger one she had a bad feeling she might need to dodge inside. But it couldn't be helped, not if she wanted to keep word of the plants from leaking to the wrong people and jeopardizing her only hope of getting her father back.

The urgency of that mission propelled her forward. She found a firefighter on a stepladder in her laundry room, scrutinizing the smoke detector. "Are you the chief?"

"No ma'am, he's downstairs. Are you the owner?"

"Yes."

"Good, he'd like to talk to you."

She swallowed a bubble of trepidation. How many men had he told? She clutched the banister with an iron grip and slowly descended the stairs. "Chief?" she said, spotting another firefighter scrutinizing a second smoke detector. "I'm Kate Adams, the home owner." She slid a glance toward the fruit cellar and her breath froze in her throat at the sight of the open door, light pouring out.

The chief climbed off the chair he was standing on and shook her hand. He wore the same heavy jacket and bunker pants as the men in her yard. "Afternoon, ma'am. As you can see, you've had a false alarm."

"Yes, um—" Of its own volition, her gaze strayed to the fruit cellar. She snapped her attention back to the fire chief. "Any idea what would've caused it?"

"I suspect high humidity. We get a few of these kinds of false alarms every summer, when the weather is muggy and the home owner isn't running an air conditioner or dehumidifier." He ran his hand through his shaggy hair, leaving it disheveled. "Looks like your greenhouse operation there"—he jutted his chin toward the fruit cellar—"is the culprit."

She resisted the urge to hurry over and shut the door. No reason to draw more attention to it. He clearly had already inspected the room, and if she looked concerned about that, it would only spark his curiosity.

"What you growing in there anyway?"

Kate fluttered her hand as if it were a trifle. "Herbs I'm studying. I work at the research station."

"Right, okay. I figured it might be something like that when I didn't recognize the plants."

Yeah, she bet he did. She casually walked over to the door. "The plants need the constant humidity for optimum growth." She'd been careless to leave the door open—Tom or no Tom. Thank goodness he'd already left the research station when the alarm call came in, and that she was only contending with a false fire alarm, not a burglary. She glanced inside the cellar and quickly tallied the plants, then blew out a breath as she closed the door. All were still there.

"If you plan to continue growing the plants here," the fire chief said, "you'll need to run a dehumidifier in the main area of your basement, maybe add a ventilation fan, to avoid future false alarms."

"Yes, of course, I'll take care of that today."

The chief nodded. "We'll get out of your hair then. We reset your smoke detectors, but the fire alarm will need to be reactivated with your security company once you take care of the humidity problem."

"I understand. Thank you."

"Kate?" Tom's voice sounded from the top of the stairs.

Kate prodded the chief toward the stairs, her heart hammering. "Be right there."

Tom started down anyway. "What happened?"

"False alarm," she said cheerily, hoping the chief didn't elaborate.

"How? She hasn't been home." Tom directed the question to the chief and sounded deeply concerned.

The chief started up the stairs, thankfully prompting Tom to about-face. "Humidity from the plants she grows."

Kate's foot missed the bottom step. She was so cooked.

189

Except . . . aside from the back of his blazer growing a tad taut, Tom didn't react. Three steps up, she figured out why. He was, no doubt, waiting until he had her alone.

Sure enough, the instant the chief and the other firefighter let themselves out, Tom turned on her. "What are you growing downstairs?"

She laughed, although even to her own ears it sounded fake. "Plants for my research, of course." She quickly changed the subject and edged them toward the door. "Any more leads on Caleb?"

He sighed. "No, not yet."

She ignored a twinge of guilt at using the boy's plight to avoid Tom's question. At least she hadn't lied.

She would have if she'd had to though, because if Tom had an inkling of what she was up to, he'd shut her down in a heartbeat and she'd never see her father again.

*With God, all things are possible.*

Kate startled at the Scripture that whispered through her mind. Except somehow it felt more like an admonishment than a beacon of hope. She chewed on her bottom lip, feeling less certain of her decision than ever.

"My friend with NSA is running the sketch Caleb left behind through a sophisticated face recognition software and database he has access to. I'm hoping a name will pop."

Kate blinked, focused on what Tom was saying. "That's great."

His forehead wrinkled. "Are you okay?"

"Yes, of course." She smoothed her shirt and tugged at a strand of hair. Then, cluing in to how nervous she was acting, she shoved her hands in her pant pockets. "Why do you ask?"

Tom smiled sympathetically. "Two close calls in one day have got to be unnerving."

"Yes, I'm happy this was a false alarm." Her gaze strayed to the kitchen window facing the street and her heart sank. "Oh, no."

"What?" Tom glanced out.

"Harold, our illustrious town newspaper editor, just showed up. Now my false alarm will be front page news!" She choked. What if he reported what caused it and Crump or someone from GPC read it? The second they read "high humidity" they'd suspect exactly what she was growing. "Can't you stop him from reporting it?" She turned pleading eyes to Tom. "People are going to think I'm growing pot or something."

Tom chuckled. "I doubt that."

She felt a little sick that Tom trusted her so completely that the possibility she might have her father's contraband plants in her fruit cellar hadn't seemed to cross his mind.

His smile disappeared. "Although I wouldn't put it past Harold to intimate as much to try and sell more papers." Hands fisted, Tom strode toward the front door, looking ready to slay dragons on her behalf.

And his determination only intensified her guilt.

# 12

Tom yanked open the front door of Kate's house just as the newspaper editor reached the top of the porch steps.

A hungry spark lit Harold's eyes. "Detective," he drawled, as if the fact Tom was here held deep significance. "What brings you to a false alarm? Investigating those unusual plants Miss Adams is growing in her basement?"

Tom cringed at the innuendo. "Sounds to me like you're dancing on the border of a defamation suit, Harold. As you know, Miss Adams is a botanist and a researcher. There's nothing unusual about growing plants in her basement. Certainly nothing worthy of a newspaper article."

Harold smirked. "No need to get defensive. Look at it as an opportunity for Miss Adams to get some free press on her research."

"Miss Adams would just as soon not be the topic of any of your articles." Tom turned the man toward the steps.

"The fire call is a matter of public record. And I'm sure my readers would benefit from being educated on the sensitivity of smoke detectors to excess humidity in the house. Don't you agree?"

Yeah. The lowlifes growing pot in their basements would be sure to pull their smoke alarm batteries after that story. Tom helped Harold off the porch, his brain scrambling for another story to whet the newspaperman's appetite and get him off Kate's case. "Wasn't the big opening football game tonight at the high school?"

"Nice try, Detective. But it's Friday night." Harold stopped dead in his tracks and squinted at Tom. "Tell me, why are you so anxious to keep this quiet?"

"Don't you think the woman has been put through the public wringer enough in the past few months?"

"You should've just admitted you're sweet on her. I might've believed you." Harold chuckled. "But there's a story here. I can smell it." He saluted with his pencil, then veered toward a group of Kate's neighbors, still gossiping in the yard across the street.

Great. Instead of convincing Harold to drop the story, he'd stoked the man's curiosity. He was no doubt thinking about how many newspapers the last scandal involving Kate had sold.

Tom tapped on the front door but didn't wait for Kate's answer before pushing it open. "Kate?" He glanced down the hall toward the bedrooms, and hearing no response, headed for the kitchen.

Footsteps pounded up the basement stairs. "Coming. Is Harold gone?" Perspiration beaded Kate's brow.

"Are you sure you're okay?" Tom felt her forehead. "You're flushed."

The color in her cheeks deepened. "I was racing around,

trying to get things done before I go back to Patti's. I had to water plants and arrange for someone to come and replace the lock on my back door."

"I can do that for you."

"I know you could. But you have far more important things that you need to do, and Julie's husband said he could be right over."

Tom cringed at her forced cheeriness. This whole thing clearly had her rattled.

She steered him toward the living room. "Having a best friend married to the son of a hardware store owner does have its perks."

"You should ask him to bring a dehumidifier too. What kind of plants are you growing down there, anyway?"

"Nothing special. Did you dissuade Harold from writing another story on me?"

"Probably not, sorry."

She reached for the doorknob. "Well, thanks for trying at least."

He chuckled at her breathlessness. "Are you trying to get rid of me?"

"What? No, of course not. I thought you'd be in a hurry to get back to work."

"It's my day off. I just wasn't ready to take it until I'd exhausted all my leads on Caleb's whereabouts." He'd like nothing more than to spend the rest of it with her. Hold her in his arms again . . . only this time, his heart racing for a whole different reason than panic over what had her so frightened. Now that she seemed to be trusting him more, maybe she'd agree to have dinner with him.

Her fingers tightened around the doorknob, turning white.

"What's wrong?"

"Nothing, I—"

His cell phone rang the ringtone reserved for his dad. "Excuse me. I need to get that. After Dad dropped you off here earlier, I asked him to tail Crump, find out what he was up to." Or more importantly, find out if he rendezvoused with Molly Gilmore. Tom clicked on the phone. "What do you have?"

"Crump just turned into the parking lot at Sumpner's Falls. There aren't any other cars here at the moment, but it'd be a likely spot for a rendezvous."

Kate's sharp breath said she'd heard Dad's report.

"I'm on my way."

Kate caught his arm. "Wait, take me."

"No way. I have no idea what kind of situation we'll be walking into."

"Listen to me. After you arrested me for Daisy's murder and then the chief let me go, Crump took me to Sumpner's Falls to talk. Remember?"

"Yeah. Clearly," Tom said through gritted teeth. She'd sided with Crump when he tried to get her away from him, fearing Crump planned to push her off the cliff.

"He told me that Daisy showed him the place, that she'd said she liked to go there when she and God had some serious talking to do."

"So you think he's feeling remorseful? Going there to talk to God? Not a cohort?"

"Maybe. Why else choose that spot of all places to meet someone?"

"To avoid being seen."

Kate chewed on her bottom lip in that uncertain way she had.

And as much as he wanted to kiss away her worries, he feared she had reason to worry, and the danger would only get worse if his dad was right about Crump. "I need to go. I'll call you later."

Her grip on his arm tightened. "No, wait. He knows something. I know he does. And I think he'll talk to me. He took me there once before to talk to me."

"I'm not putting you at risk. Besides, you have Ryan coming to fix your lock."

The hardware store's pickup truck pulled to the curb as Tom opened the door.

"I can leave Ryan to do the job and grab the new key from him later. Please, let me come, I have a strong feeling that I need to be there. The last time we talked at Sumpner's Falls, he told me that besides Molly, I was the closest thing he had to a friend."

"The last time you saw Crump, he tried to kill you! Or so you thought." Never mind Molly's sudden appearance in town; he didn't have time to get into that with Kate now.

Kate grabbed her purse and jacket. "If you don't take me with you, I'll drive there myself."

"No, you won't." He strode toward his car. "You need to get back to Patti."

"Yes, I will. Stop, listen to me."

He dug in his heel and spun around to glare at her.

She didn't back down. "If guilt is gnawing at him," she said with a conviction that that was exactly what was going on, "I think he'll confide in me."

One glimpse at the determination in her eyes told him she wouldn't back down. "Fine, get in."

She rushed over to Ryan and gave him instructions while

Tom started the car, then dove in beside him as if she thought he might take off without her. "Okay, go."

Tom handed her his cell phone. "Text my dad and ask if there's any change."

Dad phoned back and Kate held it out so they could both listen. "He's still sitting in his car in the parking lot."

"Where are you?" Tom asked.

"Parked on the road at the top of the bend with a bird's-eye view through the trees. Wait. He's getting out of his car. He's heading toward the upper falls trail. Do you want me to follow him?"

"Park in the lot and make it look like you're there for a walk, so whoever he's meeting won't suspect anything. We'll cut through the woods at the top of the escarpment."

"We?"

Tom blew out a breath. "Kate's with me. She thinks she can get him to talk."

Tom read Dad's silence loud and clear—he'd been an idiot to cave. The instant Dad disconnected, Tom gave Kate the drill. "If there is anyone else with Crump, I want you to stay out of sight, get back to the car if you can, and lock yourself in."

"Okay," she agreed, a little too readily to be believed.

"I'm dead serious," Tom said sternly. "I do *not* want them using you as a hostage."

"You have my permission to shoot anyway if they do."

"Don't think I won't. This isn't a game."

She smirked. "You're kind of attractive when you get all protective on me."

He rolled his eyes but couldn't deny the ridiculous thrill that skipped through his chest. Considering how at news of the fire alarm, he'd instantly assumed Molly Gilmore or Crump or maybe even Jarrett had set fire to her place, his dad might've been right about him imagining connections where there weren't any. But he still hoped they'd catch Crump talking to somebody connected to GPC or to Caleb's disappearance, or both . . . just not when Kate was around.

Tom pulled to the side of the road. "We'll go in from here." He pressed a key into her hand. "And remember what I said. If we run into any trouble, I want you to hightail it back to the car."

The woods in this section of the conservation area—a mix of maples and ash—had little underbrush, which meant that although they could move quickly, they'd be fully exposed. And the trickle of the falls was scarcely loud enough to mask the crackle of dead leaves under their feet. Yet Kate kept up with him with surprising stealth.

At the sound of voices, Tom lifted his hand, bringing her to a halt behind him. He motioned toward a broad-trunked tree and whispered, "Hide behind that," then crept forward until he could see Crump and . . . Tom's heart dropped a beat. *Beady Eyes.*

He knew Crump couldn't be trusted.

He edged as close as he could get and still avoid detection but still couldn't make out what they were talking about. "You in position?" he texted his dad.

At Dad's "yes," Tom moved in. "Don't move. Police. Keep your hands where I can see them."

Crump's hands shot into the air, but Smith, or Selby, or whatever he wanted to call himself, took off.

"Hold Crump," Tom called to his dad and sprinted after Smith.

198

The guy tripped over a root, and when he stumbled, Tom lunged for him. They went down hard. "You ready to answer my questions now?" Tom asked between labored breaths.

Smith butted his head backwards, nailing Tom in the chin.

Pain exploded in his jaw, but he dug his fingers into the back of Smith's jacket, not about to let his grip slacken.

Smith surged to his feet, swinging his arms like a crazy man, then took off toward a dirt bike, leaving Tom holding nothing but his jacket.

"Tom!" Kate's panicked voice cut through the trees as a dirt bike roared to life.

Tom flung the jacket to the ground. "Run!"

But Kate snatched up a heavy branch and swung it over her shoulder, like a batter preparing to swing, as Smith sped straight for her.

The gnarly bark of the branch bit into Kate's hands as Smith's beady eyes bore into hers, the bike's fumes curling into her nostrils. She tightened her grip and swung.

Smith veered left, the tip of the branch glancing off his back tire. But the bike kept going.

Tom stormed toward her, barking a be-on-the-lookout order into his police radio, with Smith's description and location. "I told you to run."

"I thought I could stop him. I—"

Tom silenced her with a glare that said they'd discuss it later. "You're okay?"

She swallowed the rest of her apology. "Yes."

"Good, because it's time to talk to Crump." He pressed

his palm to her back and urged her toward the top of the waterfall, where his dad was hanging on to Jim. The memory of the last time she and Jim stood in that exact spot rushed back to her. She'd just learned he wasn't really Edward, Daisy's long-lost nephew. A raptor had swooped down and caught a mouse, and Jim had said that that was how he saw God—waiting up there to catch him where he shouldn't be.

*Like now.*

When she'd told Tom that Jim would talk to her, she'd thought her question about his faith earlier today might have pricked his conscience and driven him here, to the one place Daisy had always found solace. A place Kate had foolishly thought Jim would revisit to feel close to Daisy, to remember her counsel, to remember Daisy's hopes that Jim would become a better man.

The last person Kate had expected to find him with was Beady Eyes.

Tom snatched up the jacket the man had abandoned and checked the pockets. "Empty," he grumbled.

Kate drew in a rattled breath. Tom had been right about Jim. Gilmore and Wolfe must have sent him here to con her into admitting what she knew. How could she have forgotten the only other friend he'd mentioned the last time they'd stood here was Molly?

*A friend he hadn't wanted to lose.*

"Do you have to read him his rights or something before we talk to him?" Kate whispered to Tom.

"We only do that when we're interrogating a suspect who's under arrest, and at this point, I don't have enough probable cause to arrest him." He rubbed her back encouragingly. "So let's hope he's in a talkative mood."

"Yes, because I have a lot of questions for him."

"What happens now?" Jim asked Tom as they approached.

Tom motioned to his father to release Jim's arm. "We'd like to ask you a few questions."

Jim gave Tom's father a bewildered look. "I'm not under arrest?"

"No."

"So I don't have to answer your questions?"

"That's correct."

"But if you're innocent, why wouldn't you?" Kate jumped in, not understanding why Tom couldn't just haul him down to the station on suspicion of knowing something about Caleb's disappearance.

Jim ducked his head, looking like he'd rather have the truth beat out of him by a room full of cops than face her. "What do you want to know?"

His reaction gave her a smidgen of hope. "How do you know"—not knowing whether he'd call Beady Eyes by the name Smith or Selby or some other alias, she sputtered—"that man?"

Jim glanced at Keith, then Tom. "Isn't he one of yours?"

Tom looked at Jim as if he'd just landed from another planet, and the man's gaze dropped back to the ground.

"I should have known he was lying."

"What are you talking about?" Kate pressed.

"He came to me after Molly's arrest, claimed he worked for law enforcement. Asked me if I wanted to help guarantee Molly got the justice she deserved for killing Daisy."

*Right.* His real plan was no doubt the exact opposite. How could a con artist be so easily duped?

"What did you tell him?" Tom asked.

"Yes, of course. He paid for a two-week stay in an all-inclusive resort in Venezuela where Molly's father happened to be and for the round-trip airfare, so I didn't ask a lot of questions."

"What did he expect you to do?" Kate cut in.

Averting his gaze, Jim scraped his hand over his jaw. "Go to Gilmore and act as if I'd do anything to keep Molly out of jail if I could have her back." Shame, or a good imitation of it, warbled his voice. "Then I was supposed to report back everything I learned."

"What did you learn?"

"I already told you that much. That Gilmore and Wolfe are interested in your research. Gilmore wanted me to return here to see what more I could learn."

About her research?

About the amendoso more likely. Except . . . Gilmore had arranged for Jim's job at the research station months before she knew about the amendoso.

Beside her, Tom tensed, his fists clenching. "Two days ago, you told me that Gilmore paid you to disappear."

"Yeah, well, if I told you he asked me to spy on Kate, you wouldn't have let me anywhere near her. Besides, I figured Smith would fill you in. When I told him what Gilmore asked me to do, he urged me to play along, but to run the information by him first."

"It didn't occur to you that Smith might be working for Gilmore too?" Kate blurted. Last month the man had seen her in the Nagy woods within yards of the plant. He had to suspect she'd squirreled samples away somewhere.

"Not until I saw that kid's sketch. Then I started thinking it'd be just like Gilmore to cover all the angles to get the info he was after, one way or another."

"And what info is he after, exactly?"

Crump shrugged. "You know . . . what you're working on. How you feel about GPC. What you do in your free time." Crump glanced at Tom. "Who you're seeing."

"Have you reported anything to Smith or Gilmore?" Tom cut in.

"No, I demanded an explanation for the kid's sketch the minute he showed."

"What did he say?" Kate asked.

"He swore he didn't do anything to the kid. That he'd been trying to help him when the kid ran away."

So she'd been right about Caleb running from him.

Keith snorted. "What did you expect him to say? Admit to terrorizing the kid?"

"I don't know. I was hoping for a rational explanation. I didn't want to believe I'd been conned. But you three showed up before the conversation got very far."

"We may have saved your life," Tom said.

Crump flinched. "Am I under arrest now?"

"No, but I have a lot more questions for you. Do you mind coming back to the station?" At Jim's shrug, Tom looked to his dad. "Will you escort him to his car? Kate and I will drive around and meet you at the main lot. Then I'll need you to take her to her house so I can follow Crump to the police station."

Tom cupped her elbow and led her back through the woods. "We're missing something. It doesn't make sense. Gilmore's a billionaire. Why put his daughter's future at risk by getting caught up in his friend's pharmaceutical interests? He's got to have something major at stake."

"If Jim can be believed." Kate bent down and scratched

an itch on her leg. A few steps further, she needed to again, more vigorously. Then again. Finally she stopped and edged up her pant leg.

Angry welts covered her lower leg.

"Terrific." She fisted her fingers to resist the urge to scratch anymore.

"What is it?"

She made a face. "Poison ivy."

"In these woods?" Tom glanced around. "I don't see any."

"Trust me. It's here somewhere." She swept her gaze over the ground they'd covered. "I've always hyper-reacted to it." Seeing what she wanted, she stooped to pick it.

Tom grabbed her arm. "What are you doing?"

She pointed to some fleshy-stemmed plants with large serrated leaves. "Picking jewelweed. It's the best cure for poison ivy and insect bites." She grabbed a handful when he released her arm and picked up her pace toward the car. "In the summer, it has dainty, funnel-shaped orange flowers." She crushed one of the plants in her hand, and an orange juice squirted out. "You rub the juice over your skin and it takes away the itch. The sooner the better."

Tom unlocked the car and held open her door. "Then sit here, and we'll rub it on right now."

She sat sideways on the front seat, her feet propped on the car's side step, but still struggled to see what she was doing.

"Here, let me." Tom chivalrously rolled up her pant legs and took the crushed plant from her hands.

"The ivy oil gets onto everything," she warned. "Even my pants, so you'll want to wash your hands well, or you could end up with a reaction too."

He frowned at his hands. "Now you tell me? I had latex gloves in the trunk."

"Sorry. It is potent stuff. One time when I was a kid, our neighbor thought she'd get rid of her poison ivy by burning it. But she didn't realize that the oils would get into the smoke. She ended up breathing it in and getting a nasty internal reaction."

"No kidding?" Forgoing gloves, he dropped to one knee in front of her. "I had no idea it could do that." Tom soothed the jewelweed juice over the welts. "How's that?"

Her tense muscles relaxed at his touch, but she couldn't say the same for the butterflies swirling through her middle at how sweet he was being. "Better, thank you."

He started on her other leg and she couldn't help thinking how different their relationship could be if she gave up her amendoso research. Then she thought about her dad. Swallowing the tears welling in her throat, she grappled for something else to think about. "My grandmother used to make a tea from the jewelweed's stalk and leaves, and freeze it into ice cubes. Then use the cubes to soothe rashes and bites. It works amazingly well."

Tom's gaze lifted to hers and held. "Kind of like your father's amendoso plant, huh?"

"Uh . . ." Had he guessed she had it?

He patted her knee. "We better get going."

"Yes," she agreed a little too breathlessly.

Tom stooped at the edge of the woods and plucked something from the ground before sliding into the driver's side. "I picked more jewelweed for later. Even found ones with speckled leaves."

"The spots are from a parasite. I don't think it'll affect its efficacy one way or the other."

"Oh, I figured they were better, because your neighbor's housekeeper said her mother was always careful to pick leaves that were speckled."

"She did?" Kate's mind arced back to the day Lucetta came to help her clean and found her father's photo in a drawer and claimed he'd murdered Lucetta's mother—the healing woman in her native Colombian village, the village where Kate's father had gone to collect the amendoso plant.

"You don't remember?"

"I was so stunned by her accusation that I must not have registered what she'd said about the plant itself." Kate stared at the jewelweed leaves, her mind whirling. "I think you may have just figured out why GPC was interested in my research months before I discovered the amendoso."

"I did?"

"Yes. Folklore surrounding the plant Daisy and I were studying varied widely. But anecdotally we realized that the samples most effective in treating depression had been attacked by a specific parasite prior to harvest. We figured out that the plant's chemistry changed in response. A change that proved beneficial to indigenous people who used it for their infusions."

"Like the amendoso."

"Maybe." It would explain why the plants in her fruit cellar didn't kill bacteria. They hadn't been attacked by any parasites. Let alone a parasite that lived in South America. A parasite that might *only* live in South America. How was she going to import a parasite?

"You think Wolfe assumed you were studying amendoso?"

"No, we identified the plant, but he might've recognized similarities. Maybe hoped the plant we were working with

206

would prove as versatile as amendoso had been. Be another miracle plant he could exploit."

Tom drove around to the main lot. "Doesn't explain why Gilmore would stick his neck out to help him though."

Kate forced her thoughts back to Jim's revelations. "Do you think Crump's really on our side?"

"I wouldn't count on it. I'm concerned that he's playing us from both ends as he claims Gilmore's doing."

"You don't think someone from law enforcement or government, maybe, could have asked for his help?"

"Oh, I can believe that part, but if Smith is legit, why'd he run away? I identified myself as a detective."

"I suppose you're right."

"And only a crooked cop would scare a kid into running away from home."

She shivered at the deepening shadows, at the thought of Caleb out there alone. "How do we fight a crooked cop?"

"Very carefully."

# 13

The streetlights scarcely pushed back the darkness as Tom parked his car in front of the B and B an hour later with Kate still sitting in the passenger seat. Her suggestion that the B and B would be a better place to talk to Crump, away from the listening ears of potentially corrupt cops, had been a good one. Tom nodded to his dad, who'd followed Crump here to ensure he didn't give them the slip, while Tom quickly took Kate by the station to retrieve her laptop, which thankfully hadn't been breached. But somewhere between the station and her home, she'd convinced him that *she* should be in on Crump's interview too.

More precisely, his uneasy feeling about dropping her off at her house in the dark with Smith still at large had convinced him. If Crump could be believed, Gilmore had to have something major at stake. Why else would a billionaire diamond magnate put his own daughter's future at risk by getting caught up in his friend's pharmaceutical interests?

Signaling to his dad to keep a lookout a while longer, Tom rounded the car and opened Kate's door.

"There seem to be more cars in the B and B's lot tonight." She hitched her laptop bag and purse over her shoulder. "I hope we'll be able to find a private place to talk."

Tom guided her to the door. "If not, we can suggest dinner somewhere."

"That wouldn't be any more private." Kate's stomach grumbled.

Tom chuckled. "Maybe not, but your stomach seems to like the idea."

Blushing in that incredibly appealing way she couldn't seem to help, she clacked the door knocker. "I skipped lunch."

The B and B's bubbly, gray-haired owner, Betty, opened the door. "Come in. Come in. Jim told me you were coming." She held the door wide. "A woman friend was waiting for him when he got home and he asked me to have you two wait in the dining room. Said he'd only be a few minutes."

Tom didn't like the sound of this. He knew he shouldn't have trusted Crump. "Where is he now?"

"They're in the back parlor. They needed some privacy, he said, but he didn't want to take her to his room. Such an honorable young man."

"Hmmm." Tom stretched his neck to see further down the hall and figure out which door Crump might be behind.

Clearly Betty was oblivious to who Crump's woman friend might be. Kate hooked her arm through Betty's and led her to the dining room table. "This is perfect. I needed to talk to you about the translation you did for me." She set her laptop bag on one of the chairs, pulled out a pad and pen, then sat opposite Betty. "Do you recall reading anything in the pages that talked about how to select which plants to use?"

"How do you mean?"

"For example, did the writer mention anything about choosing plants with speckled or spotted leaves?"

Betty motioned to Kate's bag. "Do you have it with you? *Moteado* or *manchado* means speckled or spotted. I can glance through it for you."

"I don't have it with me tonight, unfortunately. I'd hoped it might have stuck in your mind if he'd mentioned it."

Betty shook her head. "No, sorry. But I did find one of your pages here the other day. Meant to call you, then got distracted with visitors." She pulled open a drawer in the credenza. "It must have blown off the table while I was working. It was under the china cabinet. Afraid we don't clean under there too often."

As she pulled a sheet of paper from the drawer, Tom edged back into the foyer, hoping to catch a glance of Crump's guest. He had a bad feeling it was Molly, but he didn't want to mention Molly to Kate tonight if he didn't have to. She had enough to stress over without adding fears of what the woman who tried to kill her might be up to now. Tom could worry enough for the both of them. He could hear the murmur of voices but couldn't make out what they were saying.

Kate squealed and he rushed back into the dining room. "What's wrong?"

Betty had slipped on her reading glasses and was looking at a typed page.

"The missing page talks about the plants needing to have speckled leaves," Kate explained excitedly.

Betty set the paper on the table and pointed to a word. "Right here, see? Give me your pad and pen, and I'll translate the whole page before you go."

"Would it be all right if Kate and I brew a pot of tea?" Tom cut in.

Betty pushed to her feet, looking ready to bustle out. "Oh my, let me get that."

"No, no," Tom and Kate said in unison.

"You translate," Kate finished. "I can get the tea."

Tom followed her to the kitchen and glanced out the door at the opposite end of it, torn between barging in on Crump or taking a moment to tell Kate that Molly had been seen in town this morning and might be the woman friend in the next room. He doubted she'd take the news well. And if by some miracle Crump could be trusted, interrupting his conversation might jeopardize Molly's faith in him. Eavesdropping would be more helpful, if only the walls and doors in these old Victorian houses weren't so thick.

"What's going on?" Kate filled the kettle and set it on the gas stove. "Are you worried Crump is going to skip out on us?"

The chirp in her voice declared how much Betty's find had lifted her spirits, which wedged a new concern into Tom's thoughts. Despite his warnings, Kate was still trying to figure out what made the plants so special. Tom eased the teacups she'd picked up from her hands and set them on the tray. "I'm afraid—" The creak of a door and click of stilettos sounded from the hall.

"Sounds like she's going." Kate hurried to the door he'd just been at. "Don't you want to see who it is?"

Tom caught Kate by the waist and pulled her back. "We might not want her to see us. Wait here." Tom padded quickly down the hall, but the pair had disappeared. He hadn't heard the front door open. Did Crump take her to his room after all?

211

"Oh, you're welcome, dear." Betty's voice carried from the dining room.

*Crud.* He skidded into the room at the same time Kate entered from the kitchen.

The tray in her hands crashed to the floor. "What are you doing here?" she demanded.

A long-haired blonde stood next to Kate's laptop bag, brazenly flicking through the papers in the outside pouch with her blood-red fingernails.

Kate lunged at her. "Get away from my bag!"

Tom grabbed Kate. Crump gripped Molly's arm and yanked her away from the bag.

"Let me go." Kate fought against Tom's hold, her focus lasered in on Molly. "Don't you know who she is?" Then to Molly, who'd transformed from the innocent-looking, dark-haired, Snow White look-alike she'd been her last time in town to a nose-in-the-air, blonde socialite, Kate hissed, "You've got some nerve coming back here."

"She was just leaving." Crump steered the woman to the door.

"She's still jealous, I see," Molly said airily. "I hear self-esteem issues are epidemic in women whose fathers abandoned them as a child. How sad. I feel so sorry for her."

Kate's muscles bunched beneath Tom's palms. "I'll give you something to feel sorry about," she shrieked, lunging for the woman.

Tom tightened his hold on Kate's arms, drawing her against his chest, hoping to soothe the sting of Molly's nasty comeback.

Kate lashed out at him. "How can you let her parade through town like she's not a murderer?"

"A murderer?" Betty gasped, dropping the teacup shards she'd collected.

Molly snorted. "Kate has a vivid imagination. Thinks I know so much about nasty, deadly plants. When really"— smirking, she tapped her index finger to her temple—"I only know about good ones."

"Take it easy," Tom said, close to Kate's ear.

Thankfully, Crump hustled Molly out before she could do any more damage.

Kate stopped struggling, and Tom eased his grip, then quickly texted his dad to follow Molly.

The instant Crump returned, Kate laid into him. "What was she doing here? How could you talk to her after what she did to Daisy?"

Crump shot Tom a helpless look.

Not wanting to talk in front of Betty or the other guests who were bound to traipse down to find out what all the commotion was about, Tom motioned to Crump to close the door to the hall and directed Betty toward the one that opened into the kitchen. "Could you see to the tea? We'll clean this up."

"Was that Molly Gilmore?" Betty sounded dazed. "I didn't recognize her with the blonde hair. I never would have—" She shot Crump a horrified look. "And you."

"It isn't what it looks like," Tom reassured, coaxing her out the door and closing it behind her.

Kate gaped at him. "You act like you're not surprised Molly is here. Did you know she was in town?" Her voice inched higher. "And didn't tell me?"

*Like you didn't tell me about my dad.* She didn't say it, but Tom heard the accusation in her tone. Deserved it too,

213

considering his only good reason for not telling her sooner, besides not having a breathing moment between everything that had transpired today, was that he hadn't wanted to upset her. Or spur her into doing something stupid. He rubbed his ribs, still throbbing from where she'd pummeled him. He had no doubt she would've done something stupid.

"I didn't know," Crump insisted, not seeming to realize she'd been accusing Tom. "She was waiting for me when I got back. Claimed she couldn't bear not seeing me."

"You don't think that's why she really came?" Tom prodded. Crump had traded in his Porsche Boxter for a pickup and opted for a rundown farmhouse over a condo—not the kind of lifestyle changes that would appeal to a woman like Molly, even if getting back together with her was the lie he'd fed her father.

Crump glanced away, his left eye twitching. "I suspect her father got word from Smith about how antsy I got after seeing that kid's sketch."

"You're assuming Smith is on Gilmore's payroll," Tom clarified. Although whether GPC's or Gilmore's probably didn't make much difference.

"Who else's would he be on? If he's really a good guy like he said, why's the kid running from him?"

Tom blew out a breath. "Until I find Caleb, I'm not sure we'll know the answer to that."

Kate scrabbled up the papers Betty had written on. "You expect me to believe that you're only pretending to still be interested in Molly so you can get evidence against her?"

"Yes." Crump's voice cracked. And as good a con artist as Tom knew him to be, he had to admit that Crump's distress seemed genuine.

Kate stopped her frantic activity, her gaze narrowing in on Crump's for a long moment. "I don't believe you." She clasped the papers to her chest and turned to Tom. "I'm sorry, I can't do this."

"Kate, wait." Jim Crump blocked the dining room door. "I know I don't have a track record for honesty, but please, hear me out."

Right, as if she hadn't already betrayed Daisy's memory enough by even thinking he cared about justice. Kate stuffed her papers into her laptop bag, unable to bring herself to look at him. Her insides were still trembling from the sight of Molly Gilmore standing ten feet in front of her, without an ounce of remorse for the life she stole. Worse than that, she'd had the gall to riffle through her papers and accuse Dad of abandoning her when it had been Molly's father's bosom buddy who'd driven Dad from their home. "She killed Daisy, nearly killed me. How can you pretend that doesn't matter to you?" She swiped at the tears leaking from her eyes. "Unless it doesn't," she added caustically.

Tom brushed the back of his hand along her arm. "Hey, sometimes we force ourselves to do things we hate because it seems like the only way to make things right."

"How does not telling me Molly was back in town make things right?" Suddenly she didn't feel the least bit guilty about concealing the plants from him. He clearly hadn't changed at all.

His expression looked pained, but she braced herself

against its impact. Squinting instead at Jim, she was taken aback to see the anguish in his face too.

"Daisy was the only person who ever believed in me, believed I was a good person, deep down in my soul, even though she knew the worst about me. She made me want to be that person she believed me to be." He turned away and whisked his fingers across his eyes before meeting her gaze once more. "You had that same kind of faith in people. It's why you refused to believe Daisy could have killed herself, when all I'd been worried about was that your sleuthing would expose my own secrets."

She let out a disdainful snort. "That faith in people was why I couldn't see what Molly was, or you for that matter. I know better now. Like Tom so often likes to remind me, 'people are rarely what they seem.'"

Tom cringed. "I envied your faith in people."

"We both know I was a foolish idealist."

He combed his fingers softly through her hair. "The world could do with a few more idealists. You've shown me that it's better to trust and risk being a fool than to live in constant mistrust."

She shook her head. "Do you honestly think you can believe anything he tells us?"

Tom's pure blue eyes looked deep into hers, not probing but inviting. Inviting her to see for herself. "Honestly? No, I don't. But I do believe we'll know more after we hear him out."

She wrapped her arms around her middle, unable to turn away from the entreaty in his gaze. Now that the shock of seeing Molly had passed and the crushing sense that she'd be betraying Daisy's memory to spend another minute in

Jim's presence had eased, she had to admit she'd like to hear what he had to say. She wasn't about to give him a shred of information about her research or whichever plant Gilmore was really interested in, but he might know something she could use to get to see her dad. And whether she wanted to be or not, since she'd convinced Tom to bring her along in his car, she was at his mercy. She slumped into a chair. "Fine. I'll listen."

"Okay." Jim took a seat on the opposite side of the table.

Tom scooped up the teacups she'd shattered, retrieved a tray of cookies and tea from the kitchen, where he must've explained their need for privacy to Betty, and then claimed the place next to her.

"When I was in Venezuela," Crump started, "I visited an emerald mine Gilmore recently acquired a majority share in. My guide told me that about a year and a half ago a strange affliction struck the miners."

"What does that have to do with Molly killing Daisy?" Kate muttered.

"Maybe nothing." Crump smoothed the tablecloth in front of him. "But when I asked Gilmore about the incident, he didn't want to talk about it. I mean, *irately* didn't want to talk about it."

Tom straightened in his chair, his face white, and looked intently at Jim. "A dozen people died?"

Crump nodded.

"How do you know that?" Kate couldn't keep the shock from her voice.

"It was in the papers." Tom shrugged as if being familiar with the situation was no big deal, but there was no mistaking the strain in his voice or the disturbed look in his eyes.

"Yeah," Crump went on. "Apparently the incident made international news. The emeralds from this mine are among the best in the world, and two of the mine's biggest shareholders, who'd been touring it at the time, died in the outbreak. Of course, that's probably how Gilmore was able to swoop in and gain a controlling interest."

"Is that why you think he didn't want to talk about it?" Kate didn't bother to mask her skepticism. "Somehow I can't see a businessman like Gilmore being ashamed of taking advantage of the situation."

Crump fiddled with a spoon, his gazed fixed on it. "Neither could I." He set the spoon back on the table and met her gaze once more. "When I mentioned his reaction to Molly, she said that he'd been on edge lately, which she blamed on trouble with the mafia."

"The mafia?" Kate exchanged a look with Tom, her heart hammering at the thought of the sudden deaths of Patti's parents last year and of Patti's mother's ties to the mafia.

Tom's head nodded almost imperceptibly, his eyes assuring her they'd discuss it later.

"Yeah," Jim went on. "Apparently the mob mines diamonds illegally, then floods the market, which devalues Gilmore's holdings. And there isn't much he can do about it."

"I still don't see what that has to do with why Molly would kill Daisy or why they'd be interested in my re . . . search." Kate caught herself scratching her poison ivy rash, her mind veering to what she'd told Tom about good plants growing next to bad ones.

Her breath stalled in her throat. What if a toxic *plant* caused those miners' deaths? Amendoso came from Colombia— next door to Venezuela—and might have been used to treat reactions to a poisonous plant in the same vicinity, the way she'd used the jewelweed.

And Wolfe would have known that.

And could have recognized the "strange affliction" as such a reaction.

Kate sat up, excitement welling in her chest. It might explain Gilmore's interest in her research, especially if he feared some ruthless crime boss would use the toxic plant against his mines.

She darted a glance at her laptop bag, her fingers itching to start researching this "strange affliction." If it was caused by a plant that Wolfe thought amendoso could counteract, studying it might offer some clue to what made amendoso so special. Some clue that would help her sway Tom's colleagues into letting her see her dad.

She stole a glance at Tom, who watched her too closely for comfort. He'd do whatever he could to keep her safe, even if that meant stopping her work. And she couldn't stop now. Not when she was so close.

# 14

Sweat slicked the back of Tom's neck as he escorted Kate out of the B and B following their discussion with Crump. The only reason he'd recalled those deaths at that Venezuelan mine was because they'd been the topic of an article that had caught his former FBI partner's attention mere weeks before he was killed. At the time, it had seemed as if Ian latched on to it to score a date with a pretty botanist. But considering that botanist's name had turned up in Kate's father's arrest file and Gilmore now owned the mine where the deaths occurred, maybe Ian had stumbled onto something bigger than he realized.

Clamping his cell phone, Tom motioned Kate to stop on the porch, then scanned the shadows. The web she was caught in was getting more tangled by the second, and he feared he wouldn't be able to free her. Remaining on the porch, he phoned his dad. "Where's Molly now? Did you manage to tail her?"

"She left town. I turned back once she passed Hamilton. I doubt she'll return. Not tonight, anyway."

Kate's exhalation told Tom she'd heard Dad's assurances. Tom squeezed her hand and started down the steps. "Thanks, Dad. Good to know."

"Learn anything useful from Crump?" Dad asked.

"I think so. We have lots of research to do. I need to stop by the station first, but if you could start an internet search on mining fatalities in South America, especially unexplained ones, that would be a huge help."

"I'll get right on it."

Tom pocketed his phone and opened the passenger door for Kate, mulling over what to do with her. He doubted she'd let him take her back to Patti's without a fight. And taking her back to her house to pick up her car sounded like a worse idea. Molly might be long gone, but he still had no idea where Smith had holed up. The update he'd gotten from dispatch a few minutes ago, on his BOLO request, said they'd found dirt-bike tracks ending at the road that bordered the south end of the conservation area, above the falls. Smith had probably loaded his bike onto a truck and taken off before patrol cars had even been alerted.

Tom rounded the car's hood, and as he slid behind the wheel, Kate clicked off her phone. "I ordered the dinner for three special at Sum Yung's. It'll be ready by the time you're finished at the police station."

Smothering the smile that tugged at his lips at her determination not to be sidelined, he accepted her plan without argument. At least he wouldn't be worrying about her.

He parked in a dim corner of the parking lot where she was unlikely to be noticed. "You can wait here. I won't be long." He hurried inside to Hutchinson's desk. Kate's sketch of Smith that Tom had asked Hutchinson to cross-reference against law enforcement personnel sat on the corner. Clearly the man didn't understand the meaning of "keep the search low-key." Tom snatched up the paper and tucked it into his pocket. "Any luck?"

"Sorry, no matches to anyone in the local detachments, regional, provincial, or federal. Doesn't mean he's not one of us, though. Could be undercover."

"Yeah, okay. Thanks for trying." They only sealed the records of deep undercover cops. The ones investigating men who'd threaten to kill an officer's family to coerce him to do the same database search he'd just had Hutchinson do. The ones investigating organized crime.

Liking the idea of Kate staying at Patti's less than ever, Tom edged toward the window, his gut churning. If Gilmore or GPC were connected with organized crime, they could end up being a hundred times more ruthless than they'd already been.

Assured no one was skulking around the parking lot, Tom let himself into an empty conference room and put in a call to Zeb.

"Some people have lives outside the office, you know," Zeb said, in lieu of hello.

"You get an ID on that sketch I faxed you?" The first chance he'd gotten, Tom had forwarded Kate's doctored version of the lemur sketch to replace the one he'd had his dad send this morning.

"Nothing yet, sorry."

Tom told Zeb about Crump's rendezvous and Smith's hasty exit when Tom arrived, then filled Zeb in on Crump's story about Gilmore and the Venezuelan emerald mine.

"What makes you think I'd be interested in this?" Zeb interrupted.

Tom gripped the back of a chair to stop himself from hitting something or slamming Zeb with a few choice words. "You're NSA and you're telling me you're not interested in a plant that kills anyone who breathes in the smoke when it's burned? It's a terrorist's gold mine. Pun intended."

"Yeah, I got that. But what's a toxic plant from Colombia got to do with the kid you're trying to find?"

"Colombia? Who said anything about Colombia?" That tingly feeling that told Tom his buddy had made a telling slip prickled Tom's neck.

"Venezuela, then, whatever."

Oh yeah, he was definitely onto something. "Because the kid had a sketch of the man who paid for Crump's trip. And the mine now belongs to Jeremiah Gilmore—the father of the woman who tried to kill Kate."

"Ah." Zeb drew the word out to three syllables.

"Don't 'ah' me. I know you know a lot more than you're telling me. And if you're withholding anything that could help me locate this boy, so help me, I'll—"

"You'll what? Give me a break, Tom. You know I can't talk about an ongoing investigation."

"Right." Tom grinned at the confirmation. "Thanks." He clicked off and hurried back out to his car.

Kate was gone.

Pulse racing, he checked the doors. No sign of damage. He glanced every which way. *Where is she?* She wouldn't have opened the door to a stranger. Except maybe it hadn't been a stranger.

He whipped out his phone and pressed the link to her new number.

The sound of the phone rang in his ear and echoed from

the sidewalk on the other side of the parking lot. "Hey, keep your shirt on!" Kate strolled across the lot, carrying two bags from the Chinese takeout place. "You were taking so long, I thought I'd save time and pick up our dinner."

"Good idea," Tom managed to mutter without sounding like he was tamping down the herd of elephants that had rampaged through his chest at the sight of his empty car.

"I called Patti to let her know I'd be late too. Learn anything helpful?"

He relieved her of the takeout bags and set them on the floor behind her seat as she climbed in. "Unfortunately, no." Unless he counted Zeb's subtle confirmation that Gilmore or at least the incident at the mine he now owned was being investigated by US intelligence.

Kate reached for the door handle. "Then let's hope your dad had better success with his internet search."

Tom caught her door before she could pull it closed, then, cupping her face, kissed her soundly. "Don't disappear on me like that again. You almost gave me a heart attack."

Her lips curved into a smile beneath his as she kissed him back. "It's nice to be missed."

The sweet amusement in her voice curled around his heart, and it took everything in him to resist the urge to deepen the kiss right there in the middle of the police station's parking lot. He brushed his thumb over her rosy lips. "Definitely missed." He rounded the car to the driver's side, and the sight of her gaze tracking him reassured him that she was finally ready to trust him again. Trust he'd need more than ever if he was going to keep her safe.

They drove to his house in silence and found his dad combing the internet for information. Still mulling over the implications of the NSA's interest in the plant that killed the miners, Tom set plates and cutlery on the dining room table as Kate opened the takeout containers. "Dad, why don't you fill us in over dinner on what you've learned so far. Then we can divvy up between the three of us any searches that still need to be done."

Dad clicked the print icon on his computer for the third time since they'd gotten there, then swung his desk chair around to face the table. "The deaths at the mine were blamed on toxic smoke from plants tossed into a cooking fire."

"Really?" Kate returned an unbitten egg roll to her plate, her voice spiking excitedly. "Did any of the articles give the plant's name?"

Dad loaded his plate with the deep-fried shrimp and not enough of the vegetable dishes. "Yeah, the indigenous people call it *diablo piel*."

Kate frowned. "Devil's skin?"

"Because the plant's oil turns the skin hot and red on contact."

Kind of like the pepper sauce Dad was smothering his shrimp and rice with. Tom tugged it from his hands and passed him the carton of chow mein. "You've never heard of diablo piel?" Tom quizzed Kate.

"No." She turned back to Dad. "Did any of the articles give its Latin name?"

"Not that I recall." Dad reached behind him and snagged a page from the printer tray. "The details in initial reports were sketchy. This one came out in the *Washington Review* a couple of months after the incident." He pushed aside the takeout boxes cluttering the middle of the table and laid the sheet where they could both read it.

"By the description of people's reactions, sounds like the plant could be poison ivy," Tom said, his mind drifting to the doctoring he'd done on Kate's slender legs this afternoon.

"Doesn't match the plant's physical description." Kate pointed to a paragraph further down the page. "I'll have to go through my taxonomy book to figure out what this is. It doesn't fit any plant families I'm familiar with. But neither did amendoso." A giddy excitement returned to her voice. "And this says diablo piel is native to Colombia."

Tom didn't like the sound of where she was going with this.

"If amendoso grew near this diablo piel, the locals might've used amendoso as an antidote, like we use jewelweed for poison ivy and dockweed for stinging nettle."

Dad stopped his fork halfway to his mouth. "You think Gilmore wants amendoso as an antidote?"

"It fits. Amendoso purportedly cures everything, and since GPC was studying it, Gilmore's buddy would've heard all about the folklore." Kate snatched up a pencil and started underlining details in the article. "If I could arrange to import some diablo piel plants, I might be able to figure out why amendoso is—*was* such a miracle plant."

Tom choked on his food, then coughed it loose. "No way! Vic almost killed your father to get his hands on the amendoso. What do you think Wolfe would do if he heard you were experimenting with diablo piel?" Tom shoved his plate aside, his appetite gone. "Or hasn't it occurred to you that the plant wasn't tossed into the fire by accident?"

"Of course it has! After what Jim said about the mafia, I assumed they were responsible."

Tom scrubbed a hand over his face. He doubted it, but

he had no reason for thinking Gilmore was behind it other than the fact he now owned a majority share in the mine.

"Or drug lords," Dad cut in.

"Drug lords?" Tom repeated, not bothering to mask how far-fetched he thought the idea sounded. "How do you figure?"

"Sure. In lots of those South American countries, guerillas shoot anyone who doesn't toe the line. Local officials speculated that too many workers were abandoning farming coca for cocaine production in favor of working the mines, and the attack was a warning."

"But that wouldn't have anything to do with Gilmore." Kate sounded confused.

"Maybe not, but did you read to the bottom?" Dad pointed to the article. "It says a similar incident occurred twenty years ago."

"Really?" The trill in Kate's voice told him she hadn't missed the significance of the time frame—around the same time her father had been arrested for stealing company secrets when he didn't deliver the amendoso plants GPC had sent him to Colombia to retrieve.

If his father had been trying to convince Kate diablo piel wasn't connected to amendoso, this wasn't the way.

Dad pushed his dinner plate aside and grabbed the stack of pages from his printer tray. Thumbing through them, he continued, "Twenty years ago, coca farming was rampant. The Colombian government blamed the mine incident on drug lords. At their request, the US government got involved." Dad pulled a page from the middle of the stack with a picture of a plane flying low over a field. "Here it is. They bombarded coca fields with herbicides from the air. Some speculate they

227

also tracked down and destroyed sources of diablo piel so the drug lords wouldn't be able to pull the stunt again."

At the *Colombians'* request. Given Zeb's slip of the tongue earlier, Tom suspected this wasn't news to him.

"Now with the new biofuels law," Dad went on, "palm farms are replacing the coca farms, so herbicide use has been curbed—"

"Which gave the plant a chance to resurge," Tom muttered, remembering Ian talking about this very thing and wishing he'd paid more attention, because he was beginning to suspect that whatever Kate's father got himself mixed up in might also be what got Ian killed.

And now Kate was tangled in it too.

Pushing aside her plate, Kate reached for her computer bag.

Tom surged to his feet and jerked the bag from her hand. "You can't research this. It's too dangerous."

She jolted at his adamant tone. "Who's going to find out? Your computer forensics guy just finished assuring us not more than three hours ago that there was no spyware on my computer."

Tom tightened his grip on the bag's handle, his heart rioting at the thought of her ending up like Ian, as if Vic Lawton's death hadn't had him anxious enough.

"Tom . . ." She drew his name out a couple of extra syllables, concern creasing the delicate skin around her eyes. "What's wrong?"

He slumped back into his chair and rubbed his forehead. "My partner took an unusual interest in the mine incident just before he died. That's why I knew twelve people lost their lives when Crump mentioned it."

"The same partner that died from a car bomb?"

"Yes, his name was Ian." And until today, Tom had thought Ian's curiosity about the plant in the newspaper story had been feigned as an excuse to entice the sultry Latina botanist he'd met in a bar to meet him again. Now . . . he didn't know what to think.

Compassion filled Kate's eyes. "You said that a spy who'd pretended to be his girlfriend set the bomb."

Tom's breath heaved from his chest. "Yes." He didn't want to mention that Zoe's name and number had also been in Kate's father's file, let alone mention her father's uneasy reaction to the name.

"A Russian spy? Do you think she was after information on the plant?"

Tom shook his head, buying himself an extra moment to consider her second question. "She wasn't Russian. South American."

"Spying for organized crime? Drug lords?" Dad speculated.

"Maybe." Tom gritted his teeth as he recalled how the FBI agent in charge of Ian's murder investigation had confiscated all of Ian's electronics and papers. He'd always assumed Zoe had been plying Ian for information and turned on him when she realized he'd caught on to her. But if that information was connected to a potential biological weapon, was it any wonder Zeb had obliged his request to hide Kate's father without a squawk? And Tom had played right into their hands. Only . . . he wasn't so sure anymore if that was a good thing.

The next morning Kate rushed through her shower, bleary-eyed from the late night at Tom's scouring the internet for insight into what Gilmore and GPC were after. She yanked on her black pants and favorite purple blouse and hurried down to the kitchen. Patti and Jarrett already sat at the table, eating breakfast. Kate glanced at the stove's clock. "Tom's not here yet? He said he'd come get me first thing to take me to pick up my car." She probably should've argued when he'd insisted on driving her home last night, but she'd been too unnerved by his concern—almost unnerved enough to tell him about the amendoso plants she was harboring.

She'd almost let it slip a couple of times, but with the connection she now suspected existed between parasites and enzymes and diablo piel and amendoso, she was too close to the answers she'd been looking for to take that risk. Not after he'd nearly burst an artery at the prospect of her typing "diablo piel" into her web browser.

Jarrett dug a hand into his pants pocket. "Parker called while you were in the shower when you didn't answer your cell. Asked if you could drive Patti's car today instead. Which I was going to suggest anyway, to give Patti extra legroom. I picked it up from my mechanic's last night." Jarrett dropped the car keys next to Kate's juice glass, then reached across the table and squeezed Patti's hand. "And Serena won't pull any more crazy stunts. I promise you."

A blush bloomed on Patti's cheeks, reminding Kate of her own reaction to Tom's unexpected kiss in the police station's parking lot. Its fierceness had stemmed from fear, she knew, but it'd roused a yearning in her soul so deep that she hadn't known what to do about it.

Except to kiss him back.

The instant she'd seen his panicked face as he frantically scanned the parking lot for her, she'd known what he feared and had tried to make light of it to hide how her own heart had thundered at his concern.

She sipped her juice to cool the heat climbing to her cheeks. "Did Tom say why he couldn't make it?" She hoped it was because of a promising lead on Caleb's or Smith's whereabouts and not something bad.

Jarrett picked up the copy of the *Port Aster Press* that lay on the other side of his plate and set it in front of her. "He figured leaving your car in the driveway would make it look like you're home to any potheads looking for an easy score."

"What?" Kate's gaze dropped to the front-page story. "I don't believe this! Harold makes it sound like I'm growing marijuana in my basement."

"You should sue for defamation," Patti said.

Jarrett shook his head. "Wouldn't win. The slimeball has couched his words enough to leave the piece wide open to interpretation."

Molly's spiteful face flashed through Kate's mind, and an icy shiver rippled over her skin at the thought of how *she* might interpret the article: correctly. Thank goodness she'd left town last night. Kate silently prayed she didn't come back and that Jim Crump didn't tell her or anyone else about the story.

"Kate, are you okay?" Patti's cool touch jerked Kate's attention back to the table. "You've gone as white as a sheet."

"I'm fine." She downed her juice. "You just about ready to head out?"

"Don't you want to eat breakfast?" Patti shifted a plate of toast Kate's way. "There's plenty."

Kate didn't think her roiling stomach could handle any-thing, but she dutifully added a sheen of jam to a piece of toast and took a bite. Had Tom guessed what was really in her basement too?

The thought of how he'd feel at learning she'd kept the plants a secret from him suddenly made her feel downright ill. Never mind that she'd kept the secret "to make things right," just like Tom had defended Jim's meeting with Molly. Using the same argument wouldn't stop him from being hurt. Or from being angry about the risks she was taking.

Was that the real reason he hadn't wanted her driving her easy-to-spot yellow Bug? Was she putting Patti in danger too, just by being here?

Kate glanced from the news story to her assistant. The fact that neither she nor Jarrett had asked what kind of plants she did have in her basement suddenly struck her as odd. Did Patti suspect amendoso? Had she and Jarrett discussed as much?

"Where are you off to today?" Patti asked Jarrett.

"More meetings." He pushed his chair from the table and rose. "I should get going." He gave Patti a peck on the cheek. "Don't overdo it today."

"I won't. I can work from a stool."

The ordinary conversation mocked the wild suppositions flying through Kate's head. Seeing the affectionate glance they exchanged, Kate wondered how she'd ever thought Jar-rett was only interested in Patti's money or their research. He clearly adored her.

Kate quickly finished her toast. "We might as well go now too."

The entire drive to the research station, Patti chattered

about the evening she'd spent with Jarrett and how he'd apologized for Serena's actions. She wasn't the least bit curious about the false fire alarm or the plants in Kate's basement or what had kept her out until almost midnight. And as glad as Kate was about not having to field any questions, the lack of them made her strangely uneasy.

Her mind veered to what Crump had said about the mafia giving Gilmore trouble. She'd immediately thought of Patti's mom's connections and had planned to talk to Tom about them after they left the B and B. But with everything else there'd been to look into, she'd totally forgotten.

Was it a coincidence? Or did the mafia somehow tie in to all of this too?

She should have told Tom that Patti's father had died soon after he posted his questions about amendoso to that forum. Patti wouldn't like what he'd probably do about it, but at least she could reveal the existence of Patti's plant without raising any suspicion of the others.

Kate twisted her suddenly slick palms around the steering wheel. She'd tell him the next time she saw him.

Instead of parking in the back lot where she normally would, Kate pulled up to the front door so Patti could use the wheelchair ramp and avoid the need to navigate the stairs on her crutches.

Marjorie, the receptionist, flagged Kate the instant she stepped into the foyer. "This woman called first thing wanting to ask you about a plant in her horse pasture she's worried might be toxic."

"Why me?"

"Probably because you're the only researcher whose name she knows." Marjorie made a sour face. "Thanks to Harold."

*Right. This morning's article.*

Marjorie bustled around from behind her glass partition and prodded a tall, mousy-haired woman in dusty jeans and a plaid shirt toward Kate. "I told her to bring it in."

The woman's dark brown eyes lifted to Kate's. "I'm worried for my horses and hoping you can identify," the woman said with an accent Kate couldn't place.

"I'll do my best." Kate glanced from the woman's empty hands to the reception area. "Where's the sample?"

"Oh, I not want to risk touching."

A smart enough precaution, but it would've been faster to use a pair of old gloves than drive all the way here empty-handed. "Did you bring a photo?"

The woman's gaze dropped to her scuffed work boots. "Sorry, no. Its leaves shaped like dandelion's, but how you say? Spongy."

"Succulent."

"Yes, and has white-petal flowers."

Patti hobbled up to them, her eyes widening at the description that sounded exactly like amendoso. *But out in a horse pasture?*

"If you have spare minutes, I could bring you there. It's not far."

Kate glanced at her watch.

"You should go," Patti urged, no doubt eager to learn if this woman had discovered another source of amendoso. "We don't have any meetings scheduled today."

Of course, Kate had yet to tell Patti that any plants growing here weren't likely to exhibit the healing properties she wanted to research, unless they could figure out which parasite was responsible for their speckled leaves.

234

"Okay," Kate said to the woman. "I'll follow you in my car. What's the address?"

"No address. Rented field. I'll lead the way."

Kate followed her out, and after seven minutes of following the woman's beater of a farm truck, with no sign of slowing, she realized farmers had a different perception of what "not far" meant. Kate flashed her hazards, hoping to catch the woman's attention.

The truck slowed, but instead of pulling to a stop on the shoulder, it took the next right and picked up speed again. Kate didn't recognize the area at all. There was nothing but a mix of farmland—neglected fields, by the looks of them—and woodland as far as the eye could see. No houses, no animals, nothing resembling a pasture suitable for horses.

Instinctively, she lifted her foot from the gas, trepidation rippling through her. How could she not have clued in to how conveniently coincidental this woman's sudden discovery of a plant that supposedly resembled amendoso was?

Pulling to a stop on the shoulder, Kate flipped on her hazards and fished through her purse for her cell phone to call Tom.

No signal. *Figures.* She touched the gas, keeping her gaze on the cell phone signal until it flickered into range. The gap between her car and the farm truck lengthened, as she pulled to a stop once more. She was tempted to turn around and head back, except that they'd made so many turns, she'd lost track of which way back was.

A black SUV with darkly tinted windows veered around the corner. Deciding it didn't look like the kind of vehicle whose driver she wanted to stop and offer assistance, Kate clicked off her hazards and pressed her foot to the gas.

But nothing happened.

Behind her the SUV slowed, and she hurriedly jimmied the shifter, thinking she might've accidentally knocked it into neutral.

Up ahead, far ahead, the truck's brake lights finally lit.

Kate shifted the car's shifter all the way into Park and back to Drive and tried the gas again. Nothing.

The door locks popped open.

*What's going on?*

Movement in the side-view mirror snagged her attention. Her heart slammed into her throat at the sight of three men in dark shades and ball caps, pulled low, piling out of the SUV. Kate slammed down the automatic door lock. Twisted the key in the ignition. Pumped the gas. Clicked every button on the car's console.

Nothing happened.

*No! No! No!*

Ahead of her the truck's brake lights seemed to get closer. The woman was reversing toward her. Kate laid on the horn, not wanting her to drive into an ambush too.

One of the men grabbed Kate's door handle at the same time the locks magically popped back open.

Screaming, she ripped the keys from the ignition and speared them between her fingers.

The man yanked open the door, piercing her with icy blue eyes, and cuffed her hand off the horn.

Kate jerked back her other hand and drove the fisted keys into his face.

Howling, he stumbled backward, blood seeping between his fingers, but before she had a chance to do anything more, a second guy lunged through the passenger door and clamped an iron fist around her wrist.

She twisted and turned, fighting to release the seatbelt that had her pinned behind the wheel.

The buzz-cut guy immobilizing her arm whipped out a jackknife. "We have your father, and if you want to see him again, you'll come without a fight."

Her heart jerked, and for a split second, she stilled. But the steel blade slicing through her seatbelt kicked her common sense back into action. She rammed her elbow into Buzz-cut's nose and then swung toward the door to slam a well-aimed kick at the other creep.

The kick never landed.

# 15

"What do you mean Kate's not back yet? Where'd she go?" Tom hauled down his voice. The last thing he needed was the research station's talkative receptionist speculating about his concern over Kate's whereabouts, especially given the ridiculous aspersions he'd heard flying around A Cup or Two this morning, thanks to Harold's news article.

"A horsewoman needed her to identify a plant she was afraid might hurt her horses."

"A woman?" *So not Smith.* Tom sucked in a full breath. "Did you get the woman's name and address?"

"No. She said the plant was in rented pastureland anyway."

"Did Kate know the woman?"

"I don't think so."

Tom's pulse ratcheted up. "But the woman asked for Kate by name?"

"Yes, I figured she'd seen Kate's name in this morning's paper." Marjorie ducked her head. "You know what I mean. The article did say she worked here."

Yeah, he hoped that was the only reason the woman had asked for Kate. Turning away from the reception window, he whipped out his phone and dialed Kate's new cell number.

She didn't answer.

He tapped his fingers on his thigh, waiting for the beep. He should've picked her up this morning, like they'd planned, and brought her to work himself. Then she wouldn't be out who knows where, with who knows who.

*Beep.*

"Kate, this is Tom. Call me as soon as you get this message. It's important."

He and his dad had dug deeper into the fatalities at the mines and discovered that the mine targeted twenty years ago had been controlled by the mafia—Gilmore's most-hated rival. And Tom wasn't ready to dismiss the possibility of a connection to Gilmore. Not with his former partner dead, thanks to his curiosity about what caused the more recent fatalities.

Tom pulled up the tracking app he'd installed on the phone he'd given Kate for exactly this kind of scenario. The GPS locator zeroed in on a back road about fifteen miles away—surrounded by farmland.

He blew out a breath. Okay, she'd probably left her phone in the car while traipsing into the field to look at the plant. He'd give her a few minutes. He turned back to the receptionist. "May I speak with Patti Goodman?"

Marjorie buzzed the lab and asked Patti if that was okay. At Patti's yes, a security guard escorted Tom past the locked entrance beyond the reception area and delivered him to the lab door.

Patti sat on a stool at the counter in the large-windowed lab looking at something through a microscope. "What brings you here?"

"I wanted to talk to Kate. What can you tell me about this plant she went to see?"

Patti's hand jerked, knocking off the microscope's slide clip. "Uh, nothing really. The woman was afraid to pick it. It didn't sound like anything native. But she said the pasture wasn't far away. She shouldn't be long."

Patti talked rapidly, even for her. Nerves? Or being herself? One thing was for sure, he wouldn't call fifteen miles "not far away."

"I know about your family's connection to organized crime. If you know something, now is the time to speak up."

Her face paled. "Know something about what?"

He glanced at his phone screen. Kate's phone hadn't moved. He didn't like it. He pulled out his car keys.

Patti glanced at his phone's screen. "What are you doing? Tracking a suspect?"

"No, keeping tabs on Kate."

"You can see where she is?" Patti's face blanched even whiter, and she suddenly swayed.

"Easy." Tom caught her arm and steadied her. "Are you okay?"

She hunched over the counter and clasped her head between her hands. "I feel dizzy again. Really dizzy."

"Just since coming to work?"

"Yes." She buried her head in her arms. "I need to lie down. Could you drive me home?"

He dialed dispatch. "You need to go to the hospital. You might have been exposed to more toxin." Tom glanced at the items on her workbench. "What have you touched since coming into work?"

"Please, I just need to lie down."

He requested the ambulance, then clicked off and glanced again at Kate's location pictured on the screen, still unmoved. He gripped Patti's arms and peered into her eyes. "Are you being straight with me?" Her timing had been uncomfortably convenient if her goal was to delay him getting to Kate.

Patti's eyes widened and she looked utterly stupefied.

Staring at her, Tom fought the urgency in his gut. The voice that said the sudden episode was too convenient. Because as much as he wanted—no, needed—to start searching for Kate, this whole chain of events seemed to have started with Patti's dizziness. Or had she feigned it at Kate's house too, to cover her going downstairs to spy?

No, the doctor said it was due to a toxin.

*What am I doing?* Tom dropped his hold on her. "I'm sorry. I'm worried about Kate." Everything in him wanted to race to his car that second, but he couldn't walk out on Patti in this condition. She couldn't have faked that pallor.

Within minutes the paramedics arrived, escorted by a security guard.

Tom squeezed Patti's arm before heading for the door. "I'll check in on you later." He glanced at his cell phone screen for Kate's latest position and choked at the offline notice—LOCATION UNKNOWN.

An emergency call blasted from the paramedics' portable radio. "Car ablaze, unknown number of casualties."

Dispatch detailed the car's location. Heart thundering, Tom stopped in his tracks, his gaze colliding with Patti's. "That's where Kate was."

Tom swerved to a stop at the roadblock. Black smoke billowed in the air, and the toxic combination of plastics, rubber, and fuel clutched his throat. The image of Ian's burning car in the shopping mall's parking lot blazed through his mind. Fire trucks and patrol cars lined the shoulders of the secluded road, the surreal swirls of red and blue emergency lights a terrifying beacon in the smoke layering the air. Hundreds of yards beyond them, a medevac helicopter set down, its blades whirling.

That meant it was bad. *Really bad.*

Tom jumped out of his car and raced toward the scene. Two officers grabbed him.

"Is Kate in there? She was driving that car."

"You need to calm down."

"Don't tell me to calm down!" They wouldn't have called in an airlift unless they'd seen someone inside. He scanned the fields. Not a horse in sight. *Or Kate!* "Let me go!" He shoved the officers aside and ran to the firefighters spraying the burning vehicle with the full reach of their water. "Is she in there?"

Someone's arm locked across his chest and hauled him back from the heat and smoke. "Let 'em do their job."

"She's in there, isn't she? They have to get her out!" He fought against the guy's hold, his blood curdling at the hiss of the water vaporizing the instant it touched the flames. He fixed his gaze on the driver's window, praying for a glimpse of life. But as the water knocked down the flames and the haze of smoke thinned, his heart withered at the sight of the blackened remains. "Oh, God, not again." He dropped to his knees, squeezed his eyes shut, sorrow strangling him. "Please, don't let this happen, God. Not again. *Not again.*"

"C'mon, you need to step back. Let the firefighters do their job." The officer still clutching his shoulders urged him onto his feet.

Tom blinked, waited for the man's face to swim into focus. "Hutchinson?"

"I'm sorry, man. No one could've survived that."

Tom tried to swallow, but tears clogged his throat. "I loved her."

"I know you did." Hutchinson escorted Tom back to his car.

His legs were rubber. His mind a muddled mess. He closed his eyes, straining to block out the screams he'd never heard. He never should've suggested she drive Patti's car. He should've picked her up like he'd said he would. He clutched Hutchinson's arm. "Kate was following a woman. You need to call the research station, get a description of her and her vehicle, put out a BOLO. She may have seen what happened."

Or been party to it.

"What's he doing here?" Hank Brewster's voice bellowed from behind him.

Tom pivoted on his heel, launched himself at Hank, grabbed him by the collar, and rammed his back against a patrol car. "What are *you* doing here? Checking up on GPC's work?"

"What?"

Tom flung off Hutchinson's attempts to rein him in and shook Hank like the pathetic puppet he was. "You heard me! The mayor doesn't care who gets hurt as long as he gets GPC's tax dollars and re-election. You're nothing but his lackey."

Hank shoved him away. "You don't know what you're talking about."

Tom pounced again, grabbing fistfuls of shirt, as a fire-storm exploded in his chest.

Hutchinson's hand fell heavy on his shoulder. "Tom, this won't bring her back."

Tom scrunched a disgusted scowl at Hank and, unclench-ing his fists, shoved him away.

He stalked toward his car, Hutchinson on his tail. "Leave me alone. I want to be alone." He slumped behind the wheel of his car, his gaze fixed on the swirling helicopter blades, his mind blank, except for a kernel of hope that as long as those blades kept beating, the firefighters thought they might recover a living person.

He wasn't sure how long he stared at those blades thrash-ing the air, but suddenly the bird lifted, without the paramed-ics ever leaving the cockpit.

His eyes blurred, he pushed open his car door and walked woodenly toward the gutted car, even though he couldn't bear the thought of Kate's torched corpse being his last image of her. His partner's had already haunted his dreams for too many months.

Hutchinson blocked his path. "There's nothing to see. The heat was too intense. Forensics will need to—" He shook his head. "We'll find who did this. Officers are already canvassing the area. A tip line will be set up. Let me drive you home."

"No. Thanks." Tom stumbled back to his car in a daze, knowing he should be out there too, searching for leads, but . . .

He needed to be near her. He fired up his engine and drove to her house. The darkened windows didn't seem right. In the months he'd known her, even in her deepest grief, a light had shone from within her. A ray of hope that made him believe anything was possible.

He wanted to go inside, and remembering she'd had the lock changed, he drove downtown and parked in front of the hardware store. He glanced in the rearview mirror, scrubbed the dirt streaks from his face, then went in. Ryan waved to him from behind the counter. Clearly he hadn't heard the news. Tom didn't feel like telling him. "I came to pick up Kate's new key for her."

"Oh, sure." Ryan pulled an envelope with Kate's name on it from the cash drawer and handed it over without question. And why would he question? Everyone but Kate seemed to know how much he'd loved her.

"Thanks," he mumbled and hurried back out before Ryan could ask any questions. He drove straight to Kate's house and wavered only a moment before letting himself in. The security alarm was off. Ryan must've forgotten to arm it after changing the lock.

Tom walked from room to room, flipping on every light switch, turning on every lamp, until light chased the shadows from every corner. He paused at her desk and lifted her sweater from the back of her chair. Pressing its softness to his cheek, he inhaled the delicate lavender scent that was uniquely hers. *Kate, what am I going to do without you?*

His legs crumpled and he slid to the floor, his face buried in her sweater. After a long while, he forced himself to return the sweater to the chair and wandered to the kitchen. Her answering machine sat on the counter. He pressed the button that would play her outgoing message, and her sweet voice filled the room.

Tom curled his fingers around the cell phone on his hip,

overwhelmed by the crazy urge to call and leave a message so she'd call him back. The sound of the beep knocked him to his senses. He released his phone and turned off her machine.

His gaze fell to a leaf on the floor. Then a dirt smear. A trail of dirt and plant bits from the top of the basement stairs to the front door. The firefighters must've tracked it in yesterday morning. Except . . .

Tom cocked his head. Something didn't make sense, but his fuzzy brain struggled to pinpoint what. His gaze snapped to the new lock on the back door. *The firefighters used the back door, not the front.*

Tom flipped on the basement lights and raced downstairs. The fire chief had said that Kate's alarm tripped due to humidity from the plants she was growing. Tom tore around the bottom of the stairs toward the fruit cellar. The door stood open. He flipped on the light inside. The room was empty, except for a rickety table covered in a dusting of potting soil.

His heart plummeted at the thought that streaked through his mind. At the memory of how agitated Kate had been yesterday when he arrived. How hurried she'd been to see him leave . . . *She'd been growing amendoso plants.*

*Behind his back.*

He shoved the table against the cement-block wall. How could she? She knew how worried he was for her safety. Never mind adding this to the equation.

He crossed his arms over the throb in his chest and buried his fists under his armpits. He didn't want to believe she'd lied to him. But there were plants here yesterday morning! The fire chief had said as much. And whoever secreted them away had probably killed Kate too.

Tom slapped off the light and bounded up the stairs. He

made short work of turning off all the lights and headed for the door. He caught himself before touching the alarm pad. Whoever stole the plants might've left prints. He glanced at the front door, thought of the door handle on the fruit cellar door, and texted Hutchinson, telling him to send over someone to dust them all for prints. He needed to talk to the fire chief.

A couple of firefighters were hosing down their truck as Tom pulled up to the station. With any luck they hadn't heard whose car had burned outside their district, let alone know his connection to her. He needed answers, not pity. Tom jumped out of his car and flagged down the chief. "Can I talk to you for a minute?"

The chief pulled off his helmet and swiped a handkerchief across his face. "What's up?"

"The false alarm at Kate Adams' place yesterday. Can you describe the plants you saw?"

"Better than that." The chief reached into his truck and pulled out his cell phone. He tapped the screen a few times and then turned it toward Tom. "Since I'd never seen anything like them, I wanted to look them up."

The image of amendoso plants glaring back at Tom crushed the air from his lungs. He wasn't sure what hurt more, the fact that she'd kept the secret from him or the realization that she hadn't felt she could trust him with it. He'd failed Kate worse than he'd ever imagined.

# 16

Tom clutched the steering wheel, welcoming the feel of his fingernails cutting into his palms, the only part of him that hadn't gone completely numb.

"Kate, I'm sorry. So sorry. I promise you, I will find who did this. Somehow." After this morning's newspaper article hit the stands, someone must've put two and two together and figured out exactly what Kate was growing in her basement.

*Patti.*

Tom floored the gas pedal and roared out of the fire station's parking lot. He knew she'd been trying to stall him from going after Kate. He sped toward the hospital.

Twenty minutes later, a nurse escorted Tom to Patti's bed in the ER.

The doctor examining her turned. "Ah, Detective Parker, good call sending Patti to us. There was an acute increase in the toxin levels in her blood."

Tom looked at Patti, stunned. She hadn't been faking?

Her eyes were red and swollen as if she'd been crying. "Is it true?"

Tom stared at her, his mind scrambling to make sense of the question. "Is what true?"

"Kate." Her voice cracked. "Was she—?"

Tom gripped the bed rail. For a moment, it was all he could do to hang on, feeling as if the ground had washed out from under him and he might never stop falling. He swallowed hard, finding his voice. "Yes."

Patti burst into heartrending sobs. As the nurse tried to comfort her, the doctor ushered Tom into the hall.

"I'm sorry about your friend."

Tom nodded, unable to get another word past the boulder in his throat.

"Given Patti's fragile emotional state, I think we should keep her under observation for a few more hours. In the meantime, you will probably want to have her hand lotion brought in for testing."

Tom braced a palm on the door frame, his legs feeling as if they might buckle. "You think it's the source of the poison?" This could be the lead he needed to track down Kate's killer.

"She said she'd used it without thinking this morning. Apparently she'd been avoiding using it while her friend was staying with her, because of her friend's sensitivity to the fragrance, which would correspond with her interim decline in symptoms."

"Okay, yes, I'll do that." Tom returned to the room and was relieved to see that Patti had pulled herself together. "What can you tell me about the hand lotion you mentioned to the doctor?"

"What does it matter now?" Patti dabbed at her eyes, her hands trembling.

Tom scrutinized her, uncertain how much to read into her peculiar response. "Patti, someone is poisoning you. He needs to be stopped."

She turned her tear-splotched face up to him and searched his eyes. "She's gone. I know how much you loved her. How can you care about anything else?"

He fisted his hands and dug his teeth into his trembling lip. "Kate's death wasn't an accident."

Patti's mouth gaped. She splayed her hand over her throat. "You think? Oh." Her gaze bounced around the room like a frightened mouse. "The lotion was from our lab. All the labs were given a bottle, but Kate couldn't tolerate the fragrance so she told me to take it home."

"Who supplied the bottles?"

"Central supplies, I guess. No, wait. They were compliments of GPC. That's right. They had a meet-and-greet event to introduce themselves, share their vision for their partnership with the research station, that sort of thing. That's when they handed out the bottles."

"Were they labeled to go to specific people or labs?"

Patti's forehead scrunched, as if she was trying to remember. "No, I don't think so."

Didn't matter. They could have slipped the toxin into the bottle once the women returned to the lab with it. He'd had a bad feeling the poisoning tied in to GPC's interest in the plant. But their people obviously hadn't done their homework, or they would've known Kate wouldn't touch the stuff. It explained why they'd been lying low, waiting until the poison had taken care of her for them.

Proving the theory was another matter.

"How long was the bottle in your lab before you took it home?"

"A week or two maybe."

"Who else had access to your lab during that time?"

She blew out a breath. "Maintenance, cleaning staff, our supervisor. Lots of people tour through too."

"Okay, what about at your house? Who's been there since you brought the bottle home?"

"You and Kate and Jarrett."

"That's it?"

"Well . . . and my housekeeper and gardener."

*The housekeeper and gardener who'd taken an early, extended trip south.* Tom grimaced. "Can I borrow your house key and security gate remote? I need to get that lotion to the lab. And I'll want the names of your employees and a number where they can be reached." But first, he needed to find Jarrett.

Patti swung her legs off the bed and reached for her crutches. "I'll go with you."

"The doctor's not ready to release you yet."

The Lone Ranger's theme song—reserved for the police chief—blasted from Tom's phone. After the accusations Tom had flung at him a few hours ago, Hank would only call if he had new information on the attack. Tom hoped. He snatched up the phone. "Yeah?"

"Did you see Kate today?"

Tom's heart clenched at the sound of her name. He closed his eyes against the pain.

"We need to know what she was wearing."

Tom tried in vain to swallow the bile rising to his throat.

After the inferno that had engulfed the car, would there be any clothes left to identify? He turned to Patti. "What was Kate wearing?"

"Black pants and a purple blouse, flat brown leather sandals," she answered automatically, but a spark of hope lit her eyes.

Tom blinked back a sting of tears and repeated the description to the chief, adding, "A gold watch. No, that got drowned by the ditch water. A fine gold necklace with a cross pendant." She almost always wore the necklace, and of anything, it would have withstood the heat of the flames the longest.

"A purple shirt? You're sure?"

"Yes." He sank to a chair and cupped a hand over his eyes. "You actually recovered scraps of clothing from the fire?"

"No, Tom, we didn't recover a body."

Tom groaned. There hadn't been much left of Ian after the bomb blast either. Zoe had seen to that.

"Do you have any information that might help us?"

Tom's mind flashed to the plants, the secret she'd died protecting. "What do you mean?"

"I mean," Hank said impatiently, "are you aware of any reason why someone might want to make it look like she's dead?"

*Look* like she's dead? Tom's heart did a thundering roll through his chest. "She's not dead?"

"All we know is that she wasn't in the car."

Tom blinked. *She wasn't in the car. She wasn't in the car!* "You're sure?"

"Tom, focus."

He reined in his soaring heart. Okay, yes, he still needed

to find her. Molly Gilmore probably wanted her dead. GPC too. But to just make it *look* like she was? "What are you thinking?"

"Someone went to a lot of trouble to make sure we couldn't discern who, if anybody, burned in that crash. If it hadn't been for the quick emergency response, she would've succeeded."

*She?* Tom's grip tightened on the phone. "She? As in Kate?" His voice pitched higher. "Kate did not stage her own death!"

"Okay, calm down."

Hank's patronizing order set Tom's teeth on edge. "What about the woman she'd been following? Any luck locating her?"

"No, but we found an unregistered black pickup abandoned two miles from the site of the fire."

That news caught Tom by the throat. What was he supposed to look for now?

Kate rolled over in bed and pain exploded in her shoulder. She jolted awake, only she couldn't seem to open her eyes. She rocked onto her back, straining to pry them open, straining to remember what she'd done to her shoulder. She was so tired. Her mind drifted and sleep tugged her under once again.

The next time Kate woke, she heard a female voice. It was too quiet to make out what the woman was saying. Had she imagined it?

Her mind was so fuzzy. Her throat felt as if she'd swallowed a wad of bubble gum that was still sticking her molars together. She licked her lips. "Thirsty," she rasped.

A drinking straw slipped between her lips. "Sip. It's water."

Kate didn't recognize the female voice, but desperate for something to drink, she obeyed, savoring the feel of the cool liquid trickling down her throat. She blinked open her eyes, and the woman's face swam into view. "Where?" Kate wanted to ask more but had too much difficulty making her voice cooperate. The room was small and poorly lit and smelled faintly musty.

"Safe," the woman said. "Rest now. We'll talk later."

Kate squinted at the peeling wallpaper and tried to make sense of the woman's words. "Safe from what?" It was no use. She was too tired to think. She closed her eyes and rolled onto her side but immediately sprang back, crying out in pain. "My shoulder?"

The woman reached over her and adjusted a bandage. "You have a burn."

Kate nodded as if somewhere deep in her mind that made perfect sense, but she couldn't remember why. Her eyes drifted closed again and her mind slipped back to her childhood—the day she'd visited her dad in his lab. She'd been so excited that she'd accidentally knocked over a flask and got a chemical burn on her arm. Dad had rushed her to the sink and stuck her arm under the tap, sprayed water on it forever.

*We have your father.*

Kate jolted at the harsh voice that intruded on the memory. Her eyes flew open, her gaze skittering around the room as memories of the ambush flooded her mind. Where were the men who said they had her father?

The woman who'd given her the water hurried to her side. "Are you in pain?"

254

"Who are you?" She seemed vaguely familiar, but Kate couldn't remember where she'd seen her before.

"A friend."

Kate blinked a few times and squinted at the woman's mousy brown hair that somehow didn't seem to suit her dark complexion and coffee-colored eyes. "You're the woman from the research station. In the truck." She pictured the pickup speeding backward toward her car. "You came back to help me."

The woman perched on the edge of the bed and patted Kate's hand. "You're remembering? That's good."

Kate recoiled from her touch. "Who are you? You're not a friend. I don't know you."

"It's okay. You can trust me. I want to help you."

Kate strained to remember what happened after the woman came back. A man yanked her out of . . . an explosion. The car exploded. Kate retreated closer to the headboard, pulling the sheets to her chin as if they could shield her. "Who are you? What happened to the men?" She didn't dare ask about her father. She had no idea if this woman had saved her from the men or was working with them.

"It's okay. You're safe here."

"Who are you?" Kate repeated, hating the terror rising in her voice.

The woman plunged her fingers into her hair and pulled it from her head—a wig. She unclipped the pin that secured her real hair, and with a shake of her head, raven-black locks tumbled over her shoulders. "I'm Zoe Cortez."

Tom stared at the charred remains of Patti's car sitting in the police garage. *Kate wasn't in the car*, he reminded himself, but the reassurance didn't stop the smell of smoke from coiling down his throat and turning to acid in his stomach.

Then where was she?

Half a dozen officers were combing for clues in the area where the car had been abandoned, but once the medical officer confirmed no one had died in the car, the accident reconstruction team had made quick work of their onsite analysis and towed the car here for more extensive forensic investigation.

The cavernous garage felt like a tomb despite the bright fluorescent lights and the country music station playing in the background. A pair of legs stuck out from beneath the jacked car. A second investigator, an older guy named Tate that Tom recognized from years ago when he used to visit his dad at the station, pulled something from beneath the dash. He acknowledged Tom with a nod as he carried the blackened cigarette-box-sized object to a shiny steel table set up behind the car.

Tom peered over his shoulder. "What did you find?" Remnants of melted wires and unidentifiable objects filled half the table.

"A tracking device."

"You mean like those systems that allow you to locate your car if it's stolen?"

"Yes. It comes standard in a number of cars these days, but not this one."

Tom pulled out his cell phone and clicked Patti's name in his contacts. "The owner's father was security obsessed.

256

I wouldn't be surprised to learn he'd had it installed when she bought the car."

Tate shrugged. "Doesn't mean someone didn't use it for his own purposes."

"What do you mean?"

Tate's bushy mustache seesawed as he scrutinized the surface of the box. "These devices can also disable part of the electrical system. Might explain why she stopped in the middle of nowhere."

"Hello," Patti said on the other end of the phone.

Replaying Tate's words in his head, Tom hesitated. Patti had done a convincing job at the hospital of seeming bereft over news of Kate's apparent death, but he couldn't shake the feeling that she'd been trying to delay him from going after Kate this morning. Maybe delay him long enough to remotely stop her car and give her cohorts time to kidnap Kate?

"Hello? Tom, is that you?"

"Yes." Tom's fingers tightened around the phone as he debated whether it was wise to show his hand. If he were speaking to her face, he could at least read her body language as she answered his questions.

"What's going on? Have they found Kate?"

"Not yet." His gaze strayed to the blackened car, his insides roiling at the thought of how terrified she must be. "How do you activate your car's tracking system?"

Two full seconds passed before Patti responded. "What tracking system?"

"The one installed in your car." *You expect me to believe you didn't know?* "It's not standard issue. You would have had to buy it as an extra. Perhaps your dad did?"

"No-o-o." She sounded stumped. "I bought the car after my parents died."

Tate motioned Tom's attention to a computer screen showing a projection of the object under the stereoscope.

"Hold on a second, Patti." Tom looked at the image and, holding his hand over his phone, whispered, "What am I looking at?"

"The device's circuit board." Tate tapped the tip of his pencil on some faint printing in the bottom corner of the image. "This part was manufactured two months ago."

Tom uncovered the phone. "Patti, when did you buy the car?"

"Eight months ago."

"When's the last time you had it"—recalling Jarrett's "spontaneous" decision last Sunday afternoon to take the car to his mechanic buddy, Tom stuttered—"serviced."

"Jarrett just picked it up from his friend's garage last night. Are you—?" Her voice quavered. "Are you saying his friend put a tracking device in my car?"

"Possibly. Do you know what garage Jarrett took the car to?"

"No."

"Do you know where Jarrett is now?"

"No, I—" Her voice edged higher. "I've been trying to call him ever since I got to the hospital. He's not answering my messages."

"Okay, take it easy. If you hear from him, find out where he is and let me know. But don't ask about the tracking device, understand?"

The audible gulp that sounded over the line suggested she understood all too well. "You think Jarrett—?" Her question broke off in a sob.

"I don't know what to think."

"The toxin," she blubbered. "He's in the house all the time. He could have put it in the lotion."

"Do you honestly believe that?"

"I don't know. Who else could it be?"

Yeah, but whose payroll was Jarrett on? "You should be safe there. Keep your call button close at hand, and I'll alert hospital security. If Jarrett shows up, it's important that you don't give away your suspicions. Understand?"

"Yes."

Tom's neck muscles spasmed at the thought that she could be playing him again. "I've got to go. I'll be in touch." Stretching the pinch out of his neck, he disconnected and immediately called the hospital. And prayed that calling Patti hadn't been a mistake.

Next he called dispatch. "This is Detective Parker. I need a BOLO on a black Cadillac Coupe, license plate KING 2."

The female dispatcher gasped. "Jarrett King?"

"Yes." Tom should've known the vanity plate number would be recognized as the mayor's son's. "Notify me as soon as he's spotted." He palmed his keys, needing to get on the road looking himself.

Tate pried open a small, round metal piece of the device with tweezers. "Interesting."

"What?"

"Someone was not only tracking the car. He was listening in."

Tom groaned. This had GPC written all over it. Only they were interested in what a pair of researchers might discuss on their way to and from work when they thought no one could hear them.

"Nasty!" An excited cry came from beneath the car. A man in greasy coveralls rolled into view. "A trigger mechanism." He handed a soot-blackened object up to Tate.

Tate set it on the table and brushed at the soot with a fine paintbrush. "I figured it was a bomb."

Tom's legs buckled. Bracing his hands on the table, he locked his knees, reminded himself again that unlike Ian, Kate hadn't been in the car.

"Whoever installed the tracking system and listening device," Tate went on, "likely expected the explosion to destroy the evidence."

Staring at the trigger mechanism, Tom clawed through the emotions clouding his thinking. It didn't add up. The use of a bomb meant the perpetrator had to have counted on Kate taking Patti's car. But why would he? Up until Tom called the house this morning, she'd intended to drive her own car. Which raised the question: Who was the real target? Kate? Or Patti?

Or had the whole thing been a decoy to hide Kate's kidnapping?

Jarrett and Patti and whoever they might have told were the only ones who knew Kate would be driving Patti's car this morning.

Tate spouted theories about who could've designed the bomb. "I'll have a better idea once I run a chemical analysis to determine what explosive material they used."

Tom didn't have time to wait for chemical analyses. He needed to find Kate before whoever took her decided she was too much of a liability alive. Tom left the investigator his business card. "Call me as soon as you know anything definitive."

Tate slipped it into his shirt pocket. "I thought Clark was heading this investigation."

"He is," Tom said, having no idea if it was true. "But I'm working a different angle. I think this is connected to another one of my cases." He jogged toward the bay door before Tate could ask any more questions. Since being sideswiped by Kate's disappearance, his missing teenager case had slipped from his mind, but the fact Kate had seen Smith—the guy in the kid's sketch—could mean Smith had decided she'd become a liability.

Tom climbed into his car, his insides racing with the need to take action. To do something to find her. Find them both.

He needed to interrogate Jarrett. Tom tried his number. The call went straight to voice mail. Now what? Hank would take his badge if Tom tried to strong-arm the cell phone company into giving him a location on Jarrett's phone. If Hank had heard about the BOLO for King, he was probably already hunting Tom down.

Tom dropped his head against the steering wheel and drew in a deep breath. There had to be another way to find Jarrett. *Yes!* Tom grabbed his cell phone and dialed Zeb's number. NSA might not have authority over Canadian cell phone companies, but if anyone could push the right buttons, Zeb could.

Zeb picked up on the first ring. "*Tom*, how are you?"

Tom's heart hitched at the odd note of sympathy in his friend's voice. He shook away the ridiculous notion that he'd heard about Kate. It was a standard greeting. Tom swallowed the automatic response he'd usually give without a second thought. The line remained silent, except for the sound of his heart pulsing in his ears, too fast and too shallow. "Kate's missing."

"Missing? Hey, I'm sorry. I know she meant a lot to you."

*Meant.* His heart crunched into his ribs. "She isn't dead!" Feeling himself being pulled under by another wave of fear, Tom clung to the only thing that would keep his head above water—anger. "You know a lot more than that."

"What?"

"You heard me. Kate had the missing plants. And now they, along with her, are *really* missing."

"I see."

"Don't '*I see*' me. I'm not an idiot. I know why you jumped at the chance to hide her father." Tom paused, waiting for a response.

None came.

"Your silence speaks volumes, old friend."

"What do you expect me to say?"

Yeah, what did he expect? Zeb worked for NSA. All information was dispensed on a need-to-know basis, and Tom didn't *need* to know. "I'm sure your friends at the CIA have been looking for those plants as feverishly as GPC. And I think I know who took them." And Kate. "I just need you to have his cell phone pinged and give me the location. You owe me that much."

"Whose phone?"

Tom read out the number.

"Hold on a minute."

Tom stared at the thunderheads piling in the sky as he waited. They couldn't compare to the ones amassing in his chest as one minute slid into two, then three.

"Okay, Tom, he's on Ridge Road, somewhere between Caramel Street and Mary."

*At Patti Goodman's place?*

"But you didn't hear that from me. And Tom, don't do anything stupid. He may not be your guy."

Tom jammed his phone into the dash mount and backed out of his parking spot. "I'm sure in the six minutes and forty-one seconds it took you to get me that address, you also figured out that the phone belongs to Jarrett King, the son of Port Aster's mayor. You remember him?" Tom needled. "The man who's been championing GPC's partnership with the research station at any cost."

"Like I said," Zeb responded coolly, "I'm sorry about your girl. But you know how these things work."

Tom thought of Zoe Cortez, his partner's murderer. How the NSA seemed to know where she was yet hadn't arrested her. "*Yeah*, I know exactly how these things work."

# 17

"I'm trying to help you." The woman, who'd perched on a chair next to Kate's bed, sounded as if she was holding on to her patience by a thread.

Kate stared at the wig, still clutched in Zoe's hand, then at the door, noting its flimsy lock. She strained to listen for any clue as to what might be beyond the door. From the coffeepot-sized watermark on the bureau top and the mirror-sized patch of faded paint on the wall above, it looked as if she was in a cheap motel room. But she couldn't hear any voices or water pipes groaning or traffic sounds. If Zoe thought she'd fall for another one of her lies, she had another think coming. She couldn't believe she'd fallen so completely for the horse-in-danger plea at the research station that she hadn't grown suspicious until they were in the middle of nowhere. Of course, all she'd been thinking was that this woman had amendoso growing in her horse pasture. What an idiot! Clearly Zoe had set her up, feeding her a line sure to make her jump. She had to be in cahoots with those goons in the SUV. "Do you work for GPC?"

"Kate, listen to me. If I was a bad guy, why would I blow up your car and then take care of you?"

*Because you want to know where the plants are.* But Kate kept the thought to herself. She wasn't admitting to anything. She fisted the sheets in her hands, summoning her courage to face whatever was on the other side of that door. "What do you want?"

"The same as you. To keep the plants out of GPC's hands."

"I don't know what you're talking about."

"You don't have to be afraid as long as we keep you out of sight. GPC will think you're dead. With any luck, it'll be days before the detectives realize there were no bodies inside the car."

Kate's breath stalled in her chest. "The police think I'm dead?" *Tom thinks I'm dead.* She sprang from the bed, reached wildly for the night table, the desktop, the bureau top. "Where's the phone? I have to call Tom. Tell him I'm safe."

Zoe didn't move from the edge of the bed, just shook her head. "I can't let you do that."

"But you said you weren't a bad guy!"

"Kate, I know this is scary for you, but I promise everything will turn out all right if you just cooperate."

Right, cooperate. Her brain might be fuzzy, but did this woman really think she hadn't clued in that she'd been drugged? Kate backed toward the door, realizing too late she had no shoes on. Didn't matter. She had to get out of here. Except she had no idea where here was.

No light seeped past the window shades, not even a street-light. So maybe this wasn't a fleabag motel like she'd first thought. No matter. She just needed to get away from Zoe and find a phone. "I already told you. I don't know anything about any plants." The doorknob dug into her back and she reached behind her, twisted the lock.

"You're a terrible liar, Kate."

"Yeah? That makes two of us." She spun on her heel, yanked open the door, and plunged straight into a wall of hardened muscle. "Let me go!"

Sausage-sized fingers clamped around her wrists and held her at arm's length, rendering her barefoot kicks useless.

"Help! Somebody help me!" She took quick inventory of her surroundings. A long hallway with at least four other numbered doors opening off it. So this was a motel. Or at least used to be. The paint was peeling and water stains marred the threadbare carpet.

Men came running. One from either end of the hall, carrying—she gulped—*guns*.

"It's okay," Sausage Fingers assured. "Everything's under control."

The man with the buzz cut nodded and slithered away. The other man met her gaze and his familiar icy-blue eyes sent a chill through her heart.

She choked down a gasp. It was the man she'd punched with her keys.

He touched the angry red stripes on his cheek and smirked. *Oh, God, who are these people? Save me, please.*

Tom sped out of town toward the Goodman estate, but as he turned onto Patti's street and spotted a motorcycle bouncing down the driveway of the old Potter place, he realized

266

that his assumption hadn't been accurate. Jarrett wasn't at Patti's. He was next door. The question was, why?

Had he stashed Kate's plants there? He couldn't have moved them on a motorcycle. But the cycle explained why the BOLO for his car had been fruitless.

Tom parked at the end of the driveway, not wanting to risk getting his car hung up in the deep ruts but knowing he wouldn't have a hope of stopping Jarrett from getting away, short of shooting him, if he decided to take off.

As Tom checked the weapon in his shoulder holster, Zeb's edict replayed in his head. *Don't do anything stupid. He may not be your guy.*

Did Zeb suspect it was a wild goose chase?

It was the only decent lead he had. Climbing out of his car, Tom spotted Crump's black pickup parked in front of the dilapidated side porch. Perfect. The two most likely pawns of GPC and Gilmore, both in one place. This was no wild goose chase.

Tom hurried the few hundred yards down the overgrown driveway, sticking close to the cover of the shrubs and long grasses along the side.

Crump stepped out of the house and Jarrett ambushed him. Grabbed Crump by the jacket and slammed his back against the wall. "Where are they?"

Crump thrust up his hands, not even trying to fight Jarrett off. "Where are who?"

"The plants you took from Kate's house."

Crouched behind a bush at the edge of the side porch, Tom froze. Jarrett didn't take the plants? Tom peered around the bush. He'd clearly intended to, and someone—maybe Crump—beat him to it.

Crump shook his head, confusion furrowing his brow. "She didn't give me any plants."

"I never said she gave them to you," Jarrett growled.

Crump shrank back against the side of the house, his hands held high. "I haven't been anywhere near her house." He motioned to his pickup. "I've been buying lumber."

Jarrett held him pinned to the wall with one hand, center chest, and pawed through Crump's jacket pockets with the other. "Then who'd you call?" He pulled out a cell phone and thumbed through the screens.

"No one." Crump's face had gone white, his gaze fixed on the phone, making Tom wonder what he was afraid Jarrett would find on it.

Jarrett shook his head at the phone and with a disgusted snort shoved it back in Crump's pocket. "Then you won't mind if I take a look around."

"Be my guest." Why wasn't Crump protesting? Did Jarrett have a gun Tom hadn't seen?

Jarrett stormed into the house, leaving Crump to stumble off the porch, quaking. Tom started out from behind the bush but immediately stepped back when Crump pulled his phone from his pocket. Curious to hear who he'd call, Tom waited as Crump punched in a number.

A second later the phone on Tom's hip vibrated. He checked the screen. *Crump?* Tom disconnected the call and stepped into view. "What's going on?"

Crump's eyes widened in panic, then his expression dissolved into relief. "Jarrett's here looking for Kate's plants. He must be working for GPC, along with his father. You know Wolfe's got the mayor wrapped around his little finger. Did Kate really have the plants GPC is after?"

"I don't know." Squaring his jaw, Tom eyed the house for a glimpse of where Jarrett was at. It'd be less risky to wait outside and get the jump on him as he came out, but as the seconds ticked by, Tom worried he'd slip out another way. He padded through the kitchen and scanned what had once been the living room but now looked like a workshop, outfitted with sawhorses, a drill, pry bars, a hammer, buckets of nails, even a table saw. Crump obviously took the owner up on her okay to start work right away.

Jarrett appeared at the top of the stairs.

Tom stepped into view, his weapon in hand. "Keep your hands where I can see them and come down slowly."

Jarrett complied. "Crump gave me permission to come in here. I'm not trespassing."

It took every ounce of self-control not to grab a two-by-four off the pile on the floor and pummel the man until he told him everything. Tom waited in silence until Jarrett stepped off the last stair. "On the ground, face down."

"What?"

"You heard me."

"You're making a mistake," Jarrett said, but he did what he was told.

Tom holstered his gun, then yanked Jarrett's arms behind his back and snapped on a pair of cuffs. He hauled him to his feet and shoved him down to sit on a stair. "Where's Kate?"

"At work."

Tom grabbed him by the collar and pressed the back of his head against the stairs, letting his fist weigh heavy on his throat. "You do not want to play games with me."

"Okay," he gasped, and Tom eased off on his throat. "I

admit I went looking for Kate's plants. But I don't know where she is. I swear."

"Who took her?"

"I don't know."

Tom leaned his weight into him again. "Try again. You had a tracking system installed in her car, planned the whole thing."

"Planned what whole thing?" he choked out.

"What are you doing?" Patti screamed. She clomped her way across the room like a crazed woman and swung a dirt-caked crutch at Tom. "You're going to kill him."

Tom released Jarrett and grabbed Patti by the arms. "How did you get here?"

Crump stepped into the room with Patti's supervisor, Darryl, a linebacker-sized man Tom didn't want to mess with. "I drove her. She needed a lift home from the hospital." Darryl's gaze flicked from Jarrett sitting on the stair, clearing his throat, to Tom's hands circling Patti's arms. "What's going on?"

"A police matter. If you were taking her home, why bring her here?"

She tugged free of Tom's hold. "I saw your car at the end of the driveway and asked him to stop." Her knuckles on her crutch handles whitened. "Since that runaway had been hiding here, I thought maybe Kate was too."

Tom scrutinized her, his suspicions returning that she was in on the kidnapping.

"Yeah, we're all worried about her," Darryl said. "What are the police doing to find her? She could have wandered away from the accident in a daze. Have you checked other hospitals? Maybe someone picked her up and took her to another hospital."

270

Tom wished it were that simple. "Trust me"—his gravelly voice betrayed his personal interest in the case—"we are exploring every possibility."

Darryl grimaced in Jarrett's direction, clearly wondering why Tom was wasting his time here.

Tom turned back to Patti. "You came here thinking I'd found Kate and seeing me interrogating the man you'd accused of poisoning you less than two hours ago, and you didn't think twice about defending him?"

Her face blanched and so did Jarrett's.

"You can't believe that," Jarrett pleaded. "I'd never do anything to hurt you. I love you."

Her eyes shone. "You do?"

"I do," Jarrett said, although he sounded pained to admit it.

Patti's crutches clattered to the floor as she tumbled into his lap in an exuberant hug.

Tom pried her arms from around his suspect. "Then who tampered with her hand lotion? Besides Kate, you're the only one who's been in the house."

Jarrett's gaze shifted to the door. "Crump was there."

"What?" Panic flashed over Crump's face. "She was already dizzy when I walked in the house!"

"Stop it," Patti blurted. "I already told you, it could've been tampered with at the research station before I brought it home. People are always touring the labs. Tell him, Darryl."

Tom's attention jerked back to Darryl—who himself had access to the lab. And who a few months ago moonlighted with GPC doing mushroom research. Interesting that he should volunteer to drive Patti home from the hospital today.

The man shrugged. "Sure. We get student groups taking

tours. Have had a few GPC reps through in the past four or five months. One day I even caught one of the researchers giving his girlfriend the grand tour."

"What was her name?" Jarrett demanded at the same time as Tom.

"I don't remember names. She's that hairdresser from downtown. You know, the one who wears her hair all poufy and layers on the makeup."

"Serena?" Tom asked.

Darryl nodded. "Yeah, that's it."

Patti gasped.

Jarrett shook his head. "She must've flirted with some guy to gain access to the lab." His gaze reached out to Patti. "I'm so sorry. I—"

"I knew it couldn't be you!" She tugged on Tom's arm. "You can uncuff him now."

"That's *not* why he's in handcuffs." And just because he may not have poisoned Patti didn't mean he hadn't been party to Kate's kidnapping. He'd been searching for her plants! "You need to go home," Tom ordered, suspicious that she'd been deliberately wasting his time.

"What about Serena?" Patti rooted herself next to Jarrett. "Aren't you going to question her?"

"Interrogating Serena is not my priority," he said between gritted teeth, straining to keep his anger in check. "Finding Kate is."

Patti ducked her head. "Of course, I'm sorry. I—" She glanced sheepishly at Jarrett and back to the ground. "You're right."

Tom pulled out his phone and quickly called Hutchinson. If he could confirm that Serena was behind the poisoning and that it had nothing to do with Kate, it would at least narrow down the leads. With any luck, the sight of a uniformed officer walking into her shop would compel the woman to confess on the spot in hopes of leniency. With the wide assortment of hair product chemicals stored in her back room, he should've guessed she'd been behind the poisoning the second she confessed to slashing the tire.

Darryl edged toward the door. "I need to get back to work. Patti, did you want me to drop you at your house?"

"That's okay." Crump waved him off. "I can give her a ride when she's ready, so she doesn't have to navigate the driveway on those crutches again." He walked Darryl out.

Patti bit her bottom lip, looking far less certain of herself than she had a few minutes ago. "Do you think Jarrett knows where Kate is?" she whispered.

"Jarrett was about to tell me what—"

Jarrett's cell phone vibrated a call alert.

Tom reached for the phone, but Jarrett quickly pivoted and tried to snag it himself with his cuffed hands. Tom beat him to it.

"Are you crazy? What do you want with my phone?"

Tom swerved away and clicked connect. "Hello."

The screen said "private call." Whoever was on the other end must've recognized that his voice wasn't Jarrett's, because it immediately disconnected.

Tom's thumbs flew over the buttons. "What's your password?"

"Forget it."

*Fat chance.* Not when the number of whoever had Kate might be in Jarrett's contact list. Tom unlocked one cuff and relocked Jarrett's hands in front of him, then handed him the phone. "Input your password or I'll arrest you for obstruction of justice."

Jarrett rolled his eyes. "You need a warrant to look at someone's phone, you know." But he input a password and handed it back anyway.

Tom scrolled through the contacts list, but aside from family and Patti, it was empty. He checked call history, but there were no records of calls to or from anyone other than family and Patti, which was clearly not the case.

Only someone with something to hide had this kind of sophisticated security on his phone. He grabbed Jarrett by the collar and pinned his back to the stairs. "Where is she?"

"You're too close to this," Jarrett said calmly, not even trying to push Tom off, despite his hands now being positioned where he could. "You're not thinking straight."

Tom's fist tightened on Jarrett's collar, twisting it taut. "I think I'm finally thinking straight." He'd trusted Patti and Jarrett too easily.

"Take a step back a minute—"

"I'm not stepping back." Not from Kate. "If they want to stop me, they'll have to kill me."

# 18

Kate fought to wrestle free of Sausage Fingers's grip. He obliged by depositing her back in the motel room, then, with a flick of his head, summoned Zoe into the hall. Kate put her ear to the cracked-open door.

"He can't find them," Sausage Fingers hissed.

Kate clapped a hand over her mouth, her heart hammering. Were they talking about the plants?

"You need to find out who she's trusted with the code besides Parker," Sausage Fingers ordered.

At the sound of a hand slapping hold of the doorknob, Kate jumped back. Spying her sandals in the corner, she snatched them up and yanked them on. "What do you want from me?"

Zoe's eyes danced with mirth. "Your dad told me you'd always been a little spitfire."

Kate dug her teeth into her lip, not about to give in to this woman's scam just because she happened to guess what Dad used to call her. Since Zoe's connection to the men who claimed to have her father was no longer a secret, Kate should've guessed Zoe would try tricking her with that ploy again.

"Kate, I want to help you." Zoe let out an exasperated sigh. "But I need you to help us too. Your dad gave up everything to keep those plants out of GPC's hands. Do you really want it to be for nothing, after all these years?"

*No. Never.* Kate fisted her hands. This woman knew how to push all her buttons. But she wasn't falling for it. Zoe probably worked for GPC, playing the same kind of angle on her that Jim figured Smith had played on him. "I don't know anything about any plants."

"Yes, you do. And you probably think GPC already has most of them—the ones Vic Lawton stole from your father. The ones the police never recovered after the accident."

Kate blinked. How did Zoe know that was her father? No one but Tom and his witness protection contact knew, except . . .

*Peter Ratcher.*

Dad's former colleague had seen her through the window of Dad's hospital room. He must've gone back to GPC and told them, just like Tom had feared.

"But think about it, Kate," Zoe went on. "If GPC had that many plants, why would they concern themselves with the few you'd managed to scrounge up?"

Kate couldn't help the way her brow furrowed at Zoe's question. *Yeah, why would they when . . .*

"They would've just killed you like they did Vic, and their troubles would've been over," Zoe voiced her thought.

Kate gulped, feeling as if the walls were closing in on her. They were going to kill her as soon as she told them where the plants were.

"We know you had the plants, Kate. What did you really expect to accomplish by hiding them?"

Kate pressed her palms to her ears to shut out the taunts clamoring in her head. Had she really thought she'd get her father back?

Believing she could had given her purpose. Hope. It had helped the loneliness not hurt so much.

"I'm working with the men who are protecting your father, Kate. I need you to trust me."

No. She should've trusted Tom. She'd used the plants as an excuse to shut him out so he couldn't hurt her, when deep down . . . Oh, she'd been such a fool.

And isn't that exactly what he'd said? That it was better to trust and risk being a fool than to live in constant mistrust? Over and over again he'd proven how much he cared about her. *Loved her.*

That truth, the depth of what his love really meant, washed over her like a cleansing spring rain. Scripture whispered through her thoughts. *Love rejoices with the truth, always protects, always trusts.*

And because she didn't trust Tom with the truth, he thought she was dead.

Something exploded inside her at the thought. She stalked toward Zoe. "You blow up my car. Drug me. Hold me prisoner. And you want my trust?" Kate snatched up the table lamp, whirled toward the curtained window, and hurled it at the glass. Only then did it register that there was no glass. The window was boarded up from the outside. Her insides crumpled, but she refused to give Zoe the satisfaction of seeing it. She schooled her features, then turned back to Zoe and glared. "Trust is a two-way street."

Zoe actually looked remorseful. "You're right." She typed something into her cell phone.

*She has a cell phone.* Kate's heart galloped. If she could subdue Zoe without Sausage Fingers hearing, she could call Tom for help. Kate glanced around the room, looking for something she could use to gag Zoe. Spotting the open washroom door, she hitched her thumb over her shoulder and backed toward it. "I need to use the facilities." She hurried into the small room and closed the door. It was pitch black. She felt along the wall, flipped on the light switch. The lone bare bulb flickered, then sizzled out. Great. She felt along the other walls for the towel racks. There had to be a hand towel she could use in here somewhere. Her palms skimmed over something squishy and she scarcely swallowed a yelp as it scurried away.

Slowly her eyes adjusted to the darkness, and she could make out the towel racks, the bare shower rod, the bare shelves. She opened the cupboard under the sink. Toilet paper was not going to cut it. Dropping her head against the cold porcelain sink, she almost gave in to the urge to cry.

*Lord, I've made a mess of everything. I was afraid. Afraid you'd let me down if I asked you to bring my dad back. Afraid to let myself care about Tom.*

Another Scripture verse whispered through her mind— *Nothing is impossible for God*—and with it swept over her an amazing calm, a clarity of purpose. She drew a deep breath and opened the door.

Zoe stood in the center of the room, watching her. "I have something to show you. You'll probably want to sit down."

Kate took her time crossing the room to the bed. Was there a pillowcase on the pillow? If she could slip it off without Zoe noticing, she could use that as a gag. Kate sat on the edge of the bed, within reach of the pillow. Yes, it had a pillowcase.

"I want you to know that I would've liked nothing better than to tell you this sooner, to show you the proof, but my superiors prefer as little as possible be revealed."

"Whatever."

"I am working with Tom's friend, who helped your dad return to hiding."

Kate's throat closed up. Was this another ploy? Or was this woman telling the truth? Kate couldn't breathe. How would GPC know what Tom had arranged?

"Our people recovered the plants Vic stole. Tom doesn't know that. They didn't think he needed to know, although I suspect it would've saved us all a lot of grief."

Kate's insides jigged erratically, feeling like chop suey, but she didn't let on that she believed a word Zoe uttered. She wasn't sure she did. Although everything in her wanted to.

"Your father is recovering well from the accident. He woke up three days ago."

Kate couldn't help it. A cry of happiness bubbled out of her. But she quickly pressed her lips together again, stripped any emotion from her face.

"I hope I don't have to remind you that this is top secret and you can't tell anyone." Zoe turned the screen of her cell phone toward Kate. "This was taken a few minutes ago to prove I'm telling you the truth. You can see the date on the newspaper your father is holding."

Kate gasped. "You kidnapped my father?"

"No, we took him to a safe house at Detective Parker's request."

Her hopes rose. Even Peter Ratcher couldn't have known that. "Can I talk to him?"

Zoe snatched back the phone before Kate could type in a number. "They don't think that's a good idea."

"Why?"

At Zoe's stuttered evasion, the truth slowly filtered through Kate's brain, splintering her silly hopes. "Because you're afraid he'll tell me you're lying, that you're holding him against his will. He sure looked like a hostage to me in that picture." She grabbed Zoe's arm for another look at the screen, but Zoe jerked free of her hold.

Kate gasped. "It's not even him, is it?" Other than those few hours in the hospital, she hadn't seen him in twenty years. The guy in the picture could be anyone with a bandage on his head.

Zoe's pained look told her all she needed to know. Zoe couldn't be trusted.

But if Kate could snatch the phone, she could call Tom. Her heart squeezed at the irony that after weeks of keeping him in the dark about the plants, he was the one person she knew she could trust.

Zoe sighed. "Your dad took a serious blow to the head. His memory is . . . sketchy."

Kate's breath came in short, rapid bursts. "You're saying he doesn't remember me?" She pressed her lips together, forced her breathing to slow. It was a ploy. If they wanted her cooperation, all they had to do was take her to her father. She eyeballed the phone Zoe was twisting in her hand. Maybe if she appeared to cooperate, Zoe would let down her guard long enough for Kate to snatch the phone.

Zoe's gaze looked genuinely apologetic. "I'm sorry. But the doctors do believe his memory will come back in time."

Kate pressed her fingers to her temples. Her head was pounding, trying to keep all the lies straight. "What do you want?"

"I want to know who took the plants you were growing in your basement."

"What are you talking about?" Kate avoided looking at her, couldn't help the involuntary twitch triggered by her lie.

Zoe rolled her eyes. "Do not run me in circles on this again, Kate. We know yesterday's fire alarm was caused by high humidity in your basement. It doesn't take a rocket scientist to figure out what you were growing down there. I'm sure you knew it wouldn't take long for GPC to put two and two together too. You were smart to move them right away."

Kate's jaw dropped. "I didn't move them."

Zoe cursed. "Then who did?"

🌿

The dust in the air of the old Potter place was so thick, Tom could hardly breathe. In fact, could scarcely *think straight*. He glanced out the window at Darryl hiking down the driveway and Crump unloading more lumber from the back of his pickup and prayed he hadn't held on to the wrong man. Everything in him wanted to get out there looking for Kate. But Jarrett had to be behind the device that crippled Patti's car and made Kate a sitting duck.

Tom stalked over to the stairs where Jarrett was still sitting, handcuffed, surprisingly not complaining or asking for a lawyer. Tom bristled at the possibility that Jarrett was deliberately keeping him preoccupied. He planted his hand on the stair's newel post to keep himself from clamping his fingers around Jarrett's neck. "You came here looking for Kate's plants. Plants you, or one of your cohorts, would've had to break into her house to know were missing."

Patti's mouth dropped open. "You broke into her house?"

"No, I borrowed her key," Jarrett said coolly, as if taking the key without Kate's knowledge and bypassing the alarm system wasn't a crime. "After hearing the fire chief blamed humidity for the false alarm, I thought she might be growing those amendoso plants you wanted to study."

"No, she would have told me," Patti cried.

"What makes you so sure?" Tom asked. Patti had gone to a lot of trouble to research the plants online for Kate, but once Kate realized the plant's connection to her father, she would've shied away from sharing anything more about it with anyone.

Patti's gaze shifted away from him.

"Did she talk to you about it recently?" Tom pressed.

Patti chewed her bottom lip, her gaze glued to the floor.

A *yes* if he'd ever seen one. "I need to know everything she said to you."

Jarrett leaned into the conversation, looking way too intent to hear Patti's answer. Or to influence it.

"It's just . . . Kate asked me not to say anything more about our plans to either of you. That's why I tried to stall you from going after her this morning."

So he hadn't imagined that much. "What plans?"

"I want to study the plant for my thesis. I asked Kate to help me convince the university committee."

*Thesis? Kate's missing and Patti's blabbering about a thesis!* "What does that have to do with the woman who lured Kate into the countryside?" Tom demanded.

Patti covered her mouth with a trembling hand, apparently oblivious, until now, to the woman's role in the plot. She slid her hand down her throat and splayed it against her chest. "I thought the woman might have found another patch of amendoso and figured Kate would be a while checking it out." Patti must've read his skepticism in his eyes, because her own flared. "It's true. My dad found the plant years ago. Kept some in the solarium, thinking one day he'd incorporate it into a landscape plan."

Tom resisted the urge to shake his head. Did she really expect to pass off the plants from Kate's house as ones her father had been growing for years? "So the plants are at your house?"

"Just one. It wasn't until Kate noticed it a couple of days ago that I finally scrounged up the courage to tell her about my thesis idea."

*One plant. Could that be all Kate had had?* He'd have to search Patti's house before he'd be convinced that was all she had. There'd been at least a dozen soil rings left behind on the table at Kate's.

Then again, if Kate's plants were at Patti's house, Jarrett wouldn't have come over to Crump's looking for them. So maybe Patti *was* telling the truth. "Who else knew you had the plant?"

"I don't know. I'm sure my dad showed it to many clients over the years."

"What about the man in the sketch Kate printed out?" If Patti's father told Smith where he'd found the amendoso, it might explain Smith's sudden interest in Verna Nagy's property. "Was he a client?"

"What sketch?"

"Kate never showed it to you?" Tom unfolded the copy he'd stuffed in his jacket pocket, finding it difficult to believe Kate wouldn't have shown it to her when she'd taken it around to the other neighbors. "Do you recognize him?"

"Yeah, actually, I do. Darryl gave him a tour of the lab about six weeks ago."

Tom's limbs thrummed with nervous energy. The pieces were coming together, but what if it wasn't in time to save Kate? "Do you know his name? Have his contact information?"

"No, I only saw him in passing."

Tom showed Jarrett the sketch. "How about you? You know him?"

Jarrett scarcely glanced at the paper. "No."

"You didn't look." Scrutinizing Jarrett's blank expression, Tom snatched up his ringing cell phone. Before he got the phone to his ear, Kate's panicked voice clutched his heart.

"No, you have to let me—" she screamed, sounding as if she was fighting for the phone, maybe her life.

Then the line went dead.

# 19

"I want roadblocks set up on every road within a ten-mile radius of the tower that bounced Kate's cell phone signal," Tom ordered as he sped toward the sparsely populated rural area. He'd had to release Jarrett, against his better judgment, or risk wasting precious minutes. Rain pummeled his windshield, and from the look of the road, the area had been getting hammered for a while. Tom flicked his windshield wipers to high and tried not to think about how easy the weather would make it for Kate's kidnapper to track her if she'd managed to get away.

"Outside a four-mile radius, her phone would've picked up another tower," the sergeant on the other end of the line reasoned.

"And you know as well as I do that if they're already on the move, even ten miles isn't enough. Did you get the photograph I sent?"

"Yeah, all units have been notified to be on the lookout for her."

"Good. I'll want to know the location of every abandoned building they could've holed up in within that area."

"On it. We've set up the command post at Wilson's Feed Mill."

"Okay." Tom glanced at his GPS, unfamiliar with this corner of the region. "I'll be there in seven minutes."

"So what's the deal on this woman? She experimenting with a new designer drug or something, and double-crossed whoever was funding her?"

"No. She's a research scientist." It irked him how quickly such ridiculous rumors spread, and with them the risk of exposing the plants she'd been trying to hide and the true story behind them.

Yeah, he was doing a lousy job at protecting her all around.

What had she been thinking following a strange woman into the countryside? She was too trusting. His mind flashed to the soil remnants in her basement. Trusting of everyone but him.

"So we could still be facing organized crime here?" Reynolds pressed.

Tom twisted his clenched hands around the steering wheel. "I don't know."

The rain eased, then stopped by the time he pulled into the muddy feed mill lot, but the clearing skies wouldn't help when the sun set in less than three hours. He parked next to a pair of cruisers, where two officers were poring over a map spread on one of the hoods.

Sergeant Reynolds, the officer he'd been talking to on the phone, introduced himself and immediately jabbed a red pencil at the map as the younger officer stepped aside. "We're here. And I've circled the most likely places they'd hide her.

There are at least half a dozen old farmhouses or barns, one restaurant, one scrap dealer—that's not abandoned, but I figured there'd be tons of places to hide among all those old cars—and an old motel that's been boarded up for years." He pointed to each location on the map as he recited them.

"I'll head this way first." Tom traced a route that would pass a couple of the houses, the restaurant, and the motel. "In the meantime, one of your men can scan this route. But"—Tom caught the eye of the other officer—"don't stop. I don't want them to know we're onto them. Scan the driveways for any sign that a car's been in them recently or for any sign of life inside, then report back. Okay?"

"You got it." He practically leapt into his car and sped off.

"Have backup standing by," Tom said to Reynolds, then took off in the other direction.

The driveway of the first abandoned house he passed showed no signs of recent traffic, and neither did the parking lot of an old fish and chips shop. With every minute that passed with no more calls from Kate or any sign of where she'd been, the weight pressing on his chest gained another ten pounds.

Nearing the motel, his heart did an unexpected flip. Was that mud on the road tracking out of the motel lot? He slowed to a crawl. The ruts in the driveway were definitely recent. Looked like one vehicle had been in and out. Maybe a second one. He didn't dare stop for fear of tipping them off if anybody was still around. Instead, he turned into a driveway fifty yards past the motel, and edged up just far enough to get a look at the back of the motel parking lot. No cars.

His hopes plummeted. Was he too late?

He turned back onto the road and passed the motel,

traveling the opposite direction. With how thoroughly all the windows were boarded, it'd be next to impossible to see a light on inside. A woodlot bordered the back and east side of the motel property. Tom parked just past it, at the entrance to a farmer's field, and phoned Reynolds, reluctant to use the police radio in case the kidnappers were monitoring their frequency. "Yeah, I think I found where they were. The old motel. I'm parked to the east of the property and I'm going to sneak over and take a closer look."

"Do you want me to send backup?"

"Have a couple of cars stand by just out of sight. No lights. No sirens."

"Will do."

Tom sprinted along the edge of the woodlot, doing his best to avoid the muddy low ground. The fifty feet of open parking lot between the bush and the motel's side wall was the risky part. Tom peered at every window for any sign of a sniper watching the building's flank. Seeing nothing, he sprinted across the open lot, then pressed his back to the wall and peered carefully around the corner.

Outside the rear entrance, tire tracks divulged where a van or SUV had been parked. From this distance, he couldn't make out footprints.

Squinting at the back wall as best he could from the corner, he searched for any sign of a lookout. Every window was boarded. He quietly hurried toward the rear entrance and spotted man-size boot prints in the mud. At least two different sizes, and a smaller set. A woman's.

His pulse quickened. She'd been here. Maybe still was.

He snatched his weapon from his shoulder holster and edged toward the vandalized door. Someone had clearly used a pry bar to get it open, but judging from the wood, the breach hadn't been recent. Of course, the kidnappers could have merely taken advantage of a former intruder's handiwork.

Tom pressed his ear to the door but couldn't make out any sound. All senses on high alert, he eased it open. The hall was dark and dank. He flicked on his flashlight and edged along the wall, listening intently for the slightest movement. He felt as if spiders were crawling down his neck but ignored the sensation, scarcely daring to breathe, even though his light would give him away long before his breathing.

He tested the first door and paused to listen before moving on to the next. He repeated the action, again and again. Halfway down the hall, a door gave way at the turn of the knob. He flicked his flashlight about the dark room.

The mattress was bare and caked in a thick layer of dust, as were the night tables and bureau tops. He crouched down and shone the light under the bed. A cockroach scurried under the floorboard.

A few rusted hangers hung in the otherwise empty closet, and the bathroom was likewise empty.

He bit back a curse. Kate was out there somewhere, terrified, and he was wasting precious time. If she'd been here, she was long gone now.

The echo of her cut-off plea squeezed his chest.

Stepping back into the hall, his light beam caught the outline of a muddy boot print on the wall across the hall, as if someone had been slouching against it. Watching that room? Or maybe standing guard at this one. Hope charged through his veins as Tom tested the door. The instant it opened, his flashlight's piercing beam revealed the same setup as the last room, and his chest fell.

He swept the light through the closet and bathroom and turned back to the hall, ready to call in a forensics team to try to lift prints.

But something different about the room niggled the back of his mind. Years in the FBI had taught him to never underestimate those God-sent vibes, so he took another look, moving the light from bed to night table to bureau. Nothing registered, but a strong sense he was missing something important pressed on him. That and the slightest whiff of lavender that he didn't want to believe was his imagination.

He rechecked the closet. A thick layer of dust coated the rod. He flicked his flashlight back over the bedside tables. *Yes.* Dust was missing from the furniture in the room!

He punched in Reynolds's number and relayed his theory about the dusted room. "I need a forensics team at the motel pronto. Tell them not to pull into the lot. I want footprint and tire casts and whatever fingerprints and other trace evidence they can find." Heading for the door to take a closer look at the footprints outside, Tom glimpsed a disturbance in the dust on the bathroom floor—the vinyl floor that they'd apparently neglected to sweep. Without stepping into the room, Tom focused the light beam on the floor. His breath hitched. Was that writing?

He angled the light another way until the beam lit the dust once more. "Z-O-E." His heart slammed into his ribs. *Zoe?* The *same Zoe* who killed his partner? The Zoe in Kate's father's police file? The Zoe that Zeb hadn't wanted him talking to? That Zeb hadn't arrested, even though they'd apparently been bugging her phone?

Tom whipped out his cell phone and hit Zeb's number. It flipped immediately to voice mail.

"Zeb, you have about five minutes before whatever case you have on Zoe becomes international news. I suggest you call me." Using his phone's camera, Tom snapped a pic of the name scratched in dust that could only mean Zoe was Kate's kidnapper. And from how uneasy Kate's dad had gotten when Tom brought up the woman's name in the car outside the research station last month, he'd probably been dodging Zoe for twenty years, along with GPC and who knew who else.

Tom's phone rang. Hank, not Zeb. Tom clicked it on. "Yeah?"

"We just had a call. Someone sighted a woman fitting Kate's description running from a diner near Cooper's Corners. A patrol car is on its way."

Tom raced from the room. "Thanks. I'll brief the investigators arriving here and then—" His phone beeped an alert to an incoming call. He glanced at the screen. *Zeb.* Tom skidded to a stop, not wanting to have a conversation with Zeb in front of the arriving officers. "Then I'll head straight over," he finished saying to Hank, then clicked over to Zeb's call.

"What's going on?" Zeb demanded the instant Tom connected.

"You tell me. I found where Kate's kidnappers were holding her, and guess whose name was written in the dust on the floor?" Tom managed to make his voice sound nonchalant when everything in him wanted to beat his "friend" to a pulp.

"Not a clue. Who?"

"Zoe." Okay, his caustic voice gave away his true feelings, but he didn't bother to tone it down. The man was lying

291

through his teeth. "I know you've got her phone bugged, so I'm guessing you've known all along that she has Kate. And didn't tell me. Am I right?"

"Has anyone else seen her name?"

"Are you asking me to tamper with evidence?"

"National security could be at stake."

"In case you've forgotten, I live in Canada now, and the only security I care about at the moment is Kate's. Where is she?"

"Okay, okay. Yes, Zoe had Kate."

Tom's stomach buckled. "What do you mean *had*?"

Kate's already rampaging heartbeat escalated at the distant sound of police sirens. She hadn't heard Zoe's men behind her in a long while, but she hadn't dared stop either. But the deeper she plunged into the woods, the more she feared they'd drive to wherever the woods ended and wait her out.

She staggered to a stop. Hunching over, she clutched her thighs and tried to catch her breath. *Please, Lord, let those police be looking for me.*

Zoe had been so worried that her cut-off call would give the police enough to find them that she'd rushed them out of the boarded-up motel without bothering to tie Kate's hands. The second Kate saw the dense woods bordering the parking lot, she knew she was looking at her last chance to get away.

Kate reached down and pulled a twig from her sandal, wincing at the barb it left behind in her mud-caked foot. The sirens wound down and she quickly straightened, straining to pinpoint the direction they were coming from. She rotated

360 degrees, suddenly unnerved by the fifty-foot trees that looked exactly the same every which way she turned. Never mind that they seemed to be playing Ping-Pong with the sound of the sirens. *Which way?*

The sirens went silent. She rotated again, feeling more disoriented than ever. In every direction, nothing but trees and shrubs and muddy, rotting vegetation armed with biting twigs met her.

Were the police at the motel?

The sirens hadn't sounded as if they came from behind her. Except by the time they stopped, maybe they had been.

She visually traced her footprints back a dozen yards but couldn't bring herself to follow them. A gust of wind rustled the leaves overhead, sprinkling raindrops on her already soaked clothes. Shivering, she briskly rubbed her arms. There hadn't been any signs of civilization around the motel. If she went back and the police weren't there, she might have to walk miles until she found a phone, and it would be dark soon. She'd be better off moving forward. If she veered right, she should eventually reach the road.

Hopefully, before nightfall.

Fixing her gaze on a distant tree to her right, she strode toward it, then repeated the tactic, praying she was headed in the right direction. *I will instruct you and teach you in the way you should go; I will counsel you with my loving eye on you.* The words of a favorite psalm—God's words—whispered through her mind, and she quickened her steps.

In no time, the way ahead grew lighter and her hopes surged. It had to be the edge of the forest. She broke into a jog, and the trees soon gave way to shrubs and brambles. She hefted up a heavy stick and slashed her way through.

She was going to make it. She was going to get out of here and get back those plants and keep them away from GPC. Her father's sacrifice cost their family everything. No way was she going to let it be for nothing.

Her heart cracked at the thought of her father at the mercy of Zoe's people . . . if that really had been a picture of her father Zoe had flashed at her. Kate gripped the stick with both hands and whacked at the bush. She'd know soon enough, when she found Tom.

She didn't believe that her father wouldn't remember her. If the man Zoe's people claimed to have was her father, the real reason Zoe wouldn't let her talk to *him* had to be because she knew he'd tell her to do anything it took to keep the plants out of GPC's hands.

Like he had.

*You never know what you'd do until you're in the situation.* Keith had been referring to Tom, but after weeks of feeling more utterly abandoned than ever for learning her dad had chosen to protect a plant over staying with her, she was beginning to appreciate what had driven him. Kate unleashed her anger on the bushes blocking her path until the slam of a car door stopped her cold.

She shrank back. She couldn't outrun Zoe's goons again, not in her sandals. The strap had already rubbed her skin raw. And she'd barely managed to outrun them the first time. She dropped to her belly and army crawled to the edge of the field, gritting her teeth against the sting of brambles slashing her arms and face.

Her breath caught at the sight of a dark sedan parked at the field's entrance. The taillights looked a lot like Tom's. The interior light momentarily flicked on.

*It is Tom!*

"Tom, wait!" The car's engine drowned her shout as she plowed out of the bush. Fighting off the prickly branches snagging her hair, she screamed again. She broke free, only to lose a sandal. "Tom!" She snatched up her sandal and hopped after him, waving with her free hand as she fitted the sandal back on.

Only he didn't see her.

His turn signal flicked on. The car rolled forward.

She waved both hands wildly. "Tom, wait!"

An engine roared behind her.

Kate's heart catapulted into her throat at the sight of a dirt bike speeding straight for her, the driver's face hidden by a black visor. *Smith?*

There was no way she could outrun a bike. Not in the open. She scrambled back into the bushes, dove behind the roots of a giant fallen tree, and hunkered down. "Please, Lord, let Tom come back."

The dirt bike engine quieted to an idle. She could hear the driver swatting aside the bushes like he might come after her on foot.

She pressed her hand to her mouth, her pulse roaring in her ears.

What was she doing? She couldn't just sit here. She snatched up a rock and a sturdy stick to use as weapons.

"Police! Keep your hands where I can see them," Tom shouted, loud and insistent.

Kate's heart leapt. *He came back!* Gripping her weapons, she edged around her shield of mud-caked roots for a better look.

The dirt bike sat idling not more than fifty feet from her. She couldn't see the driver or Tom.

"Hands up, I said. Don't move." Tom's voice sounded mercifully closer than it had moments ago. "What's so interesting in that bush, huh?"

He didn't know she was here? Kate scrambled toward him through the underbrush. "Tom, it's m—"

"Don't even think about it," Tom ordered, low and menacing.

She froze.

A gunshot cracked the air.

# 20

Tom's second shot winged the bike racing away through the field on one flat tire. He radioed in the suspect's description and location, then plowed into the bushes. "Kate? Where are you?"

"Tom!" Kate sprang out from behind a fallen tree and hurled herself into his arms. "I knew you'd find me!"

He buried his face in her hair and shuddered at the thought that Hank's call that she'd been spotted elsewhere might've been a hoax to lure him away. "It's okay." He tightened his hold, relishing how right she felt in his arms, snug against his heart. "It's okay. You're safe now. Are you hurt?"

Her head shifted from side to side against his chest. "Just scratched up. After I called you, my kidnappers were in such a hurry to get away that I was able to run off." Her words tumbled over each other against his shirt. "I lost her in the woods."

He pulled back enough to look into Kate's eyes. "Zoe?"

"You saw the clue I left?"

He rubbed away the chill that shuddered through her arms. "Yes, you did good. I'm proud of you."

"Ouch." She jerked her right arm from his touch. "The arm's sore. A burn."

"Sorry. Let's get you into the car and warmed up." He looked into her eyes and added sternly, "Then I want to know everything."

Her eyes glistened with tears. "You'll hate me."

He cupped her face. "Not possible." He hoped her remorse meant she understood now why he'd been so protective, why she needed to tell him everything. But looking into her bottomless green eyes, he felt compelled to do something else first. His gaze dropped to her lips as his thumb traced their soft curves. "I went crazy when I thought I lost you," he whispered. "I don't want to lose you." He dipped his head and claimed her mouth, gently at first, then more insistently, his love for her spiraling into a whirlwind in his chest.

He started to pull away, but her fingers glided through his hair, drawing him back. The sweet taste of her lips, and her even sweeter surrender, made him hunger for more. He kissed the salty tears glistening on her cheeks and the nasty scratch marking her forehead, and then drew her head to his chest and pressed a kiss to her hair, his heart bursting with relief that she was safe in his arms.

"Thank you for not giving up on me," she whispered.

"Never." But as much as he'd like nothing better than to stand here for hours and hold her in his arms, he needed to call off the search, get her warm and fed and cleaned up and checked out, and get some answers. Lots of answers.

"Let's get you out of here." Tucking her safely against

his side as they walked, he called the sergeant directing the search to tell him she was safe and to get an update on the suspect on the dirt bike.

"The local police haven't spotted him," he reported to Kate. "Did you recognize him?"

"I assumed it was Smith, but with the helmet on, I don't know."

"I don't think it was. This guy had a different build and a different bike." But something familiar about the guy niggled the back of Tom's mind, just out of reach. "Was he one of your kidnappers?"

"Not one I saw. There were three men. All big guys. Muscle-bound big, not fat. But bigger than the guy on the bike."

"Can you remember anything else about them? Hair color? Tattoos?"

"They looked fairly clean-cut, short dark hair, dark pants, black windbreakers, ball caps."

"Did you see what they were driving?"

"A black SUV with tinted windows. There was an *A* in the front license plate number."

"That's good." Tom passed on the information to the sergeant.

Shivering, Kate climbed into his car.

Tom shrugged out of his jacket and dropped it over her shoulders.

She looked up, her lips quivering, her haggard gaze clinging to his. "They said if I ever wanted to see my dad again, I needed to come without a fight."

"What?" Shock kicked the question up a few decibels higher than she needed to hear. He squeezed her shoulders and held her gaze. "It had to be a ruse." *Had to be.* Zeb would've said something.

"I thought so too, but you have to call your friend. Make sure Dad's still safe." Anxiety pinched her voice and rammed her words into each other. "Zoe showed me a picture on her phone of a man holding today's paper, but I couldn't be sure it was my dad. Not after all these years and the burns he got in the accident."

Not knowing what to think, Tom quickly rounded the car and slid into the driver's seat, turned on the engine, and cranked up the heat. Zeb tracking Zoe instead of arresting her, especially after he had to have known the woman had kidnapped Kate, was one thing. Zoe knowing Kate's father was still alive and in protection was beyond explanation.

At least, any explanation Tom wanted to contemplate.

Kate twisted her hands in her lap, her fingers turning white. "They wouldn't let me talk to him. You have to call your friend. Right now. Please."

"Okay, yes." Opting to remain parked in the field a few more minutes, Tom punched in a call to Zeb.

The call rolled to voice mail.

"Call me as soon as you get this," Tom said, and disconnected. He squeezed Kate's hand. "I'm sure your father is fine. My friend would've told me if he wasn't." Tom hoped that was the truth.

"But GPC knows he's alive. If they don't have him, they'll be looking for him all over again. Peter Ratcher must've told them he was alive after he saw me in Dad's hospital room, before your friend took Dad away."

The tension in Tom's shoulders eased a little at her logical explanation. Yes, that had to be how Zoe knew. She'd been working for some kind of biotech company when Ian was dating her. It wasn't called GPC, but maybe it was an American subsidiary. He'd have to check that out. It made a whole lot more sense than Zeb leaking the information when they'd gone to so much trouble to keep her father's existence a secret.

"We have another problem, Kate. Your kidnapping is a police matter that needs to be investigated. The details will be a matter of public record. It could be tough keeping your father and the amendoso plants out of this."

"The . . . the . . . plants, right. But can't you investigate? And keep the stuff that needs to stay quiet off the record?"

He squeezed her hand. "Oh, you can count on my investigating, but Hank won't like it. And he won't let me head the investigation. Not given how I feel about you."

Her gaze softened. "But . . . but as far as he knows, we aren't even dating."

Tom stroked the back of his fingers across her cheek. "Except Hank knows that's not by my choice."

She ducked her head, but when Tom pulled the car onto the road, she reached across the seat and put her hand on his arm. "I'm glad he let you come find me."

Tom exaggeratedly arched a brow at the ridiculousness of her statement. "They would have had to put a bullet in me to stop me from coming after you."

A blush rose to her cheeks.

Grinning, he took a moment to relish that she finally understood how deeply he cared for her. He hoped she remembered that fact when he grilled her about the plants missing from her basement. Grilling he needed to do off the record. And he had only about thirty minutes—the time it would take to drive back to Port Aster—before Hank started asking where she was.

"Tell me everything you remember Zoe and these other men saying to you."

"She seemed to know who you were, your background, which surprised me. I mean, she heard me say Tom into the phone, but she knew it was you. Right away, she said to her guys, 'If Parker is half the detective his former FBI partner was, he'll show up within the hour.' Do you know her?"

"Yeah." Tom clenched his fingers around the steering wheel, not wanting to tell her how. She'd been frightened enough. She didn't need to know this woman thought nothing of murdering people.

"I heard her tell one of the guys that if you got one look at her, you'd shoot first and ask questions later."

He chuckled wryly. She had that right. And hopefully was smart enough not to mess with his woman again.

"Why? What did she do to you?"

A disturbing thought flashed through his mind. What if the kidnapping wasn't about Kate and the plants? What if it was about getting to him?

He shook his head. No, that didn't make sense. What could Zoe possibly gain by goading him, after all this time?

"Tom?" Kate pressed.

He fixed his gaze on the threatening-looking clouds. Maybe he should tell her. She still hadn't admitted to harboring the plants. If she knew what Zoe was capable of, she wouldn't hold anything back. And he needed to know everything if he was going to keep her safe.

With a gut-wrenching sigh, he said, "Zoe is the woman who killed my partner."

"Tom," Kate gasped. "I—" Struck afresh by how close she'd been to the same fate, she clamped down on her lips in a vain attempt to still her trembling chin. No wonder he'd kissed her like there was no tomorrow when he found her.

"Zoe didn't threaten me," Kate whispered. "She kept insisting she was trying to protect me. But I didn't trust her." Kate gingerly touched her upper arm. "I remember fighting off two guys a second before my car exploded. That's how I must've got burned." She strained to pull up more memories but finally shook her head. "I can't remember anything after that until I woke up in the motel room."

"They must've given you a knockout drug." Concern laced Tom's voice.

She rubbed her forehead. "Might explain the headache."

Slowing the car, he glanced worriedly from the road to her. "I should take you to the hospital."

"I'll be fine. I . . ." Kate caught herself squirming. She'd promised herself she'd tell him everything, trust him with her secret, and she'd put it off long enough. She took a deep breath and plunged ahead. "Zoe kidnapped me because of the amendoso plants I'd secretly dug up. I'm sorry I didn't tell you. But I knew you wouldn't want me to keep them. I thought that if I could figure out what was so special about them, I'd have enough leverage to convince whoever I needed to let me see my dad." A sob burbled up in her chest as another Scripture verse whispered through her mind: *My ways are not your ways.*

Tom's expression softened. He reached for her hand and stroked his thumb across the back of her fingers. "I can only imagine how hard it's been for you to learn your dad is alive and then have him torn away."

"I'd do anything to see him again. At least . . ." She dropped her gaze. "I thought I would do anything until the choice was telling Zoe where the plants were or maybe never seeing him again." She blinked back the moisture pooling in her eyes. "As desperately as I want to see him, I knew my dad wouldn't want me to give in to them. Not after all he's sacrificed."

Tom pulled his car off the road and turned in his seat. "I hate to have to be the one to tell you this, but they already have the plants." His expression held such undeserved compassion, she was speechless. "Within an hour after your car was torched, I found your cellar had already been cleaned out. It's probably why Zoe didn't try very hard to stop you from running."

"You already knew I had the plants?" She threw her arms around his neck and hugged him. "You're a good man, Tom Parker. All you wanted to do was protect me, and you're not even reaming me out for keeping them a secret from you."

He cupped her face a tad sternly and drew back enough to look her in the eye. "What aren't you telling me?"

Laughter bubbled up inside her. "Zoe's people didn't take the plants."

"Then who did?"

"I did. I asked Ryan to move them for me when he changed my lock."

"Where are they?" Tom flicked on his turn signal and returned his hands to the steering wheel. "We need to get them. Turn them in, before anyone gets hurt."

"No, wait, don't you see? It's perfect. Zoe knows I didn't move the plants because I was with her. And I put on a convincing act of looking as if I thought someone stole them when she told me they weren't in my house. She probably thinks her competition beat her to them. She'll turn her sights elsewhere."

He whacked off his turn signal and rammed the shifter into Park. "Maybe, but for how long? And if she's with GPC, who would she think is her competition? The mafia? The threats aren't going to stop until those plants are gone."

"Gone where? To the same people you gave my father to?" Her voice rose hysterically, but she couldn't help it. "If Zoe got to my father, what makes you think she won't get to the plants too, if we hand them over?"

The muscle in Tom's jaw did its irritated little two-step. "We don't know that she actually got to your father." His cell phone mounted to the dash rang, and he glanced at the screen. "It's the chief, probably wondering where we are. When I thought you died in the car explosion, I accused him of being the mayor's lackey. He's going to want to know who kidnapped you and why."

"So he can catch them? Or so he can spin the story to suit the mayor's agenda?"

"I don't know. GPC went too far this time. There's no way he can spin this into something self-inflicted." He tapped the phone screen on. "Yeah."

"We just got a tip on a teen that's holed up in someone's boat house."

Tom sent her a hopeful glance. "Get a description? You think it's Caleb?"

"Hard to say. The woman was hysterical. Called him a

murderer. Two officers have been dispatched, but I figured you'd want to know. It's near your location."

"Where?"

Hank relayed the address. "Near the Community Center."

Tom input the address into his GPS and swerved onto the road. "Okay, I'm on my way." He clicked off the phone and bit back a curse. "The woman probably watches too many crime shows and will get the responding officers keyed up into believing the kid's armed and dangerous."

Kate's heart raced as fast as Tom's car. "So you think it's Caleb? Do you think he knows enough to help us connect Zoe and Smith and GPC to Vic's murder?"

"I hope so. But let's pray they didn't hear the call over the police radio and try to get to him first."

Kate shivered at the thought of facing Zoe and her goons again.

Within minutes Tom was slowing for the small town. Kate pointed to the gas station lot. "There's one of the patrol cars."

Tom stopped at the light and scanned the lot.

"Aren't you going to pull in and talk to them?"

The light turned green and Tom drove past. "No, something tells me that Caleb will avoid any vehicle or person that smacks of police. If he trusted us, he would've called weeks ago."

"Then what are you going—" A flash of movement between the houses caught her eye. "Did you see that?"

"Down!"

Expecting a rain of bullets, Kate dove for the floorboards.

"I think I know where he's headed." Tom swerved right.

Kate edged up a fraction and spotted the top of a baseball backstop. "Why am I ducking? Did you see Zoe?"

"No, I didn't want Caleb to see you. This road leads behind the community center and ends at a picnic area with a boat launch. Caleb's bound to veer this way to avoid being seen."

"What makes you think he won't avoid us too?"

"Because I'm going to look like someone who'd help him. You can sit up now."

She peered over the lip of the window. He'd parked behind a stand of trees. "How?"

Tom eased his jacket from around her shoulders. "By helping you."

"Huh?"

Tom flipped down the car's visor and pointed to the mirror.

Mud smeared her cheeks. Her hair was a wet, bedraggled mop. She glanced down at her damp clothes, muddy and torn. "Oh, I get it."

He reached across her and opened the passenger door. "Hurry out and make it look like you've lost your footing on the muddy bank. I'll take another drive around the picnic area and come to your rescue."

The cold air slapped Kate's damp clothes as she stepped out of the car, and suddenly the thought of wading in her open-toed sandals through the long reeds that could be harboring snakes and who knew what else made her stomach plummet. But Tom had already driven off. She squinted downriver. Would Caleb follow the river this far? He'd have to figure it would be safer than walking near the road, especially past the community center.

Her foot slipped and she let out an involuntary yelp as her rear landed hard. She cried out a second time for appearances sake, and upstream, the reeds rustled feverishly.

Panic rocketed through her. What if it was Zoe? And now Tom was gone.

She clawed at the ground to pull herself up, only to smack her hand onto a dead fish and let out another attention-drawing yelp.

The bush to her right rustled.

She shrank back, the deafening sound of her choppy breaths sending her pulse jackhammering.

A young man burst from the bushes and extended his hand.

Caleb? She eyed him warily. *Must be.* He didn't look in any better shape than she did. Clasping his hand with all her strength, she whispered her thanks.

"How'd you get here?" he asked as he hauled her up the bank.

Her mind scrambled for an explanation. She had no boat, bike, or car, and he'd never believe she'd been out running, considering her sandals. "I—I had a fight with my boyfriend."

Tom chose that moment to drive up to them, and the teen stepped in front of her protectively.

Tom jumped from the car, brandishing a first aid kit. "What happened? Are you two okay?"

"We're fine," the teen said dismissively.

"The lady looks cold." Tom didn't make eye contact with either of them, and Kate took his she-was-a-stranger-to-him act as confirmation the teen was Caleb. Tom set the first aid kit on a nearby picnic table and removed a small packet that he unfolded into a shiny blanket. "Here, wrap this around her."

Caleb hesitated a moment before accepting the blanket, which Kate urged him to wrap around them both, then pressed the ends into Caleb's free hand, essentially tying them together. Spotting a patrol car through the trees, head-ing their way, she gasped.

Caleb's gaze tracked hers, and he tensed beside her.

"Could you give us a ride?" Kate blurted to Tom.

"Sure thing." Tom opened the back door and motioned them inside.

Caleb eagerly followed her in, no doubt figuring it was the lesser of two evils.

But sliding across the seat, Kate realized he'd clue in to the scam the instant he saw— Kate did a double take. The small computer that was usually mounted to the console was gone. Tom must've hidden it.

Tom closed the door behind them, and as he rounded the car, Kate sank lower in the seat, thinking he wouldn't want the patrol car spotting them.

Caleb seemed to be thinking the same, because he sank down even lower.

"Where to?" Tom asked, passing the patrol car.

"Oh." Kate met Tom's gaze in the rearview mirror. What was she supposed to say?

The door locks clicked with an ominous *thunk* as Tom swerved onto the main road. "Okay, we're past the patrol cars. And I want to help you, Caleb, but I need to know why you're running."

"I don't know what you're talking about." Caleb flung off Kate's grasp and vainly tugged at the door handle. "I was just helping this woman."

"I'm Detective Tom Parker," Tom said patiently. "I'm pretty sure you saw something that you're afraid to go to the police about and maybe afraid for your life. Am I right?"

Caleb's shoulders sank.

Kate reached across the seat and squeezed his hand. "You can trust Detective Parker."

Caleb shook his head, wild-eyed. "No, they're all crooked."

"I found your lemur sketch in the old barn," Kate said. "And I recognized the face. We think—" She bit her lip, mentally sorting through how much to say. "The first Friday in September, Vic Lawton's truck plunged over the ravine near Turner's Hollow and he died. The police said it was suicide, because he'd been distraught over causing another man's death." She choked on the last word. Her father hadn't really died, and despite all Vic had done, she felt bad that he went to his grave believing he'd killed him.

Caleb grew fidgety, his gaze darting from window to window, his face pasty.

"We think the man you sketched was involved, but we don't have any proof. I was hoping you might have seen something that could help us," Kate said.

Caleb shook his head violently. "They said they'd kill my family if I went to the police."

"Who said?"

"The guys who ran that guy's truck off the road and killed the driver."

Kate gasped. "You saw them kill the driver?"

Saying nothing, Caleb pulled his knees to his chest and drew the foil blanket tight.

Kate exchanged a glance with Tom in the rearview mirror, then softened her voice. "I know you're scared, but you can't keep running. Your parents are worried sick."

His gaze slammed into hers. "Are you a cop?"

"No, I'm a research scientist. And . . . " She hesitated, not wanting to make Caleb privy to more than he needed to know, but something told her he'd be more forthcoming if she did. "This man and his partners . . . we think they want to kill me too."

His eyes widened.

"Please, Caleb, we need to know what you saw."

"I was mountain biking through the woods and heard a crash," he said quietly, his gaze fixed on the back of the passenger seat. I sped toward the sound so I could help, but by the time I got to the truck, two guys were"—Caleb's voice quivered—"they were smothering the driver. Not trying to help him." He turned his face to the window. "They saw me and chased after me, shouting that I better not talk or I'd be the same, and so would my family."

"And the face in your lemur sketch?" Tom interjected. "That guy was one of them?"

"No, I didn't see their faces. I raced away on my bike, but when I got to the road at the top of the hill, the guy I sketched was standing there, looking over the whole thing, like he was standing guard. He said he wanted to help me, but I didn't believe him. I took off on my bike through the woods on the other side." Caleb's whole body was trembling now. "I thought I got away too. I figured they'd never be able to identify me. But the next night, I spotted the guy sitting in his car down the street, watching my house. I freaked. I figured he was there to kill me."

"Why didn't you call the police?" Kate whispered.

"Because just before I snuck out the back, I saw a guy on a motorcycle stop and talk to him."

Kate didn't miss the way Tom bristled as he slowed the car and shot a look over the backseat. "You recognized him as a cop?"

"Might as well have been."

"What do you mean? Who was it?"

Caleb wrapped his arms tighter around his scrunched-up knees, his gaze darting warily from hers to Tom's. "The mayor's son."

# 21

At Caleb's admission, Tom screeched his car to a stop at the side of the road. "I knew there was something familiar about the guy on the dirt bike." He snatched his phone from the dash mount and tapped Patti's number.

Kate grabbed the back of his seat, looking as panicked as Caleb, sitting beside her. "Who're you calling?"

He held up his finger, shushing her. "Patti, this is Tom. Is Jarrett there?"

"Oh, Tom. Did you find Kate?" Patti wailed. "Is she okay?"

He hesitated, not sure he wanted Jarrett's contacts to know just yet. Then again, chances were they'd already heard it over the police radio.

"Yeah, she's good. Can I talk to Jarrett?"

Kate tugged on his shirt. "You think that was Jarrett on the dirt bike?" she whispered. "But he rides a bigger bike than that thing. And do you really think he's after the plants?"

"I know he is," Tom hissed, covering the phone's receiver.

"How?"

Tom glared at her to stay quiet as Patti responded to his question.

"He rushed out soon after you. Said he was late for a meeting. Are you bringing Kate here?"

"No, we need to question her."

"Oh, right, of course."

"Did Jarrett say where he was headed?"

"No, sorry."

"Okay, thanks." Tom clicked off just as a patrol car slowed behind him. "Get down!"

Kate and Caleb dove to the floor, tucking the blanket over them as Tom waggled his phone to the passing officer so he'd know he didn't need assistance.

The officer nodded and sped away.

"Okay, all clear." Tom turned to the backseat. "As for Jarrett going after the plants, I know because I caught him roughing up Crump."

"He might've thought Jim was making moves on Patti."

"No, he demanded to know where Crump had hidden the plants. By now, he may have figured out that Ryan moved them. Where'd he take them?"

"His cottage. Oh no! I told Patti that Ryan changed my lock." Kate named an address on the shores of Lake Erie.

"Who's Crump?" Caleb interjected.

"It's not important." Tom typed the address into his GPS and pulled back onto the road. The last thing he wanted to do was bring Kate and Caleb along, but there was no time to waste. And no one close enough he'd trust with their lives.

"You're sure it was Jarrett King you saw outside your house before you ran away?" Kate asked Caleb.

"Yeah, I'd know his bike anywhere." Caleb recited the motorcycle's features, right down to the detailed pinstriping.

"You said yourself," Tom reasoned with Kate, "the mayor is desperate for GPC to come to Port Aster. Jarrett's his son and Patti's boyfriend—the perfect errand boy to ensure you cooperate."

"I know," Kate whispered close to his ear, "but Patti has had an amendoso plant in her solarium that Jarrett's known about all along. If he's working for GPC, why didn't he hand it over long ago?"

"Yes, Patti told me." Tom took the corner too fast and almost clipped a car in the oncoming lane. He swerved back into his lane. "And that she asked you to supervise a thesis on it."

"But I didn't agree to—"

"Wait, hear me out. Patti's a smart girl. She's got to know that a lone plant is not going to be enough for that scope of research. Don't you see? She said it so that you would reveal your stash of plants."

"You think she's in on it with Jarrett?" Kate's voice hollowed out. She was no doubt thinking of how she hadn't believed Molly could've been conning her either, and the woman had turned out to be a murderer. "But what about Patti's dizziness? The doctor told us himself that he found toxin in her blood."

"It sounds like that might have been Serena's doing."

Kate gasped. "I knew she hated Patti for stealing her boyfriend. But enough to poison her?"

"I don't have confirmation on that, yet." Tom's phone rang. He clicked it on. "Yeah?"

"Where are you?" the chief demanded. "The officers said you never showed up."

"Did they find the kid?" Tom deflected as Caleb and Kate started murmuring in the backseat.

"No. What happened to you?"

Caleb shrank toward the door, clearly worried he was about to be outed.

Trouble was, if Hank really wanted to know where Tom was, he need only call in a locate request on his car or phone. The employee being asked to run the locate wouldn't blink an eye over passing on the information if the chief of police said it was life or death. Tom squinted at the patrol car that'd passed him, now a dot on the horizon. Had he been told to drive by? "Kate doesn't feel well. I need to take her to the hospital," Tom improvised and prayed he was wrong about Hank being the mayor's lackey.

"Okay, but you need to get more information out of her. The trail's running cold on catching these guys."

"I will." He clicked off the phone. "It's okay. I don't think he suspects." He hoped.

"Do you think Patti will warn Jarrett you called?" Kate's voice wobbled as if she still didn't want to believe Patti would do her any harm. It warmed his heart to see her loyalty to her friends as strong as ever.

"I don't know. She could be in the dark about what Jarrett's up to. He could've used her as a pawn by suggesting the research project idea to her."

"Except she said it was her idea. That he tried to dissuade her."

Tom shrugged. "He could've told her to say that, thinking you might be suspicious of his motives. And let's not forget his sudden decision to send Patti's car to his mechanic's last week—the car you were driving when you were kidnapped.

I don't think that's a coincidence." Tom noticed a car in his side mirror that had followed behind him too long for comfort. He took the next right without signaling, and as the voice on his GPS spouted "recalculating," the other car continued straight on the other road.

"What's wrong?" Kate peered out the back window.

"Just making sure we're not being followed. It's okay."

"It's not okay! Nothing's okay!"

"It's going to be okay. We'll get these guys. Your instincts are good, Kate. You told me from the beginning that you didn't trust Jarrett." Tom glanced at his cell phone screen, his grip on the steering wheel tightening. Still no message from Zeb.

Apparently, Kate's instincts about Zeb had been dead-on too.

"But how will you prove any of it? You said yourself the chief's in the mayor's back pocket, even with Caleb's testi—"

"I'm not testifying to nothing," Caleb blurted. "They said they'd kill my family."

"Your running away is killing your family," Tom said, more harshly than he'd intended. He softened his tone. "Don't worry. We'll give you and your family protection."

They drove in silence for a few minutes, and then Kate sprang forward and grabbed the back of Tom's seat. "If Jarrett is working for GPC, who'd he think Crump was working for?"

"Good question. Smith must've told Jarrett that Crump had stopped cooperating with his bogus 'help the government' story."

"But where'd Jarrett think Crump would take the plants?"

Tom mulled that question around in his mind for a few minutes, thinking about everything Crump had told them

317

about Gilmore, and tried to line it up with what he knew about Zoe and the explosion that killed his FBI partner. "To the mob, maybe, or drug lords."

"Crump? He's a con artist, not—"

"I didn't say Crump had the connections, but if your antidote theory is right, that's who Gilmore would worry about getting their hands on it. GPC too." And NSA had to be worried about the lot of them. An antidote to diablo piel would be worth its weight in diamonds if some two-bit terrorist group decided to use it as a biological weapon. It explained why investigators left Zoe in play after she killed Ian. They were hoping she'd lead them to the whole enchilada. Tom's gut churned at how Zeb had played him.

"Whoa," Caleb crooned, sounding awestruck.

Whereas Kate looked as green as Tom felt. He should've demanded answers from Zeb long before now.

"Do you think my dad knew? Why didn't he tell the police? The government? Somebody?"

Tom stared at his silent cell phone and fisted his hand around the steering wheel. "Apparently he knew that not even the government could always be trusted."

Kate jerked forward once more and peered over Tom's seat and out the windshield. "Why are you slowing down? The cottage is another dozen houses down the road."

Tom jutted his chin toward a wide, sandy corridor that led to the lake and the black pickup parked there.

Kate's heart jumped to her throat. "That's not Crump's truck, is it?"

"No, different plate number." Tom cruised past, scanning every driveway and turnoff.

Swallowing hard, Kate did the same. "That's Ryan's cottage just ahead on the left. The blue one." She scanned the road beyond. "I don't think Jarrett's here."

Tom pulled into Ryan's driveway without comment and squinted at the cottage.

Kate tugged at the car door handle, but it wouldn't budge. "Unlock the door!"

"Wait."

"What are we waiting for?" She jabbed uselessly at the door lock button. "Jarrett could show up any second. We need to get the plants out of there now!"

A guy in a dark blue windbreaker dashed from behind the cottage and through the backyard of the neighboring house.

"Stay in the car," Tom ordered, then leaped from the vehicle and chased after him.

Kate lurched over the back of the driver's seat and slapped the master door lock. "I have to get those plants before anyone else comes."

Caleb's gaze darted to the surf pounding the sandy beach beyond the cottage as he reached for the door handle.

She grabbed his arm. "I need you to watch my back. Okay?"

His gaze jigged to the street, the cottage, then finally to her. "Please."

At his single nod, Kate shoved open the door. "Okay, let's go."

He hurried after her. "You gonna break in?"

"Ryan said the spare key's behind an abandoned wasp nest, under the front awning."

Caleb sprinted past her and searched the corners of the awning. "I don't see a nest."

Her heart hammered louder than the pounding surf. "It's got to be here." She jumped onto the stoop and looked for herself. *No nest.* "Maybe it was the back awning." She raced around the side of the cottage, dodging boulders and downed tree branches, with Caleb on her heels. She'd break in if she had to. No way was she leaving without the plants and risking GPC or the mob getting hold of them. Her father's sacrifices would not be in vain.

The wind off the lake whipped straight through her damp clothes, chilling her to the bone. Tom had disappeared. The beach was empty, save for seagulls scavenging among the debris and fish corpses washed ashore by the waves. Yet somehow she felt more exposed with nothing but the lake so wide she couldn't see across it and empty cottages on either side of them. There was no one to hear a cry for help beyond a lone fishing boat bobbing in the water, not far from shore, braving the ominous black clouds amassed on the horizon.

"There's the nest." Kate pointed to the top corner of the awning. "Can you reach it?" Two minutes was all it would take to snatch the plants and get them back to the car. Then they could leave the second Tom returned.

Caleb hauled over a deck chair and gingerly poked his finger around the wasp's nest. "I got it!" He handed her the key with a triumphant smile.

With a quick glance in the direction Tom had run off, Kate peered through the window of the French door that opened into an L-shaped, open-concept living, dining, and kitchen area that filled the entire side and half of the back of the cottage. Assuring herself that the rattan furniture and glass accent tables appeared blissfully undisturbed, she slid the key into the lock.

At the rumble of thunder, Caleb crowded into the cottage behind her.

The place wasn't as muggy as she feared it might be. Hopefully Ryan hadn't forgotten to steam up the sauna before shutting in the plants. It would be enough of a setback that they'd have had nothing but a lone incandescent bulb for light for the last twenty-four hours. "This way," she said to Caleb and turned down the hall, except . . .

No light shone from the sauna's window.

Kate's heart tumbled. Had GPC already gotten to the plants?

Gripping the doorknob, she peeked in the window. At the sight of the plants lined up on the cedar platform, she blew out a breath. "They're here. We'll need a couple of boxes to carry them out," she said to Caleb, leaving the door closed. "I'll grab the recycling bin I saw at the curb. You see what you can find in the shed out back."

As Caleb sprinted out the back way, Kate hurried out the front door and snatched up the blue box.

A black SUV rumbled down the road toward her, and she darted back to the porch. But the door wouldn't budge. At the crunch of tires, her pulse ratcheted up. Caleb raced around the corner and immediately skidded to a stop, then backed away, his panic-stricken gaze fixed on a point beyond her.

She shot a glance over her shoulder. Zoe, Jarrett, and Smith hulked into the yard.

Fear icing her veins, Kate tried to think. If she could get

inside and lock the door, she could call 911 and find a bat or a broom handle or something to hold them off until Tom or the police got here.

All at once, Jarrett and Smith drew guns and aimed them at her chest. "Freeze!"

# 22

Tom clambered up a sand dune, searching for his runner. He couldn't have doubled back without Tom seeing him, and Tom had a bad feeling the guy was headed for the pickup they'd noticed on their drive in. As Tom reached the top of the dune, the guy darted into view.

Tom sailed down the sandy hill toward him and lunged.

They hit the ground with a bone-crushing thud. The guy flung a handful of sand in Tom's face and roared to his feet. Blinking against the sting, Tom curled his fists into the guy's shirt. The guy—Peter Ratcher?—hammered his heel into Tom's knee and broke away.

Tom doubled over at the pain. He should've known GPC's salesman was behind this. He'd shown him Baxter in the hardware store's surveillance tapes when investigating the counterfeiting case, before he knew Baxter was Kate's father, and if Peter had thought he was seeing a ghost then, he would've put two and two together when he'd seen Kate with Baxter in the ICU.

A *pooft* sliced the air, followed by a kick of sand.

Tom dove behind a log and drew his gun, scanning for the sniper. He couldn't be far, not with a silencer. He spotted the shooter aboard a small fishing boat a hundred yards off shore as a second *pooft* took down Ratcher. Tom got in three shots before the boat sped out of range, but not before a third shot ripped through Ratcher's arm. Ugly red stains bloomed on the leg of his tan-colored pants and shirt.

Tom raced to his side and dragged him to cover behind another wave-battered log that had swept up on shore. "Who's shooting at you?"

Ratcher shook his head. "I don't know," he rasped.

Tom pressed his palm to Ratcher's leg wound. "Did GPC send you here? What were you doing at that cottage?"

A black SUV careened around the dune onto the hard-packed beach.

"Get down!" Palming his gun once more, Tom took a bead on the SUV's closest window.

Two armed men in full tactical gear barreled out of the cab. "Police! Drop the weapon. Now."

"I'm Detective Tom Parker," Tom announced, laying his gun on the log and then slowly opening the flap of his blazer with two fingers to show them his badge.

Kate must've called them and explained the situation, because they took him at his word and focused on treating Ratcher.

"What were you doing at the cottage?" Tom grilled once more.

"Nothing. I wasn't at a cottage. Just out for a jog."

The officer doing a pat down pulled a lock pick out of

324

Ratcher's hip pocket. "Yeah? You always carry lock picks with you when you jog?"

"I found it on the beach."

Tom shook his head in disgust. "Hold him for questioning after he's treated. I'll check out the house, then meet you at the hospital." He'd half expected to see Kate and Caleb pounding down the beach by now, despite the gunshots. As he turned to head down the beach, he glimpsed the back of the one officer's flak jacket. *RCMP.*

Federal police? They didn't deal with break-and-enters in this region, unless they were connected to organized crime. Was he wrong about Gilmore and GPC being behind Kate's kidnapping? Tom hit the beach at a dead run. At the sight of a frantically waving Caleb racing toward him, full-blown panic exploded in his chest.

Caleb stopped, hands on his knees, and gulped big breaths. "The guy who was spying on my house. He's here. So's Jarrett King and some woman. They're holding Kate at gunpoint."

"Where?"

"The front of the cottage. We were gonna grab the plants so we could leave as soon as you got back."

"Okay, run up the beach. The officers Kate called should still be there. Tell them what's going on and that I need backup."

Caleb grew more wild-eyed than ever. "Kate didn't call anyone!"

Tom's heart tripped. "Okay, stick with me." He blasted back to the cottage, then, motioning Caleb to stay out of sight, edged along the side until he had a view of the front yard.

Zoe lifted her empty hands placatingly. "Listen to me,

Kate. This isn't what you think. We just needed to stop you. The house might be booby trapped."

"*Right*." Kate's response sounded sarcastic, but she snatched her hand from the doorknob and scowled at Jarrett, who still held a weapon on her. There was no sign of the third guy Caleb had mentioned.

"You're lower than pond scum," Kate hissed at Jarrett. "How could you use Patti like this?"

He shook his head. "I didn't think it would go this far. It was the most expedient way to get answers and ensure she was safe."

"How did you figure out I'd be here? You better not have hurt Ryan."

Tom's grip tightened on his gun. She was stalling for time, waiting for him. Trouble was, he was still outgunned and his phone was in his car on the other side of the yard. If he didn't think there might be some merit to the booby-trapped warning, he'd break in the back door and call for backup from inside the house.

"Kate." Zoe's urgent voice drew Kate's attention away from Jarrett. "We haven't hurt your friend. We found you by tracking Tom's cell phone. We want the same thing you do—to keep these plants out of the wrong hands."

Kate snorted. "From where I'm standing, I'm *looking* at the wrong hands."

A whisper of a smile rippled across Zoe's lips. "Have you heard of Juanita Lopez?"

Kate jolted at the name of the woman her father had been accused of murdering.

"I can see that you have. She was my older sister. I was studying medicine in DC when the fire destroyed our village. I came to Canada to make certain she didn't die in vain."

Tom snorted at that piece of fiction. If Zoe was interested in justice, she never would've killed Ian.

"I work for the US government, and Jarrett and"—Zoe motioned in the direction the third guy must've wandered—"Smith work for CSIS. Do you know what that is?"

*CSIS!* Tom's mind whirled. *No way. Zeb would've told me.*

"Canada's spy agency," Kate said, thankfully not sounding like she believed Zoe either.

"That's right. Due to the international nature of GPC's work, we've been coordinating efforts to close this case. Detective Parker's friend with the National Security Agency was monitoring related electronic communications, which is why he was able to connect us with your father."

Kate crossed her arms. "You're lying. If my dad was on your side, you would've let him talk to me."

Zoe's lips pressed together in a grim line.

"Drop the gun," a man's voice hissed into Tom's ear as cold steel nudged his ribs.

Tom brought his arm down hard on his assailant's gun hand and plowed his boot into the guy's kneecap.

The guy—Smith—dropped to his knees with a howl. Tom shoved his face into the dirt, then wrenched his arm behind his back and snapped on a handcuff a second before Jarrett appeared.

Tom hauled Smith to his feet, holding him as a shield, and closed the distance between him and Jarrett, all the while aiming his gun at Zoe so she didn't get any bright ideas about grabbing Kate. "Drop your weapon."

"Detective, we're working with your friend, Zeb. We were trying to explain to—"

"Oh, yeah? Interesting thing is . . . Zeb isn't talking. You have anything to do with that? 'Cause I heard you claim you work for the US government, but here's another little-known *factoid*—government employees don't kidnap witnesses and blow up their cars and drug them."

"We didn't kidnap her. We asked her to come with us. And when the car blew up, we took her into hiding for her own protection."

"A convenient excuse, considering *you* blew up the car."

"No, I swear we didn't," Jarrett said to Kate, not Tom. "I asked my mechanic to put in a device that would allow us to track and disable the car and to listen in on conversations. That's all. He's done work for CSIS before. But clearly Wolfe got to him. Probably offered him twice as much money to add a detonation device to the upgrade."

"Right. Just like Zoe didn't blow up my partner's car."

Zoe winced. "That bomb was meant for me as much as Ian."

Tom's blood boiled with enough heat to detonate the lot of them right here.

"My questions around the pharmaceutical world about diablo piel had clearly made the wrong people nervous," Zoe went on as if she actually expected him to believe her. "That's why the FBI sent me into hiding and upped their surveillance of GPC."

He hitched up Smith's arm. "And how do you explain him? Government agents don't drive men off the escarpment."

"I didn't!"

Tom clamped tighter on the man's arm. "Caleb saw you, and you followed him back to his house to make sure he didn't talk."

"No, he saw me because I'd been tracking GPC's men."

"If you saw who killed Vic, why didn't you arrest the men responsible?"

"That's not important right now," Zoe interjected.

"Quiet," Tom blasted. "I want to hear what he has to say."

The man twisted around and looked Tom in the eye. "I didn't see them do it, and until we have stronger evidence against Wolfe, we didn't want him to know we were onto him. I was trying to help the kid when he came racing out of the woods. I don't blame him for being scared. Once I figured out who he was, I kept watch on his house to make sure Vic's murderers didn't get to him."

"But I saw you trying to buy Verna's property," Kate blurted.

"He posed as an interested businessman to try to figure out why GPC was interested in it," Zoe said, sounding impatient. "Now step away from the cottage so we can see what we're looking at here."

"No, this is private property. You have no right to be here. If you're really who you say you are, you can come back with a search warrant."

Imagining what Kate figured she'd do with the plants in the meantime, Tom would've chuckled if the situation weren't so serious. He cleared his throat. "Seems to me if you were really CIA, you'd have known what GPC was interested in."

Zoe scowled. "Yes, biological weapons. Twenty years ago, we suspected GPC of experimenting with diablo piel. Trouble was, any proof we might've found burned up with their research lab in Colombia."

"You had Baxter."

"At the time, we didn't understand amendoso's significance.

We figured GPC's posturing about Baxter's theft was a front to deflect attention from what they'd really been doing there or to frame him as a researcher gone rogue."

Kate stomped her foot, her eyes flaring. "My dad would never have been party to developing biological weapons."

"Well, unfortunately, he didn't stick around long enough for either of us to figure out we were on the same side. Then with the eradication of diablo piel, GPC eventually fell off our radar . . . until you accused Molly Gilmore of killing your head researcher."

"Because her father and Wolfe were friends?"

"Yes. Before Tom's partner was killed he raised suspicions of Gilmore's link to at least two diablo piel incidents he'd profited from. But twenty years ago, the plant was everywhere, so even with Ian's theory, we'd had no reason to think GPC had supplied Gilmore with the plant."

"So . . . what? You think Gilmore sent his daughter to kill Daisy as a favor? That it would somehow help GPC's partnership bid?"

"We don't know for sure. GPC had already approached the research station about partnering before her death and were turned down. They petitioned the mayor for support, but it wasn't until after Daisy's death that the facility decided to consider the partnership offer and it went public."

"They needed the positive PR after having their head researcher of depression treatments supposedly kill herself," Jarrett spoke up.

"Since Gilmore profited big time from using diablo piel, which GPC likely supplied him," Zoe continued, "we figure Gilmore owed him. If not for Kate's sleuthing, investigators may have suspected Crump with his record of conning old women out of their money, but not a soul would have suspected Gilmore's daughter."

"Then after your revelations about amendoso," Jarrett said, "NSA started monitoring all related internet traffic. It didn't take long to trace one of GPC's senior researchers, a researcher who'd been in Colombia twenty years ago, to an exchange with Patti's father about the unique plant he'd found growing right here in Port Aster. We soon concluded that GPC was looking to profit off an antidote."

"The NSA deleted Patti's father's inquiries on that forum? Shut down the blog Patti found?"

"We couldn't afford to have anyone else stumble upon them."

Jarrett holstered his weapon. "But then you got too inquisitive—and everything unraveled."

"You're blaming this on me?" Kate's voice rose indignantly, and she slipped her hands behind her back.

The black SUV carrying the officers that had commandeered Tom's suspect squealed to a stop in front of the cottage.

Kate's gaze shot to Tom's, her shoulders twisting oddly. "They're the guys that kidnapped me." The door behind her suddenly gave way, and she took a step back.

"Get away from the house," the officers shouted, jumping out of the SUV. "He's rigged it to blow!"

Tom shoved Smith into Jarrett and raced for the porch. "Kate, don't move," he shouted at her as she teetered in the doorway. "Ratcher was here. That's who I chased. These guys took him into custody. If they say it's rigged—"

"How can you trust them?" Her voice pitched higher. "If these guys are cops, why didn't they just say so when they kidnapped me?" Kate snatched up the recycle bin sitting just outside the door and, looking ready to close it, set the bin on the floor behind her.

Zoe stopped the stampeding officers with a lift of her hand, then patted the air as if that would calm everyone's tempers. "We didn't explain because we'd hoped we wouldn't need to reveal this much."

Kate shook her head at Zoe, then held Tom's gaze, silently pleading with him to listen. "The cottage isn't rigged, Tom. I've already been inside. I've seen the plants." She glanced over her shoulder and nudged the bin further behind her with her toe. "Ratcher must've figured out they were here and come to get them for GPC."

"Ratcher works for Gilmore," the officer with a nasty gash on his cheek declared.

"What?" Zoe, Jarrett, and Tom said as one voice.

"He just told us, because he's scared spitless that Gilmore will send someone to the hospital to finish him off. Gilmore's been paying him for months to do his dirty work. He figures he knows too much and that Gilmore sent the sniper to make sure he didn't talk."

"But he works for GPC," Kate said, still hovering in the doorway. "Gilmore and Wolfe are friends."

Zoe slanted her attention toward the officer and lifted an eyebrow as if equally curious for an explanation.

The officer held up his hands as if to say "don't ask me." "I'm just telling you what he said. Ratcher claims Gilmore's daughter heard about the false alarm at the house yesterday afternoon and zoomed over in time to spot Ryan loading amendoso plants in his truck. She followed him out here and then told her father, who contacted Ratcher."

Kate closed her eyes in a slow blink as if she couldn't believe she hadn't guessed as much. "That's what she meant by that smirk at the B and B last night." Kate's gaze shifted to Tom. "Remember? When she said she only knows about good plants."

"Yeah, well, her father goes for a lot less subtlety," the officer said. "The car bomb was supposed to take you out. The cottage explosion was supposed to take care of Ryan."

His heart racing, Tom scanned the porch and entrance for trip wires, then circled his hand toward his chest. "Kate, walk carefully toward me."

"Tom, I've been inside already. He's lying or Ratcher's lying. Someone's lying. If my dad trusted them, they would have let me talk to him." Her voice broke. "I can't let the wrong people get their hands on them. Not after everything my father sacrificed."

Zoe and Scarface finished a whispered conversation, then Zoe drilled Kate with a deadly serious stare. "Can you smell propane?"

"No." She nudged the bin a few more inches along the entryway behind her with a shift of her foot.

"Ratcher purchased a propane barbecue tank, likely set it in the room where the plants are, and rigged a trigger to ignite the gas. Did you go in the room where the plants are?"

Kate's eyes widened, and she squeaked out, "No."

"The trigger could be something as simple as a broken lightbulb," the officer added. "The second you flip the light switch, the filaments spark and ignite the gas."

Kate gasped. "The light was out."

Tom glimpsed a shifting of shadows behind her. "Where's Caleb?"

She whirled toward the back of the cottage. "Caleb, no, don't go in there!"

Tom hit the doorway at a dead run as a deafening explosion ripped through the house.

Tom's face hovered above hers, a halo of light shining around it like an angel's. He was pleading with her, but she couldn't hear his words, couldn't hear anything. Then everything went dark, but Kate could feel his breath whisper across her ear. Suddenly his words crystalized. "I love you. Don't leave me. Don't you dare leave me. Promise you'll marry me. Say it."

*Yes.* Kate struggled to make her answer audible, but her vocal cords refused to cooperate.

"About time you woke up."

*That wasn't Tom.* Kate slit open her eyes at the sound of Patti's voice, but the instant the light hit her, her head throbbed and she squeezed them closed again. "What happened? Where am I?"

"Ryan's cottage exploded and your big, handsome hunk of a fiancé saved your hide. You're in the hospital."

"Fiancé?" Kate's eyes sprang open and she pushed herself into a sitting position so fast her head spun. *It wasn't a dream?*

Laughter filled the room. Male and female.

Kate grabbed her pounding head and sank back to her pillow. "You shouldn't tease about something like that." She squinted past Patti, trying to make out the dark-haired man standing beside her. His laughter hadn't sounded like Tom's. Her heart jolted as recognition settled in. Jarrett.

Patti squeezed her hand. "I'm not kidding, Kate. Tom's been sitting at your bedside night and day for three days, telling you to wake up because the two of you have a wedding to plan. You don't remember him asking you?" Patti shot Jarrett a worried look. "He's not going to handle that news too well. You might want to fake it."

Light glinted off a stone on Patti's finger, catching the corner of Kate's eye.

Kate focused in on Patti's left hand and gasped. "You're engaged? To who?"

Patti wrapped an arm around Jarrett's waist. "To Jarrett, of course."

"But he's a . . . a . . ."

"Spy?" Patti filled in.

Scrunching her eyes against the painfully bright light, Kate peered at him. "Is that really what he is?"

"That's privileged information, I'm afraid," Jarrett said.

At the memory of the showdown outside Ryan's house, Kate's heart shattered. "Well, we may have kept the plants out of GPC's hands, but now they're lost forever, along with whatever incredible medicinal value they could've given the world."

"Not completely lost. There's still the one from my solarium," Patti reminded her. "Of course, Jarrett already turned it in."

"Just doing my job," he said. "And for the record, I'm sorry I didn't do a better job of protecting you."

"Was that supposed to be your job?"

He shrugged. "Not exactly."

"His government contract expires at the end of the month, and he's decided not to renew," Patti gushed.

Jarrett hugged her to his side. "So we can live a normal life."

"You're not just saying that?" Kate needled. "So you can pretend to *not* be a spy?"

Jarrett laughed. "I see you've acquired Tom's distrustful tendencies."

Her stomach fluttered at the mention of Tom's name. Had she imagined his warm hand cradling hers as she slept? His soothing voice whispering in her ear? "Where is Tom?"

"I sent him home to have a shower and get some sleep. I'm sure he won't take time to sleep, but at least I convinced him that he should be better groomed the next time his bride-to-be feasted her eyes on him."

Kate giggled. But at the vision of herself walking down the aisle alone, she immediately sobered.

"What's wrong?"

Tears blurred her eyes. "I wish my dad could walk me down the aisle."

"That could be arranged," a voice boomed from the doorway.

"Tom!" Their gazes joined in a toe-tingling tango. His eyes radiated a love so pure it stole her breath. And his mile-wide smile filled her to bursting. How had she doubted for a single moment that she could trust this man?

"Hi, beautiful. Miss me?"

Reflexively, she reached up to smooth her hair and panicked when it wasn't all there.

Tom rushed to her side and caught her hands in his. "It's okay, sweetie. It will grow back."

Her gaze dropped to the thick white gauze swaddling his hand. "You're hurt."

He shrugged one shoulder as if the injury scarcely compared to singed hair.

But suddenly the whole scenario crashed through her mind. Caleb disappearing down the hall with a recycle bin for loading the plants. The whiff of propane. The explo—

"Caleb! How's Caleb?"

"Doing well," Jarrett said. "The explosion threw him clear into the other room, and he escaped with only minor burns on his legs and a broken arm. He's already home."

"He is?" Kate searched Tom's eyes. "I should've listened to you. I'm sorry. I didn't think anyone would get hurt but me." She fingered the gauze wrapped around his hand, the explosion replaying across her vision. Tom had lunged for her, shielded her body with his own, as a ball of fire swept over them. The smell of smoke and things she didn't want to imagine filled her nostrils at the memory of him snuffing out her burning hair with his bare hand. She tentatively patted the new hairdo once more.

"Hey." Tom danced his fingers through her short locks, coaxing her gaze back to his. "I happen to think you look cute in the pixie cut Serena did for you."

Kate gasped. "Serena cut my hair?" Her voice spiked higher. "While I was unconscious?"

"It was my idea," Patti admitted. "And you kind of consented in one of your half-conscious moments. I didn't want you seeing it all burnt away."

"But . . . but you asked *Serena*? Didn't she try to poison you?"

Patti wagged her head from side to side. "Yes and no. Turns out she wasn't trying to kill me. She added disinfectant to our hand lotion during a tour of the lab she'd sweet-talked one of the techs into. She said she knew you wouldn't use it because of the scent, but she figured it would make my skin go gross and repulse Jarrett into breaking up with me."

Jarrett kissed her cheek. "Instead it brought us closer together."

Kate collapsed back against the pillow, having trouble taking in everything that had transpired while she was sleeping. "So what happens to Serena?"

"Since she confessed, she'll probably get a gazillion hours of community service." Patti grinned.

"I finally convinced her that spending an evening chatting at a gala fund-raiser for my dad's mayoral campaign followed by a good-night kiss scarcely constituted a date. And the idea that we ever had been or ever would be a couple was all in her head."

"Speaking of couples . . ." Tom pinned his gaze on Jarrett and jerked his head toward the door.

Jarrett chuckled. "I think that's our cue to scram. Glad to see you awake, Kate. I'm sure we'll see you again soon."

Alone with Tom, Kate suddenly felt shy. And at a bit of a disadvantage. Had she really agreed to marry him?

Tom reached into his shirt pocket and dropped to one knee.

Her breath whisked from her chest in a gasp.

"I know this isn't exactly the most romantic setting, but I can't wait another second to do this properly." With a trembling hand, he held out an exquisite diamond cluster set in a delicately etched gold band. "Since the day I lost my FBI partner, I've had this paralyzing fear of making another wrong decision. A decision that could cost the life of someone I deeply care about. But I have never been surer of anything than how I feel about you. From the moment I met you, I admired your unwavering faith in your friends. I longed to be someone you could trust and hated that my decisions destroyed that trust."

Her heart ached at the agony in his voice. Curling onto her side toward him, she reached over and trailed her fingers through his dark hair. "I know you were only trying to protect me."

"Yes." His voice cracked. He swallowed hard. "I can't help myself. I can't imagine life without you." He searched her face, his love in his eyes, the diamond ring trembling in the space between.

She smiled teasingly. "Did you have something you wanted to ask me?"

He jolted, clearly not having realized that he'd forgotten the most important part of his speech.

"Kate Adams Baxter, I love you more than words can express. Will you do me the honor of being my wife?"

Her throat clogged with tears at his use of her father's name, a name she hadn't used in twenty years but whose honest worth he'd helped restore in her mind and heart. She cupped a hand over her mouth.

He started to look a little worried at her hesitation.

Not wanting to cause him a moment's more distress, she lunged into his arms. "Yes!"

Her IV line tugged painfully at her skin, and the IV pole clattered against the bedrail.

Rising quickly, Tom rescued it and then perched on the edge of her bed. "Now, where were we?" He took her left hand and lovingly slid the diamond ring onto her finger, then cradled her in the crook of his arm and brushed a chaste kiss across her lips.

The love shining in his eyes made her insides cartwheel. She clasped his face and drew his mouth back to hers, pouring all her love into her kiss. The taste of him filled her as he enfolded her in his arms and deepened the kiss, stirring a longing that begged a lifetime to satisfy.

Pulling back, he traced his thumb along her bottom lip, pure contentment sparkling in his eyes. "I forgot to mention that I did it right this time and asked your father's permission first."

Joy exploded afresh in her heart. "He's awake?"

# 23

Tom watched quietly from the sidelines as the doctor checked Kate over. The nurse had insisted on the examination before she would allow him to wheel Kate to her father's room. Tom was still furious with Zeb for letting him believe Kate died, but he had to give him credit for how quickly he'd managed to arrange her father's transfer. This reunion was the best gift Tom could give her. But from the way Kate's gaze kept straying to his, she clearly didn't understand how bad her concussion had been. He hated the thought of how quickly that might change once her pain meds wore off.

His cell phone vibrated. Glancing at the screen, he said, "I'll be right back. I need to take this." He slipped into the hall and found a private alcove to take the call. Tamping down the irritation that had swelled in his chest at the sight of Zeb's name, he clicked Connect.

"Hey, I got more good news for you." Zeb's cheery intonation only irritated Tom more.

"Oh?" Tom said without a trace of enthusiasm.

Zeb snorted. "Don't tell me you're still mad at me?"

"Are you kidding me?" Tom exploded. "You let me think the FBI thought my partner was selling secrets. That his girlfriend was a spy."

"Hey, she is."

"For our side!" Tom hauled down his voice. "I thought she killed Ian. You're lucky I didn't shoot her on sight."

Zeb chuckled. "You're too good an officer to stoop to a personal vendetta."

"Don't be so sure," Tom growled, contemplating how he might pay his so-called friend back.

"Hey, I thought you were a believer. You're supposed to forgive me. You know how these cases work. My hands were tied."

"Yeah, I get why you did it," Tom conceded, knowing Zeb had probably revealed more than he should have. "And I forgive you. But you're still a jerk."

Zeb laughed. "I can live with that."

"What's your news?"

"We've gained joint government approval to fund Kate and her dad and Zoe to head up additional research on amendoso for its medicinal benefits."

Tom's throat soured at the thought of seeing Zoe in Kate's lab. He'd spent too much time demonizing her as Ian's killer. He cleared the unpleasant taste. "That is great news. Kate will be thrilled. Thanks for letting me know."

"Consider it a wedding present."

Tom grinned. "Okay, you're not a jerk. I appreciate you championing the suggestion to include her."

"Afraid I can't take all the credit. Zoe's the one you owe the thanks to."

*And an apology.* Tom felt gutted. He pocketed his phone,

then, rounding the corner, came face-to-face with the very woman he'd spent the past year despising, in between despising himself for failing Ian.

"There you are." Zoe's cheery tone sounded strained. "The nurse said I'd find you over here."

"I hear I owe you my thanks." He cringed at how insincere he sounded.

"Zeb called you?"

"Yes."

"I was on my way up to see Baxter now."

Tom nodded.

Zoe shifted awkwardly from one foot to the other. "I guess I'll see you around." She turned to leave.

"Wait." He dropped his gaze as she pivoted back his way. "Was Ian just . . . a job to you?"

"No!" The denial sounded as if it'd been ripped from her soul. "We didn't have much time together before . . ." She blinked repeatedly, swallowed. "But I was falling in love with him, and I think he felt the same about me."

Tom lifted his gaze to hers, sensed the moisture pooling in his eyes as he offered her a bittersweet smile. "He was head-over-heels in love with you."

The corner of her lips trembled upward. "He was a good man."

"He was."

"And he thought the world of you. Once we realized the significance of what he'd stumbled on to, he hated that he couldn't tell you what was going on. He said you'd always had his back."

Tom swiped at the tears that leaked from his eyes. "I felt like I let him down."

Zoe reached across the divide between them and squeezed his hand. "You didn't. I'm sorry you've been so tormented by this."

"Did Gilmore plant the bomb that killed him?"

"We believe he was behind it, yes. He has a lot of connections. Someone in the loop could've easily informed him about our suspicions. Proving it turned out to be more difficult, but with Ratcher's testimony, we can charge him with several counts of conspiracy to commit murder, which will hopefully loosen the lips of a few other witnesses that can help us prove Ian's theory. Wolfe is already negotiating a plea bargain in exchange for a full confession."

Good. Tom was glad to hear the convictions didn't rest on Kate's testimony. She'd been looking over her shoulder for too many months already. "Anyone admit to killing Patti Goodman's parents?"

"No, that appears to have truly been an accident. But police will review all the evidence in light of the new information."

Tom stuck out his hand and clasped Zoe's in a friendly handshake. "Thank you." His thoughts flashed from her tortured expression following the blast that killed Ian to how tortured he'd felt watching Kate's car engulfed in flames. If not for Zoe and her men, Kate may not have made it out. For the past few days, he'd been imagining a dozen different choices he might've made if he'd been in Zeb's or Zoe's or Jarrett's position, but would the outcome have been any better?

One man was dead, but Baxter, Caleb, and Kate were alive and safe. The bad guys were in custody, and some amendoso plants had even been salvaged.

As Tom reached Kate's room, the doctor stepped back from the bed and hooked his stethoscope around his neck. "You're doing well. I don't see any reason why you can't visit your father's room. But move easy. Your head is going to give you trouble for a while yet."

"I will. Thank you, doctor!" Kate swung her legs off the bed the instant the doctor turned, clearly eager to see her dad, but all Tom wanted to do was hold her in his arms and relish that she was finally out of danger.

"Hold on," the nurse scolded, hurrying in with a wheelchair. She set it beside the bed and locked the wheels. "You're not going anywhere without this."

Tom helped Kate make the transfer from bed to chair and then tucked a blanket around her legs. "I can take over from here," he said to the nurse.

"I still can't believe he's really here," Kate blurted as Tom turned her chair down the hall.

"Here. And looking forward to seeing you."

"So he isn't in any more danger? Have they arrested . . . who have they arrested? With all Zoe's and Jarrett's revelations, I've lost track of who the bad guys are."

Slowing his pace, Tom bent to bring his mouth close to her ear and lowered his voice. "Turns out that after one of Wolfe's researchers found Goodman's question about amendoso online, Wolfe confided in Gilmore. When Gilmore learned Wolfe wanted to partner with the research station, he set up the plan to kill Daisy, hoping to put an end to the research that he feared would turn officials' attention on him."

"Turn their attention more than murder?"

"Yeah, well. He didn't count on you figuring out it was murder."

"So GPC really had been developing biological weapons twenty years ago?"

"It turns out that when Wolfe discovered diablo piel's weapons potential—a capability he claims he didn't think would be lethal—he proposed to Gilmore that he use it to make the indigenous people working at competitive mines too ill to work and too scared to return. The idea was that Gilmore benefitted by crippling his competition's production, and then GPC could come in and save the day with their wonder drug and, by gaining international publicity, fast-track FDA approvals."

"They were far enough along in their research to go into production?"

"Not really. They needed cash. Wolfe figured the international community would step up to the plate once they saw amendoso's capabilities."

Kate shuddered. "But the miners died before GPC had a chance to play hero."

"Yeah, and worse for them. Investigators quickly traced the cause to diablo piel. Only, like my dad said, they assumed drug lords, not Gilmore, were responsible."

"So Gilmore and GPC escaped being implicated."

"Not quite. Gilmore did. He wasn't on their radar at all back then. But because Wolfe panicked, fearing they'd trace the diablo piel to his lab in Colombia, he arranged for your father to bring enough samples back to headquarters and then had the lab torched. But he hadn't counted on a fire in a remote Colombian village making the international news."

"Why did it?"

"Because of its proximity to a prime area for diablo piel. A pilot flying over to spray herbicides spotted the fire and

346

reported it, fearing it might spread into the fields and cause worse devastation than the mine incident. When your father heard the reports in the airport, he knew it was GPC's doing."

"If the government knew GPC had been proliferating biological weapons already twenty years ago, why didn't they shut them down?" Her rising voice left no question about how inept she thought they'd been, and unfortunately attracted too much attention from the patients shuffling along the hallway.

Speaking even more softly than before, Tom said, "They had no proof. Your dad's story was their only lead." His lips grazed her ear, and he had to fight the urge to kiss her senseless right in the hallway. "They arranged for him to go into witness protection, but when the detectives working his case died soon after, he spooked."

Kate pressed her palms to her head.

Tom stopped the chair, panic blazing through his chest as he hunkered in front of her. "What's wrong?" He took her wrist to check her pulse. "Are you getting pains? Dizzy?"

Kate's gaze turned apologetic, and she shook her head. "No, it just seems that if Dad hadn't disappeared, this could've been resolved twenty years ago."

Tom steered her wheelchair into a small alcove to give them a little more privacy. "More likely, he'd be dead. If Wolfe or Gilmore had no qualms about killing cops, you can be sure they would've taken care of your father at their first opportunity."

A shudder rippled across Kate's shoulders.

"To add to Gilmore's motivation, he likely didn't know whether his competitors—which happened to be organized crime—had figured out he was behind the attack. If he thought your father sold out to them to make a quick buck, he likely spent a few years turning over every rock to make sure the plants were truly gone."

"Did they arrest the men who killed Vic and threatened Caleb?"

"Yes."

Kate let out a grunt of disbelief. "All this happened while I was sleeping?"

Tom stroked the furrows creasing her brow. "No, it happened because you refused to let the bad guys win." He wheeled her out of the alcove and pressed a kiss to the top of her head. "Once the chief learned the extent of the federal investigation that had been going on right under our nose, he offered a humble apology for letting his ego get in the way of letting me do my job."

"But I don't understand. If Lemur Face saw Vic get killed, why did he let you guys conclude otherwise?"

Tom chuckled at the nickname that he suspected the beady-eyed CSIS operative would never live down. "Smith didn't see the guys actually kill Vic, and because he didn't want Wolfe to realize the police were onto him, he chose not to call in a tip. But he did manage to unearth outstanding arrest warrants on the pair and had them picked up a few days later."

"But by then Caleb had run away."

"Yeah, and it wasn't until after Jarrett reported the lemur sketch you'd doctored that the feds realized Smith had become our prime suspect in Vic Lawton's murder." Tom paused outside her father's room and came around the chair so he could look into her eyes once more. "We're here. Are you ready?"

Kate pressed her palm to her chest and took a deep breath. "Yes?"

He chuckled. "Are you asking me?"

Kate's dad must've heard them talking, because the next moment a rusty voice filtered through the doorway. "Katy, is that you?"

Kate sprang from the chair and rushed into her father's arms. "Daddy!"

Tom's future father-in-law beamed, and Tom felt as if his own heart might burst at the joyous reunion. He wistfully imagined one day having a daughter of his own who would love him with such abandon.

"Katy," her father began, "I'm so sor—"

Kate pressed her fingers to her father's lips. "It's okay, Dad. I understand why you did what you did." She buried her face against his chest. "I hate the time together that we lost, but I don't want to waste a second of our future dwelling on it. You told me to never forget that you loved me, and I didn't."

"My Katy, I'm so proud of you." He wrapped her in his arms, tears streaming down his face. "How I've missed you."

Tom whisked a tear from his own cheek. "Well, it sounds like you'll have plenty of time to get reacquainted." He filled Kate in on Zeb's phone call.

Kate turned from her father's embrace, her eyes widening. "The government's okay with us experimenting on the antidote to a biological weapon?"

Kate's dad, who'd already been apprised of the proposed plan by Zoe, hugged her to his side. "You heard what the man said, and I can't imagine a better job than working side by side with my daughter."

"According to Zoe," Tom interjected, "in her village, they'd rub the amendoso juice over exposed skin just like you did with the jewelweed on your poison ivy rash."

"So our theory was right?"

"In part. Whether ingesting it would help victims who'd inhaled toxic smoke is unknown. The researchers who studied the plants CSIS recovered from Vic Lawton hadn't realized the role parasites play in the process."

Kate turned back to her dad. "Did you know they were experimenting with biological weapons?"

"Not at first. When my boss sent me to assess the lab and bring back samples, I was under the illusion the researchers on-site worked for a university. I hadn't been involved with the project before that. When I saw news of the fire, I figured GPC wanted to make a mint off the plant's pharmaceutical value and was corrupt enough to kill anyone who got in their way." He shook his head. "But after Zoe and others started interrogating me, I realized a lot more was going on and I didn't know who I could trust."

Kate blew out a breath. "I know that feeling." Her shy smile, directed his way, turned Tom's insides to mush. "All Tom wanted to do was keep me safe, and I was so focused on needing to find out amendoso's secret that I was afraid to trust him. And God. I thought figuring out the secret would be the only way to convince the authorities to let me see you, but . . ."

Her father nodded. "Isn't it funny how often what we think we want is really only how we'd imagined getting it? For me, that was staying away to keep you safe." He squeezed her hand. "Makes me glad that sometimes God says no so he can give us what we truly desire."

Beaming, Kate held out her hand to Tom. "Like having my father at my wedding to this wonderful man."

Matching her beaming smile, Tom pressed a kiss to her

cheek. "And you'll even get the opportunity to figure out amendoso's secret after all."

"What about Molly? Can you prove she murdered Daisy now? Will the prosecutor bring new charges?"

"Unfortunately no, but the missing evidence in her attempted murder of you has mysteriously shown up. I suspect that whichever lowlife in our department conveniently 'misallocated' it got nervous when the hammer came down on Gilmore. Molly's lawyers are now leaning toward a plea bargain far less generous than the one offered three months ago."

"It won't be enough for taking Daisy's life."

Tom brushed his thumb across her cheek. "But thanks to you, the truth has prevailed, and the Lord will see that justice is meted out, his way."

Kate nibbled on her bottom lip. "Daisy always used to tell me that I needed to trust God in everything. And now that I've finally learned that lesson—well, am learning—I know she would want me to trust him on the verdict."

Tom smiled. He felt like a better man just standing at her side. Reaching out to take her into his arms, he tumbled into her gorgeous green eyes.

# Epilogue

TWO YEARS LATER

Kate pushed through the door of A Cup or Two and smiled at the tinkle of the doorbell, fondly remembering the many times she and Daisy had trundled through the door for "a spot of tea," as her dear mentor had liked to call it. If she were to see how Kate trundled along now, with only three weeks before her little bundle of blessing was due, Daisy would be urging her to take just the right combination of herbs to encourage an easy delivery. Kate inhaled, relishing the shop's soothing aromas, grateful they no longer made her queasy as they had for the first five months.

"Over here." Her friend Julie waved from their usual table near the fireplace.

Kate spooned raspberry leaves into a cup and brought it to the girl behind the counter.

Beth, the shop's owner, joined her with her rosy-cheeked toddler in tow. Her eyes twinkled as she glanced into Kate's cup. "I guess you're praying that Tom's skepticism about all our herbal teas won't be vindicated?"

"Trust me"—Kate smoothed a hand over her expansive belly—"this time, he's praying I'm right."

Beth chuckled. "Husbands hate to see their wives in pain and be helpless to do much about it."

Kate's spine tingled. It didn't matter that she and Tom had already been married for more than a year and a half. Whenever she thought of him being her husband, joyous little goose bumps erupted. As she imagined Tom fretting over her in the delivery room, Beth's little guy rubbed his eyes and buried his face against his mother's shoulder, looking ready for a nap. Kate tousled his fine blond curls. "Whatever the pain, it'll be totally worth it."

"Absolutely."

Kate carried her tea to the table, and Julie gave her a once-over with a widening grin. "I love getting together with you. You look like a bigger beached whale than me."

"Give yourself a few weeks," Kate said teasingly as she braced her hands on the back of the chair and awkwardly lowered her bottom to the seat. She couldn't have been happier that her former roommate and dearest friend would be having a child within weeks of her. And after two years of long days in the research lab, she was ready to enjoy this new season of her life.

"I saw your dad at the library yesterday. He said that he's all moved into his new house in town and is over-the-moon excited about becoming a grandpa."

"Oh, yes. Tom's dad too. And his sister about becoming an auntie." Sipping her tea, Kate smiled to herself at how lavishly the Lord had blessed her with family once more.

Julie's gaze lifted above Kate's head, and before a word was spoken, Kate sensed Tom's approach. "How's my famous wife?" His warm breath whispered across her cheek as he squeezed her shoulders.

"Oh no, did that reporter who called mention me in his article after all?"

Grinning, Tom tossed a glossy national news magazine onto the table. "It was a bit more than a *mention*." Jeremiah Gilmore's picture filled the cover with a headline about the trial. Tom tapped his finger to a smaller heading beneath the picture.

"Herbal Researcher Kate Parker Solves More Than the Mystery of Plants," she read, stunned. "What is this about?"

"All the cases you've solved." Tom flipped open the magazine to an article about how her sleuthing had solved Daisy's and Vic's murders, a counterfeiting case, and poisonings and culminated in the conviction of Jeremiah Gilmore for several counts of manslaughter and a list of other charges. "It also talks about the promising results the depression treatment you developed with Daisy is getting in clinical trials, but I like this part the best." Tom pointed to the end of the article and read, "Over the course of her informal investigations, Kate uncovered numerous secrets harbored by the small town of Port Aster and endeared her heart to the town's lead detective." He brushed a tender kiss across her forehead and murmured, "Who prays her sleuthing days are now behind her."

Kate gasped. "It doesn't say that!" She searched the article for the spot he'd been reading.

He chuckled. "No." He stroked her swollen belly. "But

one hundred percent true. The thought of keeping two of you out of mischief is making me miss my beauty sleep."

"Wait until the baby comes," Julie chimed in. "You won't remember what a good night's sleep is."

Kate squeezed Tom's arm. "Nothing to worry about. You already look great to me!"

# Patti's Favorite
## Chocolate/Cream Cheese Cupcakes

| | |
|---|---|
| 8 oz | cream cheese, softened |
| ½ cup | sugar |
| 2 | eggs |
| 1½ cups | chocolate chips |

| | | | |
|---|---|---|---|
| 2¼ cups | all-purpose flour | ½ cup | vegetable oil |
| 1½ tsp | baking soda | 1½ cups | water |
| ¾ tsp | salt | 1½ Tbsp | vinegar |
| 1½ cups | sugar | 1½ tsp | vanilla |
| ⅓ cup | cocoa (unsweetened) | | |

| | |
|---|---|
| 3 Tbsp | sugar |
| ¾ cup | chopped walnuts or pecans |

## Instructions:

Preheat oven to 350° F and line 2 dozen medium muffin cups with paper liners.

For the cream cheese mixture, combine softened cream cheese with ½ cup sugar and eggs in a small bowl and mix well. Stir in chocolate chips, then set bowl aside.

In a large bowl, mix flour, baking soda, salt, 1½ cups sugar, and cocoa. Combine oil, water, vinegar, and vanilla, then beat into the flour mixture for 2 minutes. Fill muffin cups half full, then top each with a large spoonful of cream cheese mixture. Sprinkle tops with sugar and nuts.

Bake for 20 to 30 minutes or until cream cheese mixture is golden. Let cool 10 minutes before removing from pans.

# A Note from the Author

*Dear Reader,*

*I hope you've enjoyed the Port Aster Secrets series as much as I enjoyed writing it. I'd love to hear from you— what surprised you, what made you laugh, and which secrets you managed to guess. You can email me at connect@SandraOrchard.com or find me at Facebook .com/SandraOrchard.*

*As you've probably guessed, diablo piel and amendoso are fictional plants; however, the other plant details in the novel are true. Don't burn poison ivy. Inhaling the smoke really can kill you.*

*Throughout this series, Kate struggled with trust. Her father's faked death left her scarred and feeling abandoned. And she struggled to truly trust God. Have you been hurt or abandoned or felt as if God is too out of reach to care about you? Kate's feelings and yours are natural, but there is a healing balm better than any herb or tea—God's Word. In his Word, we uncover the depth of his love and the magnitude of his promises.*

*If you'd like to explore the issues raised in this book and the others in the series, you can find study guide questions along with other bonus features, such as location pictures, character interviews, and deleted scenes, at www.SandraOrchard.com/bonus-features. I'm also happy to participate in book club discussions via Skype or FaceTime. If you're interested, send me an email.*

*God bless.*

*Sandra O*

# Acknowledgments

Working with my editor, Vicki Crumpton, and the Revell team on this series has been a fabulous experience. A huge thanks to each one of the many staff members who play a role in delivering these books into readers' hands. You are tremendous encouragers and a delight to work with.

My deepest thanks goes to the Lord for inspiring the stories I write and blessing me with incredibly supportive family members, friends, and colleagues.

And thank you to you, my readers. I've said it before but can't say it enough: with more books than ever vying for your time, I feel truly honored that you choose to spend a few hours reading mine.

**Sandra Orchard** is an award-winning author of inspirational romantic suspense and mysteries, whose novels include *Deadly Devotion*, *Blind Trust*, and several Love Inspired Suspense titles, including three Canadian Christian Writing Award winners and a *Romantic Times* Reviewers' Choice Award winner. Sandra has also received a Daphne du Maurier Award for Excellence in Mystery/Suspense.

In addition to her busy writing schedule, Sandra enjoys speaking at events and teaching writing workshops. She especially enjoys brainstorming suspense plots with fellow writers, which has garnered more than a few odd looks when standing in the grocery checkout debating what poison to use.

Sandra lives with her husband of more than twenty-five years in Ontario, Canada, where their favorite pastime is exploring the world with their young grandchildren. Learn more about Sandra's books and check out the special bonus features, such as deleted scenes and location pictures, at www.sandraorchard.com. While there, subscribe to her newsletter to receive subscriber-exclusive short stories. You can also connect with Sandra at www.facebook.com/sandraorchard.

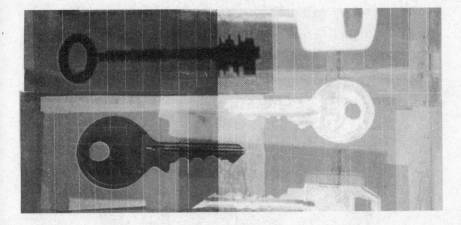

## MEET
# SANDRA ORCHARD
## AT
# WWW.SANDRAORCHARD.COM

You can learn more about Sandra's books and access special bonus features, such as deleted scenes and location pictures.

Connect on Facebook **f**

www.facebook.com/sandraorchard

More twists and turns and secrets await
in Book 2 of the
**PORT ASTER SECRETS** series!

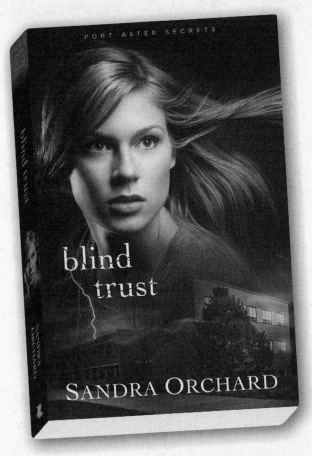

"*Blind Trust* is a fun, sometimes quirky whodunit, full of everything
a mystery lover is looking for, including a dash of romance.
If you enjoy mysteries as much as I do, you won't want to miss
Sandra Orchard's second installment in her Port Aster Secrets series."

—**Lisa Harris,** *Christy Award finalist and author of* Dangerous Passage

# Be the First to Hear about Other New Books from REVELL!

Sign up for announcements about new and upcoming titles at

## RevellBooks.com/SignUp

Don't miss out on our great reads!

Revell

*a division of Baker Publishing Group*

www.RevellBooks.com